About the author

Per Olav Verås was born in the United States to Norwegian parents. Raised in New York City he now lives in Norway, where he pursues his two passions-writing, and teaching. *The Syphilis Artist* is his debut novel.

Author photo credit: Frank Skaren

THE SYPHILIS ARTIST

PER OLAV VERÅS

THE SYPHILIS ARTIST

Vanguard Press

VANGUARD PAPERBACK

© Copyright 2021
Per Olav Verås

The right of Per Olav Verås to be identified as author of this work has been asserted by him in accordance with the Copyright, Designs and Patents Act 1988.

All Rights Reserved

No reproduction, copy or transmission of this publication may be made without written permission. No paragraph of this publication may be reproduced, copied or transmitted save with the written permission of the publisher, or in accordance with the provisions of the Copyright Act 1956 (as amended).

Any person who commits any unauthorised act in relation to this publication may be liable to criminal prosecution and civil claims for damages.

A CIP catalogue record for this title is available from the British Library.

ISBN 978 1 80016 229 7

*Vanguard Press is an imprint of
Pegasus Elliot MacKenzie Publishers Ltd.*
www.pegasuspublishers.com

First Published in 2021

**Vanguard Press
Sheraton House Castle Park
Cambridge England**

Printed & Bound in Great Britain

Dedication

Dedicated to my father, Olav Verås.

May 9, 1945

"Aldri redd for mør-

kets makt… kjemp for

alt hva du har kjært… dø om så det

gjelder…"

This is a work of fiction. Names, characters, businesses, places, events and incidents are either the products of the author's imagination or used in a fictitious manner. Any resemblance to actual persons, living or dead, or actual events is purely coincidental.

Acknowledgements

To my friends I hold close, who read my manuscript, I say thank-you.

To my creative friends in Coverks, in that small hidden place, in a valley in Southern Norway, in a little building in the shadow of the mountain, where the door is always open, I say thank you.

To my children and wife, I embrace each of you, as a candle embracing a flame. Hvala ti, Ahmed Lindov. *Nekome rat, a nekome brat...*

Rune Mortensen, you inspired me.

To Margaretha Krug Aase and Erling Dugan, a very special thank you.

And to my friend Andreas Olav Hansen, whose voice lingers, whose touch fades, who lifts a pencil to the canvas, who embraced my hallucination, I whisper her words, *La vita è più dolce con te.*

I would like to thank the unknown author of the urban love song, the stirring Bosnian *Sevdalinka*, and those words which so moved me. Lyrical words awakening a song long forgotten. Lingering words sung by a sweet, forgotten voice whose whisperings over the wide fields of Prijedor awaken Andreas Olav Hansen to a shattering, and staggering, truth.

Illustrator: Martine Johansen

I walk across a field of flowers, a bright summer's day, there is the scent of mint, and in the near distance, the buildings, desolate and rust-coloured, where the killing occurred. I walk with a small crowd of silent survivors, who are no longer prisoners. I will go inside the empty buildings, and think, can whitewashed concrete walls testify to the evil, will they speak?

— Mia Miraja *Hansen*

Preface

A dream.
    I am a black bird circling overhead, looking down, at a town in ruin. Rubble-choked streets in a black scene littered with dust; strewn bodies, laying like broken sticks. Animal corpses bloated, and bursting, purple formless bodies filling with gas. The stench of death and dead children with glass eyes, wide, and staring, like porcelain dolls' faces, alabaster white, where their silent collective scream rises into the smoke-filled sky. There is no god who has heard them cry, no angel of mercy has come to their rescue. Skeletal buildings smoking, and burning, cratered with holes, where there emerge wild-eyed men, drunk and screaming, because their pockets are full of looted treasure. I see in my dream not a single tree with leaves, all skeletal, like the hungry dogs, stray, and the scene shakes me, because there is a magnificent stone church whose dome is broken. I see the altar, where the dome lays, and there I see myself, a boy, hiding, with the girl, the girl with the red vest embroidered in gold. It starts raining in my dream. The wind and rain blow in through the shattered windows; there are deafening explosions, like the rumble of earthquakes, one after another. There are corpses and mangled bodies and children lying still in the streets, littered corpses and the smell of burning, and then a silence, dreadful, as the girl in my dream whispers her mother will find us.

I
THE WAY I WAIT

A little, hidden place in a town in Norway.
    Where I write these words.
    Where the memory of those events lingers, where I will reach back, and meet her.
    I will hold her close, again, and again. I will look into his eyes, in this stillness, and weep, as he wept. I will wait.

The little sounds of a pencil

Bang!
    The hammer's sharp blow on the iron anvil. The brief igniting sparks flashing my hooded shadow on the pine-timbered walls.
    Whose walls are the colour of dark tea, in whose shadows her naked form lays.
    I know she watches me.
    Again, and again, each strike flattening the blade's edge.
    I see my hand pulling the blade through the candle flame; I dance its point on my chest, the blade glowing white, where I trace the letters of the word, the runic letters so I know where to cut.
    I cut through the skin, the flesh splits, the blood spurts. I cut the letters; the iron smell fills the dark place, where I hear her soft cries.
    The way I drop the knife, whisper her name, as moonlight catches her face's half glow, because she is hidden in shadow, and the winter's night has frozen her stare.
    I see the body hanging head down, the naked body with long hair, blonde, like a horse's mane, the way the body swings back and forth. A storm blows in off the North Sea, a frozen wind shakes the limbs.
    Her body aglow from the full moon's light, the way the blood runs down her cut neck, to the bone-white snow, the ankles bound by rope, under the tree limb.
    The fir tree standing by itself, all alone, on the forests' edge, where a cliff drops to the sea, and the spray of salt from the ocean fills the night with the taste of a knife's blade.
    Thinking about this nameless woman I fucked.
    A paper bag hiding my face, with cut-out holes for my eyes.
    Straddling her, on the edge of the creaky bed, posts knocking violently against the timbered floorboards.
    They never see my deformed face.

The way she moaned, the way the porcelain oil lamp shook on the night table.

The way the shadow of the lamp's flame cast our shapes on the wall. *They told me what I want to know.*

And then, when it is all over, the silence. She picks up her things, takes the pencil sketch I drew of her, gives me a crisp five hundred crown note, and leaves. The sounds of her bare feet on the steps, the tick-tock of the grandfather clock. I take the bag off my head, turning to the window, the candle's burning down, its dying flame flickering.

My reflection mirrored on the window's glass.

Levi says I look like Jesus, in the shadows.

On the way out the door slams, I hear the nameless woman yell an obscenity. In the dark except for the shadows on the wall, the shadow of my outstretched hand, as my fingers, like thin dead branches, appear out of nowhere, flickering by candlelight on the wall. As my piano fingers reach for my face, lightly tapping my forehead, running down the bridge of my nose, where they trace the deformity. I hear a distant melody, the tapping of fingers on keys, this disease plays with me.

It all happened so quick.

The little sounds of the pencil sharpening are like what you hear when you rub your thumb and forefinger.

These little sounds fill the pine-timbered spaces of my grandfather's house. I feel the sun lingering just atop the mountain, the way the escaping light stabs my eyes, the way my mind sees the valley distant, great rolling mountains running to the sea.

As the day vanishes to night.

I will light candles, so they know I am here when I hear footsteps at the door. There will be a knocking, feeble, at the door, they know to enter.

They know to take off their clothes, hanging them up on the brass hooks, as they put on the robe, walk up the three flights of steps to my room, in this little attic with the box window.

Where I wait for them-*The Syphilis Artist.*

In my grandfather's room, where the shadow of the candle throws itself, and her neck, tensed like a bow's quiver, reveals a fine ripple of muscle.

Like the ripple of a soft, blowing wind off the ocean. She sits so long the old clock stops ticking, the sun steals back into view. Light stabs into the valley, stabbing my eyes, above those great cliffs of granite.

Where the sea gulls sail, and the fog lifts, and a little titmouse flies in through the open window.

I have no need for light because all I see is shadow.

My favourite weather is a cloud-filled heaven because a thousand shades of grey steal across the sky, and the sun has stopped stabbing my eyes.

Where teardrops fall, one by one, as I whisper their names. "Haakon... Tor-Inge... Bent..."

There is a place on the old desk drawer where I take out the matchbox and the little candles.

As I do now, lighting three candles, whispering each name.

Wandering in and out of dark places

When I close my eyes, I see things. In the dark.

As dark as that room over at Hercules, the room with no lights.

Going down the steps, knowing he waits for me. Seventeen years old.

Everything was damp, there was the feeling I was entering an abyss.

Swallowed up in a maelstrom of small, desperate acts, as when this faceless man said he will shoot up in the park and asked me for a needle.

I told him he had mistaken me for someone else.

"Ok, I don't do drugs all the time. Just forget my name, ok?" "How old are you?" he asks in a drunken slur.

"Seventeen... I need the money."

"Just a fucking twink. That's what you are."

I gave him a clean needle, he tried to kiss me. "Fuck off, no kissing," I told him sharply.

It's a cheap fix, he says he's injecting himself ten times a day, I tell him he'll be dead before he's thirty.

He tells me he's going over to the police station on Christian Frederiks Place to get his needles, then over to the shooting gallery by the docks.

"You're the kid with the *syph*. Can I catch it? Can I?"

"You know, it's not too hard to kill a man, to tell the truth," I say matter-of-factly.

"What do you mean by that?" he asks nervously.

"It's not hard to kill a man" I whisper. "You have killed a man. You have killed yourself."

Then he really starts yelling, so I leave him.

I was just a kid at seventeen, wandering in and out of dark places, all these cheap fixes.

I ran down Karl Johann yelling, in the night. Run down almost by a tram.

I was running, escaping, toward the alley.

Running around the thieving little gypsies, they were everywhere, I didn't care, stuck-up brats with greased hair, it's like they were everywhere, freeloading off their dad's money.

I couldn't get away from them fast enough.

I swaggered off in an alleyway off Storgata, falling down, on my knees, head bowed, in the dark.

A stray black dog watched me, I saw his eyes, I took off my dark glasses, his eyes locked to mine. I wept.

I closed my eyes. When I opened them, the dog was gone, I saw myself, seven years old, like a scene in a movie. I had been chasing the girl, the girl in the red vest embroidered in gold, in the narrow stone alleyways of Split, where I yelled for her. "Mia, come back to me!"

I have never felt such things before, the way the marble felt, rising in ancient columns, my footsteps clapping the flat stones. I want to sit her down on the stone floor under the Roman arch, where the light pillars down, and draw her likeness.

I refused to enter that old church

I opened my father's cold, tightly clutched hand, his lifeless fingers on the gun's trigger, how death had frozen his fingers like stone.

I wept as each finger cracked, as I bent each finger back, one by one. Released from his grasp, I took the German Luger and hid it.

The way the finger's snapped, the echo of their breaking, like little sticks.

I refused to enter that old church.

I stood outside, smoking a cigarette, waiting for the singing to end.

On that cold and overcast Sunday in March, bundled up in that old fisherman's coat. The church bell rang, the doors opened, they streamed outside with Levi leading the pall bearers and the single white casket.

Just a few people passing around me like a black stream, walking senseless, as the wind picked up, and the sky darkened.

I was a hooded presence; they stared away from me. They were shadows, that much I saw.

I heard their voiceless footsteps.

I made out the casket as the retreating sun glistened off the brass handles. They thought because I could not see that *I couldn't hear*.

Someone whispered, "He killed *Little Harold*. The *Syphilis Artist* killed his own father."

Another voice. "They say the police found Grandfather Olav in the rocking chair. Levi said in the sermon Harold wanted his father's ashes to be buried with him, in the same casket."

"Poor Crazy Olav was as stiff as a board when they found him. The old man must have died of shock. They say his hand grasped Harold's hand so tight that they couldn't pull the fingers apart."

A wind gust blew away a ribbon from my father's coffin.

I saw it fly off, up into the grey sky, where the sunlight stabbed down, from a break in the clouds.

A silky white little ribbon flying away, like a black-headed gull, whose wings white-tipped, vanish in the clouds stealing into the fjørd.

Clouds black like my soul because I refused to enter that place.

My father Harold, and my grandfather, Olav, may they rest in peace.

The way I wait

The way the little virus crept up on us, the little, mischievous thief. Now that a year has passed, like a day.

Now that the new church bell rings.

Now that a year has passed since that day in March when the little virus began its mischief.

An odd mischief because its awakening led me to this place, this old farmhouse.

Where I sit at this desk.

The way I wait out these minutes and hours, the way time passes.

The way I had cut the electrical wires, and the only sound is the *tick-tock* of the grandfather clock.

And the tolling of the bell, here in the valley, where a shadow has passed.

As the passing of a cloud, as when a great darkness lifts, as the light breaks through, like the shattering of a black curtain, made of glass.

The window is open, in blows the wind.

Now that the mystery has been solved, the way I sit. The way I wait.

The way the church bell has stopped ringing. Eleven o'clock on a bright sunlit morning, a Sunday.

The way the candle played its glow on the window, the only point of light in this old house, on this hill, on the forest's edge.

Where he came to me, emerging shadow like out of the woods, knowing I was waiting.

He can in one instance smile, a lovely, devious smile, and in the next instance change into a joker's face, with burning eyes, and teeth hard clenched. Because he has you alone, in the shadow, he has a knife.

In remembrance.

In remembrance of the stillness.

In remembrance of her whispers, as I lift this pencil to this paper, the way the pencil sketches, my eyes shut, so I can see.

In remembrance of my father.

My hands grasped tight, bare-knuckled; my teeth clenched so my cheek muscles on my face ripple.

The way I release my fingers and allow my right forefinger to feel the place where she kissed me, on the cheek, as I turned away because I couldn't look into her eyes, I could not allow her to kiss me.

As the policeman took her away, and her fingers left my grasp. The hard-muscled officer with the featureless face in the powder-blue shirt.

The way he pulled her from me, ripping her grasp from mine.

I held tight; I just would not let go. I was carried on a stretcher on the shore, I felt the sun on my face. I heard the waves gently crashing, the scent of the sea. I told her I had a dream, I was with her again, on the island of Pag, in her mother's stone villa, overlooking the sea. I told her I want to go back, I want to whisper in the dark, again.

She whispers, "When you open your eyes you will see me again, I promise, Andreas."

As I yelled her name, the way she wept, as they took her away, in the patrol car, her protests filling this little valley.

Where the church bell's echo is carried, and never quite escapes.

The new church bell made of bronze, whose echo rings in remembrance.

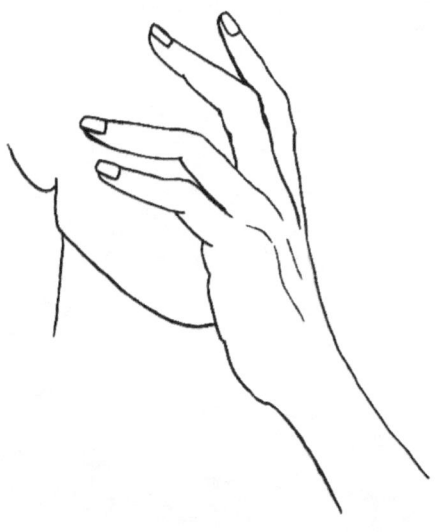

The memory of things are hallucinations

The way I now sit, a calm settling in me, the way I knew all along, the way she knew.

A year has passed since the sudden shutting down of things, the way I write by candlelight, with a worn pencil scribbling on a yellow pad, at this desk, in this old house, thinking back.

How it has all come to this, how the seasons pass, how the memory of things are maybe just hallucinations.

A year has passed since the stillness began.

The glint of light on broken glass

Men had forgotten the stillness in their hearts.

Men had forgotten the little tapping on their hearts, the sound a butterfly makes, with its wings, fluttering, as you open the window on a midsummer's night, and it escapes, where the glint of light plays on broken glass. That stillness fills my heart, I am happy.

* * *

The matter is settled, I know how this story ends.

If this absolution is hallucination, so be it.

At least I am its author. To that end I feel strong enough to lift this pencil, it is a moment worthy of some words.

Or maybe worthy of a pencil sketch, a simple sketch, just some unbroken lines, the up-stretched arms and hands, the eyes gazing upward, pleading.

Everything worth saying was yelled out, in that room, with the jail cell, in the shadow of that sorry, pleading little shadow kneeling at my feet.

Bleating like a sheep just as its throat is cut, the wild little hysteria broken by the police siren echoing in the distance. The way this shadow prayed to me as if I were the master of his destiny.

No one heard those shouts.

A benign immensity of unstained light flooded in the room; his hands stretched up to me.

The shaking, grasping hands I gripped tight, whose grip I released as I placed them over my bare chest, over my heart, so he could feel it beat, pounding quick, like a water hammer.

No hand reached down from the clouds to lift this soul, no one meets me, but the little memories I have collected, the hallucinations waking me up, in the night.

Those memories whose truth I finally accept. A truth my shadow could not accept or imagine because for him it was all my hallucination.

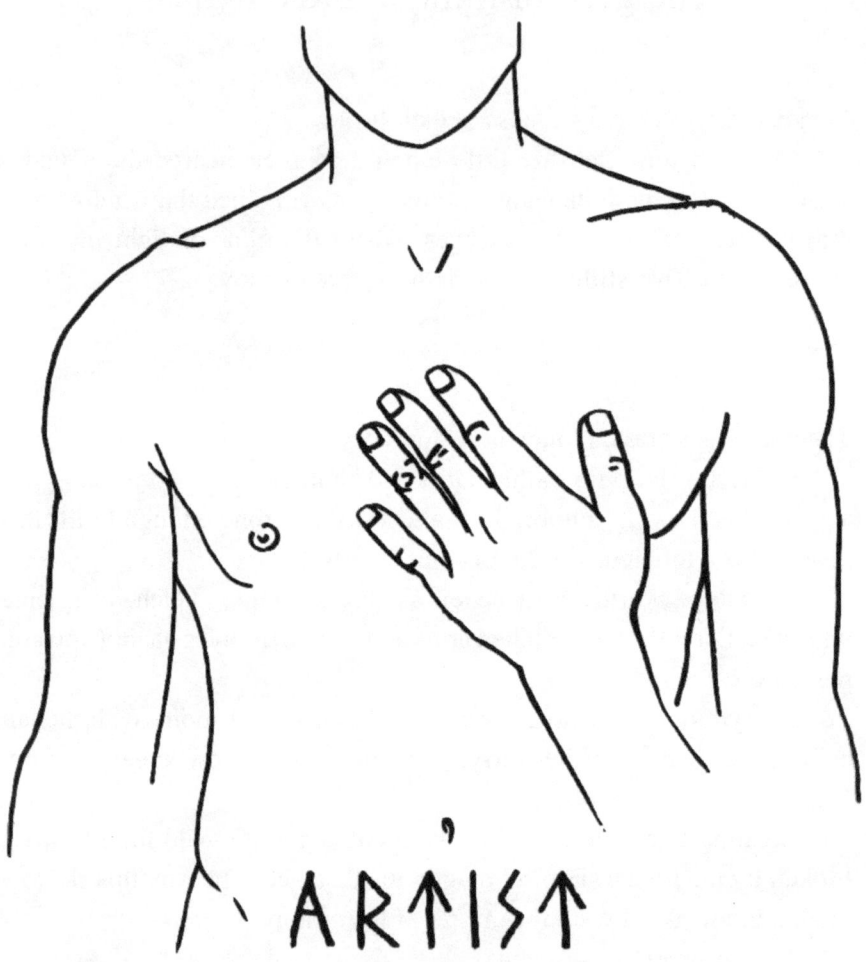

How big is the field of Prijedor

There was a man once, a man with a dark complexion, eyes-tinged honey brown, a quiet, lingering voice, who raised his gaze to the heavens.

Who searched the distant dry hills, the way the sun-scorched down, the way the dry grass burned, so the smoke rose up, and the fires sent up tendrils of smoke, like a thousand grey snakes, up and up the little whirlwinds made their holy ascent.

To the cloud-filled sky where the rain fell, on his quiet, serene face, on his eyes, where his tears intermingled with the falling cold drops, stinging the places where he was cut, where the body was torn.

* * *

There was a man once, who looked over the burning fields of Prijedor.

He knelt in the ruins of an alleyway, where the broken buildings lay skeleton-like, bereft of windows, glass splintered, in shards strewn on the street, cutting into children's feet, as they played their mindless gambols. How the little ones laughed and played with their red and blue marbles. There was a little shadow following the man, hiding behind the broken walls. The man called out to the children, they fled, because the man wept, as he gazed out over the distant burning fields, and the children cried back he shouldn't weep, it was all just a dream. A hallucination.

You lie down your head, on a midsummer's light, the night falls effortlessly, a black curtain descending senselessly.

You lie down your head, there is no place where I can say the light ends, and the darkness begins. The way I close my eyes, the way the light escapes, the way there is infinite light, when the eyes shutter, the way all this made no sense to Lena, who said I was crazy.

Some words come to me, words of a poem I had forgotten. Words meaningless, yet full of meaning, somehow, I recite them from memory.

Mani me se prijedorcanko
mlada djevojko
siroko je Prijedor polje
umorices se
duboka je Sana voda
utopices se
There is a letter I must write.

How it has all come to this

Looking out the window to the forest, black as coal, where a flange of spruce trees stands straight and still like sentinels at guard. Trees pencil-thin with forlorn, broken limbs, up stretched, needles sharp, the cones in little clumps, hanging down, heavy laden.

There is a tree standing by itself, in the yard, a tree I know well. The lower limbs hang thorn less, the way it stands, mocking me now. The tree I named 'Olav' as a boy, after my grandfather. It must be two hundred years, the way I rolled its needles between my fingers, the way I climbed up, scratching my thin skin, along its flaking, scaling bark, eagerly reaching its heaven high crown sitting like a pyramid.

Where I screamed out for joy, my playful little gambol shaking its limb, because I was just seven, scampering about in my grandfather's yard, and I had climbed to the top! I could take in the smells of the sea, the brine sweeping in the fjørd, as my nose itched and tickled itself with the tree's sharp, intoxicating smell.

These biting elixirs come now to haunt.

I have lately lost all sense of smell, and the only thing I feel between my fingertips is the point of this pencil, sharpened quick, so my letters are thin, scratch like, filling the page with thoughts sharpened by years long past.

I am not sure if the tree is dead. It has given up something inside, it waits for me. This skeleton whose shadow wakes me up.

A windless night, not a sound is heard. The clanging of the clock downstairs, twelve bells, midnight. I wave my pencil back and forth like a conductor's wand with the ringing.

The way everything had come to a halt in Oslo.

The way I locked the door on my flat. I knew I would never open that door again. I took the little red book from my coat pocket. It was a little book of poetry sent to me by the publisher, entitled "New Norwegian Poetry." I just ripped out a page, tacked it on the door with a wad of gum I was chewing. I put on my glasses. I made out some sentences by a Norwegian poet named Anne Helene. I read the lines out loud. "Drink up… what is good is always taken from us…"

The way I stood there, weeping.

That I had been thinking about so many things, standing at that door, my thoughts in knots, like the twisted fisherman's line, the one I strive to untangle, sitting in that boat, my father's shadow over me, a hot sun-bright day in the fjørd. The hard flapping of the mackerel's tail, the knowledge the creature was gasping its last, the way tears formed in my eyes because I knew my dad was getting upset; he didn't say anything, he didn't know. The fact that I was losing my eyesight, how it came and went, I didn't want to upset him. I couldn't make out the knot, the way the light reflected off the flat sea, like shards of glass, splintered little things come back to haunt. When he slapped me in the face, I looked away.

I looked away, to the place where the waves break white, far off where the coast bends and the light plays at night from the lighthouse, where the glow extinguishes itself like a lover's faint caress, when fingertips play on your chest, and nothing but a lover's sigh stirs you.

I will sing the song she taught

I stare at the ceiling.

I feel for the little mirror by my side, lift it above my face, what do I see?

My face a shadow, I make out two points of light, faint, where the candle's glow reflects a glint in my eyes, like the way a match's flame reflects off broken glass.

I squeeze my eyes again, and again, my eyes ache, it was no use, I can't see my fingers, as I wave them like little pencils in front of my face.

I touch the paper bag covering my head, feel where I had cut the holes for my eyes. This is what greets them, a man hiding his face, in the big empty room downstairs, with my easel and canvas, by the glowing fireplace. Where I start a birch fire, where their clothes drop to the hard-timbered floor, and they sit, facing me, on the stool.

I will remember to take off this bag, neatly fold it, and place it in the jar with the letter.

A year has fled since that day, sitting on the steps at the library, a year stretching to a lifetime of memories, the way I have nothing more to say.

* * *

Leo will come by. He will drive me to that special place.

In the meantime, I close my eyes, I will not sleep. I will go back, to that day, in this house, and play again the scene. There is nothing more than that, since she is gone, and Kahal Gibran once said *"Remembrance is a form of meeting."*

I will meet her again, and again, and again. I will hold her close, again, and again. I will look into his eyes, in this stillness, and weep, as he wept.

I will climb to the altar of that great mountain, the pulpit rock, and lie still, my gaze affixed upward, in the sun blinding light, the sky as frozen cobalt, clean and blue and biting.

I will sing the song she taught, as she holds that special flower whose petals are pressed in these pages.

Petals lavender, sweet-smelling, the flower she held close to me, as she whispered its elixir would still me, my soul would fly free, if I would just close my eyes, inhale deeply, escape with her as she sang those words.

Those foreign words in a language from far away, words song to her by her mother, in that stone villa overlooking the sea.

I will feel in my hand the book he passes to me, as he reads the words written in the preface, from the leather-bound *The Picture of Dorian Gray*. Leo has read the words so many times he recites them by memory, as my fingers feel the worn page, feel for the hardened little clumps of wax, where the candle dripped. *The artist is the creator of beautiful things. To reveal art and conceal the artist is art's aim. The critic is he who can translate into another manner or a new material his impression of beautiful things. The highest as the lowest form of criticism is a mode of autobiography. Those who find ugly meanings in beautiful things are corrupt without being charming. This is a fault. Those who find beautiful meanings in beautiful things are the cultivated. For these there is hope.*

Opening my eyes in the dark

The clock chimes twelve times, the ringing in my ears die down, it is past midnight, black outside, my thoughts settle.
    Opening my eyes. In the dark.
    I remember my name. Andreas Olav Hansen.
    I make out the candle's glow, on the nightstand, by the little box window. In my grandfather's old pine-timbered bedroom, walls the colour of black tea, where they look up, see the candle's faint glow, and know I wait for them.

* * *

The letter is written, I sign my name in flowing black ink.

Andreas Olav Hansen
A.O.H.

There is a drawing I make now, on the backside of the paper, a figure I will not describe.
    It will be known to her, the way my pencil flows like it has a life of its own. This figure known by this whittled-down pencil, just a stump after all these years. Cerulean blue, how it glides, a moment now as teardrops fall, one by one. It is appropriate my tears admix with the blue, the cerulean from my tears, as the light plays on the paper, the way she will touch where my pencil made its mark, where my finger traced her form, as she lay on the sun-warmed sand, and I lifted my pencil to the canvas.

I don't need to see you

It all came back, there, how I stood in front of that clean white door where my face's reflection spoke to me. I was startled, I saw my face, the hair hanging to the shoulders, the pale, mournful eyes, blue as the sea, behind those John Lennon specs, the ones Lena told me I never should remove because I was blind without them.

"Andreas," she said, "put them on."

"I don't need them," I protested.

Lying naked by her side, on those clean linen sheets, in that fancy hotel room off Karl Johann. Just me staring at the ceiling, in another place, that place hidden in me, where secrets are written on pieces of paper and stuffed in little cracks, in stone walls where I move shadowless.

"I want you to see me, Andreas. I need you to see me."

"I don't need to see you."

She climbed on top of me, the way I know she searched my face, for something I can't give her. She grinds senseless, like some fucking machine, trying her best to excite me, the way her little protestations and sighs just lose themselves, because she pleasures herself, she doesn't need me, she has never really needed me, or anyone, for that matter.

"If you don't put on your glasses, Andreas Olav Hansen," she says, grinding in quickening tempo, squealing, like some wild alley cat, "you can't see my face!"

Taking my revenge by throwing her off me, just before she comes.

The silence. The shock of my violence. The way she retreats to the bed's edge, puts on a robe, and I sit next to her, reaching my hand, to her face, where the tears run. Where I touch my fingertips and whisper, "That has been your problem, Lena. You have never understood that I don't need to see. I don't want to see."

I put on my clothes, left the room.

"Goodbye, Lena," I whispered at the door.

I missed you

It was a Saturday morning in March, cool and clear, hearing my clogs *klak klak* on the pavement.

The way there was no one on Karl Johann when I walked alone to the train station, no one in sight.

Scanning the harbour, a postcard-worthy site, no one was around.

Smelling the sea, how the salt enlivened me, arching my neck up to the sky, just craning my head around, sniffing, smelling, sensing something striking me. It was an oddity of emotion, like the way Lena reminded me we are alone now, and then reminding me she felt always alone, so the new situation wasn't so odd, was it? We Norwegians, after all, like to keep our distance.

Three white-tipped gulls cawed and capered in a pyrrhic dance like circus acrobats. High above the still plate of ocean, blue metal grey like a sheet of glass.

I stopped, removed my dark glasses, squinted as the birds alighted in the blinding sunlight. My eyes ached, I could not stand the light—the sun rising like a monster orange distant and huge on the horizon.

In me was awakened just one single thought. No longer am I alone, we are all alone. I thought it was a sort of odd karma, now that my countrymen hid themselves.

* * *

Lena had sent me an SMS. It came as a shock. She said I had to go right away, before the trains stop running, travel south and see my father.

He had been staying with my grandfather, in the old house. She said my father called her, asked about me. He saw the news about the virus, he said he was not feeling well.

He wanted to tell me something important. Right after I read the SMS, she called me. I did not want to talk. Hearing her voice struck me through and through.

It had a seriousness I was not used to hearing, like finally, she had decided to care for someone.

"You tell him something for me, can you do that?"

I waited several minutes before I answered.

"What do you want me to say?" I asked, awkwardly. "Lena? Hello?"

She was not there any more. Just like Lena.

I wanted to know what she desired to say because it would allow me to say those things, to a father who had closed himself off to his son, a son who hadn't spoken to his father for seven years.

I wanted to say I told Leo the Greek that if something happens to me, to make sure she finds these notes. She will know where I locked them.

When everything shut down, I had left instructions with my dark-eyed friend, the librarian-posting a little yellow post-it note on the glass door of the library.

"So, what are you reading, these days, Leo?"

"Kafka."

This dark-eyed man whose eyes grab you from behind his glasses. This sallow-skinned man speaking in monosyllables, who told me once he was a loner and that I am the only person he has told that to.

Sitting on the steps outside the library. "Thank you for picking me up at the train station." He grunts a noise, a guttural monosyllable.

"Is it true, that I am the only person you have told that to?"

A pause so long my eyes catch seagulls dive-bombing over the church tower, the pine-timbered tower erect and white and glistening in the sun-spangled light. I put on my glasses, my eyes adjust, I stretch out my right forefinger, following the lead bird, up and down and sideways as the birds careen, darting quick, caw-cawing. I take out a pencil and my little notebook.

The way I sketch, the sounds my pencil makes, the way Leo just breathes, his sighs lingering in my shadow, as he reads his Kafka, from that worn paperback, which he takes from his back pocket, and thumbs to a page, as I sketch, the sounds of his finger sweeping the pages, and then the silence, as he reads to himself. I hear how he whispers to himself; he knows I hear the words. He cannot help himself.

"I am a cage in search of a bird."

His words whispered, as the cawing of the birds fade, and his voice rings, and rings, the way I repeat those words, again, and again, as I pull close to his face, see those dark glasses where he hides himself. He cannot bear to take off the glasses.

He cannot bear to look in my eyes, as I remove my glasses.

On these sun-warmed granite steps where there is no one to be seen, no vehicles moving in the street, no sounds but the seagulls and their squawking, and the sighs from this dark-eyed man, whose presence fills me with happiness.

"I wanted to say hello."

I take the book from his hand. I place it in his back pocket. "I missed you."

The way he sighs at my words, there is a moment when he turns to me, a moment etched in my memory, as when he says, "I like how quiet things have become."

"The virus has shut things down, so you have this big empty library with all your books. You could not be happier."

He looks like a raven

Awakened by the distant clanging of the church bells.

I got wearily out of the bed, from under the heavy wool blanket; the cold floor attacked my bare feet, I coughed.

My chest hurt, I felt for the cigarette in the pewter dish on the night table.

I found the matchbox, I held the little paper box to my ear, I shook the box.

It has a pleasing sound, the little wood sticks, the way I shake the little box. My trembling fingers take out a little matchstick; I light it so the flame dances in my eye like the glint of sunlight.

Sharpening the pencils, with the pocketknife, by the fireplace, watching the little shavings caught up, in the rising smoke.

My little solace, I thought, as I sit in my underwear, taking my time, smoking, calming down. The bells had stopped ringing — not a sound but the beating of my heart, the way it beats inside, the *tick-tock* of the old clock downstairs, the way these sounds fill this house.

* * *

I hear a mysterious sound, a creaking open of a door, from downstairs in the landing.

Hard footsteps, someone walking back and forth, footsteps slapping the timbered floor. I recognise the voice, the meek and whispering voice.

"Andreas Olav Hansen! Are you home?"

I put on a robe, leave the attic for the stairs, go down the narrow steps to the second floor, past the landing, my father's bedroom with the desk facing the glowing window. *The old jail cell in the bedroom, bars like broomsticks, where my mother locked me inside.* I scrape the frost from the frozen glass, look out.

The forest down below the house just a swathe of black, formless, like a blanket, the snow falling lightly. A March dusting, here then soon gone.

Down another flight of narrow steps, unsteady, my knees ache, I take my time. Levi surprised to see me, I see his fleshy face, the startled face, the way his tiny mouth opens halfway, words silent on his lips, as this little priest follows my slow, deliberate steps.

This man with polished black shoes and dark eyes, standing in the doorway. He holds a briefcase in his gloved hands. The way the light glinted off the big silver crucifix pinned on the lapel of his black wool coat.

He looks like a raven.

It was his eyes I caught, those black, tiny eyes sitting deep in his face, the way they stared at me from the distance, only to turn away from me, as I came to him, he looked away from my face.

I look down at him, he pulls some glasses from his jacket. He put them on, when he looked up at me, I see his eyes, enlarged, like black marbles.

"I am sorry about your father," he says, as he opens the briefcase, takes out a document from a folder.

"You need to sign this, it is just a small matter. Your father had insurance; funeral expenses will be covered up to twenty-three thousand crowns."

Levi, always looking out for me.

I can't read the writing, what the hell, I sign where he points his finger, he puts the document back in the briefcase, buttons his coat, turns to the door cracked open. Snow blows in; he lingers with his back to me for a moment.

Then he turns, looks up from the floor, removes his glasses, and in a slow, pained expression says, *"What solace is there in the memory of a father who takes his own life? I am sorry for your loss."*

In my dream he weeps

I lie shaking in my wool underwear; nothing keeps me warm. I get under the down blanket, pull it to my neck.

Not a mouse's whisper is heard, just the clang of the old clock, downstairs, ticking, as it happens to do now.

Tick-tock, tick-tock, tick-tock, the way the forefinger of my right hand stretches up, in the darkness, and marks each bell, counting, for amusement, just tapping the air.

I count ten bells, *the sun has set*, the passing of time marked by the bells, and the fading shadow of a candle's light.

I did not want to come to this house. There is a reawakening in the silence.

The way I found my father, the way I woke up, calling for him.

The way I scrambled down to the room, thinking it was all hallucination, I had dreamt the scene, my mind was playing tricks.

* * *

In my dream he weeps, I heard his voice calling my name, a gentle sighing voice.

Through the open window, where the wind blew in, the white curtains fluttering and whipping in this room, a summer day.

In my dream I am a boy, a midsummer's night, in my grandfather's house, just as the sun slips down, the light plays on my face like a feather.

I got out of bed, there was the train set on the floor, the locomotive with the little red caboose was going around and around on its track. I was happy in my dream; I was in my grandfather's house.

He is a shadow, kneeling, by the great tree.

He is on bended knee, he turns. I kneel next to him, curious, as I see his face, a clean-shaven face.

A shadow hooded, his eyes I see, hard blue, intelligent eyes locking mine. I see the hole in his right temple where the bullet entered, a clean, little hole. He holds a little white flower.

"Lily of the valley," he intones, his voice full of sadness. "For your wedding," he continues, as he turns from me, and picks more of the flowers.

"You know Father, I can never marry."

"You know she likes flowers. You told me so."

He turns in my dream, holding the flowers, arranged in a great bouquet, hanging with those little poisonous red berries.

He lies down the flowers, stretching his finger to my face, to my nose, to the place where the bone is broken.

"You know, Andreas. Her mother made me a promise once."

He touches my face. The place where I feel my father's touch, the little dimple where the nose bone had melted away, that place he has touched so many times, in my sleep.

In my dream, I reach to my face and grasp his hand. It is cold, and dead.

I hold tight his finger as I guide it to his shadowed face, to the temple, where I trace the little hole, as my father releases my hand, as he pulls me to himself, as he weeps, and weeps, and the sobbing convulses me, in my dream.

In the silence, his trembling words strike through me.

"I am sorry, Andreas. I am sorry I took you on that train. I am sorry, my son."

The way I am a boy in my dream, the way I break down, the way I see the girl in the distance, she calls my name.

The girl with eyes the colour of the sea, the girl with a red vest, embroidered in gold.

"You know her name, Andreas."

*　*　*

The way my father's voice fades, as the wind blows the tree, as the sun has set, and the light is extinguished.

The way I see myself, the little boy huddled in the tree's shadow, holding the little white flowers, with those poisonous red berries, in my dream, I slip them one by one in my mouth.

In my dream my father's voice lingers, I see his outstretched hand as our fingertips touch, as my right hand, grasps tight his, as he releases his grasp and takes his finger to the little hole in his temple.

I hear his last plea, as a cold wind rushes up the valley, as he fades into darkness.

"Andreas Olav Hansen. Discover the truth, find who did this. Make him kneel at your feet. Make him feel my beating heart."

In the distance I spy a silent black mass around a grave, where I see the priest's long white robe fluttering, like the white ribbon that fluttered from my father's grave, a silky white banner trimmed with gold, with a name.

As my thoughts slip away and I see before me the girl, coming toward me, the girl with olive skin and eyes the colour of the sea. Hair fine like Konavle silk, straight and black, the way she has come up to me, in my dream.

The way she whispers, as I see her eyes, moist with tears. She tells me she loves my father.

"My mother has told me he is a good man. My mother has told me he has written her letters."

I know this girl's name.

I take her hand, press it to my face, to my cheek, where I feel its warmth. I whisper her name, as she unfolds a letter.

There is the little white flower pressed between the pages, it drops to the ground and the girl kneels, picks it up, brings it close to me.

"Take this, in remembrance," she says.

I kiss her hand, its warmth disappears, the scene fades. The only sound I hear is the *tick-tock* of the grandfather clock.

A reawakening in the silence

The way I knelt on the floor, the crimson stain faded, where the blood pooled, the way it dripped between the cracks into the cellar, where I had gone down with a candle.

Where the earth was cold to my bare feet, where I touched the drops, coagulated wax-like between my fingertips.

Where the drops ran, cold, as I knelt in the frozen ground, and wept.

There is a reawakening in the silence, the way dreams catch you, the way the happy little dreams turn on you in the night.

There is a reawakening when the lights grow dim, when the shops close, when the whole world spins on another axis because a little virus has chosen to do some mischief.

There is a reawakening, in this room, in my grandfather's farmhouse, here on this hill, where I have entered as an uninvited guest.

There is a reawakening of something in my past which I had forgotten.

* * *

The way I knew what I had to do, on that cold day in March, when sunlight grows ascendant on the horizon, and the fog lifts over the valley, when a stillness invades your heart.

You hear your father's voice.

The world has spun upside down.

The little mischievous virus awakened a stillness loud and clanging, its echo waking up the children in this little valley. Mothers locked the doors.

There was a thief among them. A thief hiding in the shadows. A wolf in the night.

The way the shadow crept up to the windows, in the stillness, knowing they were locked in their rooms. The way the shadow knew how to steal into the night when they slept.

The way the stillness allowed me to finally hear the voice calling me.

The way the stillness allowed me to stretch out my hands, my fingers tapping, lightly touching, a finger's breath from their hearts.

Where I sat on the stool, facing them, in a fire's glow, in that room, where I found the two bodies.

In remembrance of the stillness, so I hear their words, their awful, halting words, as I sketch the face, the way the light plays on their tears.

As they whisper their secrets.

Be not afraid, Andreas

In remembrance of the little purple lupins, the little flowers, scattered all about like drops splashed unto a painter's canvas, in the place called Salmetid, where I walked barefoot in the cool moss.

I smelt lavender, and the scent of the forest after a summer rain, when the sun alights atop the trees, and glides down, to touch the flesh.

She cups her hands on my face, kisses me ever so gently on my lips. The woman whispers in my ear, "Be not afraid."

Where her sighs echoed still, her words in remembrance.

My fingers stretch out, trembling, stretching nearer to her face.

Her jet-black hair falling down a swan's neck, her eyes wide, the colour of the sea.

Her shoulders bare, a fresh cut rose in a low-cut bodice between her breasts. Her wedding gown of finest silk and gossamer, glistening like dew dancing on a spiders web.

Now, breath to breath, the steam of my trembling voice condensing on her rose cheeks. I smell lavender, the scent of the forest after a summer rain, when the sun alights atop the trees, and glides down, to touch the flesh.

She cups her hands on my face, kisses me gently on my lips, and whispers again in my ear.

"Be not afraid Andreas."

She kisses my neck where the cut had slit the vessels and the lifeblood had run from me. I had been skeletal white like a ghost; her magical kiss healed my neck, so the cut disappeared.

Colour came back to my face. My pupils widening, focusing in and out of this spectral vision, as her gown falls to the ground and roses grow magically around us, her naked form wraps me in her embrace, as angel wings grow from her sides, enfolding me. Her whispers tinged with ecstasy. "Paint and live again."

I knew what to do.

Where I left my heart

Where is the island between hallucination, and memory, the place of truth, where my mind can settle?

Where is the island, where she undressed, this girl, in a red silk vest embroidered in gold, the girl with olive skin and eyes the colour of the sea, whose voice calms me, a voice touched by an accent from a place far away, where I left my heart?

Where is this girl whose clothes drop to the stone floor, as I sketch with my pencil in my artist's pad, and I think my father was right, it is a dream?

And where is this girl who can whisper in my ear that I did not kill my father, whose body I found in this house, whose front door I entered, on that afternoon, a day in March, when I stood at the door, wavering, should I knock, and step inside? What would I find?

There is a wolf in the forest

What would awaken in me, in the stillness of this forgotten place, in this valley where the sun escapes, the way this place hides itself in shadow?

On the forest's edge, where the fir and spruce rise like sentinels and the granite cliffs of gneiss are seen distant, rising steep in the fjørd, that straight and narrow fjørd where I rowed that little boat.

On that day I wanted to get away, far away, into the North Sea, because I heard my father shouting at my mother.

I clapped my ears, slapping my hands over my ears, but still, her shouting stabbed into me, the way I rowed, so my hands and fingers blistered, I could not lift a pencil for weeks.

The way the wind blows, the way the shadows form, the way dreams shake you awake, and you don't know what is real, because you are afraid.

There is a wolf in the forest.

It could be me.

It is him I see, my father, I see his face

It all started when something awakened inside me. There was a photo exhibit in one of the small studios in Grünerløkka.

Photographs from the Balkan war.

This was an exhibit in memory of all those who died defending the Bosnian city of Prijedor from the genocidal Serb aggression in 1992.

There was a picture of a bomb-cratered alleyway between the ruins of shattered apartment buildings, a lonely, hooded man walked bent at the shoulders on the rubble-stroked street. The picture was entitled "Prijedor, May 1992."

When I saw the picture and beheld the lonely man, I fell to my knees. The man, on his knees.

Alone.

The way the wind blows, the way the shadows form, the way dreams shake you awake, and you do not know what is real, because you are afraid.

* * *

The way you find your father, and beside him, your grandfather.

In that room downstairs, where the clock ticks.

Where I have nailed the door shut, where I dwell every minute, the way the room haunts me, but I cannot run away.

The man hooded; the man bent at the shoulders.

The man on the rubble-stroked street. Where the distant ravens circled above the man's head, high above, as my gaze alighted downward, where I see myself peeking from behind a broken stone wall.

The way you find your father, you have just stepped off the train, a smiling friend has picked you up at the train station, you are happy because your father has a secret to tell, and you will see him.

You will tell him you are sorry, even before he invites you in, the first words coming from me, as I stand on the stone slab, where the rose bush climbs up on the trestle.

You will sit in the old room, *"the beste-stua,"* with the big fireplace roaring, your eyes will lift from the floor, and meet.

We will share a can of beer to settle things, he will light up, the way he crosses his leg, and rocks, back and forth.

Looking out the open window to the garden, exhaling streams of smoke, the way the room fills, the smoke so thick I lose him, but for the fire's glow, and the creaking of the chair, as he rocks back and forth.

This is how it always goes.

Words won't be spoken, there is enough in the smile, the knowing, the way his right upper lip puckers up, his right cheek filling with air, a half-smile because that is enough for him.

I know it's all going to be right between us from now on, that will be my thought.

The way no one meets you at the door, the way you enter the house, you are terrified to see your father, you are terrified of the secret he has to tell.

You are terrified because in your mind's eye, you saw yourself peek from behind a broken stone wall, you saw the ravens above, black scratch marks against a smoke-filled sky.

From where your dust-filled eyes turned, to catch the hooded man bent on his knees in the stone-filled street.

You see his eyes.

It is him I see, my father, it is his face.

I saw shadows, I was seven years old

I removed the paper bag from my head.

I felt my face, I had not taken a shave in several weeks.

The way my fingers tremble feeling the stringy beard, how I let myself go, at thirty-three years, lying in this bed, in this dark room, on this hilltop.

Like a black curtain falling, all I see is shadow. The doctor's report says it was a suicide.

The report came in a letter, in my father's mailbox. Maybe I can accept that, somehow.

Maybe there is a place for me, somewhere.

They will find these notes, I will lock them in the desk, my father's desk.

The way these days move, the way no one is out and about, I have been lying in bed, days and weeks on end.

There is a thought I should get back to Oslo, but the trains aren't running.

* * *

Treponema pallidum.

The sound those syllables make as I whisper the words in the dark fills me with dread.

My mind plays tricks on me, and the only thing that settles me is taking up a pencil, to a canvas, and sketching, so the sounds of my pencil drown the voices screaming inside my head.

I saw shadows, I was seven years old.

Her naked form was a blur but when I closed my eyes, I saw her.

When I felt her, this girl, in the stone villa on a hill, in a library of books, where she places the pink flower, the palo borracho, behind my ears, and whispers I will draw her, with shut eyes, as my fingers touch her face, and circle her moist lips, and tremble on her unformed breasts.

As she glides my hand down, further, and whispers I will draw a masterpiece. "You don't need eyes to draw, only your heart."

She says my fingers will feel every part of her, this girl who guides my trembling hand on her body, skin soft and warm and smooth to the touch, where my fingertips linger, and my touch is as light as an ostrich feather.

A fear stalks me, the girl tells me not to be afraid as she guides my trembling hand over her unformed breasts; the skin is smooth as silk, my fingers fall to her hips, where her hand places my fingers in the space between her legs.

Do not be afraid, Andreas. Just be still, what I do is an exercise so you will discover the beauty in stillness, the beauty in another's face, as you allow your fingertips to rest on my flesh. My mother tells me we are so much more than flesh and blood, Andreas. My mother whispers we are miracles, we have life, we have passion, we can love. My mother prays to the Saints, she is a Catholic. Mary will protect us; we are God's creation. She says we are holy, and what men do in the dark, when they drink too much, how they cannot even look at a naked woman before they think impure thoughts, this is evil.

The girl tells me her mother takes people's clothes off, people who hate one another.

"They remove their clothes; she makes them stare into each other's eyes.

"Then she paints their portrait."

You remember my mother's name

Her mother is a doctor and an artist.

But we must leave soon, she says, because her mother's friend Jedranka was taken prisoner. She is a doctor in the hospital.

I hear the girl's voice in the wind and the scent of sea salt off the ocean.

Sunlight stabs my eyes; it still hurts in my arm where her mother gave me the injection. The girl whispers her mother's name.

"You remember my mother's name. It is Marija. And my name is Mia." I think my father has led me into a trap.

Mia tells me we will take the train to Belgrade, and then north to the town, Vukovar, to a hospital.

It will be a great adventure, it will just be a few days, then we can go back to Norway.

I have a secret to tell you

I was born a Pinocchio.

It was my nose.

Where the nose bone had melted there was a little saddle, like a finger had reached down from the clouds, a finger touching the wet clay of my nose, as I emerged from my mother's womb.

Pressing, leaving a little mark.

The Oslo boys spit on me, called my mother a whore. My mother was ashamed of her son.

It was all my fault.

She locked me in an old jail cell, with iron bars as thick as broomsticks, in my grandfather's bedroom and threw me a pencil and a sketchpad.

Where I knelt on the hard-timbered floor and drew lines, and circles, and shadows, where one day there appeared the face of this girl.

In my grandfather's room where the old bed headboard is made from the church altar, hand-carved with roses, prickly roses of low relief carved in pine, so when my fingers run over the carvings I think of the girl, I know her name.

The girl with a red vest embroidered with gold, who places a finger to my deformity, on my face, where my nose has melted away.

All I see is shadow

I have a secret to tell.
   All I saw was shadow.
   It is as if I didn't want to see any more.
   When I closed my eyes, on a sunlit midsummer's night, I saw her.

* * *

A tradition, in this room, on a midsummer's night, a tradition, every year, coming back, to this room, to the silence.
   Lying alone on the bed sheets, naked, the window open, the lace curtains billowing in.
   Closing my eyes, trying to remember.
   There was something moving inside my little head that wanted out.
   Here, in my grandfather's pine-timbered room, walls the colour of dark tea, on a bed whose headboard is carved with rose petals, she lies down next to me.
   The little box window is open, the curtain flutters in.
   In my vision my eyes are closed, I am afraid to open them.
   Her tight black hair flows down an olive, slender neck, her rose lips moist, and shining, her blue eyes the colour of the sea, as newly cut lapis lapida.
   She whispers she wants to go to the forests of Fontainebleau and lie down in the grass. She whispers about the old man, the black-muzzled Muslim in the mythic world of Baghdad who visits rich friends with fezzes, and plays draughts and drinks black coffee, in a bug-ridden shop, and ends up in Seville, Spain, prostate in the shadows of that great edifice, the Giralda tower.
   Where he climbs the ramps and looks over the city. There is the Guadalquivir River crossed by nine bridges.
   She tells me Gustave Eiffel built the oldest, the Trina, in 1852.

She whispers, "When you open your eyes you will see me, Andreas. You are not blind." She kisses me lightly on my lips, playfully, and whispers in my ear she has gathered the pink flowers, the fabled palo borracho, of that great tree, the chorica speciosa, and has taken them in the Reales Alcazares, to a palace.

"Palo Borracho… Palo Borracho… Palo Borracho," I whisper back, my lips kissing her neck, entranced by this woman, who holds me in her spell as she caresses my long hair, teasing my blonde locks from my shoulders.

She hears those words, and stills my heart, as she places her fingers to my lips. "Be still" she whispers, as her finger traces over my face.

I have a new nose, I am happy, the way my heart beats, the way I feel the sunlight filtering through the curtains of the room, on a midsummer's night, where a little titmouse sits perched on the windowsill, where the sun sits crowned on the distant mountaintop, ready to sink.

As it escapes, and the light disappears, and she vanishes, leaving me, alone, in this pine-timbered room where there is an old jail cell, black iron bars like pencils, where my mother locked me in as a boy and threw in a pencil, and sketchpad.

* * *

I have another secret to tell you.

The old priest Torbjørn told me my mother infected me with a disease, upon my birth.

The old priest Torbjørn said I was born blind. Infected from my mother's womb.

Levi says I must bow down on my knees, at the altar, and whisper a prayer.

Levi, the little man with raven eyes, says Jesus will forgive my father, Jesus will heal my broken heart.

It was like there were millions of tiny worms twisting inside me, in my infant eyes, and infant brain, because this disease, syphilis, takes the shape of a tiny, microscopic worm.

I felt the little worms exploding inside my head, my father had read up on the disease, told me I needed shots of the antibiotic penicillin.

But my mother wouldn't allow me to get treatment, because at seven years of age my nose bone really started to melt away—it took the shape of a saddle.

Something happened to me on my birthday, when I turned seven, it haunts me.

* * *

There was a shadow, in a dark room. I screamed, then there was silence.
I was marked.

I weep, no one asks me why

I will kill a man, or he will kill me.

A fear stalks me, in the lingering shadow of twilight, as I reach up my fingers, trembling skeletal fingers with yellow tips.

I wave my fingers, like the way the wind sways leafless branches, in this darkening room where I will light a candle.

Where the shadow my fingers make on the wall is like the way the winter's sun casts itself through the sticks in the forest, where I walk all bundled up in the old fisherman's coat, and my silent breath is like the steam from a roiling copper kettle of tea.

No one sees me, but a wolf, whose presence I feel, eyes black as a raven. Where is the wolf now?

Behind a tree, behind a window, staring in.

Sneaking quick-footed, foot pads light as leaves, daring not to betray his presence.

I wonder why he stalks me; I wonder why the raven circles above.

I wonder why the locals turn their faces from me, staggering like an old man with bones bent at the knees where sometimes the pain is too much to bear.

So, I weep, no one hears me cry. I weep, no one asks me why.

* * *

I look away from the sun, shards of light stab my eyes. I turn my head to the ground, my face hooded, my shoulders stoop.

The way the sun glints off broken glass, the way the light stabs, the way I escape into the shadows.

You would think a man who has not quite reached middle age should have a spring in his step.

You would think he would come home to a meal and a warm bed and a lady who kisses him on the lips.

A woman who forgives him for all his misdeeds and impurities, who removes the paper bag from his head and stares into his eyes and sees how they long to stare back.

A woman who is not frightened of my face, who can see past this thing I have done.

Who can stare in my eyes because there lies my heart.

She must know I love her; she must know my beating heart is a spring, all wound up.

She must know I live to die each day for my little thin pencils, sharpened to a point.

So, I can lift my hand to the canvas, so my fingers can dance.

The dance of fingers sketching her face, the left hand reaches its fingers, and touches.

The right hand grasps the pencil like a conductor's wand, and sketches. My eyes closed, since open I see but shadow.

When I shut my eyes, I see colour, I can see the hard blue of the sky hinged upon the flat sea.

* * *

I can see the way the blue fades, like the changing of a foxes' coat, when the summer sun disappears, and the cold winter's glow dances on the fur.

The eye of an Arctic fox, the way it stares, how this animal came to me, one day, just sneaked up from behind.

On that outcropping of rocks in Bodø, on that brisk summer's day, when my eyes were sharp, and I saw out over the flat ocean, shivered as the wind stole into my old wool coat.

An immutable grey vastness sickled over by the pale frame of thought.

I had an idea that I was a drop in the ocean. I had an idea I was meaningless.

I had the idea no one would remember me, but for the memory of my footprint, where I walked barefoot on the beach.

Where they would make out two sets of footprints, because he had found me, and his memory is like a footprint on the shore, which the cold North Sea washes away.

As it rolls in, and the waves mount, and the wind blows in cold and harsh, and the skies hard blue shifts to metal grey.

My students were off, making their landscape sketches, in the shadow of those great mountain peaks, rising like shards of broken glass, when something stepped lightly behind me, I felt a presence, breathing.

I turned, and there sitting still on that mottled stone was the little blue fox with brown eyes.

We just stared for a moment into each other's eyes.

There is a way the light shimmers on its fur, charcoal black, so the blue-tinted hairs stand on end, charged like the sky.

As, when the northern lights whipped across the black and starlit Bodø sky, the dark harbour alleyways I walk, searching for that art gallery on Sjøgata.

There was that big mural named 'Phelgm' depicting a troll on a building. They say one of my students had hammered my drawing 'The Lady From Eiken' with a rusty nail on the gallery wall.

I reached out my hand to the little fox, and the animal just looked at me, considered motionless my gesture.

The fox eyes locked mine in a frozen stare, a moment passed, and then the animal turned away, walked off, so his vanishing form disappeared. A black speck swallowed in the distance by the whitening sand of the beach, on the shore in *Mjelle*, where my bare feet felt the ocean, the cold waters touching me, like the coldness of her touch, when it pulled away from my grasp.

* * *

It was the way Lena stared at me, how her face changed, when I came from behind, touching her bare shoulder, my fingers lightly tapping her neck, in the pleasing manner she loves.

How still she stands, her back to me.

Standing naked by the curtained window in that tiny apartment, when she parted the curtains, and the cold winter light streamed in, from behind some clouds.

Oslo washed over by a faint glow of the morning sun rising in the east, like some phantom giant finger lighting a match above the Trinity Church.

The building red-bricked, and glowing, just a finger's length away, in whose shadow I have often taken my lunch.

It was the way the warmth in her body left, the way her skin turned pale, as she turned to me, withdrew, looked down and said in a quiet voice, "I never expect I can love you, the way you would love me. I am sorry."

I hear distant melodies

Lying in this bed, just staring, the way they play, I hear Grieg, distant, I hear melodies unheard.

My fingers are my instrument.

The way the glass quickens me from my dreams, the way my fingertips tap like my father's fingers, on the piano keys, when there was music in this old house, and Grieg's Sonata in A minor echoed on a midsummer's eve.

I get out of bed, tossing aside the wool blanket, nothing seems to keep me warm. Standing barefoot on the floor, shivering in my wool underwear, a day in May, days lengthen, soon midsummer.

I go to the odd little square window on the wall facing east.

The way the light stabs in this little box, casting itself on the pine-timbered planks, black as tea.

The way the little virus has closed things down, the way I leave this house, walk through the forest to town, the way no one is out, the streets are empty. The silence.

* * *

There is a thought, the way I know what I must do.

I will wait.

Leo had come to the house with a warm pot of *lapskause*.

"You should not be alone," he says.

The way Leo's breath is like a little, sweet wind, the way it touches my face, I breathe his words.

"You know you should not be alone. You are not a strong man, Andreas." I think of the man, the Nazarene, whose eyes watched over the meek.

I hear the bells ringing. The clanging of the bells ringing in the valley. "I thought maybe you would be in church, today. It is Pentecost."

On a spring day, I can lay on the floor, and wait, as the early light creeps up my face.

I can lay still for hours, feeling the morning's faint light, just a hint, like the girl's touch, the way her fingers touched my face, hands smooth as silk, warming to me as her whispering soothed my fear, as I hid myself, in that dark place.

I must go downstairs and start a fire, put on my coat, pour myself some hot coffee from the kettle.

I need to see light

There is only one window in this attic bedroom.

The small little box window cut out hastily, in the autumn of the year 1918, when my grandfather's sister Hanna lay coughing in this windowless room. "I need to see light," she cried.

My great-grandfather Torkyl abided by her dying request and cut a hole in the wall.

The dim autumn light stole in with the cold air.

Twelve-year-old Hanna lay feeble in that great pine bed hand-carved with rose petals.

And died, as a child going to sleep, smiling grimly, the last images being the light dim, the shaking of leafless branches, her hand going limp in Torkyl's grasp.

I feel around for the coat, it's laying on the night table where I put it.

There, I find it, I put it on, that great blue fisherman's coat with brass buttons. Leo says I will become just skin and bones because I am not eating.

He had checked up on me.

"I am sorry I didn't go to the funeral."

The way I listen, his voice lingering, waiting for my reply. Around Leo, I do not need to talk.

He hears the way the wind rushes into the room, the way I crack open the little oven door, the old, soot-black Jotel, where I lay a few birch logs and light a little fire.

Ladling water from the bucket into the pot, placing it up on the oven. "They say you killed your father."

I reach out my hand to the mirror's glass, to the reflection of my face, I see my outline. Levi says I look like Jesus.

My fingers tap the mirror where my face's shadow lingers,

to the place of my nose's reflection, the mirror, flat, betrays no deformity. Retreating my tapping fingers to my face.

I feel the place on my nose where the bone melted away. It is just a little mark.

It is more than just a mark.

The way the little place on my face burns in me, the way I had dyed my hair, the way I painted my face. Trying to hide what lay hidden behind the mark, the poison infecting every waking thought.

"Andreas, I am frightened for you. Your disease has awakened. You need to see the doctor."

* * *

On a face whose eyes hide themselves in the shadow of my hoodie, and those oversize dark glasses, so that I can walk the streets, in my imposed exile from this world, without much attention.

"They say you walk alone, like a monster, people stare at you from a distance."

"Leo, we all stare at a distance, now."

I take a pencil, a little sharpener, and the pocketknife from my coat pocket, and stare out the window, my shadow on the glass.

The ladies will look up, and see me in my old wool fisherman's coat, my face hidden by that black hoodie, as they appear on the worn path at the forest's edge.

They will see the old farmhouse, they will wonder what kind of person lives in this falling apart old place, where I cut the electrical wires.

Where I held my father's hand.

Where I lie still, where I stare out the window, where I lift a pencil.

Where in a dream his last words come to me like the flitting of a titmouse's wings, as the tiny bird flutters into the room through the open window, flitting back and forth, in this cage where I sit at the desk.

As it escapes back out, a rose's faint scent lingering in the sun-warmed air.

The only heat comes from the little Jotel oven in the bedroom and the fireplace downstairs.

There is no light, only here in this little attic bedroom, where the candlelight plays my shadow on the window.

The rooms are dark, the memories of what happened between these walls play like the shadow of a black cloud passing a full moon.

When not a sound is heard, as when I lay naked and silent in bed, staring at the ceiling, because he has just left, and the creaky sound of the door's closing fills me with sadness when the door shuts.

"Leo, something happened to me when I was a boy."

"The doctors said you were cured."

"I don't mean that, Leo. There was something else."

* * *

In the stillness, I hear a woman singing.

I wonder at the meaning of the words.

It is a hymn to a thousand murdered poets.

It is a hymn to the oppressed, the poisoned air they breathe, the unsmiling faces and nameless graves where the woman are buried like litter.

It is a hymn to the footprints of blood where the prosecuted stumble in the dark, in chains, naked in the forest, where they are shot.

In the forest where the shadows dwell and the gunshots ring out and the dead vanish in the night.

I light up a cigarette, fill my cup with hot water from the pot and stir in a teaspoon of instant meat broth.

There is a faint scent of frangipani, fragments of dreams, the play of fingers on ivory keys, the straying fingers tapping the keys, black and white, in the stone palace where the melodies echo filled my spirit.

Where I sat on a stool, and lifted my pencil, to the canvas, as she sat in the light, stabbing through the holes between the stones, so her face vanished, and I struggled to see.

"Andreas, close your eyes in the light."

"If I can't see, how can I draw?"

We are children. My father has taken me on a train, to this place. He tells me I have a disease; I have syphilis, a woman will give me shots of penicillin.

I open my eyes.

I see shadows, bars like pencils, I am in the jail cell.

Lying on my back, on a mattress. I squeeze my eyes again, roll my pupils around, my eyes coming in and out of focus.

I get up off the mattress on the floor of the jail cell.

Standing naked, in this jail cell, in my grandfather's bedroom, grasping cold iron bars.

I scream and shake the bars.

I don't remember how I got here.

I squeeze my eyes again, open them, make out a candle burning in the middle of the floor.

I feel the biting of a million ants on my skin.

I see my grandfather in that jail cell, in Grini, lying on the floor, looking up at the threads hanging in the ceiling.

I feel the cold iron bars of the cell, my hands desperately feeling for the lock.

The door is locked, and when I try turning the key my shaking fingers fumble, and the key drops to the floor.

Crouching down on the floor, my arm stretching out under the bars across the floor, feeling for the key.

I can't reach it. I hear a woman's voice.

A woman's soft voice, calm, coming from the shadows.

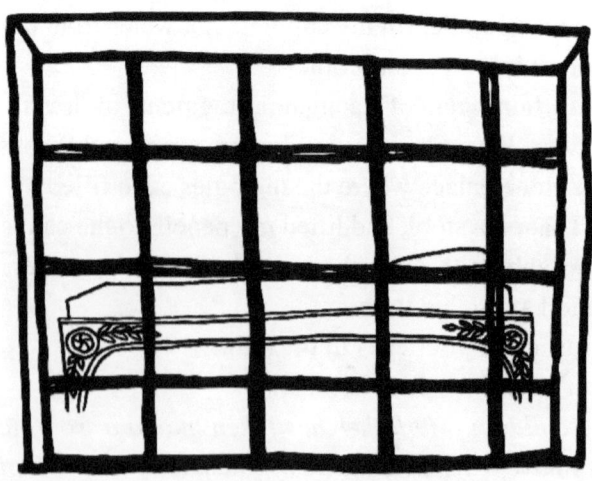

A nightmare from which I have never awoken

There is a scene that plays in my mind.

A nightmare from which I have never woken. It begins when I was seven years old.

The doctors said it was brought on by syphilis. Maybe I am crazy.

They say I have a morbid imagination. Only one person could tell me the truth, and that was my father.

"He was around here last night," my father said.

"Here, in your grandfather's house," typing on his old *Corona* typewriter at my grandfather's desk.

"Svein wanted to tell me something but said he forgot, he had to take his son to a soccer match."

"What happened, Father? You can tell me."

My father looks at me like he has seen a ghost, rips the paper out of the typewriter, locks it in the desk drawer. "Oh, I was writing just some dribble."

I tell my father about my dream.

I am a black bird circling overhead, looking down, at a town in ruin. Rubble-choked streets in a black scene littered with dust; strewn bodies, laying like broken sticks. Animal corpses bloated, and bursting, purple formless bodies filling with gas. The stench of death and dead children with glass eyes, wide, and staring, like porcelain dolls' faces, alabaster white, where their silent collective scream rises into the smoke-filled sky. There is no god who has heard them cry, no angel of mercy has come to their rescue. Skeletal buildings smoking, and burning, cratered with holes, where there emerge wild-eyed men, drunk and screaming, because their pockets are full of looted treasure. I see in my dream not a single tree with leaves, all skeletal, like the hungry dogs, stray, and the scene shakes me, because there is a magnificent stone church whose dome is broken. I see the altar, where the dome lays, and there I see myself, a boy, hiding, with the girl, the girl with the red vest embroidered in gold. It starts raining in my dream. The wind and rain blow in through the shattered windows; there are deafening explosions, like the rumble of earthquakes, one after another. There are corpses and mangled bodies and children lying still in the streets, littered corpses and the smell of burning, and then a silence, dreadful, as the girl in my dream whispers her mother will find us, they will not shoot her, because she is a doctor. "She is a Serb-Croat, she has friends on both sides, that will help." she says.

"You had a seizure, Andreas."

My father put away his writing, locked it in the drawer, pulled me up into his lap.

He had a way with me, the way he could stare in my eyes, and not say anything.

He wanted to tell me something, his eyes revealed anguish, the way he turned his face away, looking out the window, distracted by my grandfather picking ripe summer apples. I remember I was in this room, in Grandfather's old house, I had found some of my father's notes in the desk.

I remember sitting at the desk going through the drawer.

There was a colour photograph. I held the little photograph to the summer light stabbing in the window.

I saw myself, I was sitting on a stone bench, under a great stone arch, on the stone floor of a great stone palace. *Diocletian's palace.*

Where a girl in a red vest sat under a great stone Roman arch, a girl with straight black hair, eyes as blue as the summer sky.

"You have never been to Croatia, Andreas. Those terrible dreams, Andreas, you have made them up. You have never been outside Norway, Andreas. It is all hallucination."

A fir tree drops to the ground

A boulder drops to the sea. A casket drops into a pit.

A woman's voice, filled with ecstasy, echoes in the mountains.

I stand on the hill, the sun at my back, a summer's morning, in my coat and sunglasses. The way I feel the sun sneak up and warm my shoulders, the way my shadow is thrown pencil-thin on the road.

I am alone on this hill.

Days and weeks and months have passed, unnoticed, since I arrived. When the doors shut when my countrymen closed the shops.

When Leo locked the door to the library, and I know he is alone, in that office.

With his books.

All because this little mischievous virus awakened itself, as if it had a plan, sneaking about, the way it creeps up, in your personal space.

I am not an old man, I am thirty-three.

The way I have lived, walking the alleyways of Oslo, the way I was alone.

The way my friends left, one by one, the way their departing words drift back, in the silence.

I want to give away that which I want most for myself.

* * *

The gravelled road winds down to the forest path, old guard stones marking the road's edge where the cliff drops.

I can go to the edge, sit on a stone, feel the rush of wind, take a smoke. There is something about rolling your own cigarette.

Listening to the sounds my fingers make, striking a match, putting the fag to my lips as the *rollie* lights up and the glow sparks.

The worn path to the waterfall runs through the forest. It is like walking in a dark tunnel.

I can see at the end of the tunnel flashes of light in the sky where the sun breaks through the treetops. If I stop and just stare long, I start seeing the outline of things.

I know the way, down the hill, coming to the rusty iron gate.

There is a sheep pasture and meadow I must cross, a narrow-planked foot bridge with rusting cables over the river.

I hear clanging bells in the distance, the sheep are up and moving about. They come to me, unafraid, I lay down in the grass, hide myself under the coat.

I can lay for hours. Just looking up, to the black sky.

A flock of sheep are snorting over me, looking down on this old blue coat with the curious brass buttons.

Then I show myself, peeking from under the coat, removing my glasses. They stare, snort, and move on.

I kiss his lips

There are places on the stones where the sun strikes and the mica flakes glitter. There is one big round stone where someone carved the likeness of a face. Where the light glitters atop the stone like a king's crown.

King Svein of Skårdal, I call the stone. I kneel in his mighty presence. I raise my hand to his nose, feeling its outline, warm to the touch.

I kiss his lips, there is a way the stone has a way with me.

This mute, unfeeling stone speaks to me, it will sit here when I am gone.

It will remember where I pressed my hand, where my tears fell, fingertips running down his lichen blotched cheeks, where the green hoary moss gathers itself, and fills like a sponge in the rain. I kneel down and drip water from the moss into my mouth, the taste quickens me.

I kiss King Svein's lips, stone eyes a finger's length from my face, where he stares into my sightless eyes.

Like that night sitting with Tor-Inge at a table in the London Pub, staring into his face, as he searched my face, and then as he waved his hand in front of my face, and I saw him vanish, as I started to shake, and call his name, because it was all beginning again.

"Tor-Inge," I cried out, "I am going blind, again! Hold me!"

"No!" he cries out, he takes me up, in his arms, something snaps inside me, like a stick.

"Give me a pencil and my sketchbook!" I shout, as I feel a pencil pushed between my fingers, and then it happens, as always, opening my hardcover sketchbook with the fancy leather binding to a page bookmarked by a ribbon, where I sketch.

"What do you see, Tor-Inge!"

As if an invisible hand guides me, lines are forming themselves, lines forming themselves into leafless trees, skeleton-like, where rope hangs dangling, and from the limbs there are formed stick fingers of figures hanging upside down, bound at the ankles, arms dropping to the ground, necks cut and slit, a forest of hanging, lifeless bodies.

Tor-Inge's soft voice, interrupting my sketching, "I see… figures… hanging… from trees, their ankles… bound by rope…" as the shaking stops, and I lay down the pencil, and stare at him, where his shadow lifts.

My eyes start seeing again, like a curtain rising, and I look down at the sketch, sharpening, I see the lines, where my pencil slit the necks, where the trees were witness to unspeakable horror.

"Andreas, Andreas, my dear Andreas. You need help. What happened to you, Andreas?"

They say something happened to me

The doctors call it psychogenic blindness. They say something happened to me.

They say my eyes can switch on and off, my eyesight can come and go. "Is it related to the syphilis?" asks Tor-Inge.

They cannot say.

But I know exactly what happened.

It started on a winter's day, my seventh birthday. I remember it should have been a happy day, because my older sister Vilde had made a big birthday cake, a *bløtekake*, with big, fat strawberries.

I saw the reflection of the seven glowing candles in the frosted windowpane as I scraped away the ice from the pane. My father hadn't paid the landlord the month's rent.

I had on those big dark sunglasses because the sun hurt my eyes.

The winter sun hung low over the dirty half of Oslo, over the east side of the river.

We lived in a shabby, run-down building, down in the alley I saw a woman all bundled up in colourful scarves fishing something out of the bin.

The gypsy woman tossed a ball out of the can, it was blue, I remember.

The few friends I had: Tor-Inge, Bent, and Rolf, were there, shouting and telling dirty jokes, around the kitchen table piled with wrapped presents and balloons.

Vilde says "Make a wish, my little brother, and blow out the candles!" as I take off the big sunglasses.

I was shocked. I saw the balloons, the red and blue and yellow balloons, I could read the handwriting on the birthday card.

My eyesight had come back, the doctors said the spots in my eyes had disappeared, after all those years in Oslo in the Montessori school when I could not see a thing.

I was finally free of those horrible, dark sunglasses!

I had taken them off, my eyes adjusting to the light, as I crept into my father's room, sneaking up on him, while he spoke on his mobile phone.

My fictional novel is about a Norwegian writer on holiday with his friend in Vienna, in 1985. There my main character Harold falls in love with a mysterious, beautiful woman, a young psychiatrist who is also an artist. They meet up again several years later when Marija happens to be travelling to Zagreb. Harold goes along, travels to her childhood home on the coast in Split where they meet Marija's family and Marija's young daughter, Mia. Marija finds out her best friend, Jedranka, also a doctor, who has been treating the wounded from the border conflict in Vukovar, is imprisoned in a camp near the hospital. Marija, in an effort to free her best friend, travels to the hospital. There she secretly coaxes Croat and Serbian soldiers to lay down their weapons long enough so that she can paint their naked portraits. In the process, the soldiers discover the futility of their hatred toward one another. Stripped of their uniforms and guns, facing one another, naked, they have nothing to hide but their own lies. In that way, Marija peels away layer upon layer of the soldiers' mutual suspicion and hatred. Then Marija is discovered for her activities, she is arrested, and imprisoned with Jedranka. I am working on the rest of the story.

My father heard me in the room, was startled, put down the phone hurriedly, collected his papers, locked them in the desk drawer, and came over to me.

"This story you are writing, Pappa, is true. It is not fiction. The dreams I have, they are true!" My father slapped me.

He was overcome with grief, taking me in his arms, as I struggled to get free.

"You hit me!"

My world went dark. I stopped seeing.

Like a light switch had been thrown. The shock of my father's violence, his anguished look just before it all went dark for me, shouting for me to come back, he had something to tell me.

I ran out of the apartment, down the steps.

Coming up the steps I bump into an old man. I recognise his voice, it is Torbjørn, the old priest.

"Happy Birthday, Andreas," he says coldly, brushing up beside me.

I stopped on the steps, I heard a pin drop, I knelt and handed him the gold crucifix. Torbjørn was a shadow, the way my eyes hurt, I made out his stern, wrinkled face.

I smelt alcohol, when I touched his hand, it was cold. He stood lifeless like a statue.

I felt a little mole on his face. He takes my hand away from his face, his face written with shock.

The way he turns, goes up the stairs, I hear his words, shrill and sharply whispered, "Happy Birthday."

I think it is strange, this old man who comes regularly to visit my mother. I run outside into the dirty alleyway, knocking over full bins, collapsing to the ground.

Getting up, feeling the walls, smelling the stink of rotting food. My hands feeling the brick, weeping, on my birthday, my fingertips coming alive.

I had a pencil in my pocket, I felt for some paper on the ground. I couldn't see a thing, just a distant light in the sky, stabbing down in the crack between the tenements.

I started sketching the scene, there was a Roman arch, a girl, sitting cross-legged on the stone floor, her face turned to the light, filtering in, just touching her face.

Aglow, eyes blue, as lapis lapida.

I am blind to colour

There are soft places in the forest, where the reindeer moss lays matted.

When I close my eyes, I see colours, reds and greens and yellows, drops on a canvas, colours I saw as a boy before I became sick.

I am blind to colour.

There is an old, mighty fir tree, a Norway Spruce, the sap runs, the sweet smell of the needles is like the smell of fresh-cut lemons.

The way the sharp needles feel on my fingertips, the way I play the little cones in my palm, feeling the round scales with my fingertips.

The way I can sit for hours, under the old giant, listening, how the wind plays through the trees, how the light touches my face.

Taking out the little sketchpad and pencil from my pocket.

Sketching, with closed eyes, feeling the pencil touching the folded little pieces of paper, the handmade paper my father bought for me in the artists' shop in Grünerløkka.

My father found me in Grandfather's garden on a summer's day, sitting by myself sketching.

* * *

He put down his beer bottle, flicked the cigarette from his mouth, looked at my drawings.

He could stare for several minutes without saying a word.

I know he admired my work, he wouldn't say anything, then after a while, he asked, "Did you really draw these, Andreas?" as he gave me back the sketchbook, and I ran off, back to the old house, where I would find that place in my grandfather's bedroom, the room with the jail cell.

Where, under the floorboards, I hid my sketchbook.

Where I hid the sketch of that girl's face, the girl with blue eyes and black hair and a round face, in a red embroidered vest with gold braid.

The girl who had seen my drawings, the girl who whispers in my ear, as I sit alone, by myself, in the forest where the light had a way of hiding itself.

I would cut the bark with my little knife, just to get the sap running.

The taste of the sticky sap on my tongue, the strong smell awakened me, quickened me, stilled my soul.

Because at ten years of age I was troubled, there was a mark on my face.

Where the nose bone melted, so when I took a mirror to my face I saw the deformity. The boys would wait for me behind the hedges of my grandfather's garden.

Then, when I walked by, they sprung out, throwing stones, chasing me into the forest. They shouted terrible things.

My mother was a whore, I was a bastard son.

There was the mark on my face, where the ugly nose, crooked, melting away, was witness to a truth my young mind could not wrap itself around.

They say I was born with syphilis.

They say I inherited the bacteria from my mother.

This contagion, this tiny worm reawakening itself, a shadow stalking me. They blame Wenche, my mother, they say it passed to me in the womb.

All I know is that my childhood is a blur, I have no memory of events, or playing with friends.

There is just the touch of my pencil on paper, in that special school where my mother sent me because I was blind.

My mother did not know I didn't want to see. I learnt to read braille, with those coloured little Lego bricks, I learnt how to touch.

All I needed was my fingers, the way they played on the little bricks.

* * *

I come to the old tree.

It is my morning ritual, extending my hand to the tree, taking out my worn pocketknife, making a mark, touching the fresh sap oozing to the surface with a finger.

I see a flash on the horizon, the sun rising, the skin on my face twitches, I feel a tear forming in my eye.

The way the light stabs in, though I have those big, dark sunglasses on. I was just a boy on my first trip to the old house.

It was before my eyesight got really bad.

I was upstairs alone in my grandfather's bedroom, about to shut the window, when a tiny egg-sized titmouse, with a red-and-white breast and charcoal wings, flew in, darted around the room, and flew out again. I saw colour!

Then all became quiet. Nothing stirred. Or spoke.

I stretched my head outside and saw the places in the grassy meadow pressed flat where the elk had lain the night before, chewing lazily those juicy red apples, fermenting the juice in his great stomach.

The sight of trees everywhere, up hill and dale, just a breath away, tall, straight- pine and fir astonished me.

There was even a small white flower, the *liseklavelia*, which blooms for only one day, a year.

As it did my first week at the old house, when Grandfather Olav brought a dozen town folk under the apple tree, to watch this spectacle of white buds opening.

I could make out down in the valley the few dozen white farmhouses with black-tiled rooftops, scattered and few and far between, like so many afterthoughts on a painter's canvas. My father was downstairs on a sofa all curled up on a couch, drinking his beer, getting all smoked up.

I looked down, saw him in the open doorway, just smoking a cigarette, staring out in the valley.

That's when I heard him say those things about my mother, how he whispered those swear words, how he didn't know I was watching him.

Back in the room on the desk, I remember there was a half-eaten apple, a Halliburton pen, sticking out of a brown stoneware bottle of blueberry ink, with a cylinder body and pour lip. I remember the label "ARNOLD'S BLACK WATERPROOF DRAWING INK, FOR DRAUGHTSMEN AND ARTISTS, LIQUID INDIAN INK."

An L and M cigarette burning in a pewter ashtray.

A vase of vibrant blue lavender stems dried and bundled, a hand-carved wooden bowl of freshly picked cherries.

I admired the bowl, it was a present from Simon Peter, the old priest, who had knocked on the door.

It was a timid knock, just two taps, and when I ran down the steps, I saw in the corner of my eye my father on the sofa, he was snoring.

Old Simon Peter just stood at the door, looking down at me, with a beautiful, soft, old man's smile.

He was ninety-three years old, with shoulder-length white hair, blue, liquid eyes the size of walnuts.

He was an expert wood carver and created leafy, flowery designs in the *rosemaling* style. He peeked, saw my father, took out from his pocket a little package wrapped in newspaper with a red ribbon.

"Give this to your Grandfather Olav, Andreas. It is a gift."

My grandfather had driven to visit his friend Helge, who lived in Tonstad. They were prisoners together in Grini, in the Nazi work camp, outside of Oslo.

The way the wind blows cold

I sit on this big stone, gazing down at the white water splashing from the waterfall, on the forest's edge, where the rocks are smooth and round.

Where I hopped happily barefoot from stone to stone, as a boy with my pants pulled above the knees.

The falls have a way of playing with my eyes, the way the light reflects the water, the way I make out the familiar, unchanging scene.

Where I sat for hours with my sketchpad and pencils, tracing the outline of leaves and trees while listening to the rustling of birch leaves no bigger than a mouse's ear.

Sitting on a stone by the thundering waterfall, sharpening my pencils with my pocketknife.

With my drawing pad and pencil above this churning maelstrom where my father took me as a boy—he told me a man can be hypnotised if he stares too long at the surging river. Pencil shavings caught by the updrafts, scattered up and blown away, far away, to the North Sea.

Now all bundled up in my grandfather's fisherman's coat—a prized inheritance, double-breasted with brass buttons.

Nothing can keep me warm, even now, when the children go in shorts, and the way I shake, and the touch of women's flesh, what is that?

I am a stick in the forest. There is a wolf in the forest.

There is a wolf in the forest, here in Norway, in this valley hidden from the sun. Where even in May, with the lengthening day, the light steals in like a thief, because shadows form quick.

The way the wind blows cold when the sun drops down, the way the sea fingers in the fjørd, the way stones rain from the sky.

The way this nameless man stalks me, this wolf in the forest.

Where the sun squints behind the clouds, and now and then peeks through, like so many knives flashing, like thunderbolts, stabbing my eyes, as I hide my face from the light.

I caught his shadow once, when he ran off, back into the forest, from behind that great fir tree near the old barn, where I had gone to collect some firewood.

It was winter, the snow lay ankle-deep, the sounds of my boots crunching betrayed my presence as I heard someone coughing.

I called out "Who is there!"

The sun stabbed my eyes; I saw his shadow, as he ran off. I found his footprints, in the snow.

My fingers traced the boot's outline, he was not a large man.

I squeezed my eyes, for a moment, shadows sharpened, I made out on the old red barn door the word "Homo."

I have a feeling I will kill this man. Or he will kill me. Is he watching me, now?

I can take a last puff from my cigarette and be done with it.

I hear the ringing of church bells

A man loses his sanity because the guilt of living peels away skin and muscle and fibre like the peeling away of so many layers of onion skin.

Like all the onions I peeled at Easter with my friends, before I left Lena.

When we boiled the eggs and coloured them yellow with the onions in that black kettle on the foot bridge.

Until what sanity remains hangs like a thread on a skeleton, with just sticks for bones, and a stone for a heart, and a crooked, misshapen nose because your mother told you a lie.

So now I am the starving artist.

Hiding in the shadow of my shoulder-length hair, in the shadow of these great mountains where I am a little stick.

Chain-smoking those fucking cigarettes, just like my father.

Treponema pallidum.

A poetic name.

I think, a *tintinnabulation*.

I hear the ringing of the church bells, — it must be Sunday.

Bells ringing down in the valley, by the bend in the river, where a raven sits atop the church tower, marble eyes black as the winter night. Watching for me, ready to swoop down and pluck out my eyeballs.

I hear the songs; I hear Levi's voice over the loudspeakers.

There is music, a band playing, a guitar strumming, children's voices in chorus.

"I am weak, but thou are strong… Lord, help me, Jesus…"

The town's folk are gathered in the square, in their automobiles. That is how they practise social distancing.

* * *

My eyes squint at the sun.

There is nothing left to do but weep.

Lena once told me grown men don't cry. Lena, who wore the t-shirt that said *With Anyone. Anywhere. Anytime* on the day I left her, when I told her my little secret, standing in the doorway of my apartment as I was about to join some artist friends at the Aker pier in Oslo.

In the town's centre the drifting echo of a prayer, a child's cry.

"I forsake the devil... I believe in God the Father... I believe in Jesus, God's son, born of the Virgin Mary..."

A man loses his sanity, little by little.

Like the way sand is blown away by the wind.

As it blew away my sculpture on the beach, in the shadow of the runes, at Husby, where the Viking mounds lay like giant turtle shells along the road.

Where my sand sculptures made something of a local sensation.

My father kept one promise in his life. And that promise he kept in the old house, on the day my grandfather died.

The doctor's report said my grandfather died of natural causes. My father had an alcoholic liver, his death was ruled a suicide. I do not know how I can run from that disturbing fact.

It would be easy to say *What The Fuck* and just end it all.

I see shadows

Feeling the rain drip down my face, hanging on my dirty blonde, scraggly hairs, drops of tears and rain dropping, one by one, into the maelstrom.

    I am relieved the police have finished their investigation and they say the case is closed.

    I told them the night the gunshot awakened me, from downstairs, I heard a glass bottle shattering.

    There came the sound of a heavy thud like a body hitting the floor.

    I raced downstairs in my underwear to the dining room and found my grandfather, in his rocking chair, like he was asleep.

    Bald-headed, bushy-eyed Olav, whose big body, shaped like an egg, lay slumped in his rocking chair.

    My father was sprawled on the floor.

    The floor littered with empty beer cans and crumpled packs of cigarettes.

    I cradled my father's lifeless body in my lap, the blood oozed from a hole in his right temple.

    He was ice cold, there was no life in him.

    I see shadows, and squint as the sun peeks above the mountains in the east.

    I step back from the edge, sit on the stone, wipe my eyes with the little embroidered cloth I always have with me.

    As I look up back at the sun, I see shadows forming themselves, stirring images from stones and trees, and there, magically, in front of me, I see the girl who lived in the stone palace, on the island of Pag.

    The girl with hair like fine Konavle silk, black as the Norwegian night.

    The girl with olive skin, eyes the colour of the sea, in a red vest embroidered in gold.

    Who first came to me in a dream. Who comes to me now.

I see myself, a boy, standing in front of the palace, the girl approaching. As within a whisper's breath, she plants a kiss on my cheek and vanishes. I think how I kissed that man, on that fateful night in the London Pub, the night Lena said she would pack her things and leave.

"Leave me, then! Just leave!"

"I can't leave you, Andreas."

Lena is like the night that follows the sunlit day. She clings to me, wants my touch.

The way teenage Lena posed for me, finding me in my grandfather's house, where I waited for her.

The way she was frightened when she removed her clothes.

"I won't hurt you, Lena, I promise. I will make a sketch, then you can pay me, take the drawing, and leave. I guess you saw my ad."

The way she sat, silent, as I sketched, the hours passing, the way the fear fled her, as I closed my eyes, extended my fingers to her face. Where they traced her form, as my hand fell to her shoulders, down her arms, lightly tapping, feeling the tension in her muscles melt, as the candle's flame cast her shadow, and the scent of lavender filled the room.

* * *

Her name is Mia.

The girl with the purple iris hid behind her ear.

The girl with olive skin, eyes the colour of the blue-green sea, hair as black as the Norwegian night.

Straight, silky hair falling on a red vest embroidered in gold.

Mia, an Italian name short for the holy name Mary, meaning mine. Mia, the girl embracing my thoughts, who came to me first in a dream. Before I started to see terrible things, and Lena told me I was going crazy.

I have something to tell you

I was in a darkened room with the girl in the red vest and an old man lying in a bed.

That mysterious girl whose face is hidden in a shadow, wearing a coarse linen dress and red silk shirt and khaki jacket inlaid with thick gold braid.

"You must be dressed and washed," she prods the old man on the bed. His eyes stared up at the ceiling.

The brown mole on his nose is the size of a pea.

His legs were cut off just above the knees and the fleshy stumps were strawberry red.

She sits on his bed, takes a washcloth from a basin and wets it. She sponges his face, wipes the mucous from his nose.

She washes his face. She starts at his eyes and wipes away the sleep. She goes to his nose.

"Blow, now, try to blow out, Grandfather." His lungs are too weak.

She puts her fingers in his nostrils to pull out the crusty mucous, takes a cigarette and lights it up and puts it between his lips.

The light of an oil lamp hanging on the wall shines down on the floor paved with flagstones.

Muslin sacks and barrels are strewn about, light stabs in through a shoebox-size window above his headboard.

She goes over to the window and looks down at the courtyard where an old shepherd wearing a yellow turban stands beneath a broken Roman arch.

She looks at the graveyard where carved stone stumps lay crooked among the long grasses and the wild irises.

I think to myself in my dream: Only the men receive carved stones. The women lie in unmarked graves, and their stones are smooth.

I know in my dream the thoughts of this mysterious pretty girl, her face hidden in shadow.

It is because of something hidden in his soul. He will not tell her, but she knows. Ever since that short old man, black from the sun, with a glass eye and turban and sandals knocked at the door.

He was eighty years and said his name was Kiril. He was from Sarajevo.

He had the photo of a man. He showed it to the girl.

He explained it was taken at Jasenovac, in 1941.

He had walked fifty miles to this house because he needed to look in the man's face. To look him in the eye. No more.

Just to look and turn away to the sea. That is all he needed to do.

When she went back to him, he already knew.

He had heard the old man's voice in the wind. The old man whose legs were cut off, the old man who had a secret to tell.

"I have something to tell you," says the old man, in a laboured voice.

"Whisper your secret in my ear," says the young girl.

She gets on the bed, draws her ear to his whiskered face, and he whispers his secret.

In my dream a ray of light reveals a tear falling from the girl's face. I see a tear falling in slow motion, like a crystal, breaking apart on the stone slabs.

Outside, in the courtyard, as the sun dropped into the sea. Worn, brown pages blowing open. A photograph.

It was a picture of the old man, the man with no legs. In the picture, he was a young man. In a Nazi uniform.

The girl in my dream lays her head down and weeps, and no one hears her cry, except me, peeking out of the shadows.

The girl lifts her hand, sees me, fixates on my face, as she gets out of the bed, walks up to me, staring at my nose, at the saddle, where the bone has broken.

Large eyes full of tenderness, blue and brown with a tinge of honey, a voice like the warm wind blowing off the Adriatic.

"I will fix this," —she pulls a warm wad of gum from her mouth, seats it over the dimple. Her forefinger taps it down and makes it smooth.

From her dress pocket, she takes out a little mirror and holds it to the nose, so I see my reflection. I am shocked to see a normal nose.

Her voice whispers now as she pulls up to me, in a voice playful, entrancing, tickling my senses. *"La vita è più dolce con te,"* the words sweet-scented.

She gently kisses my cheek.

I had forgotten my name

This morning I woke to the *tick-tock* of the grandfather clock.

I put on my clothes, the coat, my thick woollen socks and clogs, walked down the steps.

"What is my name?" I asked myself.

"I don't know," I replied.

Coming to the door I had nailed shut.

Behind the door, what would I find? What would I remember? I want to forget.

I want to remember!

Banging my head against the door. It could be another day in June.

I could just go out for a stroll with the gang, on those heady Oslo nights full of gay perambulations on Karl Johann, stumbling out of the London Pub after a night playing pool and slow sipping chilli cocktails.

Grünerløkka was my hangout, the little galleries in the back alleys stole my attention, strolling along the Akerselva, what could be better than that?

Lena didn't care, I didn't fit in with her crowd, she asked no questions.

That was all before I started seeing shadows, before the headaches, before the light stabbed my eyes and Tor-Inge said I must have AIDS.

No, I had taken the tests, they were all negative.

Tor-Inge wept when I stopped seeing his face, when it all went black, on my opening night, when he had to lead me out of the gallery, hurrying me back away from the admiring crowd, sitting me down in the men's room, giving me a glass of water.

"Andreas, you must tell me something."

I hear Tor-Inge's voice, this tall, hard-muscled man with white, short-cropped hair whose heart melts mine because he has been by my side all these years.

The others left when I started losing weight. They were frightened. My head buried in my hands.

Like a curtain falling, I see nothing, feel but his warm hand on my head, as I lift my head to his staring face, the way I smell him close to me, the perfumed scent of his aftershave, my right hand's thumb and forefinger stretched out to his eyes, whose lids my fingers gently close, as Tor-Inge settles down, a minute or two passes, I don't know. A knocking at the door. A man's angry voice.

"Are you two finished?"

"Hey, give us a minute. Just got to clean up the mess," shouts Tor-Inge.

"Tor-Inge," I whisper. I know his eyes lock mine. "Don't you remember? What happened last night?"

"You were drunk and got into a fight. There was this punk who was dunking this boy's head in the toilet."

"It wasn't that. I told you I need to get away."

"What are you talking about, Andreas?"

"I need to go down south. I need to be alone."

"Where, Spain? You remember what happened in Alicante."

"No, not Spain. Norway, to my grandfather's old house. I need to draw again. Just alone, a pencil and my sketchbook, like I used to."

"Not down in that Bible belt! You told me what happened to you there, those Jesus freaks!"

The way my fingers lightly trace his face, tapping, so gently tapping. The way a man stills himself, the way Tor-Inge melts at my touch.

Tor-Inge kisses me lightly on the lips. More hard knocking at the door.

"Hey, why don't you two fuckers get yourselves a room!" Tor-Inge helps me up.

"Let me tell you something, Tor-Inge from Drammen. I see terrible things, I have nightmares. I see boys hanging naked from trees, my father said my nightmares were brought on by syphilis and the spells I had as a child."

"You are thinking about the war. The Balkan conflict. I was with you, at the exhibit. Don't you remember what you told me?"

"What did I tell you, Tor-Inge?"

"You told me you were there. You were a boy. Your father took you on a train. Don't you have any records of the trip?"

"My father said my dreams were delusions, the doctors found spots on my brain. My father said I have never left Norway."

"Andreas. You have gone with this how many years? Since I have known you, I remember the birthday party. You were seven years old, do you remember? Do you remember what you told me?"

"No. I don't remember. Tell me."

"You said something happened to you. You couldn't tell me what it was. All you could do was cry. I had to take you away from the others, in the bathroom, calm you down. I wiped the tears from your glassy eyes, I waved my hand in front of your face. You didn't see a thing. That's when you broke free from me, I saw you leave, followed you from the window, as I yelled for you. Escaping in the alley."

Grasping Tor-Inge's hand. Looking down, my head bowed.

My name is Eirik

Moments pass, maybe ten minutes, I do not know.

I know he is watching me.

"So, what do you know about me? What have you heard about *The Syphilis Artist?*" I whisper, in a raspy voice, as I strike a wood match and relight the fag hanging from my lower lip.

I cough, damn it, I don't care.

I chain smoke, lung cancer is the least thing that will kill me.

Since I left the school, I have been rolling my own cigarettes, those king-size rollies, so what the fuck do I care what you think?

"Does my smoking bother you?" I shout, because I know he is here, he has not said a word, in this old pine-timbered parish church, along the bend in the river where his faint footsteps betrayed themselves.

I heard him enter at the appointed time, just as the last rays of light escaped behind the mountain, when I closed the leaded puckered windows.

Those handmade windows of Bavarian glass with the bull's eye whose surface my fingers slide over, again and again.

The way the wind turns cold when the sun slips away, the way smooth glass tickles my fingertips, in these shadows where I hear the drop of a pin.

He must be sitting in the back pew.

"I need the money. That is why I am here." A young man's desperate voice.

If he wants to escape, he can do it now, no one will see him leave the church at this early hour, the bar has stopped playing the loud music.

I had pulled the curtains and Levi knows I am not to be disturbed.

He must see me standing at the altar, by the big, framed canvas, as I remove a candle with its brass holder from my big coat pocket.

I kneel by a small table where I have arranged my pencils and light the candle with the glowing fag hanging from my lip.

My knees ache, I see a spark in my eye, like a lightning flash.

It is candlelight reflecting off the brass crucifix above the altar. In the distance the roll of distant thunder, there is rain on the way.

I hold up my pencil to the candlelight and see my yellow-tipped fingers, as I reach into my big coat for the little hand mirror which I hold up in front of my face, so I can see my reflection.

A hooded figure with a turned-up collar.

A thin, haggard and bearded face. I feel the saddle on my nose, the underlying sharp-edged bone, and think one day this disease will eat up my face.

To think I had not a care in the world just five years ago, teaching art to the teenagers in that private school near Vigeland, walking the parks on a summer's eve hand in hand with Lena.

Taking a beer at the Pernilla, a show at the theatre, making love with the windows open as the lace curtains billowed out into the alleyway.

Just so Lena's moans could tickle old Karl's big floppy ears, the pensionist building inspector, who knew to push his broom outside my apartment door on Saturday nights precisely at ten-thirty in the evening.

Just when my bed post started to shake. A shadow.

That is what I am.

This young man sees me in that thick blue fisherman's woollen coat with solid brass buttons. What does he see?

An unkempt bearded man of thirty plus years, this rake-thin shadow who comes out only at night and walks the streets.

When the candle burns all the way down, I will pack up my mahogany box full of whittled-down pencils and tubes of paint and walk back to the old house on the hilltop.

Where I will walk up the steps to my grandfather's cold bedroom and light a fire in the Jotel.

Watching for entertainment the black iron bars of the jail cell play their pencil like shadows on the timbered walls.

I will walk up the steps to the little attic bedroom and stare out the box window and think how the little girl turned her head to the light.

Lying in bed, her hands stretched up to Jesus.

Then her final breath, as she closed her eyes, her voice lingering, as her little brothers and sisters stared silently from the shadows.

There are sounds in the old house, I hear voices, the tapping of piano keys, the echo of a sonata, children's laughter.

When Grandfather Olav spoke of his loving mother, tears came to his large tender eyes.

I know this was a happy house long ago, my grandfather told me stories, his brothers and sisters were good people, of hardy stock.

They were hard-working, forgiving, and upright. I would have liked to have known them, but they all passed on before I was born.

Like skeleton fingers dancing all around me, as my wild thoughts swim and mock me, because I am the *Syphilis Artist*, and I know Levi has told his flock that God has touched his finger to my face, as a mark.

"They say you are a genius."

The man's voice now assertive, strangely appealing, there is the smell of aftershave lotion, and then, what can I say.

He is right behind me.

I turn around to face him.

I see the outline of a young man in an open white shirt and dark pants, clear and large-eyed, blonde straight hair on his shoulders.

I put down my pencil, the burning fag is glued to my lower lip, hot smoke spiralling up.

"My name is Eirik."

* * *

I raise my right arm and stretch out my hand, so the fingers lightly touch his face, tracing the perfect ski slope nose, the smooth, moist skin, how silken it glides under my fingers, as they explore all around the face, the sharp, angular jaw, the smooth straight hair dropping to the shoulders.

This young man named "Eirik."

I sense he is nervous, the way he looks at me.

I see his large, liquid blue eyes staring at me, this beautiful face alabaster white, like it has never seen the sun.

Levi told me he wanted a white Jesus, blonde-haired, blue-eyed, like some damn movie star.

I told Levi Jesus was dark, almost as black as piano keys, brown-eyed, full of Arab blood.

The shock on Levi's pale face and the single tear in his right eye and the moments that passed where he just stared out the window and told me just to accept his offer of twenty thousand crowns.

The young man's strained voice as I start sketching on the blank canvas. "Is it true what they say about you? Is it contagious?"

"You mean the virus. Yes, the virus is contagious."

"I don't mean the virus."

My graphite pencil sketching an outline of the Nazarene's upturned face, sliding quick on the smooth canvas, forming outlines for his up-cast eyes.

I take Eirik's hand and guide his forefinger to the hole on my nose, where the saddle dimples in.

The way his hand tries to pull away, the coldness of his fingertip on my face.

He pulls his hand away.

"Do you want it to be contagious?"

This man's face now like Munch's Scream.

Good, I think, his expression reveals some emotion, like I pinched something inside his head, where his thoughts are just a jumble of youthful gambols.

"I don't have a problem, you know. I mean, I don't care what they say."

A sudden burst of rain and the violent dancing of drops on the leaded glass windows of the old pine-timbered church.

A thunderclap strikes nearby.

There is anger in the sky, a storm is on the way. That is good, I think, no one will bother us. No one will hear us.

"I answered the ad you placed in Agder. Like I said I need the money."

Distant thunder rolls overhead as lightning flashes through the leaded windows, and then the heavens open up and the rain hits the windows.

Jesus was gay, just like me

I had gone over to the little art gallery owned by a menopausal woman with pursed lips and short-cropped red hair, as she was locking the door. "Sorry, we are closed. It's the virus." She lifts her face, meets mine.

She had never seen me without my glasses on. She gasps, like she has seen a ghost.

The way her fingers reached to her lips.

The gallery sold mostly landscapes, carved wooden spoons, and little troll dolls for the tourists. Once I provoked her. After all, wasn't provocation the essence of art?

"Jesus was gay. Just like me!" I remarked, as I left the shop.

She didn't want anything to do with my painting entitled, "Jesus kissing a man."

She stood frozen, staring at me, her mouth gaping open and closed like a fish gasping his last breath. Her mouth moved, but no words came out.

Then she put her hand over her pursed lips, the colour drained from her face and she whispers so I hear her strained breath, "We will pray for you at the guesthouse."

Levi manages the guesthouse.

He tried to convert me to Christianity one summer but gave up after he saw my paintings.

The guesthouse is a popular place for asylum seekers because Levi puts them to work, gives them a room, and some of them get lucky and get to stay in Norway. Once the police came and took away a young woman from Afghanistan because she had no visa or papers.

Levi never got over it.

Levi was wearing a suit jacket with a white shirt but no tie. He had a small gold crucifix pin on a lapel.

I saw him sitting in the lobby in his front office counting money at the cash register, he smiled when he saw me.

He invited me into the library for our usual banter. He was a friend of my father and would drive him home when he had too much to drink at the bar.

"Hello, Levi," I said.

And then I took off my big sunglasses, and he absentmindedly stretched out his hand over the counter. I didn't shake his hand.

"Oh, sorry. Forgot about the virus," he says, as he retracts his hand. "Let's go into the library and talk," he continued.

It's a cosy place, this elegant guest house with traditional Norwegian furniture converted into office space for the church. I followed him into the library, he closed the sliding door, we sat down in leather seats.

I was restless so I got back up as he poured some coffee as I checked out the old books.

I felt the fine leather-bound editions of Ibsen and Bjørnson, remembered someone said that the children's author Roald Dahl had left an autographed book here when he was a guest.

I couldn't read the words on the pages. I was getting hungry, so I sat back down and noticed on a coffee table the biscuits and coffee and last month's green covered local *History* magazine. I flipped idly through the pages and remember they had written an article about my grandfather. Levi had opened a briefcase and took out a photograph and handed it to me.

"It's a picture of the baptismal font inside the Orkdal church in Fannrem.

"It's a beautiful work of art, and I thought you would like to have it." I fished around my coat pocket for my glasses and put them on.

I saw a baptismal font with four angels standing on their toes holding up a golden baptismal bowl.

"Your grandfather was one of the prisoners who presented the sculpture to the church in 1946."

I put the picture down and looked out the window at the churchyard and the graveyard just fifty metres away, across the busy street, where cars and cyclists pass by.

The big Norwegian flag in the courtyard was at half-staff.

A drunk teenager driving 120 kilometres an hour crashed his Opel in the tunnel.

I saw in the distance a dozen young men and women, in dark suits, led by old Pastor Torbjørn in his flowing white robe, as they followed six pallbearers carrying the casket to an open pit under a big fir tree.

"It's a shame. They refuse to work for me because they say my wages are too low. So, they go out, drive too fast, and kill themselves."

The clanging of the church bell from the steeple in my ears as Levi picks up the magazine, flips through it.

"He was a great man, your grandfather. Not many men of that generation left."

I am not thinking about my grandfather and the war is like ancient history to me. He says in a self-righteous tone "Your father, I am sorry to say, was a drunkard." I slap Levi across the face.

I slap him across the face so hard the white imprint of my fingers lingers sharp on his left cheek. He does not react.

He clenches his jaw tight, so the lines of my fingers stretched even longer on his face.

The pupils of his tiny black eyes now dilating, his face revealing hurt. It was all the anger bottled up inside me. Levi is a friend.

Someone slides open the door a crack and peeks in. It is an Eritrean girl with big curious eyes spying on us.

"Slap the other cheek."

I slap him again on the other cheek.

The innocent Eritrean girl disappears. I escape outside. I will walk back through the forest, to the old house.

They will do their questioning and find out nothing

In the dark.

There is someone knocking on the front door, downstairs.

I get out of bed, there is not time for anything but to pull on my jeans, put on some thick wool socks and fisherman's coat, slip into my black clogs.

My knees are unsteady, pain me; I must be careful going down the narrow steps.

"I am coming!"

I recognise the young man's voice shouting from beyond the door. It is Rune, the policeman.

"Andy, we need to take you to Kristiansand for some questioning. All routine, you know."

It takes a minute for my eyes to adjust as I open the front door.

It is early morning, the sun has just risen in the east, I feel the cold slide into me.

There are two police officers standing in the doorway. Rune, and a woman, smartly dressed in their blue uniforms and dark ties.

Tight blue short-sleeve shirts, caps on their heads, no weapons. I see the police van parked in the grass, its headlights casting two hard beams of cold light deep into the forest.

Today I have no problem seeing, my eyes cast a hard stare at Rune's unsmiling face, who returns a hard stare, like he has discovered a new fact in the case of that unsolved mystery.

The brutal and bestial winter murder. Whoever did it used it as a symbol. The madman who did this made a statement; the horror so intense it defied reason.

I turn my gaze at the trees standing as shadowed sentinels, and the hills and meadows up beyond the house, where the invading lupins, purple-stained, are splattered like so many afterthoughts from a painter's brush.

The image of that woman invades my thoughts, and I think I must be crazy to imagine such obscenities. I see her hanging naked, upside down, her long blonde hair touching snow, her body swaying back and forth, back and forth, blood dripping on the white blanketing snow. Tied by her ankles, hanging head down with gently swinging arms like a slaughtered pig, from the branch of that lonely fir tree, in the clearing. The young woman's face as white as the tree's bark, her wide blue eyes open and fixed, her neck slit like a letter. In the meadow where the wildflowers shed wild intoxicants in the summer. I walked barefoot, feeling the moss under my toes. Where I first made love to Lena, by the little fresh brook, where the sounds the gurgling water makes are drowned by the woman's screams.

"Hurry up, Andreas," Rune says, awkwardly, as he awakens me from my daydream. "Just some routine questioning, you know. By the way, is it all right that we take you in for some questioning? You will be back in a few hours."

"Yes, that is fine," I answer.

They cannot hold me overnight in the local police station if I am not considered a suspect. They would have to take me to Kristiansand.

I remember the doctors told me I had spots on my brain.

I remember thinking the disease could do things, make me believe things that were not true. I could fool myself; others could fool me.

I imagine there may be a suspicion I was involved in the disappearance of that young woman, Ida A, because she had knocked at the front door on that cold winter's night several years ago.

I was interviewed in the local police station and released after a few hours.

I told them what I remember.

There shivered a young woman in the crack of the open door, I opened the door, my face hooded, I wore my coat, it was freezing cold, with snow knee deep. "I am not afraid of you," came the woman's voice. I touched her face, wet in tears, as her anguished voice broke. She said was a friend of Lena's, her name was Ida.

She said she was told my sauna was always fired up outside, and if she could just have a cup of tea, and spend some time alone in the sauna, and then she would go her way. "It is late, after midnight, you can stay the night," I said.

Inside the house, in the big empty room, the blazing fire warmed her up, a wool blanket draped on her shoulders, she sipped a cup of tea.

She remarked she was told I was not a dangerous man, I was gay, that if a lonely woman wanted just to lie down in a warm bed, with warm feather blankets, and hold her arms around a nameless man, a shadow, who wears a paper bag over his head, she could do that, without being taken advantage of.

I had painted a nice wedding portrait of Rune and his wife some years ago, I remember. This same Rune who fled from Trondheim to this dark valley because the authorities found out he acted in a porn film. Imagine that.

An officer of the law just had to escape. The nervous-looking young woman, she looks about twenty-one, is about to put me in handcuffs when Rune motions her hand away. "Elisabeth, this is not an arrest. No handcuffs."

It takes me a moment to take all this in, there are so many wild thoughts dancing in my head.

"Rune, give me a cigarette."

It is all just a routine, he knows it, he fulfils my request, scrambling in his pocket for the little box of Marlboro cigarettes, which he fumbles around with, taking out a cigarette, lighting it up with his gold-plated lighter.

The rising sun glistens the smooth metal of the little device, as he clicks open the lid, lights up the cigarette he has pressed considerately into my mouth. The menthol aroma of the cigarette, the way the smoke fills me, settles me; the way the smoke blows out my nostril holes must shock Elisabeth.

Who stares bug-eyed at me, then at Rune, in wide-eyed silent protest.

Before I step in into the metal cage, I feel his hand on my shoulder as I turn to face him.

I remember to spit out the glowing fag. "Forgot to check your pockets." I face him eyeball to eyeball.

There is something beautiful about him, this hard-muscled police officer, this man clean-shaven, in a neatly pressed short-sleeve shirt who calls me Andy. This man with the hard-blue eyes, and the worried face, with short, cropped hair. It excites me, the idea being put in handcuffs, I know Rune senses this, for a moment, just before his face hardens. He has never gotten used to my face.

He hasn't seen me in a while, not since their last visit, when I was driven to the local station for questioning.

No, I did not know anything about that young girl, the one who went missing in the forest, no I had not seen anything suspicious in my walks, in the woods. No, I did not know anything about the other cases, the unsolved mystery of the masked man who broke into all those houses. The houses few and far between, up the valley, where the young girls were molested at night. The way the news sparked fear, a trembling, at night, among the villagers, it was like a contagion. The man wore a paper bag over his head with cut-out eyes. The man crept in through the window, while they slept. The man moved in the shadows, formless, striking fear in the local folk, like a thunderclap. There is a shadow stalking the girls, the doors are locked, the windows shuttered.

Rune fishes around in the deep wool pockets of my fisherman's coat and pulls out what he was looking for.

"We will need to keep these."

He takes out a handful of my pencils, and the little knife, the one sheathed in the decorative leather sheath which I use to sharpen my pencils.

"Elisabeth, make sure these get to the lab" he says hurriedly, handing her the items as he gives me a gentle but firm nudge in the cage.

The door slams shut, the windowless cage starts to shake as I buckle myself in the vinyl seat and the artificial bright light from the caged ceiling lamp stabs my eyes, and I think I just have to close my eyes for a while.

The young woman Ida lies naked in my arms, under the blanket. It always happens this way. Lying by my naked body, hip to hip, a bag over my face, with cut-out eyes. She tells me she is twenty-seven years old, she has had many boyfriends. She tells me she will leave in the morning; she says she has heard stories, I can draw without seeing, that the glint of light on broken glass is enough for me. Just a touch of my hand, just the way my fingers linger, how my patrons show up at the doorstep, from all parts of Norway. It is not a secret, she tells me, that she has heard my name whispered in Oslo, in the Grünerløkka galleries, where in some little gallery one night she saw me, at the opening of my exhibit. She asks me what it is about drawing, what is so special about lifting a pencil to a canvas? I just stare in her eyes, I see the shadow of this woman, no longer nameless, who has spent the night telling me stories of her drunken boyfriends, her idle, boring, beautiful boyfriends, who have never laid quietly next to her, like I do.

I stare, say nothing, that is enough, because the sounds of the wind blowing outside is enough, and the way she breathes, that is enough, and the touch of her skin, that is enough. She cannot understand this passion, it is not logical, I have no way of describing it, I tell her a girl once touched me, a girl who visits me in my dreams, and whatever I love is my own business.

They will do their questioning, find out nothing.

The way the sun hides itself

The way the sun hides itself, the way the wind picks up before a storm.

The way the winter snow melts up in the mountains and drains in the valley, charging rivulets cold to my tongue.

Lapping the water like a dog, filling my empty stomach, while kneeling on the riverbank, in my blue fisherman's coat. Where my head sinks down in the frozen water.

My skin stops aching, my eyes sharpen, I make out a rainbow over the valley where the hot sun has burned away the fog.

A man in a hunter's uniform shot at me, once, thinking I was a bear, the way my shadow kneels on the bank. I was told to wear a vest with reflective tape.

I could never do that.

The way I limp back from the riverbank to the big house along the path in the forest, where my shadow disappears.

Where not a sound is heard. Now that it is spring, the cackling of birds on the treetops.

The way I enter the old house, and don't lock the front door, because my patrons will show up at any old hour, and I have to be ready with my easel and pencils.

* * *

The way she steals into my dreams, night after restless night, the way she wakes me up with a gentle kiss on my cheek. When I lie in my grandfather's bed, on that pine bed carved with roses.

In my dream I am a boy again, with my sketchpad and pencils.

I draw her face and the sound my pencil makes is like fine sandpaper sliding over pine. Like the old pine bowl my grandfather was always sanding, with his wrinkled sausage fingers, how he filled the bowl with Morella cherries, and counted them, one by one.

Where he sits in a chair under the boughs of that great fruit-laden tree in the yard now overgrown with weeds, and sands the bowl, and then there is silence.

A midsummer's night, he snores so I creep on my knees to the tree and cover him with a wool blanket.

I take the golden Comet harmonica from his hand, from his flour whitened fingers, and remember that strong smelling mackerel rolled in flour and melted butter he had for breakfast. The smell never left the house.

The way these dreams awaken me in that old house full of shadows, the pine-timbered farmhouse with walls the colour of dark tea.

The way my eyes open, when the light breaks through the wall of trees that surround the house, where a well-trodden path leads down to the sea.

They know where to find me

The way the grandfather clock ticks and the way the distant church bells ring, all these little things affect me.

I shiver in bed, under the wool blankets, and turn my head to the window, in the dark room. My breath is frost, I need to start a fire and warm the house. I see the morning light aglow on the window, that old window of leaded

Bavarian glass. I can stare at it for hours, how it changes colour.

The light flickers in now, and dances, and touches my face, and the dust particles in the air glitter, as beams slice like light sabres in the shadows.

There is frost on the window this morning, I make out a pattern.

It is the Anahata Chakra, the smoke grey lotus flower with twelve petals.

Shatkona, the tiny flame inside the heart.

I get up, barefoot, in my underwear, and touch my fingers to the frosted glass, my eyes squint at the sunlight playing on the glass.

I trace the figure of the Chakra, two intersecting triangles and twelve petals, petals now glowing vermilion, as the sunlight breaks above the top of the trees.

I start to really shiver; it is like I am barefoot on a frozen lake.

I press my hand and my long piano fingers against the glass. The frost melts away and disappears, and the window clears, the light is blinding.

I think of snow-covered fields, and all I want to do is sleep in bed and wake up on midsummer's day.

There is no electricity, had I cut the wires. I have no need for light. *They know where to find me.*

I like waking up, in a shiver, the way I scrap the frost from the window, taking in what little I need to see, as the sun rises.

That is what Lena could not understand. I had put away some money, I pay everything now in cash, I settled with Lena and closed my accounts. I told her I needed to escape, from everything.

"Why do you need to escape? How can you just leave? There is nothing for you in that little town, you are used to the city. You said yourself it was just full of bible-thumping holy rollers. They will not accept you, Andreas Olav Hansen."

"You never ask me questions, Lena." That was her problem.

She did not know why I had to return to my grandfather's house.

It was only in that dark house where I could lay on the bed, staring into the black.

It was only between those pine-timbered walls where I could lay still, they would come to me, I heard their footsteps up the stairs.

I saw the door of my attic bedroom open, I heard their voices, as they whispered my name.

I did not tell Lena the story, she would have taken it to the police without thinking.

That would have ruined everything.

The young woman abused in the valley, not far from my grandfather's farm, the little houses where the windows were open in the summer, where one could creep in, unnoticed.

I could not reveal to Lena my methods, that would ruin everything.

I close my eyes and whisper

The only light comes from candles and that great antique kerosene lamp.

The lamp that plays the light exactly right, as I sit at my easel on the wooden krak, by the fireplace.

The chair is covered with flowery *rosemaling*.

In that big empty room, I use as my painter's studio where there is a stone fireplace, and that old bride's bench, from my great-grandfather's time.

On that bench where they lay, by the fire, and take off their clothes.

The way the light plays over their bodies, the way my fingers stretch out, and touch their skin, fingertips traipsing as light as an ostrich feather.

As they glide down, so I can feel the distance between the nose and the eyes and the lips, the trembling lips where the lipstick is still wet. I close my eyes, and whisper, and start sketching.

I am in a shadow.

Hidden like the face of that girl hidden in the shadow of that great stone house, the girl in a red vest with gold braid, who gives me a flower, a purple bearded iris. In a dream I take the flower, and fold it in wax paper, and hide it in the pages of that special leather-bound book.

That Hamsun with five raised bands, where my fingers play, sliding on the marbled endpapers, along the gilt lettered spine.

I want to thank her, but she disappears in the shadows, and the wind opens the book, as the pages sweep by.

Black, wordless pages. I am blind in my dreams. The doctors told me I had syphilis.

I remember not wanting to see, because the light hurt my eyes.

* * *

Everything in my early childhood is a shadow.

My fingers traced raised dots on little Lego blocks, I learnt to read braille.

With the tips of my fingers, I had to learn the sound of letters, my lips whispered the sounds of words, like blue, and yellow, and red.

At the Montessori school, the boys started to spit at me, the boys who chased me in the alleyways, as I walked home from school.

Tor-Inge rescued me, pulled me from their grasp, said he was like me. That's when he told me not to be afraid.

He kissed me.

I saw my reflection in the mirror.

My nose had begun to take the shape of a saddle.

I heard stories that my mother gave me the disease, upon my birth. I asked her, she did not deny it, *she didn't say anything.*

No one answered my questions, and then one day, I woke up. I was a just a boy.

There had been a dream. I was hiding, in a room. In the dark.

I could not see, but I could feel.

I screamed, because I was back home, in Norway. And still, even here, I was not safe.

Because I was in *that* room. Where was my father?

What I felt frightened me, I remember how I ran out of the room, down a long hallway, it was a black tunnel.

I remember a man's voice, shouting, I remember running down narrow steps, outside, into the blinding, stabbing sunlight.

I remember finding an alleyway, making out rotten smells, stale urine, garbage overflowing in cans.

I fell to my knees. I did not want to see any more. I did not want to speak.

The way shadows steal over men's faces when I limp on by, all these little things affect me.

It all started with a dream.

A man lays his head down

If it had all been a dream I could wake up, back in my nice little apartment, on the east side in Oslo.

It would be summer, I would be off from school, and would not have a care in the world.

I had been drinking a half a litre of Frydenlund beer at the outdoor Pernilla restaurant on Karl Johann and then paid five crowns to use the toilet.

I looked at my reflection in the bathroom mirror.

Wearing bright summer clothes, the designer labels Lena gave as presents on my thirtieth birthday. My hair was tied up in a ponytail, there was a smile on my face. Yes, my nose was ugly, but I did not care.

The doctors had given me a clean bill of health. It was vacation time; Lena had invited me to her cabin in the mountains. There was so much excitement, with my new exhibit at the gallery, I had received positive press, there was even talk NRK would do a programme about my sketches.

I had released a book, called *PHAEDRO*, with dozens of my simple pencil drawings of the female form. Stick drawings and simple figures, minimalist representations of intertwined forms, coupling lines entangled. There was no self-identity, just spontaneous interactions of lines, the way they form when my pencil finds a life of its own.

This was all before I started getting the headaches before I saw the exhibit of photographs from the Balkan war down at the pier.

Before I changed inside, before I started seeing shadows on the wall. I had exited the Pernilla down Karl Johann, going past the popular Student Tavern where I greeted my students sitting around tables, drinking beer.

They were happy to see me. There were toasts, glasses were raised, I made a speech and Alexander B. told me he loved taking the life drawing class, the others were just shouting and laughing and high fiving.

I went over to the courthouse with its fountains and went in to admire the remarkable wood friezes of Dagfin Weienskiold.

There were ancient motifs about creation, love, and war. I marvelled at the elaborate workmanship. Each gold and silver gilded frieze was made of pine timbers glued into blocks weighing two thousand, two hundred pounds. One frieze depicted Odin, riding his eight-legged Sleipner, the fastest stallion in the world. He had a ring, the Draupne, dripping eight equally beautiful rings every ninth night. Odin's two ravens, Thought and Memory—Hugin, and Munin, flew out every day into the wide world in search of new bark for their master. They guided Odin in the twilight of the forest. Another frieze depicted three Valkyries: Alrund, Svankit, and Alvit who came flying as swans and changed into three beautiful maidens.

* * *

So, midsummer approaches, I am alone, in my thoughts.

Nature is like some wild-eyed fox, staring at me, night after night, ready to break in, tear into my neck, and carry me off into the forest.

That forest so green it is black, even in daylight.

Fir and spruce stands guard around me, hiding me from the world.

A world I escaped, on that April day several years ago when walking back through the woods to my grandfather's house I found Lena on top of bald-headed Trond, the butcher from Sirdal.

His father would be Svein Torkildsen, my father's friend, who is also a butcher.

Like father, like son.

Grinding at the hip so hard he could scrape fish scales from a flagstone.

In that meadow in the clearing with the quick tailed swallows and tiny yellow buttercups sprinkled about, where once Lena walked hand in hand and confided in me that maybe I was just too sensitive.

Something had been bothering me, she could tell.

I would need to see a psychiatrist. "There is nothing wrong with me!" I shouted.

She told me I had something like a seizure when I was sleeping, I had woken up, I had been yelling in my sleep.

She said I was yelling about someone who was chasing me, in the forest.

A soldier, she said, with a rifle. I had never been in the military; I was exempted from service.

A man lays his head down, and weeps, and no one hears his cry.

A nameless town

A tiny, little town, nameless, in a valley hidden from the sun, where light steals in quick, and then escapes.

I know why my father escaped to this place.

He could never really escape.

A forgotten town of only a few hundred towns people, a little white church along the river, pine-timbered, with a tower like a phallus, erect to the cloud filled sky.

Bone-white, noiseless houses, red barns scattered few and far between, like drops of paint splattered from a brush.

A little ribbon of a river snaking in, through the town's centre, where the church sits like a mighty king on his throne, white-robed, and a graveyard stretching to the riverbank.

Headstones smooth black like domino bricks, with gold lettering, so when the sun shines the names light up.

"Hans Hansen... Torkyl Andersen... Erling Moi."

When it pours rain from the clouds the river swells, and grows, the church basement fills with water like black ink.

Charcoal black like the ink my father used in his pen, when he sat down at his desk, and wrote by hand.

The big boulders and stones along the *grus* road to town are blotched with lichen.

Flowerless and crusting, I brush my fingers on the stones, tapping gently, as the sounds of my finger's tapping is all you hear, when you walk alone, and the silent stones mock your presence.

Because they will be long here when you are gone, and your passing was but a shadow.

As my stick of a shadow gliding by, in that heavy fisherman's coat with brass buttons.

On the church steeple top a black crow sits, watching, with eyes tiny and black and all knowing.

Where the bell will toll on Sunday precisely at five minutes before eleven in the morning, and the blank-faced townspeople will shuffle in, through the open black doors, greeting an unsmiling Torbjørn, the stern-faced pastor who must be at least seventy years old. *He has been always old.*

The virus is of no consequence, they will keep one another at arm's length. Torbjørn will see to that.

Torbjørn's face is wrinkled like the white cotton shirt I last wore on my confirmation, the shirt I ripped from my body, when the buttons snapped off from the force of my protest.

Fuck old Torbjørn.

During the confirmation ceremony, up at the altar, while I bowed on my knees, Torbjørn whispered to my mother I was going to hell.

My friends were Satanists because I had slept with that boy.

It didn't help that my mother had to take me kicking and screaming from the service, in front of the startled townspeople, as I *yelled "Jesus was a homosexual! Jesus kissed John! Your men bow down on their knees, tremble their love for this man! You drink his blood; you eat his flesh!"*

The sounds their footsteps make on the stone steps fills my ears, as I watch them, the sticks of mud, entering the church, from behind a tree, where I watch, and listen, and sketch a few drawings.

I know where they live. The young women up in the valley. In their fine dress, now, entering the church, next week there will be a communion.

The smoke of my cigarette tendrils up, along the skeletal, leafless branches,

up to the cloud filled sky, where a cold wind scatters the smoke.

The cracked bronze bell, hanging lifeless and still, like a man hung by the rope. The sound the bell makes has been replaced by an electronic recording.

Where the sound of my pencil scratching fills my ears, when the bell stops its clanging, and all there is, is silence.

I watch them.

Townspeople like matchsticks, sticks moving senseless. Torbjørn says I am one of Satan's dark angels.

He denounces my friends as Satanists because they have marched with me in the Pride parade.

When I was strong enough in my legs, and carried the rainbow flag, whose colours the wind whipped senseless in my mind, because I was colour blind, and losing my eyesight, and soon days would come when I all I saw was his shadow. As when he stood naked in the hall outside the bedroom, and I told him to come close.

* * *

A town shadowed in the valley, hidden by great cliffs of gneiss, rising on all sides, gunmetal grey like polished steel, in the winter, when the cliffs shine bright from a full moon's reflection.

A town so small tourists never stop. They do not know it exists.

Where the windows are left open, where there are no police, and an unsolved crime is an uncomfortable afterthought on everyone's mind, because it will never be solved.

A town where a man kills another man.

In the shadows, so his footprints escape into the night.

Where a man hates, in the silence, and his hating is like the force of a strong, cold wind, as it sweeps up the valley on a winter's day.

Where the little fires in the houses billow up the smoke in the little chimneys, up the black pipes to the grey sky above, where there plays just a hint of light far off, as the sun rises.

Just a hint, as the sun rises, and the smoke from the fires fill the valley, like an iron lid. Nothing escapes, no screams echoing, just the ringing of the church bell.

A town where a man can escape in a hoodie, and walk the main street at night, and enter the forest, on the worn path, up to the old house, sitting atop the hill.

Where in the attic, on the third floor, looking up at that little box window, they will see my shadow, and a lit candle.

Where from even the church, they see the house, and a candle's glow, not a day passes when they don't whisper my name.

"Andreas killed his father."

"Andreas invites women to the old house. He molests them."

"Andreas is an atheist."

I can hear if he cries

Great fir trees rise up and surround the house.

The pine-timbered policeman's house built in 1834, where my great-grandfather Hans locked up prisoners, from the common thief, to the town drunk, in the old jail cell, in the bedroom on the second floor where there hangs Great-grandfather Hansen's portrait, severe in his gaze.

It is the first thing you see when you wake up, his portrait on the wall, this balding man with bushy sideburns.

They say he was an honest, upright man.

There is no electricity in the house, I had cut the wires. *Fuck the light*. The only glow plays from candles, the old kerosene lamp, and the stone fireplace.

In the library on the second floor a window where I sit, at the desk. Unfastening the latch, pushing it open, warm breezes blow in.

A voice inside my head says, "Breathe deeply." I crane my neck out, like a turtle head come out of its shell. I think: *Soon dusk on a warm summer's eve, nothing will stir or make a sound.*

I can hear if he enters, I will wait for him.

There is a perfect view of the blue ocean fingering the fjørd, and the valley laying beyond the old church at the bend in the river.

I understood why my great-grandfather had chosen this place to build his home, since you could keep one eye on the ocean and the other eye on the land.

He told me Vikings would be buried facing the sea and the land, so their spirits would be at peace.

The sun has slipped below the mountain, I hear the strike of ten bells from the old clock downstairs.

I light a candle, still in my overcoat and boots at the desk and sort through my father's things: a Birkebanar knife in its leather sheathe. Used to sharpen his pencils. Its razor-sharp edge made from rust freechromed steel and the decorative handle from Birch, in the style of the 12th-century Vikings.

A decorative pewter plate, full of pencil shaving, called the Prim Stav, used by the Vikings to remind them of the religious holidays, like Barsok's Day, on August 24th, for the apostle Bartholomew.

Goats would be slaughtered the first day of autumn, when the trolls came out.

A lip pour glass bottle of black ink with a gold calligraphist pen, because my father wrote in black ink from an old style pen, which he dipped in the ink.

A small glass mason jar for my pencil shavings.

There was something about putting words on paper, holding a pencil between the fingers.

My father rolled cigarettes with his yellow-tipped fingers, preciously sprinkling the tobacco onto the tissue paper, licking the edge, like it was some magnificent creation.

A habit I picked up, so I take out a pouch, rolling paper, a box of matches from a drawer, roll a cigarette and light it up, inhaling the smoke, calming down. I raise up my right hand and try holding it still, over the candle flame. My fingers shake with a fine pill rolling tremor. I pick up a pencil, the way it shakes.

It startles me.

"Damn it!" I throw the pencil at the wall.

My fingers shake, my mind plays tricks, I do not know if the terror playing over and over in my mind is real or not.

After the thunder rolls there is silence

My mother locked me in the jail cell. I was just a boy.

On her trips to this place, Grandfather's old place, she would lock me in his bedroom, in the jail cell, in the dark, where I pressed myself against the bars, yelling.

I was afraid.

I heard shouting downstairs, my father yelling at my mother.

Locking up Andreas in the cell just because he did not want to go to Sunday School was wrong.

My mother yells that the sun hurts my eyes, I must get out of the sun.

There is a crack between the floorboards so I can see little of what is going on. She is yelling about the trip. She says my father should never have taken me out of the country. She yells she will never forgive him; he yells it is her fault Andreas has syphilis. I saw my mother's hand slapping my father's face. I saw him just standing there, shocked, taking it all in without a single protest, because he is afraid to stand up to my mother. She charges out the door, slamming it on the way out, as tears roll from my cheeks.

The papers texture, the sound of a page turning

Sitting in my heavy wool coat, at this desk.

My hands aglow from a full moon's light, a giant bright round disk lily white, sitting atop the black hills, enough light to make out my pencil, as it moves across the paper.

There is a flower, the five-petalled palo borracho.

I sketch it now, the sound my sketching makes on this paper fills me. I sketch because there is a memory attached to this flower.

Or an hallucination.

I cannot decide what it is.

Nothing, it seems, can keep me warm these days.

Weeks have passed, I do not know, there is food enough in the cold cellar, cans of beans, sardines with flatbread.

There is water from the well, I can go for weeks without a trip to *Rimi*.

There are some bottles of my father's homemade blackberry wine, I take a drink now and then.

Maybe Leo will come by.

How the days pass, in this old house, up in the attic, pacing back and forth, back, and forth.

Staring out the window, the little box window, just staring.

*   *   *

Lighting a candle, wondering if Levi sees the light, maybe he will come up with a warm pot of *lapskaus*. Levi wanted to take me hunting elks in Sirdal last fall before my eyes got bad. I said no. He said it would be good for me, taking a life. That would be my absolution, he said.

Let me tell you about the desk. My father had it sent from England. It has always been special to me.

The desk sits in a little oak-panelled space outside my grandfather's bedroom, tucked on a landing by the stairwell leading down a flight of narrow steps to the front door.

Shelves stacked with old books, row after row with unread tomes from my grandfather's time. *My grandfather's teak rocking chair where he read on a midsummer's night. A book, a glass of cognac, blowing rings of smoke from his mahogany pipe.*

Smelly little treasures, old, faded, dusty tomes, hard covered, leather bindings smooth to the touch.

This was my favourite place to sit, as a boy, closing my eyes, holding a big book, turning the pages, just listening as I closed my eyes.

Peeling apart the thick pages, the beautiful, coarse pages, feeling like fine sandpaper.

The paper's texture, the sound of a page's turning.

These voiceless books were my friends, I held my grandfather's big magnifying glass to the pages. There were Bjørnson's poems and Ibsen's plays, poems by Kafka.

I strained to read the letters, I discovered how to hold the book up to the summer light, so that I could make out the words.

It was magic, the why I could sit for hours, discovering words, forming sentences, closing my hands, and seeing how the words, like the markings of a pencil, created figures, and forms.

How my pencil captured my imagining, as when I wrote the words, by Oscar Wilde.

Yet each man kills the thing he loves…

I wonder who placed the flowers between these pages?

Could it have been little Hanna, my grandfather's sister, the girl who stretched her hand in the dark room, who begged for a window, so the light could enter that dark room?

Yes, it may have been her, it was also me.

I would press the flowers between the pages, take them out on my father's desk, and spend hours just sketching them in pen and black ink.

My father had a leather-bound volume of Carl Linnaeus's botanical sketches in the library, it was my favourite book.

These pages rain down now with dry, pressed flowers, harebells and sweet-smelling clover, aromas awakening, stilling me like some narcotic.

Vanilla is sweet, I pick up the strewn flowers from the desk and hold them to my broken nose, the way I close my eyes, the way I take out my little pencils, and sketch in my artist's pad.

There were *stories* in the books, my grandfather would take me up in his lap, in the rocking chair. *He read to me.*

I loved listening to his soft voice, I fell asleep in his arms.

Then he would play his golden harmonica. I heard the music in my sleep. It was a beautiful melody.

Dear God, I have it good, thank you for everything I have received…

A gentle man hiding a sorrow, my father's father, who kept a secret from his son.

Who played a melody on his harmonica, the words of the song on my lips.

A man needs to remember so he can forget

I had no mother who loved me. She locked me in the jail cell.

I had a father who slapped me in the face, because he could not face up to my mother.

I had a grandfather who absolutely loved me, he told me stories, he said God will take care of me.

"Grandfather, there is no God."

His large, moist blue eyes locking my itching eyes, looking up, curled in his lap.

His large hand, warm, touching my head, feeling his touch on my hair's golden locks, a boy of seven, on a summer's holiday, the window open, the light like a shining bar behind his big oval face.

Bald Grandfather Olav with the big, floppy ears.

He did not say anything to me, it was enough that his moist blue eyes met mine. Their silence was enough for me.

"Tell me about Grini, Grandfather. Tell me about your imprisonment. How the Nazi gave you the Luger. You still have it, don't you?"

He struggles to lift his body from the rocking chair, takes my hand, leads me to the open window.

There are words unspoken on his lips, minutes pass, the way he has something to tell me.

"There was a time it was so cold my fingers froze to the iron."

The way my grandfather lifts me up, sitting me on the windowsill. Grandfather's words whispered, the way he stares out, at the green, grey hills falling to the sea, from this hilltop.

"Yes, we love this country, as it rises forth, rugged, weathered, above the sea."

A long, lingering moment.

His face turned, far-off, to the place where the sun rises sharp, where the ocean breaks against the cliffs.

Too far off to see, I know he dwells on the scene, the windswept sea, though the sky appears calm.

"The memory of the evil is vanishing, Andreas."

He kneels, his big, lovely egg face and those large, blue eyes. He claps his sausage fingers on my face, a stare so benign yet awful I shake inside.

"You must never let hatred consume your heart, Andreas."

"Grandfather, I have seen something awful. In a place far away."

"I know."

"You know? What do you know? What has my father told you?" He gets back up, how he struggles with the wooden cane.

Looking out the window.

"Hope is a frail thing, Andreas. You will learn to embrace hope, to write it in your heart. Sometimes a man needs to remember, just so he can forget. So he can hope."

The way the blue fjørd runs to the sea, the way the warm wind blows in, the way the cloudless sky smiles down over the valley.

A boulder drops to the sea

My father's desk has a green leather writing surface smooth to the touch.

Hand tooled in gold leaf, of solid mahogany, cross banded with boxwood and ebony, with ribbon tied swags and festoons.

Where my fingers play, over hand-cut dovetails, where I can sit hours on end, sketching.

The desk has seven drawers, with brass ring handles, where I keep my pencils, my sketchpad; in one drawer I keep that special book. Where there lies in between the pages, a pressed flower, a purple bearded iris, folded in wax paper.

The little box window made with hand blown Bavarian glass, the leaded, puckered glass still bears the glazed imprint of my hand. Where it pressed itself that dark night, pressing so hard I thought the glass would break.

A tint of green plays through it when the sun strikes it just right, and the shadow it makes haunts me.

Here I can sit, by candlelight, with a pencil, and a piece of paper, and write. There is something about writing a sentence, hand drawing a line, just you,

a pencil, a piece of paper.

A fir tree drops to the ground.

A boulder drops to the sea. A casket drops into a pit.

I do not need to see, I close my eyes, the way the words form themselves, the etching of my thoughts on paper.

I see letters in my mind's eye.

I see words forming themselves.

I see a girl in a red vest, embroidered in gold, in a great library of books, flooded with light from an open window.

She sits in her mother's lap, I hear the mother's voice, she speaks in Italian, I know the words.

They are like honey, the way her mother whispers in a room brightly lit with yellow walls, where the floor to ceiling window faces the ocean, where I see a stone palace, distant, on a hilltop.

In the desk drawer I hide these handwritten pages, one day someone will find them.

They will read my handwritten notes.

Like the note, *"When the ladies have had a drink, after a sauna, they relax. There is a moment I put down the pencil. There is silence. Then they start talking. They tell me what I want to know."*

There is one shelf over the desk with medical texts, one of the worn books, entitled *The Merck Manual* sits on the desk.

I open the book.

There is a way I can see writing, there is a magnifying glass in the drawer.

I hunch down, the magnifying glass close to the page with the index card, placed in a chapter 'Sexually Transmitted Disease'.

I recognise my father's handwriting. "His symptoms have gotten worse. He has not been cured."

Thumbing the pages, discovering disturbing pictures of people with syphilis, faces full of sores, little ulcers on palms and hands.

There are ugly pictures of faces melting away, a hole, where the nose should have been, deformed, ugly, monstrous faces.

I close the book. In the desk drawer a little hand mirror. I take it out, hold it up to my face.

There are no sores on my face, except for the nose, saddle shaped, and misshapen. There are no ugly sores on my bearded face, or my hands, my tongue looks fine. It is just the nose, the mark, a reminder I carry a secret inside me.

A secret stalking me.

I am afraid to face this secret.

The evil that men do.

I start to shake, I am cold, it always starts this way.

"I need a fix!" I shout, as I grab the desk drawer like a madman, throwing it open, so the drawer flies out on the floor, spilling pencils, little marbles, trinkets, little tin soldiers, scraps of paper.

I am having a spell.

I remember a needle lying someplace in the drawer. There were some friends in Grünerløkka who did heroin like me, they toot before I cooked up the stuff. When you toot it goes down smooth, I know the taste, I will get that warm sensation, I will no longer feel so cold. I am looking all over for the stuff, the bag, I can't find it. I cannot see a thing; I'm thinking I'll die without a fix. I have not done drugs in seven years, now is not the time! A sort of seizure takes hold of me, a private little twitch that begins in my right little finger, and that crazy itching feeling comes over me, like a thousand biting fire ants. I stand up and rip off my clothes, shedding them in a fury, as the itching becomes worse. I start screaming, like some crazy man, naked in front of the wall mirror. I see my reflection.

I am shocked by what I see. My eyes clear so I make out my naked body. You see the scars of your youth, on your right forearm, where you cut yourself. And then that big tattoo across the chest, the letters A-R-T-I-S-T, where you cut into your chest. I stand there, staring, in the flickering shadow. Time stands still. The ticking of the grandfather clock, the way I crumble to the floor, burying my head, in my hands, the way I cry, how my sobs echo in this old house. No one hears me, no one cares. There is only one thing I know. And that secret I keep to myself.

Alone

Running barefoot, in the woods, in the wet moss after a summer rain, that was beautiful to me.

My eyesight is becoming worse. Light hurts my eyes, so I must squint outside. That is why I like cloudy days the best.

I do not fear blindness.

I do not fear this disease.

I can walk for hours in the forest, in the shade along the well-trodden path, in my coat, and boats, and high collar.

Not saying a word, just walking.

There are a few, they walk, alone, in the woods. I pass, faces downcast, my head bowed.

The townspeople shut inside.

I felt always alone among them. I am not one of them.

There is a place by the river

There is a place I go by the river where the water rushes down and drops into a pit, a chasm, where it boils and swirls, and rushes down into the valley.

I can sit on a rock, take a smoke, and stare, until I start getting hungry, and my thoughts start swimming, because I am getting hypnotised, and I think I will jump into the chasm.

I can take out a pencil and a little pad I keep in my pocket, and sketch, to pass the time, and think about the artist who stood naked on the shore last summer, by that great sand sculpture near Husby, when no one came to see him, and he just stood, with his arms outstretched.

The North Sea freezing his balls, the sand on that great naked sculpture scattered to the wind, because the people didn't want to look at this unhappy artist, they had better things to do.

Maybe that is what will happen to me.

The artist on the seashore where the wind blows sand all the way from the Sahara.

Near that great lighthouse on the shore, where I will go back one day, to that special place hidden between the rocks, and try to draw a straight line again.

* * *

The house is in a sad shape, my father let it go as he looked after my ailing grandfather.

It would be a grand farmhouse once fixed up, but there are just boxes all over of old books, a few pieces of traditional furniture, old glass-framed pictures on the wall.

Spider webs all over, mouldy yellow curtains, the ceilings are low, it is like living in a casket.

The way I move, in my overcoat, the way my knees hurt, the way the house hides me, in its shadow, startles the locals, who want nothing to do with me.

They say I am infected; they wonder how anyone can live like this.

I make my way up the flimsy steps to the attic, pull myself into the cold dusty space.

My old big canvasses are all here.

My flashlight makes out dozens of canvasses lying spread out on the floor.

In my teenage youth when I visited Grandfather in the summer, I attracted the neighbouring teenage girls to model for me.

I see those canvasses now, littering the floor like so many obscene afterthoughts.

As a teenager I discovered my talent for capturing the female form right here, in this crawl space.

I had to hurriedly paint the girls back then. That's how I first met Lena; she was my first model.

My flashlight reveals a big canvas of the Lady from Eiken.

Lying naked on a white goatskin, in a silly position, on her back, knees flexed to her chest, arms wrapped around her legs.

What a woman becomes after too infrequent dental visits, and too many bets on losing horses.

She lived down the valley with my one-eyed cousin Kjell.

Kjell would run outside every Saturday night in his underwear, at midnight, chasing her into the street, playing squeaky notes on his cornet.

His glass eye popped out and broke into a thousand pieces at the bus stop. An event witnessed by the mayor, me, and a schoolboy—the impressionable boy would never be the same again.

The Lady liked the fact I could erase a wrinkle here and there with a brushstroke, and with a dab of rose add some pink to her sallow cheeks.

On my summer holidays over the years here in town I painted so many women I saved fifty thousand crowns.

A small fortune for my efforts in erasing their wrinkles.

I erased the crow's feet from their eyes, whitened their teeth, firmed up the breasts. One day while posing and reading the magazine *See and*

Hear, the Lady from Eiken said she wanted me to paint her dark, as a brunette.

She told me she wanted a pussy the colour of black shoe polish.

Her friend Else went to Paris to a salon where they permanently dyed hers coal black.

I told the Lady I could paint her in purple polka dots, any which way she wants.

I go back down the attic steps; I shine the flashlight on the walls.

I see old framed black-and-white family pictures of my grandfather and his ten brothers and sisters. A collection of my father's pewter mugs and beer steins and my grandfather's homemade skis with leather string bindings.

* * *

This was a house full of happiness, at one time.

I step onto the landing by the front door where there is plenty of room for guests to leave their muddy boots and hang their coats.

The door on my right leads into the cosy dining room.

The brass door handle was placed higher on this door because this special room was meant just for the adults.

There is a black enamel rocking chair with a colourful floral design facing the window, lacy curtains and a traditional woven rug.

There is one of *Forland's* landscapes on the wall and a Jotel oven.

The only sound you can hear is the tick-tock of the antique wall clock.

In this room my father and grandfather spent their last hours. The doctors said it was just a coincidence my father died the same time as Grandfather Olav. The doctors ask me why my father killed himself. *I told them I had no idea.*

The light of my flashlight starts to flicker as the batteries die so I light the kerosene lamp on top of the fireplace.

The glow fills the room and I think I must start a fire, get out of these clothes, and warm the place up.

There is a black kettle hanging over the fireplace for heating water and all my cooking can be done here.

The dining area is an open area with a table and my tubes of acrylic and oil paints where I have made my painter's studio.

There awaits an easel and a canvas.

There is no refrigeration except a small crawl space under the first-floor kitchen where a cold stream ran year-round.

It is cool enough to store perishables.

There is one long wooden oak table with my tubes of oil paints, brushes, and mineral spirits.

Most special and dear to me is the *krak* my grandfather had made, a black enamel stool stylised with colourful rose painting.

Over the fireplace is my grandfather's double barrel shotgun, a *haggler*, next to a black-and-white picture from the 1950s of my father as a boy, standing proudly with a hay pick outside a barn.

Stamped on the shotgun barrel, amidst stylized, flowery markings, were the words *Special-Gewehr- Lauf-Stahl S.G.1.*

I start a fire with some birch logs and sit down close to the fire, my clothed body warming, starting to sweat.

I will remove my clothing and run outside to the bathhouse, where the steam is thick, like the fog that lays over the valley in the morning.

She waits for me, this woman who has shown up at the door, this nameless woman who says I will paint a masterpiece.

She says she has come all the way from Kristiansand, she says she will pay me handsomely.

Abdi

He pulls off in the black Audi with the brightly lit taxi sign on the roof.

The sun will be coming up shortly, Abdi will come back and wait for me at the usual time and take me home.

Here on the coast in the little harbour I come now and then, just limping around before the locals get up for their hot tea.

I can sit on a bench facing the ocean, smell the salt, roll and light up a cigarette, sketch whatever.

I can think how still it has become.

Abdi told me business has not been good, lately. He says people have kept to themselves.

"It's the virus."

"The virus won't dare infect me, Abdi. You know about me, Abdi."

"Yes, I know all about you."

* * *

I hold tight with clenched fingers my mahogany artist's box.

In my boots and grandfather's fishermen's coat, high collared, with brass buttons, falling below my knees, the only thing keeping me warm these days.

There is a pencil in my coat pocket, I feel its point.

Limping here in the shadow of these old pine-timbered houses.

It is a tunnel, the way the houses lean in, alleyways no wider than an arm's length, where the morning frost is silvered white on the cobblestones.

It can rain stones, the way the sky turns on a screw.

Leaning in like matchsticks, tightly packed houses like sardines in a tin, white as bone against the sky.

Curtain drawn windows where light veils itself half the year, where the North Sea sweeps in, where no sound is heard because it is Sunday morning, and the intoxication of last night keeps the locals in their beds.

I look back toward the alley away from the sea and see a shadow in a window above the bookshop.

I remember this place, the bookshop. I see still there sits the sculpture of the 'Leaping Gazelle' behind the window. It's a wood carving of Marshall Frederick's famous 'Leaping Gazelle', his memorial to Norwegian emigrants which he revealed at Breiavannet in Stavanger in 1958.

I go to the window and press close to the glass and look at this beautiful creature, this leaping gazelle.

Its lithe, arching neck and downcast horns, muscle and sinew locked frozen, like an animal stalked, grips me, and it is too much for me, so I step back from the window, and stretch out my fingers.

Trembling fingers wanting to touch the neck, this smooth gazelle neck, but they just linger on the glass.

I make out my reflection in the window.

A pale face hidden but for the eyes, a neck high collared and hidden, dirty blonde hair stringing down on my shoulders.

This town sleeps before the church bells ring, shadows hide behind curtains, my reflection appears in a window.

What has become of me?

I look like Per Olav, the drug addict, who once asked me if I could sell him some pills.

The thin nervous man my age with unkempt hair who lives with the other addicts, in the new house by the church, where the children are afraid to walk.

My knees give out, I drop to the ground.

I am like a puppet whose puppeteer has just released the strings. My face strikes the ground, my box opens and spills my pencils.

I lay sprawled out, do not feel any pain, just the cold earth pressed against the side of my face.

I lay there for some seconds, or minutes, I do not know.

My mind fogs over, I see the sun, and the shore, and the blue sky, and it is summer.

I am a young man of nineteen, before I became sick, my face is full of life and smiling.

My nose is just a little crooked, and Solveig's big blue eyes search mine, and she is like a gazelle, the way she poses for me and arches her back, the way the fine muscles of her neck catch the sun, her skin is smooth silk, her breasts firm, her naked body as taut as a bowstring.

When I could still hold a pencil between my fingers and draw a straight line, as the line of the horizon, where the sea meets the shore, the lighthouse stands erect. Where Solveig took off her clothes, and the wind played with me, and made me smile. I whittled my pencils to fine points, Solveig whispers the coffee is ready, as the coals twitch red. As the soot starts to turn the kettle black, as black as the charcoal I use to shape her breasts.

I can tell you this.

There is no woman in Norway more beautiful than Solveig.

A man loses his sanity, little by little

A creaking of a window opening.

Someone calls my name.

I recognise the scratchy, silly voice.

It is the Lady from Eiken.

I arch my head to the opened second story window, get back on my feet.

A white curtain whips out, that crazy woman hangs out the window, this crazy middle-aged half-drunk who keeps on paying me to make her beautiful again.

What a woman becomes after twenty years of placing bets on losing horses, chain smoking counterfeit Marlboros.

Smoke tendrils out the window from the glowing cigarette she's smoking and slides down the white timbered wall and fills my nostril holes.

The clinking of some ten-crown pieces hitting the cobble stones. "You crazy artist, Andreas! Make me beautiful again!"

The way she cackles and screams in that silly, unthreatening voice. No doubt she has had already a few beers for breakfast.

I pick up the coins, see shadows behind curtains. The locals are peeking behind curtains. *The Syphilis Artist* has returned.

I limp to the dock where I will have a smoke.

From the corner of my eye, I make out a glowing cigarette on the ground. I pick it up, there is a red lipstick smudge on the fag, I put it to my lips.

I will be knocking on my Lady's door when I need to fill my pockets again.

She'll give me five hundred crowns for a quick pencil sketch, enough to buy a slab of goat cheese, a loaf of bread, a few bottles of *Ringnes*.

There is the distant sound of a police siren.

I remember when the only sound was the rush of the river after a summer's rain.

Where I swam as a boy, on my visits to my grandfather, sketching trees and birds and waterfalls, perched on a mossy rock with my pencils and artist's pad.

And now midsummer is just around the corner, the wind breathes low on the earth, clouds will fall to the ground, it will rain, it will thunder.

I am happiest on a cloudy day, how the way the rain falls from the sky, how in the rain no one can tell I weep.

I hear rumours I am a failed artist, and my patrons throw their crowns at my feet because they don't dare to come close.

Ever since I became yellow in the face, they think I must be infected. In my baggy clothes I do not look so thin.

I look like that dark-eyed Rumanian, the beggar with the brown, creepy face who sits down cross-legged on a pillow with a white laminated sign printed in English. He never says a word.

On some days when business is bad, I can even stand outside Rimi, hide my face behind the high collar, hold out a plate, and collect a few hundred crowns.

They don't recognise me, the Syphilis Artist, and I would rather beg than go to NAV where so many other young men go to get a free handout.

Drug addicts, all of them.

At least when I beg, I can look from the corner of my eye in those dark sunglasses and stare into the soul of my countrymen.

A man loses his sanity, little by little, like the way wind blows and scatters sand, until footprints on the shore are covered up and no one knows you were there.

Like the way blackbirds scatter chicken bones from the litter and drop them on the churchyard grounds, little, tiny bones reminding one of fingers crawling up out of the grave.

The present is all there is

I need a drink.

I bang with my fist on the door at the bar. A sign says 'Closed'. It is midnight, a Sunday night, I could not sleep, there is still some light left in the sky.

A man sticks his head from a second story open window. "The bar is closed!"

I know that man, it is the old man Ludvik, the alcoholic from Stavanger. "Oh, Andreas. It is you!" he says, apologetically.

I painted Ludvik's mistress a long time ago, I remember.

When his wife discovered the painting in a trunk, he was never the same again.

"I'm sorry for your loss. Your grandfather was a good man." "And my father, was he a good man?" I shout.

I'm angry, all wound up.

I will go back to the old house, light up a fag, finish a bottle of wine, drop to the floor in my coat and wake up when sunlight stabs through the window and strikes my face.

I will take the taxi back to town and go to the church and weep over my father's grave.

No one will hear me cry, except the black birds circling overhead, and Ludvik cannot tell me if my father was a good man. And now I am afraid because a crazy idea has started to infect me, that everything, including my art, is meaningless.

There seems more meaning in a flower, then a man. Evil, how can that be meaningless?

Was it all without meaning that my mother left me, because she had slept with other men, and that ulcer between her legs infected me, as I fell from her womb into my father's hands, on that bed in my grandfather's house, that great old pine bed made from the church altar and carved with rose petals?

I want to lie all day next to Solveig again, feel her flesh against mine, a sensitive woman as deep as the Skagerak, who can throw away her mobile phone and tune everything out and just stare at a painting for an hour before saying a word.

Someone so unlike Lena. She did not know what to make of the letter I sent to her, the letter I spent two days composing, pouring out my thoughts.

I was just too intense.

I don't have friends, just lovers.

You think when someone dies that something of them is left behind.

That the imprint of that life is stamped not just in a little box in a newspaper where all the death announcements go, on newsprint sitting in discarded piles at the local *Rimi*.

No one reads the newspapers except the old timers, my grandfather's generation, and a death, what is that?

And life, can you tell me what that is? The past is dead.

The future has not come. The present is all there is.

I fear this is not a dream

In the churchyard my relatives lay side by side, in neat, manicured rows like so many sardines in a King Oscar tin.

One aunt was a teacher, but that did not help since she went senile, the other aunt went crazy because of the dark winter months and ended up in a clinic.

There was Tordis, she lived with a dozen cats, ate raw sardines for breakfast and could not get over how the copper wire she used as a clothesline got stolen every time it was put out.

One day I saw a shin bone atop a fresh pile of sandy dirt, like a flagpole. George, the gravedigger, was digging up my uncle's grave so there would be room for Tordis.

I sit on the grass by my father's grave.

Two simple white crosses stuck in the grassless dirt. The ground has sunken since the funeral.

One nameless cross for my father. One nameless cross for grandfather. I collapse into the dirt.

I happen to find a wilted rose on the grass.

The caretaker will throw everything away, in the container, the ribbons and the wilting flowers, and there will be nothing left.

No one gave flowers to my father when he lived, and I think it is all so meaningless.

I just sit atop the mound of dirt on the grave, there is no one around.

I see shadows and ghosts and now, in this fleeting moment, I imagine my father and his father, in their white caskets, in the black earth, laying side by side, like two porcelain dolls.

The weight of the earth crushing and splintering the caskets, snapping their bones the way a heavy snowfall snaps branches in the forest.

It is a cruel, unforgiving end, the way a man lies in the ground.

I open my artists box and take out my drawing paper and a graphite pencil.

I start sketching the old church, with its steeple pointed like a phallus in the shadow of a giant moon. I struggle to draw straight lines, my fingers shake.

In the shadow of the church the dead are buried in simple pine boxes.

The bell rings every passing, scattering the magpies and crows, black dots against a silver sky.

The cracked, bronze bell in the tower that no longer rings, because now a recording does the job, and the sound the false echo makes in the valley infects me, because I know it is not real.

I lay down on the wilting flowers, press my ear to the unfeeling ground, and whisper to my father.

I am waiting for a divine resurrection, a flash of light, a shaking of the earth. Nothing at all happens.

I fear this is not a dream.

I am a boy on a train

I look out the window as the train speeds into a dark country with stony plateaus, flat lands and dark valleys—so unlike the fjørds I loved. My father sits next to me, looking nervous, smoking a cigarette. An old woman sits across the aisle, stares blankly into space, lines like scratch marks in her face, holding tight unto a sack of potatoes. A boy in dirty clothes smoking a cigarette. A soldier with a red cap in uniform looking nervously around at the other passengers, his catlike eyes jumping from one face to another, his hands shaking as he sips plum brandy from a paper bag. There is no conversation among the passengers.

In my dream I think I love riding the trains in Norway, because I can play with the Lego bricks. This train is different, the train from hell. The only sound comes from the angry grating of the train's wheels on the tracks. Death is written on the passenger faces, as eyes stare straight forward, frozen by some dark spell. The old man sitting next to my father has a fleshy nose, full of red spider veins. He turns to face my father and says "It's best not to stop in my country. Zagreb is going from bad to worse." The old man takes out two mouldy cigarettes from his pocket.

His hand shakes, as he lights the cigarettes with his lighter, one cigarette falls to the floor, he picks it up, puts it back in his mouth. I feel my father's hand squeeze mine hard, I hear him talking to himself, something about my mother, saying it was my mother's fault, what a Satan she was, how she had left me alone in the apartment without leaving a word, how she was an unfit mother.

I tell my father I don't understand, because no one told me I was sick, and now I am on a train to Zagreb and Father tells me I am to get an injection.

The old man smoking two cigarettes continues his conversation with my father, who is reading a paperback and trying not to pay attention.

"Go lock yourself in a room, with a knife. Feel its edge, razor it across your neck. Do it slowly, so you feel it cut the skin, then the vessels.

Slit like a letter your tender throat spurts blood, but you cut deeper, despite the pain. Imagine you have no control, that your hands moved as if controlled by a puppeteer. You scream "Noooo!" but your ears are full of cotton, and your senseless brain has become like Frankenstein's, an unfeeling machine. You cannot prevent yourself cutting your own throat."

My father takes me by the hand, says he had heard enough, stands up and collects his bags, and tells me we are going to sit in another cabin.

The old man takes my father's hand, pulls him close, his eyes locking my father's.

"I am a Croat, born in Novi Sad. I was a watchmaker until they set fire to my shop. Boys ran down the street, shouting for mercy. The Serbs cut their necks and hung the bodies from trees."

My father breaks free from the man's grip. I am shaking inside. The image of boys hanging upside down in trees with their throats slit cuts into me. I had never heard of such things.

"Turn back. Once you step off in Zagreb you will never get back on."

The man explains that very few passengers head east to Zagreb. If anything, they all headed west here to Vienna. Going to Zagreb was like jumping off a ship in a storm without a life preserver.

Sudbanhof was where the Serbs arrived, day after day, in crowds like rats rushing up the sideboards of a sinking ship. It was the disembarkation point of thousands of exiles coming from Croatia and Serbia.

We had broken free of the man and Father drags me and our bags down the aisle toward another cabin. Everyone looks at us, stone-faced, at our fine, bright clothes, my father's face strawberry red, flushed with a fear I had never seen before.

I beg my father to take me off that dirty train, back to Norway, as he turns back to face that old man who was shouting at us, as my father slides open the door between the cabins.

The smell of diesel, the blast of wind, the rain banging loud against the train like stones, as the train squeals loud, entering a tunnel, swallowing us whole, into darkness.

The man's voice echoing in the darkness, as my father swears again at my mother, how it had all come to this, as he grasps my hand, and I felt it was wet from sweat.

"They are animals. They will end up in the hotels on the Adriatic coast and there will tear up everything. Rip wallpaper from the walls, smash televisions, tear the curtains down. Why? Because they say if they can't have these things, why should anyone else?"

Pouring water on hot stones

I see the little stone oven in the corner where my grandmother baked flatbread.

The stones kept their warmth for days; in the old days they used to ferment beer.

I get a little birch fire going with a few logs to heat the tank of water so I can make steam enough to thaw my frozen limbs.

It happens like this, every time, when I wake up with a pounding headache. My muscles get so tight and wound up like a rubber band, the only way I rewind is to go outside to the little *badstua*, that old falling apart red-timbered bathhouse with rotten floorboards.

My favourite little place, this old bathhouse, with my grandfather's handmade oak skis crossed outside over the doorframe, and all those pewter mugs on the shelf inside from my father's collection.

Countries he liked to visit on his writing holidays, like the time he went to Slovenia, to that great castle at Valenje.

Pouring water over the hot stones from my father's hand-carved spoon, that beautiful big pine ladle carved with flowers, with my initials *A.O.H* engraved on the handle.

Taking off my clothes, layer by layer. Laying them neatly on the wooden bench, a ritual, so the time escapes unnoticed. There is a way the day passes, a way one loses oneself.

Feeling the steam pierce into my naked body, feeling now empty of tears, because I had wept all day.

I close my eyes, feel with my fingertips the spoon's engraving, how my finger's feel every groove and ridge.

In the mist I see her enter the room. The world seems to have grown insane. Like today, with the sky unsure of itself. It may rain, it may snow.

One day the sun bakes, the next, the ground freezes over.

And yesterday my stringy beard dripped off sweat like wet, dripping moss, getting tired as I chopped wood out in the barn and wept to myself inside the barn with the doors wide open.

Outside shadows past by like sticks of mud shuffling past, my mind played tricks with me, it was the summer, and I was a boy again, old Mrs Gundersen peeked in, she didn't see me, because I hid myself.

I watched her nose twitch, on that hard-wrinkled face of hers, that very old woman who is so nicely dressed, as if every day is a Sunday.

Showing off that silk floral hat, the one she bought in Paris before the great war, the one she sprays with perfume, to hide no doubt my barn's rotting hay and rotten smells.

A blight she says stinks up the whole valley.

And then this ghost of an old woman disappears. Thinking I am getting weaker by the day, what will become of me?

This nameless woman who tells me she is forty-one years old, who doesn't mind looking at my face, the way she just stares a moment, looks down, then there is a moment when I think she will weep, as her head lifts, my eyes focus. Feeling the steam relax my muscles, my eyesight relaxing.

I slip in and out.

This nameless woman with crows' feet eyes who has come out of the forest to the house and knocked on the door.

Her girlfriend says I am a genius with a pencil.

The way I hid her face in the shadow of that mountain, as the sun escaped at midday when the air turned cold and I closed the barn door and lit a fire in the little oven.

The flames licking her body as she sipped plum brandy from a glass, stained with her lipstick, and I stilled her irritating little protests, because I had wiped the blood from her lips where the lipstick hid the bruise.

* * *

"Svein Eirik would kill me if he knew I was here."

It is really steamy, and she disappears and I see where the black mascara drips from her eyes, the outline of her breasts disappears in the fog.

"Why are you crying, Andreas?"

I sit here pouring water over the hot stones, waiting for some sort of absolution.

Looking at this woman, whose face passes in and out of the steam. These are the moments where time stands still, where a day passes to night. Where they come, and speak slowly, and I listen. They tell me what I want to know.

"I want to see the blue sky again. I want to hold a sable between my fingers, so I can draw a fine straight line, like the one I drew for an horizon, where the lighthouse played its beam of light through the fog, and the ocean stretched open like the pages of a book."

"You are a poet, Andreas Olav Hansen."

My father said it was a tick bite. As a boy I could not even ride a bicycle, my eyes hurt in sunlight.

Get yourself back to Oslo

In 1991 my father and mother had a big argument; my mother just left, ran off, never to be seen or heard from again.

Someone from the lawyer's office had said for me to come to the office. There were papers to sign. I was not surprised my father died penniless.

I would inherit the big old house. My sister Vilde would get the apartment in Oslo, that tiny little place looking over the park.

She was nowhere to be seen at the funeral. And my mother, where was she?

Lena had told me once that after a few cans of beer my sorrow would simply wash away.

* * *

She described letting go would be as easy as throwing leaves in the river, the river that charges with so much violence just a stone's throw away. The white water sweeps down the valley, snaking its way under the bridge and around the bend and the old timber church.

It was the chiming of the grandfather clock downstairs in that old house that woke me up. Tick-tock, tick-tock, tick-tock. Three o'clock in the morning. How I could remain in that old house, where the stain of my father's blood is still visible by the fireplace despite all my scrubbing?

In Oslo, the traffic drowned out the little noises.

In in my little apartment, where I escaped early in the morning, after a night walking the streets.

I couldn't make out the intruder's face, it was just the shadow, like a bear.

I was awakened in the middle of the night, I heard footsteps downstairs.

I wasn't afraid, really, there was a numbness to the night, the way you wake up and stumble down the steps, naked but for the overcoat.

You think it is all a dream, you are thinking no one comes to this house. I am infected, this house is full of disease.

The doors are open, let them come in if they dare.

They will see my face, that ugly face, they will think I am some monster. In the night there is a way the moon's light strikes my face.

The intruder jumped out of the shadows, pushed me against the wall, a picture in a glass frame fell on the floor and shattered.

I got up to my feet, but he was on top of me, started choking me, shouting obscenities, "You homo, get yourself back to Oslo!"

Just before it all went black, he got up to his feet, and left, slamming the front door.

Lena

The grandfather clock chimes two times.

It's two o'clock in the morning.

I get out of bed, put on some clothes from a pile tossed on the floor, go the desk and sit, find a flashlight in a drawer and shine a flashlight on the green metal tube.

I take it in my hands, feel its smoothness, a stylish cigar tube with a faded label. I pop off one end, take out the paper and lay it flat on the desk.

It is just a simple straight line. I make out my signature. I find a pencil, try drawing a straight line on the paper, my fingers shake, and I think I will never be able to draw again.

I crumble up the paper.

There is faint knocking at the door. *I am used to the knocking at all hours of the night. They come like stray dogs to the door, they know I will share a warm cup of tea, they will sit by the fire, and stare. I will fire up the bathhouse, go in, remove my clothes, and they will enter. The room is full of steam, I see their eyes, how not a word escapes our lips, all they seek is silence.*

I go downstairs, open the door. It's cold, frost lingers in the air. I shine the flashlight on the lonely figure standing in front of me.

A figure hiding behind a curtain of cigarette smoke. *It's a woman shivering in a black-zippered down jacket.*

It takes time for my eyes to focus on her face. I am not sure it is her, at first, not as I remember pretty Lena.

The only light comes from my flashlight and the glowing stub of her cigarette. I take my time just staring at her. She is used to this, my long staring spells. She's getting impatient, as she coughs and the frost in the air bleeds into the cigarette smoke exhaled from her wheezing lungs.

She has a dark tan, she has been no doubt to Phuket. It doesn't look nice, because there are lines and wrinkles around the corners of her mouth, she has bags under her eyes.

Once her skin was smooth as white as milk. I reach out my hand and touch her face. This is how we used to greet, she loved how my fingers slid down her cheeks, her neck, her breasts.

"Lena?"

I squeeze my eyelids tight and reopen them just to make sure she isn't a ghost. When I reopen them, I see she is still there, miserable looking.

Her face puffed up, her right eye swollen, her messed-up blonde hair catching the light from my flashlight. She has been drinking.

"I was worried for you, Andreas," she says, her voice weak, words whispered in despair.

"Come in, I'll light a fire. We'll warm up some tea over the fire and talk."

I close the door in the dark hallway, I put the flashlight down and fumble for a box of matches and a candle I had left on the steps.

My fingers can still strike a match, my hand is steady enough with the little box of wooden matchsticks.

I consider it a minor success lighting a flame, the way I have been shaking lately. The candle flame lights up the hallway, I see Lena checking her iPhone. She's all worked up. "I have no internet, Lena."

I'm thinking about a big mug of warm black tea, sitting by the fireplace, and have a thousand questions, but everything is jumbled up in my head, because Lena has shown up, and the way she starts looking around in the dark, as we enter the living room, how she shines the flashlight on the tea-coloured walls, on my spartan existence, how I have lived like a hermit.

With no electricity, no refrigerator except for a cold space under the floor.

I start a fire with some kindling in the fireplace, Lena pulls up my grandfather's *krak*, and sits shivering a few inches from the fire.

I don't need to wear my glasses because the light of the fire has sharpened my senses as I hang a kettle over the fire.

This is how my grandfather boiled the water. Even in the fire's glow Lena looks pale, her face caught up in some small terror.

There is a bruise over her right eye. "What happened to you, Lena?"

Her reply, whispered, eyes downcast, words of tender indifference. "I don't want to talk about it." A pause, as her eyes meet mine. "I missed you, Andreas." I remember how I held her in my arms, how perfect we thought we were for another. Before I really started to get sick, when I worked in the school, in Oslo.

Eating out in the restaurants, hopping from one museum to the next.

Lena always filled with so much nervous energy. But then there started to be talk that I had AIDS, and Lena could be infected.

Though the Oslo doctors said I was not infectious, that my sexual disease was dormant. As long as I took the regular blood work, I could count on working at my job and living normally.

Then I started shaking and getting weak.

When we peeled the onions on the footbridge last Easter a change came over Lena. My face was more yellow than the onions. I told Lena I wanted to have children.

A little girl. Lena looked at me like a monster.

My mean older sister Vilde was frightened of me growing up. She called me a little monster; she threw stones at me.

"You will never have children with me, Andreas Olav Hansen."

Lena couldn't get away from the internet, and Facebook, and a thousand distractions.

She could not even walk barefoot in the forest without feeling she had to stop and check her phone every second.

Like now when I hand her a warm cup of black tea and she has to put away her phone so she can hold the big porcelain cup between both hands.

I know what she thinks, the way her eyes fly all around, how she can't get away from the fact something has changed in me.

I'm in the mood for a smoke so I take out my little black leather pouch of *tobakk*. I take my time making a perfect cigarette.

* * *

Lena paces around nervously, looking suspiciously past the thin curtains. She takes off her coat.

Her t-shirt has skull and crossbones with the slogan 'Don't fuck with Lena'.

There's nothing to see outside, just the forest standing guard around the house and the distant lights in the valley. A tree limb starts tapping against the window, and startles Lena. She's not used to the little sounds a house make.

On the wall my shadow, as the flames play around the room. This nervous woman hiding in the shadow.

"Have you seen him? Has he been looking for me?" she asks meekly.

I'm sitting at the table, just idly sketching away, trying to capture this figure in the shadows.

I know she is thinking of that man. Trond, the butcher from Sirdal.

The way a man cuts flesh from the bone, that large bear of a man who I had only seen once, when he dragged that bleeding deer's carcass in the forest.

The bear with large hands who could knock me down, senseless. There is a place I hide in this house when I am afraid.

It is in the jail cell, in my grandfather's bedroom upstairs. Where I hid from my mother, where once I locked myself in, and hid the key from my mother so she couldn't get to me.

Lena lights a cigarette, blows smoke at me, I cough.

"He is a jealous man. If he knew I was here I would get in trouble."

* * *

When she has removed all her clothes, she just comes up to me and stands warming herself by the fire.

"Turn around Lena."

There is a flowery tattoo over her ass with a name, 'Andreas'. I run my hands down her hips.

She asks me if I have any wine in the house so I go to the potato cellar in the kitchen, lift up a floorboard, pick up a cold bottle and return to the room where now Lena has lit some candles.

There is something which slips off a man as his clothes drop to the floor. She whispers she wants to go upstairs into the jail cell, just for tonight, because she is all sexed up, like a wound spring, and she doesn't give a damn about Trond any more.

She wants to forget that butcher from Sirdal, who slapped her around, because he gets violent when he is drunk.

I tell Lena to follow me up the stairs. I go to the front door, check that it is locked, and walk up the stairs past all those black-and-white family pictures.

I just see the frames, the black wooden frames, because tonight my eyes are really bad.

In my grandfather's room, in the shadow of that great bed carved with rose petals.

Where there is a single candle lit on the floor, so the shadow of the bars hit the wall like broomsticks where Lena's legs project up like flagpoles.

The way the floor creaks, the way she gasps for air, as she yells her dirty little cat calls.

Marija

The faint *tick-tock* of the grandfather clock.

I wake up in the dark.

It must still be early morning; I remember being up all night, sketching.

I had a dream. It was winter.

I was being chased in the forest.

I was a boy chased by a wolf's shadow. A hungry wolf with burning eyes, who caught my odour in the black wind.

As the life blood ran from me, from the cut across my neck.

Where the blood squirted out, running down my neck, down my body, bleeding a trail into the snow.

A snow-blanketed meadow looking over the valley, by that great Viking mound, a sacred place where the shadow of the great fjørd stretches out like a black snake.

That great long shadow visible even in the dark because its granite walls reflected the moonlight, and the silver of the ocean was like the gleam of a Viking sword thrusting in long and sharp from the North Sea.

In the meadow with the two glowing birch trees, standing like stoic sentinels. A wooden swing stretched by rope between the trees.

Swinging back and forth, but there was no one around in my dream. I sensed her presence. Icicles of light cut around me, as tiny ice crystals danced in the moonlight, like thousands of fireflies, stirring images of places, spinning around me. Spinning faster, images blurring, as if I was in the centre of a carousal.

I saw a low hill by the sea, and a stone palace the colour of honey.

There were carved portals and balconies lined with countless flowers. It was two-storeyed, with a loggia of six arches, and eight Gothic windows, a tower in each end.

Wind stirred; the palace vanished.

She appeared at first just as a play of light on the swing, a shadow rocking forward and back, then transfiguring, as my frozen tears melted from my eyes and I beheld a full giant moon rising up at her back.

A woman in a silken wedding gown swinging, back and forth, unaware of my presence.

A beautiful, dark-haired woman with olive flesh, and honey brown eyes. She sees me. The swing stops.

Her eyes lock mine.

She stands slowly, a hint of smile on her face, as if she had been expecting me. I am too shocked to be frightened because this is the woman I was painting.

She whispers my name.

I whisper her name. "Marija."

My fingers stretch out, trembling, stretching nearer to her face.

Her jet-black hair falling down a swan's neck, her eyes wide, brown sickled with honey.

Her shoulders bare, a fresh cut rose in a low-cut bodice between her breasts. Her wedding gown was of finest silk and gossamer, glistening like dew dancing on a spider's web. Now, breath to breath, the steam of my trembling voice condensing on her rose cheeks.

I smell lavender, and the scent of the forest after a summer rain, when the sun alights atop the trees, and glides down, to touch the flesh.

She cups her hands on my face, kisses me gently on my lips, and whispers comfortingly in my ear.

"Be not afraid, Andreas."

She kisses my neck where the cut had slit the vessels and the lifeblood had run from me. I had been skeletal white like a ghost, but her magical kiss healed my neck, so the cut disappeared.

Colour comes back to my face, even my ugly nose transforms into a beautiful nose. Flesh magically grows on my bones; I feel born anew.

The snow vanishes, it is summer, the field is full of wildflowers.

My pupils widening, focusing in and out on this spectral vision, as her gown falls to the ground in slow motion and roses grew magically around us, as her naked form wraps me in her embrace, as wondrous angel wings grew from her sides, enfolding me. Her whispers tinged with ecstasy. *"Paint, and live again, Andreas Olav Hansen."*

***

She disappears and I am in a darkened room with a girl and an old man lying in a bed.

The girl whose face was hidden in a shadow, wearing a coarse linen dress and red silk shirt and khaki jacket inlaid with thick gold braid.

"You must be dressed and washed" she says to the old man on the bed. His eyes stare up at the ceiling.

The brown mole on his nose is the size of a pea. His legs are cut off just above the knees and the fleshy stumps are strawberry red.

This is the dream I had before. But it is now different.

I anticipate in my dream what happens, as she takes the washcloth from a basin, wets it, sponging his face. She sees me, only now I am an adult in the dream. She sees me, in my heavy blue fisherman's coat with the brass button, my upturned collar, my thin, bearded, face, and that ugly nose.

When she sees me, it is like she has seen a ghost. Her terrible screams of fright wake me.

Vukovar

I jump up out of bed at the crack of thunder. Rain beats loud on the bedroom window.

I am blind.

Blind though the thunder rolls and the lightning splinters and I smell a forest burning. I stumble barefoot to the door, down the steps, to the landing, feeling my way, as I knock pictures off the wall.

Glass shattering from the picture frame, splintering on the floor.

A fragment enters my foot and the pain sends shock waves up my leg. I yell for Lena.

She must have left early. I find the door, it is not locked. There is someone outside in the shadows waiting for me. The rain clouds must be right overhead.

I have a feeling something awful will happen. There was a wolf that chased me in the forest.

I stumble in the dark, toward the barn, where my father's name is notched into the door, where my fingers feel the worn places that I touched as a boy.

Where my uncles have etched their names, including Hans Hansen, that stern looking sheriff who stares at me night after night.

Where I go in the dark to feel their imprint, just to get back to reality. But they are all dead, laying like sardines in their graves, where George has prepared a casket for me. The sky opens, the rain spits down on me.

I shiver, my head pounds, a thousand aches assault me.

I have forgotten my name and why I am out in the rain, and then I come back to my senses. I clutch at my knife, swing the barn door open, smell the rotten hay.

I take a few steps, feel the worn pine floor under my feet.

In a black room where I listen. There is the smell of smoke. I hear a fire crackling in the small Jotel oven.

I crouch down.

There is a dripping on my face and I think it must be rain. But the liquid is warm, a taste of iron.

It is blood. It drips on my face, like a running faucet.

Looking up at the ceiling, my hands stretching up, as I stand up and it bumps into me.

It is the body of some animal, hanging upside down, in the barn. A deer. I feel where its throat has been slit.

Though it is too early for hunting season, the summer has not passed.

My hands feeling the smooth neck of this tender animal where the blade cut sharp. There is a shaking inside me, a terrible awful shaking.

Whomever did this knows my fears.

A thunderbolt snaps overhead. The rain pours down in buckets. The noise deafening like a locomotive.

The crack of thunder.

I must get from here. I am being hunted. I am running in the woods.

Running like a deer whose neck has been cut.

Up the hill where the fir trees grew tight together and the branches stab into me a thousand times. I feel no pain. I am a bloodied mess.

There is a silent scream in me yearning to be set free.

I do not think about anything except that ice-cold lake in the clearing, on top of this hill.

Where I will drown my fears.

I am a locomotive charging ahead; nothing can stop me.

A rifle shot. Another rifle shot exploding in a tree trunk just an arm's length away.

The tree splinters, pieces hit my face. Someone is yelling in the distance.

Someone yelling my name.

The hill levels off, I am out of the black woods, the ground is marsh. I am almost to the mountain lake.

Somehow, I know the way, I have walked these woods so many times, I don't need to see. I can't stop. This is where I have come so many times, in my mind's eye I picture the scene.

Blocks of black shadow angle in and out of the wooded hills, clutches of white birch stand like a frieze of nymphs frozen in time. The sun steals glances through openings and makes columns of light like granite pillars.

It has stopped raining; I feel sunlight stabbing down on my face like sharp pencil points. I wade deeper in the muddy underbrush, wet moss encircling my ankles, until I get to the cold water's edge.

Something strong seizes me, from the innermost depths of my being. The idea it will all end, that my life was but a drop in the ocean.

I jump in the ice-cold water.

I wade out over the sharp stones, feel the muddy bottom grabbing and pulling my bare feet, like quicksand. I yank them free, and push further out, so the frozen water is up to my waist and then I start swimming. I am swimming further from the shore.

It is a nightmare, swimming blind, another rifle shot and a man's voice shouting my name, and then I think I hear Lena's voice. My muscles cramp, I must be far out from the shore.

The sound the wind makes through the treetops becomes a whisper, I feel heavy and wasted and everything is black and then I just start sinking down, below the surface. I hear a familiar girl's voice, a whisper.

It is the girl from my dreams.

She is shouting for me, in her girl's voice, and as her voice echoes louder I hear machine gun fire and screaming.

In my mind's eye I see my body sinking deeper and deeper. It is like I am watching a war film.

A moving mass of horse-pulled carts, tractors, beat up cars, old ladies pulling bulging suitcases. Young, frightened men and children carried in their worried mothers' arms and old wrinkled men with blank stares. Suitcases thrown from second-storey windows to the street below, exploding as they land, clothes and dust blown all over, a scene right out of hell.

Frightened, the girl lost in the crowds, the girl in a red vest with gold braid, lost in the crowds just as a tank rounds a corner.

I see myself, a frightened boy, pushing through the crowd, in this ghetto, towards the girl, as wild-eyed soldiers in red caps on the tank start shooting their Heckler machine guns over our heads. I throw myself down just in time under a cart as a mortar crashes through a roof.

I am back on my feet pushing through the fleeing crowds following her toward a building, past a shot-up sign 'Vukovar' and I see trucks with red crosses parked outside a shot-up building with white gowned patients funnelling out the front doors.

I get to the building; a mortar explodes nearby and the debris blasts behind me just as I manage to reach her. I grab a hold of her in the crowded dimly lit hallway and she snakes past the fleeing patients and nurses in bloody aprons.

It is a scene of total chaos, she turns to me, her face caked with dirt, her eyes lock with mine, and without saying a word takes a chain she has been wearing around her neck, a small silver crucifix, and places it around my neck.

There is no time for me to react, she sees her mother in the hallway, this woman I recognise, pushing a gurney with a patient who yells from pain, a woman in a bloodied lab coat and surgical scrubs.

The lights are flickering, she yells for her mother and goes to her. She is picked up in her mother's arms, as I see my father, down the hallway, shouting desperately for me, as he struggles to get to me.

His forehead bleeds from a gash, I am frightened and yell for him, my hand stretching out, stretching through this wall of fleeing humanity in this hospital under siege, as his hand stretches to me over the shoulders of a young, dark-eyed man with a torn shirt and bandaged face, and my fingers stretch to grab a hold of my father's hand and I see the frightened look on his face because I am being pulled away by the crowd.

My hands stretch up to the sky

My hands stretch to the sky, as my body sinks, lower and lower, and there is a shimmering light far away, a light that dances, on the surface of this lake, this black maelstrom swallowing me whole. I hear my name.

There is a beeping sound and my eyes open to a bright, blinding light.

I breathe through a mask, I feel my chest heaving, I hear talking, I think I must be in a hospital, in the emergency room.

I feel something warm running in my forearm. And then I am out of my body, just floating.

I hear a violin playing a tone, in the distance. A mournful simple melody I have heard once before, distant, in a far-off land. I am floating in the clouds, looking down, at a field covered in snow. A white, glistening field of snow in a clearing, in a dark forest. I am floating, floating back to earth. There are hundreds of wooden crosses, nameless, sticking up through the snow.

A dead man's hand sticking up, grasping a rose. A young woman whose face is hidden behind a shawl, a woman in black, placing rosaries around a cross. I see the woman's face—it is the girl of my dreams, but now she is a young woman, as she turns her face to the clouds, and it is as if she sees me floating down to her, as sunlight breaks through a scratch in the heavens, and dances on her face. A single tear rolls down her cheek. My eyes look away and I hear the violin playing, and the shadow of a young man sitting on a stool, in a coat, in an empty room, facing a frosted window, a window through which he sees the field of wooden crosses, and I think I see in the young man's face a resemblance to this woman, and I know his name. It is Marko, her brother, his eyes the colour of honey, he weeps. As he looks out at the field of crooked, makeshift crosses, as I float down, like a feather, over the killing fields of Prijedor. Where the living, dig up the dead. Shadows placing bones in caskets, caskets placed in horse-drawn carts, wheeled away, as the women kneel at the crosses, hanging rosaries. Whose beads are caught in the wind.

I see snow blowing and see through the clouds a black shape running, running wildly through the snow. I make out the face. It is Marko, and he is running with his violin into the forest, running for his life. The air is frozen, his breath is steam, he throws off the violin, as he stumbles over a crag, and struggles to get away.

A man in a uniform with a Kalashnikov, a soldier in a red cap, chases after him. A wolf stalking him, a wolf wearing a red cap, a young man no older than Marko. The soldier stops, lifts the rifle, aims at distant Marko, as Marko stops, his exhausted body just standing, tall and proud, his eyes lifted to the sky, his arms reaching up to the sky.

His voice whispering his sisters name, and his mother's name, as a simple prayer leaves his lips. The words he whispers are in Italian, I know their meaning, I have whispered them in my sleep. The gunshot echoes in the forest. Marko's face caught in a final, fatal grimace, his outstretched arms collapsing to the earth, as my body floats, down, through the clouds, I see myself lying in a field of wildflowers, the sun shines high overhead, I know I am back in Norway, and the woman with blue eyes and olive skin lies with me in the forest.

I know this place, in Salmetid, where the river flows gentle. We are naked, embracing one another, in a field of yellow buttercups and purple irises. She is on top of me, grinding gently, in rhythm to our beating hearts, a heartbeat I hear now growing in intensity, because it is my heartbeat and a light is shining in my eyes, and I hear voices, and I know I am lying in a hospital bed. I don't want to wake up.

It was all just a dream, Andreas

A woman tells me to wake.

I recognise the women's voice.

My eyes focus on Lena, wide and clear-eyed, as she stares curiously at me. She is alone in the room, it must be the hospital, the room is brilliantly white all around, my eyesight takes a while to focus on the window where the sunlight stabs in. I see no shadows but for Lena's concerned look down on me. I am lying in a bed, in a hospital gown, there is an intravenous drip in my right forearm. I feel like I have been hit by a bus.

Lena, wide-eyed, stares down at me. She says, "You have been sleeping for over seven hours."

"What happened?"

"You passed out. During the sex."

"What about the lake? The gunshots in the forest?" She turns from me, goes to the window.

"It was all just a dream, Andreas. I drove you to the hospital myself. You will be discharged today; I have called for a taxi to take you home."

The Syphilis Artist

I get out of the taxicab, the dark-skinned driver lets me off at the harbour.

I have a doctor's appointment. I walk in town in dark glasses, my collar upturned. The sunlight seems especially intense today.

I decide to go in a roundabout way to the doctor's office, so I follow the pier down Standgata and cut across the street through some alleyways toward the park.

There is a sculpture of a boy and his boat. I loved to visit it as a child.

I pass the police station as a shopkeeper takes pots of flowers back into the shop. There is the *asylmottak* office, I walk by a few skinny Eritreans outside the office holding Styrofoam cups, sipping coffee.

A short woman in a blue burka with a stroller.

Two stubble-faced Russians with heavy accents, burning cigarettes hanging from their lips, their collars turned up, their hands in their jeans' pockets.

I know their eyes follow me, as I escape down an alleyway and disappear.

The doctor's office is in a modern office building next to the bakery, I decide to go up one flight of stairs instead of taking the elevator.

I put on my dark glasses, go inside the doctor's office where there is a crowd of people, sitting quietly and awaiting their turn to see Dr. Olsen. I don't remove my dark glasses because I don't want to be seen.

Everyone stares at me because they know who I am. The Syphilis Artist.

There in a corner reading a newspaper is the *Lady From Eiken*. She must be approaching seventy, now, that Marilyn Monroe with a wrinkled face who smokes counterfeit Marlboro cigarettes, in a shiny red leather jacket and knee-high black leather boots.

What a woman becomes after placing too many bets on losing horses. She is embarrassed to see me, I can tell, because she hides her face in the newspaper.

As I find a seat, I am not surprised to see sitting next to me hundred-year-old Mrs Gundersen, with the salt and pepper hair, in a yellow wool coat and blue felt hat. She smells of fresh lilacs, her hands shake with a Parkinson's tremor.

A baby is crying. A pleasant looking young woman who has been checking her iPhone lifts the crying baby from her lap, to her shirt. With one hand she manages to unbutton the shirt while still checking her phone with her other hand. Suddenly, the woman's breast pops out like a pink water balloon. The baby stops crying and suckles contently.

"Andreas Olav Hansen?"

A nurse calls my name, I get up, follow her through the door into the doctor's office where I sit down. At the desk, a young man in glasses wearing a laboratory coat reading from a folder. He puts down the folder, stands up and shakes my hand.

"Hello, Andreas. I am Doctor Olsen. You were perhaps expecting my father.

"He retired last year."

I sit down.

He sits down and thumbs through the folder looking for a report. Above his desk on the wall happens to be one of my early pen-and-ink drawings of the lighthouse.

"I see you have one of my early drawings on the wall."

"Did you sketch that?"

"Yes."

There is a pause as he finds a report and reads it, and stares intensely at me, because his facial muscles tighten, as the muscles above his upper lip pull a bit, and his nostrils flare. For some reason, my eyes manage to focus just fine now, and I see details, like the eight steps of that lighthouse, in that sketch on the wall, in the expensive black frame, signed with my initials: A.O.H.

He hasn't asked me to take off my big glasses.

"Well, I have been reviewing the blood work and the scans from Oslo. I am not sure what has been causing your fainting spells, the blood work and brain scans are all normal."

My father said nothing about syphilis when I was sent to the *Rikshospitalet* for brain scans. I had not seen the report from the tests and because the headaches went away, I assumed it was just a migraine.

He pulls some X-rays of my brain from the folder and stands up and places them on a fluorescent viewing box.

There are cross sections of my brain. He explains these are magnetic resonance images of the brain which were taken last summer.

"You have no lesions in your brain. As was mentioned in the letter the VDRL blood work was negative. You were likely cured of syphilis when you were a boy."

"Will I go crazy, Doctor Olsen?"

"Why do you ask that?"

I tell him I had been reading about syphilis, and how in the late stages some people suffered from dementia.

He comes over and listens to my heart with the stethoscope. "Heart sounds are all normal."

He sits down at the desk, and types on the computer.

"You were brought to the hospital because of a fainting spell during some sexual activity, is that correct?"

"Lena said I fainted. That is not how I remember it. I had a dream. I was running in the forest. I heard gunshots. There was a lake."

"Explain."

"Do you have nightmares, Doctor? Do you wake up, in a sweat, because there is a black bird, a raven, sitting on the window ledge, staring at you?"

"No. I seldom remember my dreams."

"Did your mother ever lock you in a jail cell, my good doctor?" He stares at me like I am a crazy person.

"Excuse me?"

"The Oslo boys spit on me, called my mother a whore. She locked me in an old jail cell, with iron bars as thick as broomsticks. In my grandfather's bedroom. She threw me a pencil and a sketchpad. Those were my toys, Doctor."

The doctor types at his keyboard, like a robot. "Do you know of any seizures?"

"No." *I don't tell him about my spells.*

"Are you depressed?"

"Yes. My father and grandfather died. My girlfriend left me. I lost my job some years ago, I have used up most of my savings."

"I am amazed you are not getting social benefits. You are eligible, of course."

He takes out a prescription pad from a drawer.

"I don't want happy pills."

I have learnt to love the darkness in the shadows.

I see this beautiful young man with the smooth face.

Details come and go, go in and out, because my eyes paint on some days with wide-angled strokes, like painting with a fan brush.

Like fanning the clouds at night, with a hundred shades of grey, twisting the brush in so many variegate forms, so I lose sharp details, but the edges remain where the light splits the darkness.

On other days I lick my riggers to a fine point, so I see lines and edges, like the edge of the ocean, when the light shines from the land to the sea from that great lighthouse.

On the cliff where I have sat so many times, with my easel. Where that beautiful woman Solveig removed her clothes, and posed, the wind alight on her face, dancing in those big blue eyes, when the light played a trick on me and I fashioned angel wings from waves.

On days like today my eyes paint with filberts, that flat brush with a rounded end, so I see just the edges of things, like the sharp edge of his tie against his shirt, but there is a blurriness in the middle, like when a person looks through baking paper.

"What scares you about me, Doctor Olsen?"

Olsen puts on latex examining gloves, calls for an assistant, and tells me to drop my pants behind a screen.

A nurse in uniform comes in and observes while I go over behind the screen where I drop my pants and underwear.

I don't feel embarrassed and she stares at me with a forced smile while the doctor pokes around my balls.

He finishes up, snaps off the gloves, goes back to his desk where he types some notes into the computer. The nurse leaves as I put my clothes back on and take a seat again.

"Your examination is normal. Your next round of injections will begin in a few weeks. You will be notified by mail. I have scheduled an appointment for the eye doctor.

"Also, there is a long waiting time to get plastic surgery, as you know. You will likely have to wait at least one year."

There is silence as he stares at me, and just as he is about to get up and thank me for the visit I say, "There is something important I want to tell you."

He settles back into his comfortable leather chair. "Yes Andreas?"

"I see ghosts. Shadows. I see terrible things."

"Oh?"

I tell him about the train ride, and the boys hanging from trees with their neck cut. And my dreams about the angel in the forest.

How my father said they were just nightmares.

The doctor types notes into the computer as he listens to me talk. Looking at me from the screen as he types.

"Your eyes may have been damaged by this illness. There is not much we can do except get stronger glasses. And those nightmares, the one's you say you have had since a child; I think those are best understood by a psychiatrist."

He takes out an ophthalmoscope, comes over and checks each eye, the sharp light filling my eyes like a torch.

"I do not see any changes since your last examination. Hold your hands out like this."

He holds his arms bent at the elbows, so I bend mine and he tries to pull my hands to him.

"Good muscle strength. When you start walking do you have any problem stopping, like your feet just want to move forward?"

"No."

Though my muscles ached most of the time. "The muscle tests and lab tests we have done rule out things like Parkinson's disease." I shift my weight in the chair.

He notices no doubt I am drained and informs me he is done with the examination.

"There are cases of late syphilis where the patient has signs of dementia. There can be seizures, forgetfulness, lots of things can occur. That is why they call syphilis the great mimicker."

* * *

Sitting on a park bench, facing the harbour.

Thinking about the dirty little persecutions, since that fateful day, when he found my lips, and kissed.

Thinking about the little scraps of paper in my father's old desk, how he wrote a few sentences on those scraps. He sneaked up behind me, he caught me on the sofa with Tor-Inge.

My father was never the same after that.

Scribbling sentences, dirty little accusations about his son, how ashamed he had become. I found the little scraps.

I was not the virile and strong son. Thinking I did not know he was spying, or that I would find those torn little scraps in my gambols in the old house.

I was on a street corner in Grünerløkka outside of Henrik Ibsen with a cup of expresso and a *wienerpølse*.

I noticed a thin little brown dog on the sidewalk. He was alone.

He stares with lonely and hungry eyes.

I crouched down, stretched out my hand, he came to me. He ate hungrily, looked at me with tender eyes, walked off.

There was a man standing behind me who spoke to me quietly, and left, his words lingered.

"That was a very kind thing you did," he said.

I started walking down the street, unable to speak.

I fumbled for my sunglasses to cover up the tears running down my cheeks. I cried.

I have no idea why the tears ran.

Abdi weeps

Back on the street the fire-red Opel taxi is waiting for me. The black driver gets out and opens the back door, I see Abdi, the talkative young brightly dressed man from Eritrea.

Or was it Somalia?

"Hey Andy" he calls me, affectionately, as he grabs me gently by the arm and pulls me into the back seat.

Before I can count out loud to ten, he helps me into the back seat, fastened the seatbelt, slammed the door.

"Hey, Mister Andy, you look different today. You are smiling."

"Abdi, take me on a trip. Take me to the beach. I will pay extra."

Abdi is unlike the local Norwegians; he loves to talk, he has no problem with my face, he doesn't give a damn who I sleep with. I just have to get to the beach, smell the ocean breeze.

"But Mister Andy, you know this will cost extra," flashing a broad white smile in the rear-view mirror.

"Take me to the beach, you know the place."

I pass him a thousand crown note, his teeth flash a wide, bright smile and he says, "I hear on the radio that the police will be allowed to carry weapons during the parade, and parents are told to gently remind their children of the fact."

"Abdi, where you come from, do the police carry weapons?"

The way he grins in the mirror, and shakes his head, his silence betrays the fact something bothers him.

I open the window; the wind hits my face.

I am like a dog sticking his head out of a car window, the way the wind blasts my face, blowing the snot from my nose. I love these road trips with Abdi, he doesn't give a damn, maybe he is the only one who I can relate to.

I shout above the blowing wind and passing heavy traffic.

* * *

"Abdi, tell me about your leg."

I see something is up from his pained expression in the rear-view mirror. He pulls over to a scenic overlook, stops the taxi, gets out, opens my door, unfastens my seatbelt, helps me out.

"Andy, I want to tell you something."

We sit at a park bench at the cliff's edge.

Abdi looks out at the valley, the horizon sprinkled with houses touched with spots of red and blue, little red Norwegian cabins sitting each by a little sparkling lake.

I think a few minutes pass by with silence, just him and I sitting, each wrapped up in our fractured world.

"We were beaten. Tied up day and night. I was tied up for two weeks. They cut off my right leg with a bayonet." His eyes fixed straight ahead.

"I refused military service."

The hard blue of the sky and the flaming sun and the valley green, ripened anew, the singing birds, the speeding traffic going by.

I listen to Abdi telling a story; he talks with a pained voice full of medley, in Eritrean.

The words float in one ear and out the next, while I stare at the white gulls spinning in the warm updrafts in the valley as the sun spanks and glitters off their wings.

He knows I do not understand Eritrean, except for a few words, and I think he talks just to get it all out of his system.

He's really getting into it, his hard brown eyes fixed away, at the horizon.

Then with his voice reaching a rapid clip, like he's totally lost, he starts yelling, at some enemy, in a voice echoing loud in the valley.

Yelling like an actor totally lost in the moment.

I hear some English words mixed in, something about a boat sinking, off the Libyan coast, something about children drowning under the waves.

Then, as quickly as he began, he stops. There is quiet.

He weeps.

Abdi's tears, as he turns, faces me, unspeakable anguish fills his face. I have never seen a black man cry.

There is something awful and beautiful in watching Abdi, how his ebony face changes, the eyes dropping deep socketed in his face, the facial muscles stiffening and pulling, the ivory teeth.

Abdi's mind is far away, with that caravan of corrupt traffickers driving their human cattle across the baking hot sands of the Libyan desert.

Silence, as I take out the embroidered little handkerchief from my coat pocket.

I wipe the tears from his eyes. I bend over, kiss his cheek, his wet eyes locking with mine.

"I love Norway. You have a free country. Promise Andy, promise me, you will keep it free."

"Abdi, let me whisper you something I have learnt."

I pull him close; he is startled by my aggression.

I love this man.

I turn his head, so my mouth is up to his ear and whisper, so he hears softly, "There is a way to learn to love nature by understanding art. It dignifies every flower of the field. And the boy who sees the thing of beauty will not throw the stone."

"Oscar Wilde," remarks Abdi, matter-of-factly.

We stop at Knut Hamsen's old house

I was on summer road trip back to Oslo. I was seventeen in the back seat of my father's tiny red Polo with Father driving, Grandfather in the passenger seat, the window was down, grandfather was playing some playful tunes on the harmonica. Father chain-smoking, having a good time, colourfully swearing under his breath.

They were dirty little expressions which only the Norwegian language captures, and one about a trout's vagina that particularly struck me as funny. But I was disturbed because my father had an argument with my mother, and she hit him. Which explained his bruised left eye, swollen, so he could only see through his right eye, and why he had to get away.

It made me nervous, the way he was driving, so I started smoking too, rolling cigarettes, licking the paper, watching the little tissues fly all around the car because the windows were down. Somehow, I loved this trip, because I was smoking, Father was talking dirty, and Grandfather disregarded us both. Lost in the past. There was something noble about Grandfather, a quality neither my father nor I possessed.

We had stopped at Knut Hamsen's old house in Grimstad. Wherever I went I had a little sketchbook so I persuaded my father to wait over two hours, just so I could sketch Hamsun's house. It is a grand old house, and Grandfather wanted to stop, eat shrimp, and admire the gardens. Afterwards we were walking down Kirkekarten Street when father took me to a tent, with the name 'Erotikktorg'.

It was crowded with people and filled with stands piled with sex toys.

My grandfather was too embarrassed to go inside but his face lit up when my father remarked that we would be stopping at the Hok beach in Oslo just so Grandfather could feast his eyes on the topless ladies sunning themselves.

I know my father bought a dildo by the look on his face when I asked him, back in the car driving to Oslo, as he shoved a plastic bag under the seat and Grandfather remarked that in his time people knitted their own condoms. They can't say my grandfather didn't have a sense of humour.

Our destination outside Oslo was Grini, the site of the concentration camp where, in 1945, over five thousand Norwegians were imprisoned, including my grandfather.

On a way there along E18 we passed by stubby wheat fields, girls in braids and red caps riding horses at a delicate trot and Grandfather was talking about someone who collected, dried and lacquered elk shit, sold it to tourists for 25 crowns a bag.

He thought it was funny, he started laughing crazily, the snot blew out of his nose and hit the windshield. Clouds stole over the sun as my father pulled the car outside the museum parking lot. My grandfather remarked, "The only way to have escaped the camp was by way of the smoke from the crematorium."

We walked around outside the red-timbered buildings, following a path to some memorials outside.

There were not many people around, it was a Saturday afternoon, and we let my grandfather walk alone. I watched as he stopped solemnly by a flat stone memorial inscribed with the words, 'Frihet og Liv eg ett'.

Watching in silence as we saw Grandfather sitting down on a bench, covering his face. We went over, my father sat by him, wrapped his arm stiffly around Grandfather's shoulder, said nothing as Grandfather wept quietly.

Then he stops weeping, looks my father straight in the eye and tells him matter-of-factly that the toilet consisted of two buckets. One for solids and one for liquids.

Each man slept on the floor. Shoulder to shoulder, foot sole to sole. You rotated on the floor so you didn't have to sleep next to the same stinky bucket every twenty-one days.

Some prisoners had been in the cell over one year. Every morning through a tiny hole in the cell door the German guard would shove in a safety razor.

With a piece of soap, and some cold water from a single pan all twenty-one of the prisoners would shave and soap up. Men with heavy beards went through agony. The turn to use the razor went according to age.

The oldest one first, so Grandfather was always last. The guards made sure everyone was clean-shaven.

She told me the black wolf wears a silver crucifix

A timid knocking at the front door.

I hurry out of bed, go to the window, parting the curtains to see a huge full moon sitting like a crown atop the mountain.

No doubt there is a patron at the door, with a car boot full of counterfeit Marlboros from the Swedish border.

Now she wants a fix with that crazy man who wears a paper bag over his head, with the cut-out eyes.

Somehow, with every passing full moon, they show up at my doorstep. They do not know I have a method to my madness.

The last young woman told me the black wolf wears a silver crucifix.

* * *

My mother locked me in a jail cell and threw me a pencil.

She slapped my father, when he told her he would take me on a trip, to see a doctor, in that faraway place.

"If you take him away, I will leave, and never come back!"

"Then leave! I know who you have been sleeping with! Where do you think he got this disease!"

This woman who called herself my mother, this proper churchgoing holy roller who cursed the fact I was born, who smoked and drank the nights away, in that little apartment on the east side in Oslo, when my father came home night after night from the bar, awful thoughts all bottled inside.

Because he was a nice Norwegian, wearing his emotion on his sleeve, he hadn't the balls to confront my mother when he discovered she had been sleeping with the pastor of that crazy church where they speak in tongues.

Fuck the church, fuck those crazy, hypocritical high rollers selling their snake oil and miracle cures.

They would pray for little Andreas, that this sexual disease would flee his body.

My mother would go down on her knees, night after night, and shout her hallelujahs to the great Jehovah in the sky.

There would be a shaking of the heavens, there would be rain, and a thunderclap.

And then, just like that, with a thunderclap, little Andreas, the boy with the broken nose, would be cured.

* * *

I unlock and open the door.

My eyes are not good, I see a shadow standing in front of me, a shadow outlined by a gigantic full moon sitting atop the mountain.

"I found this on your doorstep. A handwritten letter." I recognise Eirik's timid voice.

I stretch out my right hand to his face, my fingers tapping, feeling the warmth of his flesh.

I feel Eirik putting the envelope in my hand, it is no matter, I cannot read today, even with the thick glasses.

"Come in, I'll make a fire, we will have a drink, you can read me the letter at the desk."

I remember we had the Jesus painting to finish, I had taken it from the church to the studio.

He stands in the open doorway, unsure of himself.

"Come in, Eirik. We'll sit at the desk, warm ourselves up, you can read me the letter."

Eirik comes in, shuts the door behind him, makes sure it is locked.

He stands in the hallway like a tightly wound coil about to be strung. I feel it, the hard way he breathes, his body has been cut down the middle, and the two halves, hot and cold, are grinding one upon the other. There is something troubling him.

"Is it contagious?" his clear eyes locking mine.

Full of fear.

So that is what is bothering him.

I cannot tell you what happens next because there are things hidden in shadows that are not meant to be seen.

There is a place I go in the house, on that bed carved from the church timbers, whose posts are rose carvings where my fingers feel their relief, gliding gently.

Where Eirik can sit, naked, by the glowing Jotel oven, where his tears can fall, and I sit by him, my face hidden not behind a bag, but in a shadow.

And all this young man needs is someone to hear him weep, because his old friends have left him.

And I just sit there, listening, the way the fire crackles, the way the candle burns down, the way we just spoon under the thick down blanket.

This young man with the alabaster face, this Jesus, who weeps quietly, and shakes, because he was born with an affliction, and the smooth-faced men in their white collars and black robes say he is going to burn in hell.

"Fuck the church. There is no heaven, there is no hell," I whisper in his ear, as he turns in bed to face me, my face in the shadow but for the glow of my eyes, widened and fixed on his porcelain face.

This young man who stares at me, wildly eyed. *"Fuck you,"* he says, affectionately.

I go to reach for the paper bag with the cut-out eyes. "No, I want to see your face."

Eirik sits up, takes the bag from my hands, crumples and throws it on the floor.

He lays back down, his naked form a shadow on the wall, as the candle dances our shadows on the wall, where the only light now is a tiny spark I see in his eye, the light of this dying candle, when, soon extinguished, I will hear his moaning.

The way the bed shakes, the way I shake inside, because Levi says I am a marked man, and I am going to hell.

A boulder drops to the sea

Sitting at my desk, pouring a cup of coffee from a thermos.

Bundled up in my coat, up early this morning as the light stabbed in the window.

The light touched my face, awakening alone in the bed. Eirik has left.

On the desk my father's antique cassette tape recorder, the one I found in a box labelled 'for the museum'. Amazingly I got it working, it just needed fresh batteries.

I press the buttons, rewinding the tape, the scratchy turning of the little plastic cogs awakens me to a strange thought.

If I could rewind my life, back all the way to that fateful day, when I was a boy, and my mother threw my pencils and sketchbook in the jail cell, in my grandfather's room, in the very room I now sit, and if I could erase this mark on my face, and if my mother had not slept with all those men, and if my father had not started to drink, and all those terrible things, that happened, would it make a difference, if I could take it all back?

No, it would not.

I am just a leaf blown in the forest; it is like what Lena said.

I am sand in the seashore; I will be blown out to sea. I am here, then one day I will be gone, and my memory will linger on, perhaps, for a day, and Levi will say a few kind words, and the casket will drop into the pit.

***

A fir tree drops in the forest. A boulder drops in the sea.

A woman's voice, filled in ecstasy, echoes in the mountains. God is dead, religion is myth, life is meaningless.

And the touch of a woman, what is that.

The Jotel oven glows in the corner where I started a fire, downstairs there is a fire going in the studio, I remember Eirik said he would make a fire before he left.

He would sharpen my pencils, the little plates of oil paints would be ready, with all my sables and filberts as I had instructed him.

Everything would be ready for me now that the pencil sketch is ready. Eirik had stretched the huge floor-to-ceiling life-size canvas in the studio. This man Eirik, who comes to me in the night.

Who sits on the black enamelled *krak*, his porcelain face upturned, eyes as large as plums, blue as the sea, flowing locks to the shoulders, blonde, as heavenly light stabs down through cracks in the clouds, touching his face; this alabaster Jesus, who I have been commissioned to paint.

This white Jesus, in a swaddling loincloth, eyes up cast to his father, kneeling by a stone, on the forest's edge, where a distant waterfall is seen, and the fir trees stand pencil sharp and erect. *The scene I was commissioned by Levi to paint.*

I hold the letter close to my face so I can make out the handwriting as I press the button on the cassette recorder and hear Eirik's clear voice, reciting the letter.

As he reads, I take it all in.

* * *

I am writing from Zagreb. It is May 21st, 1991, and by this time Norway will have celebrated its Independence Day. It is one month since the sanctions were lifted in Serbia. I meet many people on the street and they speak about the 'former Yugoslavia'. Ha, ha! That is paradoxical because if it is 'former' then it does not exist. How can I exist in something that no longer exists? It does not make sense. I find it comforting to write you these letters.

I did not feel I could talk to you freely at the hospital. But of course, you know that in Belgrade the war was never fought. So that makes our struggle to express ourselves as artists a kind of test. It is as Grotowski once said, freedom is not whether you go to prison or not, but inner freedom, the inner possibility to survive.

Today there was no fuel so I rode the bicycle to work. I left at five and got to work at seven. A two-hour trip! My legs are so sore. Tonight Eloise, Jedranka and I will be performing our "Tales of Man and Woman."

I feel I have a moral responsibility to express myself in this way.

We are not politicians. I will have only one hour to get away from the hospital so we cannot go out afterwards as you Norwegians do and 'chat' in a restaurant. You understand why I cannot meet you. I can speak with you as we did about politics, and art, and what is happening with us.

I thought writing you a letter quiets my mind of so many things.

For you, Zagreb was an abstraction. I tell you this: When Slovenia started putting up posts with its border with Croatia and began a different currency, I felt anger.

The green forest where my father took me on walks now is black, it is an abstraction, a black fence, staring at me.

Ha, ha! My Slovene neighbour says to me, as she tells me she is now liberated, and I am not. Should I feel guilty? I do not know what I should feel.

When I was sitting at Sudbanhof, waiting for you, I read one of the daily newspapers from Serbia. An article had described an atrocity of the war committed by the Ustache, the Croatian army. It froze the blood in my veins and my heart stopped beating. It was the first time I had heard of such a thing. The newspaper described how a man had gone into his backyard, to his well, and pulled up the bucket. About three hundred cut-off testicles were found in that bucket. I felt a shaking in my body, a sort of mental convulsion.

The reaction to a scene my brain could not process, because it was so horrible. I resisted picturing it, though my imagination had to, at least for a second, when it flashed the long line of men, hundreds of them, standing naked, waiting for the knife's flash, the spattering of blood, the choking pain and terror. I tell you this: Writing it down puts an edge on this abstraction, so I can make some sense of it.

The television is on and the announcer says that a family of eight was slaughtered in a Slovenian village. He says it as a matter of fact that is no more startling than a traffic jam on the Zagreb Belgrade highway.

At that moment, I realised that darkness had come upon us.

I will have to go back to the hospital in a day. So, I will say goodbye now in writing.

We are not so different, you and I.

In my country we have four languages, two alphabets, and bombastic history lessons that pander to mutual hatred and chauvinism. You must return to Norway. It is a beautiful country whose proud, independent people I admire.

We have an old Croatian proverb: Some truths are not to be told. Please go back, and please, please, forget you ever met me.

Marija.

There is a hard knock at the door.

I turn off the cassette player, get up and walk down the steps.

I get to the door, crack it open, there is a shadow on the steps, as big as a bear.

Suddenly I feel a blow to my face, I see a flash of light, and everything goes black.

I am your sister

I hear the crackling of a fire burning.

I am lying on the floor, under a woollen blanket, a down pillow under my head. There is candlelight, the glow of logs in the fireplace.

The room aglow, the smell of my oil paints lingers.

Delicate fingers move down my forehead, dancing down my face, stopping at my bruised lips.

A finger inserted between the broken front teeth, pulling out a chipped tooth.

The insertion of a plump strawberry in my mouth. I chew, hungrily, my senses enlivening. Swallowing, my throat reeling from a dull pain.

A finger stopping, pressing deliberately on my lips. "Don't worry. You are safe now." A woman's voice.

I brood on the moment, the erotic panic of finding myself alone with a mysterious woman.

The outline of her face coming into and out of view. A woman in a black dance leotard, her hair in a bun. In a stylish red vest with gold braid.

I see her dark olive skin and her searching big blue eyes. Around her neck a crystal teardrop pendant on a silver chain. She drops her hair from a bun.

The way the girl stares out at the sea through the open window, from that ancient stone villa atop the hill, the girl in gold braid and a plaid vest with dark hair and olive skin and eyes the colour of the sea, the way she steals into my dreams.

My jaw struggling to move, feeling tight muscles relaxing, as if it had been wired shut. She presses grapes into my mouth.

Then it hits me.

"You are the woman I have been dreaming of."

This was the girl in my dreams, the girl attending the old man in the villa on the seashore.

"I found you in the doorway. You didn't come to and start talking until an hour ago."

* * *

I have a headache.

"What happened?"

I remember knocking at the door, a shadow, then everything went black.

I feel like I am on a carousel, with the room spinning. I smell incense and hear the crash of waves on the shore.

I see the girl, in a red vest with gold braid, in that room made of stone, on the bed with the old man, sponging his face, wiping the sleep from his eyes.

The old man whose legs are cut off above the knees, with the mole on his nose the size of a pea. In the stone palace by the sea.

I see myself as a boy, in the room made of stone, crouched in a corner, sketching in a pad.

My eyes fixed on the girl, as my charcoal pencil traces an outline of the room, the bed, the open window, and the sea.

Where the wind rustles through palm leaves, and the shadows have an edge, and the sound my pencil makes is a sound I have only heard once in my life.

The woman with olive skin whispers in my ear.

"I want to go to the forests of Fontainebleau and lie down in the grass." Her voice is like the wind.

I turn to her and cup my hands on her face.

She stares into my eyes, her face a finger's width from mine, lavender on her breath, her blue eyes with a tinge of honey, searching, full of sorrow.

There is a moment when I think she will cry, a tear forms in her eye, and runs down her cheek and neck, along the silver chain bearing a crystal teardrop.

I am lost in the moment.

My finger stretches out, touches the teardrop.

She is in another place, the way her eyes turn away, the way she bites her lip. I have known this woman; this is the girl born on the Island of Pag.

* * *

I cannot tell you how long I stared, just staring into her face, how the *tick-tock* of the grandfather clock chimed in my ears.

She takes a mobile phone from a leather handbag, taps the screen.

There is music playing. It is a piano melody, *Schubert's Ave Maria*, when it begins, she strikes a pose in the centre of the room, as I sit up, watching.

The fireplace is to her back so her shadow is painted large on the timbered walls. Her back is straight, her head high, her arms relaxed, slightly away from her body.

It is like I am walking on ice.

There is something beneath the surface of the dance.

She jumps, she kicks, she rolls on the floor and spins as if she were in a great concert hall. Minutes pass, I cannot tell, because nothing has prepared me for this.

She has disappeared in the music.

As the song fades, she strikes a final pose, in the middle of the floor, her arms outstretched, as she lays her head downcast on the floor.

Sitting some moments later back on the sofa, sipping warm black tea from a thermos.

I awaken to something tapping inside me, a gentle tapping, like a titmouse when he taps outside on the tree.

It was something I had been thinking about since I found the letter on the doorstep.

"I found a letter at the door. Did you put it there?"

"No, I know nothing about a letter."

A shadow on my doorstep.

I try to recall memories, but my mind hits a wall.

I feel like I have seen things a boy should have never seen, and now little pieces are coming back, like threads spinning in the wind.

My mind reaches back, to that train ride to Zagreb, and I feel my father holding my hand tight. It is all too real to be just a dream.

Now a woman feeds me, wants nothing from me.

I just want to touch her face, feel its smoothness. I feel awkward. I do not know what to think.

"Has anyone told you of the shine that sparkles from a kind woman's heart?" I whisper, to myself, just talking, not making eye contact, staring down at the floor.

When I look up her face is locked on mine.

Those wide-eyed blue eyes with a touch of green, touched with honey, eyes grabbing you, seeing right through you.

I am not sure if this woman is real, the woman from the island of Pag who haunts my dreams.

My fingers stretch out, trembling, stretching nearer to her face.

Her jet-black hair falling down a swan's neck, her eyes wide, searching, precious as newly cut lapis lapida.

Her shoulders bare, a fresh cut rose in a low-cut bodice between her breasts. Now, breath to breath, the steam of my trembling voice condensing on her rose cheeks. I smell lavender, and the scent of the forest after a summer rain, when the sun alights atop the trees, and glides down, to touch the flesh. Mia cups her hands on my face, kisses me ever so gently on my lips.

My fingers now on her face, like the way I touch a model's face and feel its contours before I make a drawing.

Putting into my fingers' memory its form so I can close my eyes and draw a likeness.

I close my eyes, my fingers linger a moment and glide down to her neck, so I capture an image of her in my mind. My hand falls away, my eyes closed, because I think when I open them, she will be gone, this all a dream.

"Your mother Marija. That is her name, isn't it?" I ask, my eyes closed.

I feel her forefinger on my lips, I open my eyes, there is heartache in her stare. For a few seconds they fill with sadness. They turn from me, she is distracted, staring away, there is something she does not want to think about.

She goes to the window, and stands, staring outside at the starlit sky.

It is a perfect still night, seconds pass, minutes pass, the grandfather clock stops ticking.

She is lost in thought. She turns to face me.

The way her eyes lock mine and search, the way a woman struggles with a secret. She comes over, kneels in front of me. She bites her lip, struggles with her words.

"Andreas. I will tell you something which you have no way of understanding, at the present. My mother, she hid in the basement. She got calls on the telephone and people left messages. They called her a Chetnik whore. They said terrible things. That is when I got my dismissal."

"Dismissal?"

"From the Zagreb Theatre. From a certain individual who said I could never return. I had told him in a letter what I thought about the war. How my mother could never have participated in the atrocities. She was a doctor. The unexplained exceptions that people had about the war was for me an admission of guilt that they too were guilty."

She gets up, my eyes have trouble focusing, she comes in and out of view, so I put on my ugly thick glasses, and I see Mia clearly now, she digs in her purse for something.

She takes out a photograph, hands it to me. A faded Polaroid picture, I pick it up and hold it close to my face, make out the date stamp. 'May 16, 1992'.

"My mother took it of us."

I would be about eight years old in the photo, a dark-haired girl a few years older wearing a silken red vest with gold trim stands happily next to me in garden.

We are outside in a stone patio. A cloudless horizon meets the ocean.

"Your father first met my mother when she was on holiday in Vienna, in 1984." Mia takes a postcard from her purse, shows it to me.

"Look at the date. It's written to my mother."

It was a drawing of the waterfront in Split, Croatia. The card was dated December 29, 1984. On the back were just a few words, in my father's handwriting, in black flowing ink.

"*Min Kjære, Marija...*" in his distinct, flowery signature.

* * *

Mia walks around the room and blows out all the candles.

The only light in the room comes from the fireplace whose embers glow faint. Shadows of the dying fire play on her face as she comes back to me, sits so our hips touch. She faces me, her liquid eyes locking mine, intense, full of feeling. And then she slips the dancer's leotard from off her shoulders, to her waist.

On her breasts and chest is a stylish floral tattoo, below her left shoulder the word 'HOPE'.

"Andreas, I need to expose myself to you."

She weeps. Her lips tremble. "*I never lost hope finding you.*"

From the corner of my eye, I catch the unusual tattoo on her right shoulder. With my thick glasses on my eyes are sharp, the tattoo is no larger than a twenty-crown piece showing a crucifix surrounded by a floral tapestry of flowers. "My mother paid a Croatian artist during a Catholic holiday to make it for me. The ink was made from my mother's milk, charcoal, and honey, a sign of my mother's faith going back to the Turkish occupation hundreds of years ago."

I pull off my shirt and wipe the tears from her cheeks. "Let me show you my tattoo," I tell her.

She sees the big tattoo across my chest, that ugly, scarred tattoo in Runes. "A-R-T-I-S-T" she reads out loud, as I feel her warm hand tracing the ridges of the scarred flesh.

It is as if I have known her for a lifetime.

"The politicians scream their angry hatreds, they interrogate, they imprison, they use Nazi tactics, they tell me I should hate my neighbour because of something time should have healed. I tell you this, Andreas Olav Hansen, a shadow reawakens itself. It will take to the streets again, if we are not awake."

She pulls away and stands back, looks at me, and the eyes are full of sorrow.

Then she turns her head to the fire, so her face is aglow.

"My mother boycotted classes, I walked together with her in the streets. She wrote letters. I couldn't convince those who pull the strings of the simple fact that we are citizens fully aware of our undeniable right of free choice." Now turning to me, her eyes locking mine.

"You cannot deny the existence of the people who walk the distance from Nis to Belgrade in forty-eight hours, nor can you deny them their free will."

* * *

I stare at her, searching for words, this woman who awakens something in me.

This girl with a khaki shirt and a red vest with gold braid who visited me in my dreams, in that jail cell, in my grandfather's room, upstairs.

Where my mother threw me a pencil, where the sound of my scratchings on the pine-timbered floor filled the day, the only sounds in the house but for the ticking of my grandfather's clock.

My mind is a jumble of scenes awakened from their sleep, my fingers start to shake, I see the little knife I use to sharpen my pencils, I take it in my hands, and in one sweeping cut, slice a mark in my palm, where the blood spurts. I feel nothing, I have no feeling in my hand.

"I feel nothing, Mia."

I begin to weep, Mia sits my side, taking a tissue to my hand. My hand feeling her face, some blood dripping down my palm on her neck, down her chest and between her breasts, like a meandering rose's stem. She just holds me, wants nothing in return, this otherworldly woman who knows my pain. Maybe several minutes pass, she is silent.

Searching in her gaze, looking deep in my eyes, as she takes my little embroidered cloth and wipes away my tears.

I weep.

* * *

There is a stillness, the ticking of my grandfather's clock, the sounds of dying embers cracking.

I feel her heartbeat, I take her in my arms and press her close to my chest, as she looks at my big tattoo, which her eyes linger on, as her fingers feel the scars on my arm where I had cut myself.

Her eyes meet mine again, and I think I am about to kiss her. She senses this, and pulls slightly away, as she struggles to find the right words, because they have been forming on her lips.

Her eyes lock with mine.

"Do you think I would have come all the way from Pag on my motorcycle to Norway, to a stranger's house?"

She reaches back into a bag and pulls out a big envelope and spills the contents on the floor. There are dozens of time-worn small blue letters, the kind my father used to buy at the post office, the one page kind you folded and licked yourself.

Mia picks up a little letter, holds it close to my face. I make out my father's handwriting.

"All these letters are from your father, Harold Hansen, in Norway. They are addressed to my mother, Doctor Marija Drovik, at the hospital where she worked in Zagreb. They are love letters, written by your father Harold. I know everything about you, *Andy*. Your father wrote how proud he was of you, how you could paint, how you are a genius with your pencils. And he wrote about your sickness."

I am shaken to my bones.

"He told me how he met my mother on holiday in Zagreb, when he visited with his friend Svein. How he had to take you on that miserable train ride you remember so well just so you could get the shots from my mother at the hospital. You see, it is not a dream. Your father wrote you had hallucinations, you saw things. Sometimes you made up crazy stories because this disease, syphilis, can do that to your brain. It is a psychosis, you can believe things that didn't really happen."

"What are you trying to tell me, Mia?"

"There is one fact that isn't a dream. *I am your sister.*"

She is light entering the dark places of my soul

The rain falls lightly, a depression in the grass where the ground sinks, fills with water.

I stand at her side in my yellow hooded rain jacket and my new green Viking boots and stare blankly at the gravestone, with my father's name engraved in gold lettering, in his flowing signature. 'Harold Hansen'.

He just wanted his name, and nothing else. That should be enough, he said. It is a rectangle of polished black marble, with his flowery signature, a simple headstone, no more. "I don't think our father killed himself." Mia pulls up close to my face.

The way she locks her eyes on you.

The way I can't help but take it all in, without protest.

This woman's presence, this woman from the island of Pag with olive skin and eyes the colour of the sea, captures me, in her embrace.

I melt, she is light entering the dark places of my soul.

How her eyes lock with mine, how she forgets my ugly face, how it doesn't bother her, how she can just stare, and search, as I lift my fingers to her face, and touch where the raindrops fall.

I walk in the meadow, where the purple lupins lay scattered on the hillside, along the bend in the river, in Salmetid, where the moss is wet under my bare feet. Where the echo of her voice, filled with ecstasy, echoes in the valley.

"The police report said it was a suicide," I remark.

"He was murdered. He would never have taken his own life."

Mia takes something wrapped in tissue paper from her coat pocket. She unwraps it, a silver figurine, a *nightingale*. She places it on my father's gravestone. She traces my father's signature on the paper with a pencil. She does this solemnly, so the minutes pass. I watch as the pencil scrapes, I make out my father's flowery handwriting bleeding through on the paper.

She finishes, folds the paper, stuffs it into her pocket and turns to me and I think she will say something. She has a way of staring into my face, just staring, lovingly, searchingly, she whispers: "We will go inside the church and pray."

Following Mia, we stroll slowly to the church.

The path to the door winds through the pretty churchyard, it is like a park, and now with spring, the flowers bloom, like so many rainbow colours sprinkled from a painter's brush.

* * *

Mia takes my hand and leads me to a bench under a tree.

Midday sunlight breaking now through the leaves, in the distance a few locals entering through the gates, collecting water cans, Mia spies them, something bothers her, her face now locking mine, as both her hands hold mine tight.

"When I arrived here, I found out where you lived from your friend in the church office."

"Levi?"

"Yes, that was his name, Levi."

Mia continues, her voice dances on the edge of a pin, the way it trembles. "There is some talk here in town that you may have something to do with the disappearance of that woman who went missing. I understand that the police took you in for questioning."

Pulling my hands from her grasp, staring up at the blinding light filtering down on me.

My eyesight going dark, the flashing of light stabbing from above, then shadows, the images of trees, black fir trees pencil straight, and stiff, in that clearing in the forest.

Where I see myself, laying hidden in the snow. In my fisherman's coat, laying still and mute like a stone, frost on my breath, because I had been running in the forest, a scared animal hunted by a shadow unseen.

A stone's throw in front of me, a naked woman hanging upside down, tied at the ankles, naked and swaying, back and forth, like a swing. I take a little stick and bite down hard because it is the only thing that will prevent me from screaming.

Shaking, like I am about to have a seizure. I see the young woman's eyes, horrible, widened eyes locked in shock, staring at me. I see the slit neck, dripping drops crimson to the snow, where a blood trail like a serpent's tail winds back into the forest. I recognise the woman, she had come to me one night, *I had sketched her, we had taken a sauna together.*

My teeth bite so hard on the stick it snaps, and the sound awakes me, and I see Mia staring at me, hearing her anxious voice.

"Andy. Are you all right?"

Continuing now, my eyes back to normal, she stares at me, concerned. "You had a spell. Your eyes rolled back; you need to see a doctor. Promise me, Andy, you need to see a doctor. You cannot live like this."

* * *

Inside the church, just Mia and myself.

Mia stands in the aisle, awed.

An old Norwegian church pine-timbered, masterfully built, with cogged tight joints, like a graceful Viking ship.

The way the light enters the thick leaded windows and plays on the altar. Handblown windows of leaded Bavarian glass, bearing the marks of their artists.

I had forgotten how beautiful this place is.

There is a crucifix four hundred years old, from the city of Lubeck, on the wall, near the altar, with the suffering scantily clad Christ figure. Mia walks over to the figure. She removes her coat, places it on a bench.

"Have you ever been to Borgo San Sepolcro?" she asks, turning to me, but I am listening to the rain outside, there is thunder, and I think I should get back. I turn back and see Mia as her hand reaches to the small hand painted Christ figure, her hands touching his feet, a wooden sculpture of a sorrowful man draped in a loincloth, wearing thorns for a crown.

I am not thinking about Jesus.

In the shadow of this Christ figure with thorns for a crown. In this church where I dreaded to come on my father's funeral.

I am torn by the shadow of this half-naked man. I bury my head in my hands. Squeezing my eyeballs tight.

I remember Eirik, that night, when I sketched his form. I remember so many things, how he drew his face close to mine, and whispered. He told me he was going away because he was afraid.

Mia comes over, sits by my side.

"My mother told me once that the Bocca Trabaria is the most beautiful of the Apennine passes, between the Tiber valley and the valley of the Metauro. There is a little town surrounded by walls, in a flat valley between hills. There are fine Renaissance palaces with balconies of wrought iron, and the most beautiful picture in the world."

"And what may that picture be?"

"It is Francesca's picture, the Resurrection. I want to see the painting one day."

I look up, she is startled to see my face now. Our eyes locking with one another's.

My jaws clenching, my anger stirring. I hate the church.

There is something about Mia that softens me, but I feel like I will explode.

"Levi has commissioned me to paint Jesus. I feel like I am losing my mind.

"I hate the church."

I struggle to get to my feet. I feel unsteady, I feel I must get away from this place, and this woman, who seeks to convert me. I pull away from her grasp and walk toward the door.

"Stop!"

I look back and see her standing facing me in the aisle.

"Don't you remember, Andreas Olav Hansen! You saw it! We hid together in the church! There were young men in uniform all around! Plastic sheets covered the church windows and there was no wood to cover the window frames! The church clock tower had tumbled down! Bodies had been floating in the water!"

She shouts now with a tone meant to awaken something inside me, something I had kept hidden.

"Bodies had been floating in the water!"

I go to a bench, sit, and feel the room starting to spin.

Mia next to me, holding my hands, unbuttoning my coat, laying me flat, because this is how it always happens. Before I get those dreams, those horrible dreams. Mia bends over me, I see her necklace, and a crystal teardrop.

Mia's tears dropping on me now, as I hear distant gunshots, the room fades, shadows invade, as my minds spins back to that fateful day.

The sharp metallic echo of machine gun fire, the shouts of soldiers in a foreign tongue.

"Hold my hand, Mia!"

I am a boy, hiding in that magnificent Catholic church, under a bench, holding tight this girl's hands. This girl Mia in a khaki shirt and red vest embroidered in gold. Mia lays next to me and places her hands over my eyes, so I won't see but I pull her hand away. I see the nuns in their black gowns at the altar, at the foot of St. Peter. I hear the nun's wailing prayers, see their anguished faces caught by light stabbing through the stained-glass windows. There are people all over lying on cots, moaning in pain. Mia's mother, in a bloodied white doctor's coat, sits by a young woman lying on a cot, and feeds her soup with a spoon. It is all a nightmare, I think, as there is shouting outside and machine gun fire, and a drunk young soldier drinking from a bottle with a red cap comes bursting into the church. He's a total madman swinging a Kalashnikov, and I want to scream but Mia cups her hand over my mouth. The soldier picks up a boy hiding in a corner. Mia's mother strides courageously up to the soldier and tries to force him out but he knocks her down as he goes from cot to cot, shooting the innocent patients, the young woman on the stretcher, a nun at the altar. The lifeless body of the small boy thrown at the altar, at the foot of St Peter.

It comes all back to me in and instant, these awful memories.

How I witnessed evil as a boy in a foreign land, how that evil hid itself all these years.

Now I know why I became an artist.

It was to escape from this world.

Mia's comforting words, awakening from my spell, her motherly eyes on mine, as she cradles me, tight to her chest, as she weeps.

"I have forgiven those awful men, what they did. The terrible things men do against one another will haunt and destroy them in the end. They forced my mother to lick puddles of water on the ground, like a dog. Evil turned men into something less than dogs." She helps me to my feet.

She leads me to the church altar.

This peaceful little Norwegian church where a raven sits atop the bell tower, waiting for me to drop to the ground.

I drop to the altar.

Besides me, on her knees, staring straight ahead, the gentle woman Mia.

"I have come to Norway to start a new life, *Andreas-Olav-Hansen*. You must forgive your mother. You must forgive those men. Otherwise, you will lose yourself. You will hate, that will destroy yourself."

I remember my grandfather whispering a prayer in Grini, in that dark cell, where threads hung from the ceiling. A prayer whose words he whispered, over and over, in the blackness.

"Never be afraid of evil's darkness."

"Never be afraid of evil's darkness," I whisper. The touch of Mia's hand on my forehead.

She kisses my forehead, gently.

"You will finish your masterpiece. This man you say you admire, this man with the gentle heart, Jesus. Then when you are finished, and the people come to see this great painting by *The Syphilis Artist,* you will have your miracle."

Her eyes lock with mine.

There is a silence that stretches itself, as the stretching of her hand to my face, when she first came to me, in the shadows.

Omarska

It is like I am watching a movie, in my dream. I am far away from Norway, away from my beloved oceans and fjørds, watching as the flat barren countryside streaks by. I am about seventeen, in a train, looking anxiously out the dirty window, as the train comes to a screeching stop alongside a platform.

It's strange because the reflection of my face in the dirty window reveals a normal nose. I am not Andreas Olav Hansen, but someone who is my doppelganger. As the doors on the train slide open, I am pushed forward and see spidery iron tentacles, conveyor belts and limbs of machinery linking one metal shed to another.

A sign on one shed says 'OMARSKA'.

I am among hundreds of shabbily dressed prisoners as we are forced off the train by a phalanx of shouting soldiers. Children are yanked from their mothers' arms. Wailing protests escalate to brawls.

A woman wearing a scarf is shot, she collapses in a puddle. I am swallowed in the crowd as buses unload wave after wave of prisoners—each face bearing witness to unspeakable acts of cruelty.

The soldiers are forcefully taking away personal belongings, an old woman's rosaries are ripped from her grasp. In my dream a soldier pulls a dozen young men from a line and directs them toward an open field.

I see them forced to lay on the ground, while a truck rolls over their legs. The screaming in my dream is awful. I find myself standing in front of a guard seated at a folding table. In my dream, behind the table, I see a white shed and next to it a red-painted shed, and in between, a soldier standing guard with a Kalashnikov. The boyish looking guard at the table is forcing the prisoners to sign their names. An innocent-looking girl holds her mother's hand as the guard registers her name.

The girl says "My name is Berina Kostadi. Make sure you spell it correctly."

A bloodied face. A beat-up man is dragged forward by a soldier who announces to the guard "This is Sinisa, the radio announcer."

The guard looks up from his paper and says "He must be killed. He's an Ustasha."

He is dragged, screaming, away. In my dream it is my turn, and when the guard asks my name, I tell him I am an art student from Zagreb. The boyish guard says he is from the town Roma and asks if I know the homosexual from Roma named Peter. The guard lets out a devilish laugh, instructs a soldier to take me away as he yells, "Go and remember that your son has been saved by Lieutenant Colonel Ivanovic!"

I am led away in the crowd of prisoners past the red-painted building. I stop to hear screaming coming from inside. I hear a soldier yelling "Gouge out his other eye!" There is a horrible old man's scream as his bloodied torturer comes out of the building, comes over to face me.

"Hey, you. Ustasha" he calls at me. I tremble, trying to make out his face as he grabs me by his bloody hand, and pulls me off the ground, where I had collapsed in fear. With how many fingers do you greet? Do you know how to turn Ustasha into a Serb?" I am an artist. I need my hands.

The guard continues. "You chop off two fingers, and he's left with three. Then he'll greet as any Serb would do!"

The monster guard throws me to the ground. Just as I hit the ground I wake up in a sweat.

There is someone knocking at the door.

The quiet room

There is a still room in the guest house across from the church called the *Stille rom*.

The figure of a heart with red handwriting, 'Stille Rom' hanging by a string on the door. I hear Mia's voice, praying in Croatian. On a small chalkboard in the hall, you can write your name to reserve the room. 'Mia' is handwritten in chalk.

I enter quietly, take a seat, she knows I am here by her passing glance. In this simple candlelit room with a large crucifix hanging, backlit, on a wall.

The smell of incense. Mia, in her red spring coat, kneeling before the crucifix.

She turns from her prayers, faces me.

Tears in her eyes. Her hand reaches, touches my face. She smiles at my new clothes and new spring coat.

"Glad the new clothes fit, Andreas."

I shaved my face, there is not a stubble left, my hair is pulled back in a ponytail, the way I had it in Oslo.

"You look like a new man," she says.

I am entranced by this black-haired woman with olive skin and blue eyes. I wipe tears from her eyes with my little embroidered cloth.

She stretches her hand to my face, I feel her warm palm slide gently down my forehead, to the cheeks. It has been so long since I felt a woman's touch on my face. She cups my face in her hands.

"You will go and have that surgery on your nose. I have spoken with Doctor Omland, arrangements have been made. We will leave by train next Friday to Oslo, I will be with you, and take care of you. I have an interview with a dance company. I am so excited!"

My mind swims around with so many thoughts. Things are moving fast, like a swift current.

I think about a sculpture in the woods, among the pine and oak trees. A sculpture, silver and glistening, of a couple suspended in the air, their naked forms coiled, entwined, floating in the air.

I want to go to Ekeberg to that great park in the woods. There is a concave woman's face, porcelain white, that just stares at you.

My fingers on Mia's face, as I close my eyes, whispering words slurring together senseless, somehow, I struggle to put words together.

The way my brain twists, the little ways the disease affects my speech now and then. So, I whisper, and my fingers, so full of feeling, glide down her hair, her silky-smooth strands, as she submits to my touch.

"I want to go to the park in Ekeberg. There is a sculpture in the woods, silver and glistening, a couple floating in the air. I need to see that."

"I have arranged for a DNA test for both of us. This way we will know for certain that you are my brother, Andreas Olav Hansen."

"How can you be so certain? The fact my father paid your mother all that money in child support, it could have been someone else."

In the candlelight of the quiet room, where our beating hearts are as one, and a bead of sweat forms on my forehead and rolls down past my face to my lips. I miss the ocean; I miss the taste of the sea.

She turns on the lights in the room. "Come with me."

She takes me by the hand, her grasp is firm. She leads me down the steps of the guest house.

No one is around.

So we go outside to the street.

It is quiet, no one is around. There is no traffic, soon the bells will ring for the church service.

I had spoken to Levi.

He drove me to town, to Lawyer Syvertsen's office. Syvertsen had been a friend to the family over the years, a man in his early sixties now, with bushy eyebrows, with a small office overlooking the pier. He had helped my grandfather with some legal matters years ago and now had some papers for me.

There was the deed to the old house, and a letter from my father which was only to be opened in Syvertsen's presence.

When I arrived bushy eyed, Syvertsen remarked I looked like a new man, with a clean-shaven face. Syvertsen went over the accounts, explained he had tried to contact me after my father's passing.

It was difficult since I didn't use a phone. He explained there was no money in any of the accounts after the funeral expenses were paid. Then there was the important matter of my father's letter.

It was sealed with a wax stamp, and Syvertsen opened it in my presence and gave it to me to read. Putting on my thick glasses, I read the three-page handwritten letter. Yes, he had an affair with Marija. Yes, he was certain he was the father. He wanted me to look up a friend of his, Svein Torkildsen.

Svein could tell me everything. My sister Vilde had known all along, had lived with my mother in Oslo, but the truth was kept from me because I was so 'overly sensitive'. Syvertsen explained to me it appeared the matter had gone through the courts but my father had kept all this secret.

Syvertsen explained he had seen similar conflicts where the daughter takes sides with the mother, and it was all very unfortunate, since my father had signed the accounts over to my mother and there was nothing provided for me except the old house. There was an inheritance tax and the farm house was protected as a landmark.

I am thinking about all this when Mia takes me by the hand and walks silently with me across the street, to the old church. We enter through the black gate. There is no one around. I hear the cawing of blackbirds in flight, they sail mischievously overhead. A crow sits atop the steeple.

She whispers: *"Bog govori: pomozi si sam, pomoći ću ti.*

"It means God will help you if you help yourself, Andreas."

I recite the words, slowly, their melody is sweet, the way the words still me.

There is something special about this white-timbered parish church. At the bend in the river where the gravestones sit like pebbles on the shore.

"A Croatian proverb, it means have faith, do something, and God will help you, really help you, Andreas. You must never lose hope, Andreas," she whispers.

I feel overwhelmed, under the shadow of that great tree, where the blackbirds cackle.

I feel Mia's hand on my shoulder. *What if this woman is not my sister?*

I open my eyes. At my father's grave, the little polished metal nightingale sitting atop the black polished headstone where Mia had placed it. I get down on my knees, close my eyes, and trace my father's gold signature, my fingers to the cold stone. I feel the lettering, seconds melt into minutes, my mind escapes.

I want to draw this woman, Mia.

I want to lay down with her in the meadow, in Salmetid, in the summer, feel the warm grass, stare up at the clouds racing overhead.

A nice picnic lunch, collecting water from the river, boiling tea in a blackened kettle, sipping from our tins, saying nothing.

My father used to tell me, that it was in silence where we found our strength.

Maybe a whisper passes between us, a poem, a story where we laugh a moment, and she turns to me and says, "I love you."

I want all these dark visions to pass, I want to wake up, with a new face, I want to live again, and teach, and walk in the Oslo parks, and trace my fingers on Vigeland's great sculpture.

George, the gravedigger

I look around at all the black dominoes sitting in row after row, by the bend in the river, how the graveyard stretches so far away.

There is a red fleck, it must be Mia, under the steeple's shadow, where my father and grandfather lay buried, by that place where all my relatives lay side by side like sardines in a King Oscar tin.

I turn around and see Levi across the street. He sees me and waves silently, as the big Norwegian flag is raised just under half mast. There will be a burial today.

So I walk past the black dominoes, around the back along the walk, and stop facing the outbuilding where George, the gravedigger, works.

Bodies for burial are prepared here by the mortician. George is a friendly short man from Holland, he dug my father's grave.

I see that the door to his little place is open a crack, there is light escaping, so I am curious as I walk over. His truck is away, he must have just stepped out, and I enter the office.

There is a strong chemical smell, so I go past the closed door of his office and open a door to the backroom. A white casket on a steel table.

George will be back soon, no doubt, and I must get back to Mia. But I am compelled to go to this simple white casket with eight white screws, little stylish screws whose ends are plastic and clover shaped, as I start unscrewing them, with my fingertips, without thinking, unscrewing by hand all eight of them, on top of the casket. The screws are just sitting in the holes, and one by one they easily come out.

I go to the door, peek out in the hallway. No one is around.

I lift open the casket a little so I can steal a view.

There is a strong chemical smell like ammonia, my eyes water. There is a sharpening of focus, a face comes into and out of view. A slim body in a suit.

I see a face, as white as snow.

A young's man's face, a man with a mohawk haircut, his waxed hair stands on end.

I close my eyes, and touch his face, my fingers lightly feeling, gliding over a face stone cold. My fingers shake, the maddening idea of death, how one day you are here, then gone. I open my eyes and see how the powder has smudged away and the skin is purple-black underneath.

* * *

The doctor says I am so overly sensitive, how even the touch of that woman's little ostrich feather on my face, after she bathes in a tub of milk and honey, before I make my sketches of her, how the faint brush of a feather stirs me to combustion.

I feel a stirring in me, my cheeks flush, my heart pounds, I panic. The thought hits me. I might be dead tomorrow.

And then I think of Oddvin, the shopkeeper who died while holding a talk about his business in the mayor's office.

He was sixty-one, a short, round man who always wore a smile. He collapsed in front of the mayor and a room full of local politicians, and here, in this room, Svein, the mortician, sponged him down, dressed him in his burial clothes.

I used to buy my pencils and artists supplies from Oddvin, one day he patched my bicycle tyre for nothing when I punctured on a tack outside his shop.

I hear a truck pulling up, a door slamming shut. I shut the casket, put the screws back, and escape through the door just as George enters wearing work clothes.

He's got his usual felt cap on, as he stands there, just facing me, as he takes a last puff on his stubby cigarette, throws it to the floor, and squishes it under his polished black shoes.

"Andreas Hansen?" he asks, curiously, in a friendly tone, with that peculiar Dutch accent. Then he laughs as he comes up close, stands on his toes, looking straight at me, a man used to looking at dead faces, a happy man who loves his work.

The way he keeps the graveyard nice like a garden, cutting the grass, and digging the graves. Making sure when the graves sink to fill in the hole and replant new grass.

He is attentive to the little things, and when he studies me, it is like he is taking measurements for a casket.

I don't mind as he circles me and opens the door to his office and explains he would like to sit and talk and eat biscuits.

He says something about the blackbirds, how they are mating in the air, now, how overworked he has become, because every week there is a new hole to dig.

Then he escapes into his office, shuts the door. He comes back outside hands me a little package.

"Holland syrup waffles. Take them." He goes back inside, shuts the door.

* * *

He is always giving me little things, especially after I sketched his girlfriend, that funny Dutch woman from Nordwiik who lived by the North Sea and sang me the new Dutch national anthem as she took off her clothes. Nervous, maybe, but I did not mind, because all I was interested in was making a nice sketch out back in the barn, by midsummer's light, when her flat chest caught the light just right, so the shadows enlarged them in a pleasing way.

George keeps that sketch on the wall in his office. I see he looks at it now, and when he turns his head to see if I am still here, I have vanished outside.

Svein Torkildsen

A bent over man with a walker came to the door this morning. There was a nurse with him, she said his name was Svein Torkildsen.

He looked around sixty, but it was hard to say.

There was a sadness about him, but I could not put my finger on it. Something stern and proud and defiant was etched in his face.

Whatever made him shuffle up to this house hung on him like the loose-fitting jacket hanging on his bones.

The way a sixty-year-old man looks like one hundred and sixty, bent over and shaking. You wonder what he thinks, what he does in life.

It took a minute before I could focus on his face and then I remembered. He had been an acquaintance of my father.

Trond Torkildsen's father.

The nurse said he didn't talk and just wanted to give me a shoebox and go. He handed me a cardboard box. He didn't look in my eyes, and the way his hand shook was enough for him.

I took the worn shoebox and when I looked back up, he and the nurse were gone.

* * *

I went back inside the house, up the stairs, to the desk where I opened the taped box with a pair of scissors.

A warm summer wind blew in through the open window and the curtains flapped like a butterfly's wings.

I shook the contents out on the desk. It was full of money. Paper money.

One-hundred-crown notes falling down like leaves.

A gust of wind blew in and scattered the notes all around the room. I watched in amazement as the notes blew around the room, caught in the midsummer's draft, whirled around and settled all over the place.

I took a moment for me to register the fact that were hundreds if not a few thousand notes scattered around the room. I got up and started the hard task of crouching down and picking up all the notes, putting them back in the shoebox.

In the jail cell there is a secret place in the floor where the floorboard is loose, so I went over, lifted the floorboard and placed the box inside.

* * *

My head swam with a thousand thoughts, but with the excitement all l could think about was sleeping, as I dozed off in the bed. The last thing I saw was old Sheriff Hansen staring at me, from that stern portrait hanging on the wall.

Somehow, I felt he kept watch over me, like the raven sitting atop the church steeple. A raven with beady eyes as black as the night, waiting for me to drop and fall to the ground.

You wake up one early Sunday morning in summer and somehow the months have flown by and the sun shines through the window.

You wake up blind, your eyes do not work, and this woman helps you around.

She washes you, and clothes you, and opens the windows and tells you to look out over the valley, how the sun shines.

The quickening of summer, the garden awakening to life, in all the variegate colours like a rainbow.

The way she sings in her sweet voice, the way I stand at the window in fresh clothes, because I had given her money to buy new clothes, and I wonder about the old man at the door, and Mia says it is a gift, and I should not think about it. She had counted the money, there was over one hundred thousand crowns, she would put it into my account for safe keeping.

You wake up after a good night's sleep, you start a fire, the house warms, and you think you have been born anew.

She shaves your face with a new razor and tells me we will soon take the train into Oslo for plastic surgery for my nose.

She holds the little handheld mirror to my face, she says my eyesight will return. She says she believes in miracles.

"I am your sister, Mia Marija Drovik, from the island of Pag, and I believe in miracles," she playfully whispers in my ear, while combing my newly washed hair.

I touch my face, how smooth it feels, and I wonder so many things.

My fingers traipse down her forehead, and nose; I feel her moist lips, I see in my mind's eye the little girl in the stone castle, the old man in the bed, how she lights a cigarette and places it in his mouth.

"How do you know you are my sister? How can you be so certain without the DNA test?"

"Because of your father's letters to my mother. I discovered them one day in a box of things my mother had prepared for me, when she was taken away."

"What happened to your mother?"

* * *

You wake up and the yellow in your face has vanished, your hand has stopped shaking.

You wake up, the days and weeks have vanished.

You wonder who brings you warm food to your doorstep day in and day out, you think of the woman who can leave without a trace.

You wonder how days pass to weeks and you long to see her again, and you think it is all a dream. You wonder how she washes you; your skin smells of lavender and olive oil and the grass is green once again.

And the angel in the forest, the angel who kisses me ever so gently on my lips, whispering in my ear "Be not afraid" appears in my dreams night after night, so I awaken in this old house no longer afraid.

She has cleaned up the house, it is full of spring flowers, the windows are open. A titmouse with black-tipped wings flew in the bedroom this morning, circled around me as I lay in bed and fluttered back out through the window.

Mia, on her way out his morning tells me I have been sleeping for days on end.

"You remember he said the doctors have ordered daily shots of high dose penicillin for two weeks, in Oslo, to cure your blindness."

I didn't remember that remark by the doctor, only that I said they had tried that before, and still I lost my sight.

"It must be all in my mind. Maybe I don't want to see any more."

* * *

You go out and she has the fire going already in the bathhouse.

You take a sauna, and the sweat pours from you, and you go outside naked under the starlit sky and the woman from the island of Pag pours ice-cold water over your body.

The woman who says she is my sister, whose name passes silent on my lips, she nudges me away, gently, when I press too close to her, she whispers she will one day move to Oslo, where she will dance in the theatre.

The woman who sleeps in my bed night, after night, keeping me warm. "I will lay next to you, my brother, and keep you warm."

I wake up in my sleep shouting. "Nooooo!"

"My brother," she says, tapping her finger on my lips, "be still, and know I am here, with you."

She whispers she will lie by my side, take care of me, she is my sister.

She tells me about her grandfather, the beekeeper. She tells me how his hives were scattered over the brown Dalmatian hills, the apiaries bursting with sweet nectar, acacia honey from the flower of that special tree. *Robinia pseudoacacia.*

* * *

"Grandfather sat cross-legged under the shade of the black locust tree, and spoke with his friends, the bees. As the hot sun baked down on the brown hills, he closed his eyes, they whispered to him."

"What did they whisper?"

"The buzzing bees whispered they were happy. They whispered they caught the flowers' scent, in the salty air, as they swept down like a fluttering black curtain, whipping and fluttering around, caught by the sweet-scented wind, alighting on the cream-white flowers that bloom for just some days. They filled their little furry bodies with the nectar, back to the apiaries they flew, bursting with happiness, because that is all they knew, flying about, tending the flowers, whose petals open, and then, shortly, close, as the opening and closing of a book."

The way I close my eyes, her fingers lightly tapping my face, her forefinger feeling lightly the place where my nose forms a saddle. The way she whispers, settles my spirit.

"I love the bees, Andreas. I love the flowers, the daffodils of spring time, when they bloom in Zagreb. *Robinia pseudoacacia,* say those words, Andreas."

"Ro-bin-ia pseudo-aca-cia," I repeat, obediently.

* * *

"I want to visit Fannrem."

I want to go to see the golden angel and the baptismal fount and my grandfather's name inscribed in gold. She tells me we will go one day, when I am all well.

She whispers she will take me on motorcycle adventure. She will finally then get to see Norway, beautiful Norway.

"It's great, on my motorbike. It will just be you and me, brother and sister.

"We'll make up for some lost time."

I daydream about that night by the fireplace when she posed for me and I made a quick pencil sketch and tell her I want to go to the place where the waves crash on the shore.

I tell her I want to walk barefoot in the mountains, in Salmetid, at that special place where the river settles and the echo of a woman's voice is heard as a psalm in the forest. She whispers I will paint this man Jesus in the church, I will paint a masterpiece.

When I paint, I close my eyes

I lift the filbert to his face, and I see him in my mind's eye, I feel his breath, there is the taste of dark tea and honey.

The wind is full of salt, blowing down the slopes, a vale spreading down the cedar hills of Nazareth.

His eyes are tinged azure blue, the tint of the sky on a clear midsummer's eve, when the windows of the old house are open, and sky opens like the pages of a book. When this morning a little smooth stone glittered on my desk, that stone she passed into my hands, she said it was a gift. She folded my fingers around the stone, its warmth like her beating heart, as I held her to me. As she accepted my embrace, and the light glimmered all about, as we stood in the hall of my grandfather's old house, where the open door let in the rose-scented air. I saw two little red buds, entwined, creeping up the trellis. A sight moving me to tears, as I dared to touch their petals, lightly, as my fingers fled back to her face. Where I felt a softness like the flower's silken petal, a scent enlivening me, as this woman touches a tear on my cheek, and whispers she and I are entwined, forever.

* * *

She bought the stone in an Oslo shop, it was lapis lazuli, and it reminded her of the sea on the shores of Pag, where she longed to return.

She misses her mother.

She misses the way the light plays at night on the flagstones in the courtyard where the doorways are arched, where her mother read to her, in that great library of books and the open window, where she looked out to the sea.

She misses the narrow streets and stone walls, the cafes and art galleries, the sand on the shore.

Walls of yellow damask, brightly lit, where she sits cross-legged, reading a book.

The Morocco binding, the way the textured goatskin presses pleasingly on her bare shin.

I smell black tea poured into a cup hand-carved from pine, passed to me in the shadow of the fire, by the river, in Salmetid, where she whispers she will sit in the church, in the last pew, and hide herself, and wait, until I am finished.

As she does now, this late night, when the sun has just set, and Levi has left us alone in this wood-timbered church.

Where my father, and grandfather, lay.

Where the black-eyed crow, the bird sitting atop the steeple, has flown off, when he saw me enter the church.

I feel the sun, the days are no longer dark, even my nose seems normal, the way my face has softened.

I know this because Mia told me I had changed, when I held her close, and she asked me not to look so longingly in her eyes, because she would soon be leaving.

I told her not to go.

The women kneeling by the crosses

She calls me naive; she tells me I am a recluse, living in a dreamworld, in that old farmhouse.

I feel sorry for myself. It was not my mother's fault that my mother got syphilis.

It was likely a man, a drunk man, full of lust, who raped my mother.

When she said the word 'rape', a change came over her, I had to help her sit down on a stone by the fire.

She spoke about her mother, how she had found letters from my father written from Norway, envelopes would come every month, with a cheque attached.

For as long as Mia remembered, they would come, in the mail.

Her mother hid them in a box in the library on a shelf, but Mia found them on her sixteenth birthday, that terrible day Mia confronted her mother.

Mia asked who her father really was, her mother was shocked, because there is a picture on the wall in the library of her father.

The man who resembles a young Omar Shariff, the man her mother called *her father* had dark eyes bearing a striking resemblance to Marko, her brother.

"Alessio was your father," her mother Marija told her.

Her mother said he died, from tuberculosis, before Mia was born, his grave was at that stone church in Pag, in the shadow of the great 15th-century Church Of The Assumption. Mia knew the story, she had never doubted the story, but why were her eyes blue?

Mia told me her mother's eyes were the colour of honey.

Allesio's were the colour of ash, darkened clay, like the brown of the river Drava, where it meets the Danube.

Mia tells me she will wait until the painting is finished, wait in this church for the answers she has been seeking.

She waits for me now, as I paint this humble man in flowing hair, hair the colour of chestnuts, falling to the bare shoulders.

His head arched to the sky, his eyes fixed at the sunlight breaking through the clouds.

I see women kneeling by the crosses, the crosses sticking up in the snow, where the woman weep, the women who have lost their sons. I see the little red-and-white wood beads of the rosaries, hanging and dangling, the faceless women hidden in shadow. I think of that place across the sea, where the killing fields lay bedecked in white, where the memory of what happened hides itself in the winter.

Let me tell you, how a grown man weeps

Let me tell you, how a grown man weeps.
    He weeps because a woman accepts him for what he is.
    He weeps because she wraps him in her embrace on a church altar. And all she asks for in return is for you to quiet your heart. Because you are in a holy place.
    There is a stillness in the air, anticipation of something like lightning, the way it flashes in the sky and you see it, and then the thunder comes rolling in the fjørd.
    An echo building and building, as your clothes drop to the floor and you stand there, in her embrace.
    Levi has locked the church door. I told him not to disturb us.
    A man weeps because she says there is divinity in each of us, whether or not we choose to believe.
    A man weeps because this woman comforts him, this woman with a crystal teardrop about her neck.
    She accepts me.
    I weep because I say I have no need for heaven or hell and Mia tells me she will pray for me and God's hell is what man creates for himself on earth.
    Evil and selfish men who have forgotten to forgive.

* * *

There is divinity in us now, in this quiet church, where Levi has locked us in, so I can paint.
    If someone looked through the window, they would see a remarkable sight.
    A naked man, and a naked woman, embracing one another on a church altar.

Where someone would think obscene things, maybe call the police, the *jungle wire* would send alarm bells ringing in the valley.

I will paint my dream, this woman with angel wings, who came to me in the forest.

I will paint by candlelight because the smell of wax and the heat of the flame on my fingertip sets my fingers in motion.

I will paint this beautiful man, Jesus, wrapped in Mia's naked embrace, angel wings as smooth as spiders' silk, in the forest by those two birch trees where the angel first came for me.

A man weeps because he has never forgiven his mother, that mother who ran off when he was a boy, who locked him in a jail cell and threw him a pencil and a sketchpad.

My fingers stretch out, trembling, stretching nearer to her face. I see shadows, I do not need to see any more.

Because my fingers have felt her body, how the black hair falls down a swan's neck, her eyes wide, searching, precious as newly cut lapis lapida.

Her shoulders bare, a fresh cut rose in a low-cut bodice between her breasts.

Her wedding gown of finest silk and gossamer, glistening like dew dancing on a spider's web.

Now, breath to breath, the steam of my trembling voice condensing on her rose cheeks.

I smell lavender, and the scent of the forest after a summer rain, when the sun alights atop the trees, and glides down, to touch the flesh.

She cups her hands on my face, kisses me ever so gently on my lips, despite my disease and my ugly face.

This woman Mia whispers in my ear. "Be not afraid."

Chiaroscuro

The play of shadows, the play of black against white.

Mia sits in the back pew, watching me paint on the big, stretched canvas.

I draw a breath of smoke from a stubby cigarette and blow it on the canvas. On the wet paint, on Jesus's face, that beautiful face where my fingers build up layer after layer of flesh tones.

The smoke talking to me, fire burns in my heart.

The way I sweat and how the feelings have come back in my fingers.

The way I paint this beautiful man Jesus. The way my fingers slide over his face, that face shining white against the black of the night.

This man who was spat upon, who turned the other cheek, who took the sins of others.

A blackbird sits atop the church steeple even now, protests my presence. There was a mocking tone to his cawing, when he saw me entering the church, and I saw his shadow atop the steeple.

He waits for me to drop and fall. She watches as I paint.

In the church, from the bench where she has been watching the last three days.

La vita è più dolce con te

Levi brought food this afternoon, a big bowl of steaming *lapskaus*.

I must not forget to eat.

"Meat and potato stew, that will fatten you up," he says affectionately.

He tells me he is amazed at this painting, how it is taking shape.

There is the smell of linseed in the church and the paint is smooth as butter between the fingers.

Windsor yellow, Alison crimson and Prussian blue, these are all the colours I need.

* * *

I hear a song, a voice in the church, like an angel singing. It is Mia's voice. She sings a Croatian melody.

The words float in the air, distant, like a river whose waters rush ahead, the only sound one hears in the forest, as the fog lifts, and you approach.

Leo found a book of poems by the Croatian poet Ivo Robic, there was one about love, how you only love once, how everything else is illusion. *My eyes closed, I walk in the forest, hooded, she follows, she sings a melody, I feel her fingers*

lightly grasping mine, I know the way, but she will guide me to the falls.

"*La vita è più dolce con te,*" her voice whispering.

"*La vita è più dolce con te,*" I whisper back, knowing these words. Sweet Italian words meaning, 'Life is sweeter with you'.

The way the words whisper, the way the wind blows, the way I think *she is my hallucination*. Barefoot, in the forest, a warm summer's day. Finding our special place by the falls, where the waters rush down the rocks, the cool spray dancing on our bare flesh, as we lie down in the moss, and we close our eyes, and nothing escapes our lips.

"I am happy for the silence, Andreas."

She tells me she came to Norway to forget. She tells me people who hate one another must first learn to forget, so they can love again. What they did to her mother, the cruelty, this was something she could never forget. But her mother told her that one day a neighbour must forget what he did to his fellow neighbour, one day neighbours must forget, so their children can play again.

"How can you forget, Mia, what we witnessed as children?"

My eyes closed, I don't want to open them. Facing her, our voices a finger's breadth apart, as we lie hip to hip, the way she embraces, without enticing me, her warmth is enough to settle me, so her words enter, as a psalm, and I want to die now, her words are wings, they take me away to a place where there is no hate. Where a man walks, hand in hand with another, and the sun smiles down, and there is no judgement but for the voice that lingers. The Nazarene's voice, lingering, as a faint echo, *love one another, as I have loved you.*

"Andreas, there is no remembering, without forgetting."

There is silence, the way the water rushes, the sound of the leaves rustling. The sun-warmed face, whose skin I touch, lightly tapping, how I know she lies by me, I feel the warmth of her flesh. There are words spoken, sweet words I cannot write down, but there are other words, I write them down in my little notebook. The notebook she will find one day, with these words, as they were meant to be found.

Lying in the moss, her words recite the known facts. There is a remembering, there will be a forgetting. She tells me I must forget that I have forgotten, I will wake up one morning, and be reborn to hope. As she woke up one morning, in her mother's stone villa, on the island of Pag, where she packed her motorbike, locked the front door, knelt on the flat stones, and whispered a prayer.

She tells me that on July 10, 1995, Serbian forces occupied the Bosnian city of Srebrenica. The city was surrounded by Serbs since 1992 and was the only free city along the Drina watercourse on the eastern border of Bosnia with Serbia. As a result, the city's population had increased sharply as people fled to Srebrenica when their cities were occupied by the Serbian war machine. When Mladic's war hordes take the city, there were over 45,000 civilians in it. The city was declared a UN-free zone in 1994. The only thing that stands between the Serbian soldiers and the Bosnian civilians are 450 UN soldiers from Holland who are stationed there to keep peace in that area. They have been in the city since the Bosnian army left it. That was the agreement between Bosnia and the UN. No soldiers in the city, and the UN must protect it. Unfortunately, the UN soldiers did nothing when Mladic's soldiers early in the morning of July 7, 1995, took their lookout points and started the journey towards the city centre. The Bosnians see this and start fleeing the city. Many believe that the UN will help them, and over 20,000 people gather outside the UN base in the hope of seeking refuge from the Serbs. UN soldiers lock the entrance gates and deny the Bosnian civilians entry. The UN soldiers see to it that the people in this group are divided, where the men are killed and women and children under the age of ten are transported to Tuzla. About half of those who came to the UN base were killed. The other group of Bosnians in the city immediately flee through the mountains towards the free areas around Tuzla. In just one week, over 8,000 Bosnians were killed in Srebrenica by the Serbian soldiers. Several thousand women are raped before being sent on to the free Bosnian territories. The Hague Tribunal ruled that the 1995 Srebrenica massacre was a genocide. It is the most documented genocide in human history. All of the Serbian leaders from the 1990s have been convicted of the genocide in Srebrenica. Today, twenty-five years after these actions, Srebrenica is a small town in eastern Bosnia. The population is almost halved compared to what it was before the war. At the entrance to the city is the 'Potocari Memorial Grove', where all the victims found after the genocide are buried. To date, about 6,500 people who were killed during the genocide in July 1995 have been buried. The Bosnian authorities are still searching for the missing 1,900. The victims are found in several mass graves that are being dug up. After the war, Serbian nationalists dug up the mass graves and transported the remains to secondary and tertiary graves. This has led to the identification work being very late. A victim is often found in several mass graves. The reason for this is that the bodies disintegrated when they were exhumed from the primary mass grave one year after they were killed. The genocide in Srebrenica is the result of a long-standing hatred that was bred where society was divided into groups, us and them. Unfortunately, the hatred that springs from Serbian nationalism lives on in Serbia today. It lives on, Andreas, because nationalism has taken root again.

Split

She was born in 1983 in the town called Split, on the Adriatic Sea. She loved the Dalmatian coast. Sitting on the shore, as a girl, because there were no fence posts or walls at sea.

The ocean did not ask you if you were a Serb, or a Croat, or question your grandfather at a police station because he wrote a book about the Nazi work camp at Jasenovac.

The ocean asked you none of these things because it was all listening, and in its depths, it hid all your thoughts. The town Split was a magical place where her imagination wandered, in and out of the walls and cellars and dark sewers of ruined palaces built by fabled Roman rulers.

There were ruins of Roman cupolas and columns and red stucco rooftops of honeycombed inns and temples with crowded thoroughfares. Creeper hung niches and pillars and narrow doors leading to courtyards and cloistered gardens. Gothic buildings with balconies and shadowed alleyways where she hid, playing hide-and-seek with her best friend Mira.

The 'monastery' was where Mia spent her childhood. It was an eighteenth-century three-storey stone palace overlooking the ocean, built in the Byzantine style, rich in arch and balcony. It had been a working monastery with three elderly monks until it was bombed during World War II by the Germans and left vacant. The roof had collapsed and the walls facing the sea had crumbled. No one knew what happened to the monks. Mia's grandfather bought it after the war for one hundred American dollars and restored it with local artisans.

The flower beds were laid out in intricate shapes and surrounded by low box hedges, with surrounding lilac bushes of leafy purple flowers. The courtyard was her favourite place. It was always sunlit and golden. It was a quiet place to go and reflect. There were statues and fragments of statues, some Roman, and carved stone slabs bearing undecipherable inscriptions.

All about was a profusion of red and blue flowers bursting from lead cisterns, leafy plants and bronze-backed ferns, many in little pots hung on lines of string tied between sculptures. On the side of the courtyard facing the ocean there was the first floor of the monastery. Through a great open door was the library, lit by the soft light of a chandelier.

There, in the corner, her mother Marija would sit, and read her stories as sunlight filtered down from the high tresses and played upon their faces.

Her mother carried an informal eloquence. At night she taught Mia how to read and write in French and Italian, on the horsehair sofa with chenille armrests. Plush and horsehair, chenille and rep were her mother's favourite materials.

And they were found in abundance in every room. For formality's sake they spoke Italian to her European guests, and Serbo-Croat to the locals. Yet her mother thought it indignant to be called an Italian since she was a Slav, and a Catholic, by blood.

Until the Croatian War started in 1991, she was a happy girl, living with her mother and her grandfather. He was her mother's father, a diabetic, and his legs had been amputated. She loved him; he was like a father to her.

She took care of him in the house by the sea as her mother worked as a doctor in the hospital. Her mother's name was Marija.

Mia never knew who her father was until she discovered the letters from my father and the court papers signed with his name.

In the jail cell

I open my eyes.

I see shadow, bars like pencils, I am in the jail cell.

Lying on my back, on a mattress. I squeeze my eyes again, roll my pupils around, open my eyes, my eyes coming in and out of focus.

"Mia!"

I get up off the mattress on the floor of the jail cell. Standing naked, in this jail cell, in my grandfather's bedroom, grasping cold iron bars. I scream and shake the bars.

I make out a candle burning on the floor. I feel the biting of a million ants on my skin, the gouging out of my eyes.

A thousand and one tortures from a thousand evildoers. I see boys hanging upside down from tree limbs.

I see my grandfather in that jail cell, in Grini, lying on the floor, looking up at the threads hanging in the ceiling.

I feel the cold iron bars of the cell, my hands desperately feeling for the lock. The door is locked, and when I try turning the key my shaking fingers fumble, and the key drops to the floor.

Crouching down on the floor, my arm stretching out under the bars across the floor, feeling for the key. I hear a woman's voice. A woman's soft voice, calm, coming from the shadows.

"My mother came to bring food for my brother, Marko. That's when I saw them order her to strip off her upper clothing."

It is Mia's voice.

Her face pressed against the jail cell.

"That's when I heard firing and saw her lying on her back. Then the evil soldier told my brother to take off his pants and underwear."

I stand and shake and know this is not a dream.

Mia's voice trembling. "Now I will make you rape your mother."

Mia continues as I collapse on the mattress, my hands grasping the bars. Her two hands grasping mine through the bars. Her voice trembling, whispered words hanging on threads, slowly spoken, words like tears, I feel her tears on my fingers.

"Andreas Olav Hansen, You saw this. You were there with me. They forced us to watch. You must accept this hallucination. Stop feeling pity for yourself. You must forgive your mother for what she did, how you were born with this disease. You and I, we were witness to evil. We live. You must wake up. Hatred rose up, neighbours forgot how to love, neighbours forgot how to forgive. Neighbours twisted by angry, evil words from the politicians. You must forgive yourself, accept yourself, for who you are."

It comes back to me

It comes back to me, in a blur, the scenes cut from one to the other, like I have hidden them in a locked vault in my mind.

Mia is the key that has opened this dark vault. I start screaming a wild, uncontrolled scream, because this woman tells me to forgive.

Then it comes back to me, that violent scene in the forest, on that winter night, I see the young woman, hanging head down, her ankles bound, blood dripping into the snow.

Her blue eyes wide and staring. I start shaking, an uncontrolled, violent shaking, pounding my fists on the bars.

My eyesight returning, a blur at first, so Ida's death stare transforms into Mia's face, her startled, caring face, looking at me from behind the bars.

She opens the door, catches my collapsing body in her lap.

I see Ida, hanging in the forest.

Hanging naked, bound at the ankles, her neck slit, I see a shadow in the forest, standing over Ida, a shadow that turns to me.

I see myself lying in the snow, in my blue fisherman's coat, barefoot, startled senseless by the scene.

There is a shadow hanging over Ida; the shadow turns, I sense it sees me lying in the snow. A human-sized raven, winged black, its beady eyes catch my presence.

Then it flies off, escaping into the sky.

Mia inserts the big old key into the latch, the bolt slides open. Mia takes me in her arms, pressing me close.

"You did not kill Ida," she whispers. "Andreas Olav Hansen! Be still!"

I am an artist, she says. I create, I do not destroy, she tells me. A shadow stalks me. Evil's shadow, as real as the hard pencil I grasp between my thumb and two forefingers. It is a shadow that followed me back to Norway, as a boy, from those terrible places where evil rose up among neighbours. It is a shadow stalking me now, a shadow in the forest, who hides here, in this old house, a shadow who knows you, by name, who takes advantage of you, as you hide yourself in the dark, as you sketch.

"What are you telling me, Mia?"

"I am telling you something you already know… there is a wolf in the forest."

* * *

"We will take the train to Oslo, to the hospital. I have spoken with the doctors and surgeons. You remember you signed the papers, you are lucky they rescheduled the surgery."

I remember I had gone to the doctor's office. I would receive penicillin injections for two weeks while in the hospital. I would be cured.

Mia helps me to grandfather's bed, lays me down gently, takes a warm washcloth from a metal bowl of water, wipes my face.

"You will paint a magnificent painting in the church of this man you secretly love. You will paint this man Jesus whose face is lovely, his heart is not made of stone, you will see again. You will see colours, no longer will you walk in the shadows. Then, Andreas Olav Hansen, you will have your miracle."

She plants a kiss on my forehead. There is a spark in my eye, I make out the crystal pendant on the gold chain hanging around her neck. I touch the pendant, hold it to the morning light stabbing through the window.

"Inside this crystal is my mother's tears, the ones I collected in a vial on the day the soldiers pulled her out of my arms. She yelled for me, as they dragged her out of her office, as I watched helplessly from the window, she didn't resist."

How did I get here?

A pleasant woman's voice, from a train speaker.

"Drammen. Please exit the train on the right-hand side. Please watch your step exiting the train."

I make out Mia sitting opposite me, my vision sharpening on her face staring at me.

I am on the Vy train, we are alone in this empty back section of the train, near the café. There is the smell of hotdogs and coffee, fresh pastry. "You slept for four hours. Just a few more stops, then Oslo. In one week, we will be walking in the park, in Ekeberg. The sun will shine, you will see your floating sculpture."

The train starts moving, I see blurred green shadows on the window, Mia has moved to the empty seat next to me.

She pulls up a tray from my seat and pours a cup of coffee from a thermos. "You can tell always who the Europeans are. They drink the espresso or the cappuccino. I prefer Turkish coffee, isn't that strange?" she says playfully.

I make the patterns of her light floral dress, she pulls out a mirror, puts it in my hand, moves it in front of my face.

I sip the coffee, it is strong, there is a feeling I am awakening to something new. Like my life is entering a new chapter.

"Take a good look at that face, Andreas Olav Hansen. Because in one week you will have a new nose."

I look out the window, the blurred passing of open fields and red barns and white houses.

The passing of black lakes, like little puddles, the shadows of distant mountains, rolling, like waves on the shore.

High-flying ravens, cawing in the summer's updrafts, flitting about, like so many black stones caught up in a whirlwind.

My mind plays with the landscape, the way my forefinger on my right hand taps the table, nervously, to the beating of my heart.

In a short time, a few weeks, I will walk in through the front door of my grandfather's old house with a new face.

I will find out if this woman who showed up one night on my doorstep is my sister.

I will discover if I killed that gentle young woman who hangs in my dreams, her lithe gazelle-like neck slit just above the clavicle, where once I played my tapping fingers. Because I had to feel her, and close my hands, and the sounds my pencil made on the canvas deafened her tiny protests.

Mia sips coffee.

"On April 6, 1941, Hitler attacked Belgrade with an air bombardment lasting three days. Over twenty thousand men, women, and children were killed. My grandmother was killed, my grandfather was never the same again. In a matter of a few days the army was defeated. A fascist state was established in Croatia. Serbia was occupied by the Germans; a puppet state under Italian control was set up in Montenegro, while Slovenia and Macedonia were handed over to their neighbours. And then in a few years, more people would be killed by their own neighbours, than by their enemies."

She looks away, as the train enters a tunnel. *"Andreas, I believe your father was murdered."*

II

HOPE

Tears form in my eyes, she takes out that special little embroidered cloth, touches it gently to my face, her eyes fixed on my eyes, and she whispers, "La vita è più dolce con te."

A Sunlit Room

I sit in a sunlit room, sipping strong black coffee, at a table in a lounge area full of flowers and hanging vines. In a hospital guestroom, by a big window, at a table looking down a few floors at a wall inlaid with rose tinted stained glass, where sunlight filters through.

I feel the bandage covering my nose. When I remove the bandages in a few days I do not think I will recognise myself.

I will have a new face.

The nurse said I had slept a full day after the operation. A new nose was fashioned in a technique known as rhinoplasty. She said I had received high-dose penicillin every day during my two weeks in the surgical ward.

When I woke up, the first thing I saw this morning, was a single red rose in a vase by my bed. I cried, because when I woke up, I was not blind.

I no longer see shadows, I see the sharp outline of things, it is a miracle.

The young resident surgeon Egeland with the beautiful smiling face takes a seat opposite me, in his green scrubs, a surgeon's mask pulled down on his neck. He is busy scribbling notes in a medical chart, looks up at me.

His smiling eyes look pleased with the result.

"As an artist, Andreas, you can appreciate the effort that went in reconstructing your nose. I must admit it looked beautiful. Buried stitches, not much swelling, it's a fucking work of art." He's back scribbling some notes, taking down my responses.

"Any pain in your face?"

"No… Doctor, I… can… see."

"Did you sleep well last night?"

"I have never slept better in my life."

"You can take off the bandage in a few days. I don't expect much swelling. You know, Andreas," looking at me now, his tone more serious, reading my medical chart, "you can thank Mia for saving your life. I mean, you wouldn't likely be here if she hadn't pulled you out that lake, got your heart beating again."

Egeland gets up, pats me on the back, walks out of the empty lounge.

"Wait!" I shout at Egeland, as he disappears in the hallway. It can't be true.

Lena had told me it was all a dream.

I remember Egeland had told me he had written all the facts in his report. Mia had pounded my heart with her fist, she had blown air into my lungs, she got my heart beating again so colour came back to my face.

On the shore of that mountain lake where she ran after me, shouting my name, where she ran into the water and swam toward me as I sank below the surface. She dove after me, pulled me up, swam my unconscious body to the shoreline.

She brought me back to life.

It made no sense, what the doctor had told me. All I remember was waking up in the hospital and there was Lena looking after me. I remembered Lena telling me it was all a dream.

* * *

"Like I said on the train you can tell always tell who the Europeans are. They will always drink the espresso or the cappuccino."

Mia's playful voice, in a red mid-length dancer's skirt and open olive-green Helly Hansen jacket, looking around at people coming in and sitting down at tables with their little plates of smorgasbord and porcelain cups of coffee.

"I am so excited. I interviewed at the dance company, they liked my Beyonce-inspired *Ave Maria*."

I stretch my hand to her face, my fingers lightly tapping, the way I see more than outlines, the shock of seeing colour.

Her face searches mine, she looks worried, and I can't read her emotions, my mind is swimming with a thousand emotions.

"Lena had told me a lie. Doctor Egeland had written in his medical report that you got my heart beating again. Up at the lake. I thought it was all a dream. Is it true?" Mia looks pained.

"All I remember is waking up in the hospital. Lena said it was all a dream."

* * *

There is a moment when a woman's eyes lock with yours, when time stands still and the tremor you feel swelling inside is silent, as you whisper, and the whisper echoes loud, so the woman knows your feelings.

My words fall senseless from my lips.

"I love you, Mia Miraja. I always loved you."

As I reach my hand to her gentle face, her eyes blue as the cloudless summer sky, eyes capturing me. There is something she hides from me, the way her eyes reveal pain, the way my words have found their way into her breaking heart. Her eyes tear, it is too much for me. She closes her eyes, unformed words tremble on her lips.

My fingers tapping, so lightly tapping her forehead, tracing the outline of her face, where the sunlight sparks points of light in her eyes, blue-green as the sea, where I see white gulls flocking wildly, pitching their wings and diving and sailing and cawing the midsummer's day.

Tears form in my eyes, she opens her eyes, takes out that special little embroidered cloth, touches it gently to my face, her eyes fixed on my eyes, and she whispers, "*La vita è più dolce con te.* I will always love you, Andreas."

How we can stare into each other's eyes, for those timeless, uninterrupted moments, as when we were children, and she sat still for me, as I sketched, and the minutes bled to hours.

"It was you who pulled me from the lake. You swam out, pulled me up, to the shore. You breathed life into me."

Mia doesn't look at me, her eyes staring out the window. "Yes, I did, my brother. I meant to tell you, there are things I have not told you."

* * *

She takes some papers out of her handbag and slides them to me.

"Sign this permission and the nurse will take blood samples from you, soon we will know. I gave my sample yesterday."

She takes out a pair of new glasses from her handbag and slides them to me. "It's a DNA test," she says, "and these are your new glasses if you should ever need them. Andreas. This is not about you. This is about your father."

"What happened in the forest?"

"Come with me, for a walk. There is a pretty hospital not far away, we can take a walk. I need to show you something."

Gaustad Hospital

Sitting next to Mia on a sun-drenched afternoon, on a bench outside the entrance to the Gaustad Hospital.

The spray of water from the fountain, in this hideaway, old brick buildings, outside the arched entrance and clock tower.

"I looked up this Gaustad hospital in Wikipedia. This was Norway's first psychiatric hospital." Mia looks at her iPhone, reads.

"It seems that during the occupation of Norway from nineteen forty to nineteen forty-five, the hospital's workers, knowing German soldiers would send their patients to concentration camps, devised a plan to save them. For months, they collected urine in buckets. When the day came that the soldiers knocked on the door, they threw the urine on every radiator and heater, creating a tremendous stink. The soldiers left and didn't return, and the patients' lives were saved."

"Why do you bring me to this crazy hospital, Mia? Do you think I am crazy?" Looking now into her eyes.

"Come with me to the wall."

She gently presses my fingers to the old bricks, under the arch of the hospital's entrance. From the corner of my eye, I see a nurse pushing a patient in a wheelchair under the arch, a patient with a blank, staring face.

I can see fine details in the worn brick, the spread of colours varying in hue, from rose to red blood, I feel the visible cracks, the coarse, ragged, brick edges exciting my fingertips where I press my bandaged face, cheek to stone, as another nurse in a tight white uniform catches my gaze, passing deliberately quick under the stone arch.

The stone is sun hot, it bakes my cheek, I sweat, my eyeballs roll back. *I sense Mia watching me. I blink my eyes crazily at her, see her horrified expression, as she just stares at me, she thinks there is a chance I am a killer, a stalker of woman and little girls, a psychopath murderer who sketches naked women and chases them in the forest, where I hang them upside down from tree limbs and cut their throats.*

I close my eyes, my hands stretching up, on the brick wall, I am in the dark, I feel that warm, slit neck, feel with my tapping fingertips where the knife blade cut quick. The lithe neck as smooth as a gazelle's, muscles tensed like a bow's quiver, the body dangling down from the rafters. The dripping blood, hot on my face, drops dripping into my open mouth because I am screaming like a madman, my voice echoing sharp like a knife blade, stabbing the darkness, in the barn in my grandfather's old house, in the valley haunting my dreams.

A still voice

"NO!"

I awake to bright light; I see a small flashlight stabbing my eyeballs with pencils of light.

I make out the room. I am groggy, my head aches.

A clean, brightly lit office, a window, a man in a white lab jacket embroidered over the pocket, 'Dr S. Paulsen. Gaustad Psychiatric Hospital'.

"You had a panic attack outside. We had to sedate you, you started to get violent."

I sit up from the examining table. "Where is Mia?"

"She is waiting in the hallway. She was very concerned."

I sense Mia sitting outside the office, I sense a tear in her eye, the way it forms, the way it drops to the floor, as she looks through the smoky glass, catching my shadow. She wants to tell me something, a secret, she is stricken.

The way a fine ostrich feather, white, as light as air, floats down out of the hard blue sky, and touches your face, the way the fine tremor of her forefinger falls from my forehead, over my spiny nose's saddle, down to my lips, where her fingers trace the movements of my unspoken words.

My lips parting, voiceless words she senses, she tells me to still myself, so I can feel the beating of her heart.

Oh, for the touch of a vanished hand, oh, for the sound of a voice that is still.

* * *

"I have read your files and scheduled some tests. You will spend the night. It appears from your records you never have never had a thorough psychiatric examination. We can administer a medication to help you relax."

"Am I crazy, Doctor Paulsen?"

"Based upon our examination what matters is not the presence or absence of false or bizarre beliefs themselves, such as these spells you may have. Many sane persons have bizarre beliefs or hallucinations. You may have a condition known as dissociative amnesia."

The doctor hands me a brown folder.

"Mia, this woman who says she is your sister, asked me to give this to you to read. She said it was important."

On the worn folder's cover my father's distinct flowering handwriting. *'Marija. A True Novel. A Work In Progress. By Harold Hansen. Oslo 1992'.* The doctor hands me a few sheets of paper from the folder.

"There was attached a letter in an envelope to you, Andreas." He reads the writing on the envelope to me.

"To my son, Andreas Olav Hansen."

The doctor leaves me alone.

Dear Andreas… know this, I love you, my son

I read my father's pencil handwriting.

Know this. I love you, my son. I never told you I loved you, but you must know the fact now. I could never say those words. How important it is to say those words!

And now that I am dead, I want you to discover in these pages the truth about what happened to us.

The awful story is here for all to read. I wrote this novel as a work of fiction, in the third person, but every page and detail, is true, based on my eyewitness account.

They say truth is stranger than fiction. I pitched the book to the publisher as fiction thinking it would be easier for me, but as you know I never became a published writer, the book was rejected. Likely, the story was pitched too soon after the actual events, I do not know.

Whatever, you can appreciate as an artist our paths have crossed, our ambitions are not so different.

You draw. I write.

I expect the public to react to my writing, I do not judge.

That was the problem with your mother. She was so quick to judge. She had no idea what you saw, and heard as we escaped the madness.

Hiding in the church, what you witnessed, how Marija and I found you, how this gentle and good woman got you back across the border.

This story will mark you for life. Much more than the mark on your face, that terrible saddle nose, from that terrible disease syphilis.

How I wept at night, feeling guilty about so many things!

As you can read yourself, the novel is about Doctor Marija Drovik; I can no longer hide these facts.

Go back one day to Pag, to that beautiful island, and that stone palace.

Mia will be there, she will see to things. I was wrong hiding these facts from you. When you were seven years of age you started with those awful, violent spells, those nightmares. You had a seizure when we arrived back in Norway.

One day you asked me what happened. The seizure erased memories of the trip, I thought you were the lucky one. I made you think your nightmares were caused by the syphilis.

I wouldn't let you relive what I think about every day. We have it good in Norway. Your grandfather, my dear father Olav, he sat me down one night by the fireplace and finally talked about the Nazis. He never said a word before to me about Grini, about how he and his fellow prisoners faced their captors. In the shadow of the fire, my dear father started telling me stories.

The first story made him laugh, until the tears started running from his face. That round, fleshy face with the big ears, how it finally betrayed his heart. All these years never saying a word. He said that there were large piles of potatoes in front of the entrance to a bunker.

It turned out to be a large underground German ammunition store. It was the task of the prisoners to carry down the heavy ammunition boxes down various steps.

There were two prisoners for each green-painted wooden box. He told me he even remembered that the handles were made of thick rope. He had to stack the heavy boxes at the bottom of this large 'potato cellar'.

He said he had no idea what was in those boxes. He didn't see a single potato. When he looked around, he discovered that this large 'potato cellar' was not for potatoes but for German ammunition. They had found a safe place for their sabotage.

It was not far from the Ullevoll Hospital. There had to be tons of ammunition and explosives in this potato cellar. Should it be blown up in the air, it would probably have been a major disaster for Oslo.

Suddenly, two of the prisoners dropped a crate down the steps so it split open, the grenades bumped down the stairs, stopping like apples between your grandfather's feet. Silent prayers passed between their lips.

Like the silent prayer your grandfather had on his lips, the day in Grini, May 9, 1945, when he was called into the Gestapo's office.

The young commandant in his newly pressed uniform standing before the newly freed prisoner, Olav. He stood at attention, saluted Grandfather, then removed his field glasses, handed them to Olav.

He sat back down at his desk and pulled out a pistol from his desk drawer. He shot himself in the temple, right there. Grandfather said he took the German Luger, it is hidden now in the locked metal box under Grandfather's bed. Make sure you have it registered.

Give it to the museum. It should never be used.

When Grandfather finished with his story, he asked me about Vukovar.

You know I, like him, kept this secret to myself. I think we sat until three in the morning, I remember the tick-tock of the clock.

I want you to visit the old church in Orkdal. There is a baptismal font with four golden angels. It was a gift from your grandfather and the Grini prisoners.

Grandfather wept when he described this beautiful hand-carved sculpture.

You see, you have seen things which a boy should never have seen. Touch the golden angels, feel where your grandfather placed his hand, and knelt, because he was thankful. He was a free man.

Never forget it was hope that guided him, hope in man's goodness.

I just couldn't face the fact I took you to that place. That hell. For me I had to write it as fiction because I face the fact of evil, that men could do such things. Grandfather Olav understood, he bore that silent evil within his heart.

The novel I have written is true, yes, I may have changed some names, but that is my freedom as a writer.

I discovered your sketches of Mia, she is a remarkable woman. Because you were sick, and needed treatment, I took you to see Mia's mother, Doctor Marija Drovik.

I first met Marija when Svein and I went on our trip several months before you were born, in the winter of 1985. In Vienna. At that time, your mother stayed in the apartment with you in Oslo. I just had to get away. There is something else, but for this you must go to your mother, Wenche.

I am so ashamed of myself. I am sorry how this story played out with Marija, the gentle artist doctor from Zagreb. What you will read will shock you back to your senses. She did not deserve any of this.

On my second trip to the Balkans in 1991, you were seven years old and I took you with me, to see Doctor Drovik. The penicillin injections she gave you did not cure your disease. As you grew older, I heard you screaming in your sleep.

About the death camp, how you were witness to unspeakable atrocity. I decided then when you were growing up in Oslo to hide these facts from you.

I decided to make you believe it was all a bad dream, that this girl you met and sketched was a fiction from your daydreams. That was wrong.

The doctors said there were spots on your brain, your eyes were diseased, there was a chance you could die if the disease advanced. Your sister Vilde left home because she couldn't look at your face.

You missed a playmate, your mother locked you up, threw you a pencil. I never forgave your mother, how she got up and left both of us.

So I let you draw, escaping away the hours, in my father's old house down south in the valley. There, in that tiny little town we could both escape. Syphilis can do that to your mind, it can make you believe things that are not true.

I wanted to forget what happened to me, how Svein Torkildsen entered into the picture, what he did. Watch out for his son, Trond!

They say the apple doesn't fall far from the tree! I want you to learn of these things now, that you can get the help you need and move on.

I passed this book on as a work of fiction, I needed to believe it didn't really happen. I had to do that for my own sanity. Now I understand I was wrong. I am so sorry, Andreas. You had a mother who left you. You had a father who never said 'I love you'.

But you have a grandfather who witnessed evil, who by the strength of his goodness, bore this evil. I do not know how his end will come; he sits downstairs now, playing the harmonica, by the fire. This letter will be placed in the desk drawer, in an envelope.

I know you will find it, it is where you have sat so many nights, with your pencil and drawings. Again, Andreas, the unspeakable things you witnessed, don't keep them inside. Get the help you need, life your life, follow your passion.

Love, your father, Harold.

What frightens you, Andreas?

The doctor comes back in, he sits at his desk, types on his laptop. "Where are the rest of the pages? *Where is the book?*"

"Mia said that's all there was in the folder."

I turn over the typed pages, see where he has pencilled in the side margins notes, scan the pages.

My eyes are sharp, things are starting to get in focus. I had nightmares as a boy. "What do you think it would be like to die in a field of long grasses and wild irises, where no one remembers the sound of your footsteps, a smooth stone marks your grave, and no one remembers your name?" I hear computer keys, the doctor typing.

"The nurse will give you a sedative. You will be hooked up to some monitors and receive an intravenous medication that will help you to relax. Then we will begin our interview with some questions. If you feel uncomfortable, or would like me to stop at any time, let me know and I will conclude my questions. Is that understood, Andreas?"

* * *

My eyes are still closed, my head flat against the table.

Her voice. "I am here for you, Andy." She has been sitting in the corner.

I am drifting away.

The doctor's distant voice. "Is there something you want to tell me, before we begin with the questions, Andreas?"

"I am afraid."

The doctor's words are calm. "What frightens you, Andreas?"

I feel a warm hand grab mine, holding it firm until the shaking stops. This is the way it happens, when the panic attacks start, when everything just builds and builds, before a storm, and I think Mia should have just slipped my hand, as I sank in the lake. I hear her yelling for me, as I float down, under the lake's surface, I hear a rifle shot, then another rifle shot, I see an arm stretching toward me in the darkness.

Mia's soft voice. "I am here for you, Andreas."

There is a tremor inside me, I don't want to wake up.

I am drifting, and drifting, in a dark tunnel, I feel my heart dunking loud in my chest, it races, and the drumbeat grows distant, and then... BANG! I hear a hammer's blow, I see a hammer tapping on a small, bent knife blade, a hammer tapping and tapping on an iron anvil, I see the hand pulling the straightened knife blade through a candle flame, and then I see myself alone, standing in the old jail cell, naked, facing the little mirror I have propped up on a stool.

I see my hand placing the knife's razor point to my chest. 'ARTIST' reads the runic letters, made by a red marker, showing me where to cut. I start slicing the skin over the letter A, the flesh splits open, the blood runs down my chest.

I cut the other letters, so when I am finished the word 'ARTIST' is seen, the letters run down below my nipples across my belly.

The blood runs from the cut flesh, I see myself in front of the mirror, this young man no longer a boy, whose face reveals anguish, an inner torment, because there is a mark, where the nose has melted away, a mark left by my mother.

I hate that woman, who hated me. That woman has made me what I am.

That mother who called me a monster, and locked me in this cell, where my shadow lifts the bloody little knife to my neck, and I hear a girl's scream "NOOO!" as I drop the knife, and I turn see a young woman, sitting crouched in the corner, naked, and weeping. It is Lena. I go over to her, manhandle her amid her protests, drag her by the ankles under me, as I force myself on top of her, kissing her violently, as she helplessly beats my bloodied chest with her hand.

"I cut myself. I was seventeen years old. I raped Lena."

"Lena?"

"Lena left me. I saw her not long ago. In the hospital."

"Did Lena file any type of report on that incident?"

"No, she said I needed help. She said I was messed up. I needed to see a doctor."

"Why do you think she said that?"

"I had been having nightmares. I was daydreaming about the girl."

"Mia? The girl in the red vest?"

"Yes. She visited me in my dreams. It was so real. I knew I had met her, but it was like she was behind a wall, in a locked room. I couldn't get to her."

"She happens to be the woman who is now here, in this room. The same woman who showed up one day at the old house?"

"Yes, I knew right away it was her."

"How did you know that?"

"The tattoo. She has a special tattoo I recognised."

* * *

"Tell me about the trip, when you first saw Mia."

"My father said I needed to get penicillin shots."

"Why couldn't you get the shots here in Norway? That would not be difficult."

"My mother didn't let him. She was embarrassed. They say it was her that gave me the syphilis."

"You think she was the carrier for the disease?"

"Yes."

"Why do you think that? Did your mother tell you?"

It was Torbjørn, the priest who said I was marked by Satan. It was Torbjørn who said I had a disease. The doctor says he has no medical records for my mother to confirm or deny my suspicions.

"How did you feel about that?"

"How would you feel?"

"I am asking you."

"Terrible. I hated my mother."

"How do you feel about women? Do you hate women?"

"No. Aren't you going to ask me about Ida?"

"Ida?"

"Yes. The murdered young woman. They found her hanging in the forest."

"That case is being handled by the police. This interview is not about that case. Do you have something to say about that?"

"She was a gentle girl. She was not afraid of me."

"Why should she be afraid of you?"

"I had nightmares growing up. I was afraid."

"When was the last time you had relations with a woman?"

"How do you mean?"

"Sexual relations."

"I don't remember. They come to the old house, you know."

"And what happens?"

"They show up at the door. Usually at night. I take them up to room, the great room with the fireplace."

"That is where you draw their portraits, correct?"

"Yes, I sit them on a stool. I sketch them."

"How can you sketch them. You were just about blind, isn't that correct?"

"I can't explain it. It just happens."

"You have a condition affecting the eye, it is called *uveitis*, but the diagnosis has never been fully established."

* * *

"Tell me about the trip. You and your father visited the Balkan countries, in 1991, is that correct?"

It is like I am watching a film.

I describe what I am seeing to the doctor. I hear him typing on a keyboard, these sounds fade and I hear a car's motor, I see myself in the back seat of a beat-up old red Lada, sitting in the back seat next to the girl Mia.

She holds my hand tight.

An overcast sky. The rain had stopped, and the clouds had left. Marija pulls the car along the side of the dirt road, on a hilltop.

She turns to my father sitting in the front seat and says calmly, "It is strange, to look down on the villages and the land."

"What do you mean? Can you get us to the border?" my father asks, nervously.

"Look, down there."

She points to what looks like a stream of ants moving along the road. "I am going to tell you something, Harold."

"You must pretend it is all a dream. Unless you pretend it is a dream, you will go mad."

The doctor's voice interrupts my dream. My eyes are closed.

"The place you are describing. Where were you travelling? Do you remember?"

"My father said he knew a doctor. Her name was Marija. She worked in Zagreb."

"Did you travel to Zagreb?"

"Yes. We took the train from Vienna."

"Is that where you got the penicillin injections? In Zagreb?"

"Yes, I remember there was an office in the hospital."

"This girl you have seen in your dreams. Where did you meet her?"

"In a stone villa. A beautiful stone villa with a library. On an island."

"Pag? The island Pag, off the Adriatic coast. Could that be right?"

"Yes. Pag. I remember that name. I remember finding my journal. I wrote we took the train from Zagreb down south to the coast."

"So you travelled south to the Adriatic coast, to the island Pag. Then can you tell me what happened afterwards? Do you remember? This would have been in the fall of 1991."

"I was seven years old."

My mind clears, it is like there is open a door to the past, and I am looking in. Pieces of this puzzle are falling into place, there is a shadow hidden in my past.

I see sunlight stabbing down in the black water, I see snow blowing, a black shape running, I make out the face.

It is Marko, I know this frightened man, running with his violin into the forest. His breath is steam, he throws away the violin, he stumbles over a crag, struggles to get up, as bullets from an automatic rifle splinter branches.

A man in a uniform with a Kalashnikov, a soldier in a red cap, chases after him. The soldier stops, lifts the rifle, aims at distant Marko. Marko stops, his exhausted body just standing, facing the distant soldier who is just a shadow.

Marko lifts his eyes to the sky, his arms up stretched. Bang! Marko's face caught in a final, fatal grimace, as his outstretched arms collapse to the earth, as his chest explodes, and the blood sprays out and I see myself, just a boy hiding beyond a tree, with the young girl Mia, who holds me tight, hiding from this soldier, who has just shot and killed her brother.

"Marko!" shouts Mia.

"We had escaped from the hospital. There was a church, where we hid."

"What do you see?"

With my eyes closed and face pressed against the table, I whisper to the good doctor, the young doctor with a beautiful face, who has spent his whole life inside a book, who has never seen boys hanging head down in trees, with their necks slit.

"I was in Prijedor. I saw terrible things. I was in the forest when Marko was killed."

A thousand shades of grey

Walking in the Ekeberg woods, where the trees stand as pencils.

The light hidden, the way it plays on my face, how I walk in and out of shadow. I can hardly bear how I feel.

I want her to take off the bandage. She hides somewhere.

The way the summer's evening draws in late, the way the light lingers in the treetops, and never quite leaves, the way something has changed in me.

It takes a moment for my eyes to adjust.

It is shocking to me, I think, *This is the first time I have seen colour.*

It is like a switch has been pulled in my head, how I walked so long in the shadows. How I could see a thousand shades of grey on a winter's night, when I shuffled, my face hooded.

The doctors cannot explain it.

I had not thought how I missed colour, because all I had to do was close my eyes. I saw her eyes, the colour of the blue sea, I touched her lips, the colour of climbing roses.

Thornless roses my grandfather tended by the door, where they crept, like drops of red splashed on the white pine-timbered wall. Clinging by their apple-green stems climbing the white wooden trellis, wood strips crisscrossed as diamond squares, where I reached up my fingers, feeling the pattern. Searching for thorns because I wanted to feel how the sharp points stuck my fingertips.

* * *

The way she looked into my eyes.

Red tremulous lips whispering words searching my soul, as she took my hand to her lips, and kissed it, the wet lipstick making a mark like a tattoo.

"You know where to find me," she said, as her stare lingered in me, because there was fear in her eyes, as she turned away, and walked down the hall, in her light summer floral dress and high-heeled shoes.

The nurse took me into that windowless room and attached the wires to my head, scrubbed the spots on my scalp where the sharp electrodes were attached.

I told her just to go ahead and shave my head. It was easier that way, attaching all those wires to my scalp, I had been through this before in the police station.

The glue stuck to my hair, easier just to shave it all off.

It took no time buzzing my scalp, as the electroencephalograph was switched on, as I closed my eyes, the only sound coming from the noisy EEG machine, as it recorded my brain waves.

The doctor said Mia had left something for me. I found a note, a package of new clothes, a 'present', wrapped up in colourful paper and ribbon.

"Happy birthday, *Andy*."

There was a brightly coloured olive-green silk shirt, a lambskin leather jacket, black designer jeans, designer sunglasses and a pair of Buffalo London jogging shoes that happened to fit perfectly.

* * *

The sun shines high in the sky. She wants me to find her.

I know where to find her.

I climb the Ekeberg stairs, flat stones leading up to a viewpoint.

The sun blinds me, I face the south west; the sun sits in front of me like a torchlight, like it is searching my new face. I think it is happy with the result, and what do I feel?

I do not know. I don't feel much has changed, even in these new clothes, tight-fitting shoes, and head shaved smooth.

I make out the islands Langøyene, Hovedøya and Gressholmen.

From the lookout the fjørd spreads out, it is like a painting. The way the islands lay, textured with trees and stones, the little white fluttering spots in the sky where the seagulls sail.

The doctor told me he had the psychiatric tests, the results would be sent to me. He said he read the files from the lie-detection tests done in the police station.

They confirmed his findings. Yes, there was a disorder, a psychosis, with delusions.

I was not a killer.

The terrible dreams of boys hanging head down, the haunting shadow stalking me in the forest, these could be explained by the trauma I experienced in Bosnia.

I had suppressed memories of the trip growing up, I relived my fears, in my night terrors.

I was not a killer.

I did not murder Ida.

I did not kill my father. The tests were conclusive. I wept.

* * *

I tell the doctor my life has been a running away from things.

It all started on my seventh birthday.

"That is when you had your first seizure, is that correct?" asks the doctor, going through the printed medical record in the folder.

"Who would kill Ida? What kind of madman would hang a woman from a tree by her ankles?"

"That question, Andreas Olav Hansen, is for the police to answer. I am not a neuropsychiatrist."

Something happened to me when I was seven years old.

"Do you remember, Andreas? Is there anything else you would like to share?"

I had been put on medication, I stopped having the spells when I was thirteen years old, according to the doctor.

"I have trouble remembering my childhood, Doctor. It is like it is all made up, everything except the dreams I had, the dreams of the girl. The nightmares from that place…"

I had been up all night, reading at my desk, by candlelight. I had found beneath the floorboards of the jail cell, a mouldy cardboard box. Inside the box a notebook, a journal. It was my handwriting, in black flowing ink, and there was an old-fashioned pen, the kind you fill with black ink from an ink pour bottle.

I had written a journal, with entries from 1995, the pages were stained and crumbled, I could barely make out the words, pages stuck together with a glue-like honey, when I pulled them apart there dropped a pencil drawing of a girl, it was Mia's face, just as I imagined it.

This Desdemona, this Ophelia, from my dreams.

A masked, white face, of chalk, lit by a candle's glow.

Spun from my dreams, where she tended her grandfather, where I sat crouched in that sunlit room, in the corner, with my pencil and sketchpad.

A journal with entries from the town known as Split, from the library of that great stone monastery with eight Gothic windows and a courtyard where the flagstones are bone-white. Where my father said there lived a friend, a woman named Marija, who was a doctor.

She would give me an injection, and I would be cured. I had written in my journal that my father told me Marija was a woman who was just a close friend, someone he had met in that castle in Slovenia, when he was on a writer's holiday.

It was not the first time he had met her, she had invited him to travel north to the island of Pag, before I was born, where she had a villa. She was knowledgeable about tick bites, and all sorts of disease, an educated doctor who would take care of me while he was on holiday.

There were entries from the train ride to Zagreb, and reading it made me shake inside. Because my dreams of that terrible train ride from hell were just as I had written them in my journal. The man smoking two cigarettes, the old woman with the bag of potatoes, the dark tunnel where my father grasped my hand when the echo of that old man's voice screeched in my ears, like the screeching of the train on the tracks, as we were swallowed into darkness.

"Yes, Doctor. It has all come back. My father made me believe none of it happened."

"Why do you think he did that?"

"I don't know."

One day can change everything

One fantastic day can change everything.

One brief moment, the way she touches you, the way her eyes linger on you, and turn away, from this place, this look out point, where I sit on a bench and see stretched out the great and happy city Oslo.

In this city where one day I looked up from a cocktail I had idly been stirring, and Tor-Inge says, "I love you, and only you."

One brief moment, one kiss, from a man, years ago, in the London Pub. The stillness.

My sunless exile, all those motherless years, in the dirty alleyway in Grünerløkka, the dirtiest place in all of Oslo, where I touched the graffiti littered walls with my fingers, and closed my eyes, and wept, because this was my hiding place.

I hear a woman's voice.

"Hello, my name is Mia. Mia Marija Drovik. Do you mind if I sit here?"

I open my eyes and see her standing in front of me, in dark sunglasses and a dreamy blue Catherine Hammel dress. Her arms wrapped playfully around her head.

She sits down, takes an apple from her purse.

"Here, have an apple. You look hungry. You know, Andreas, you can take off the bandage on your nose."

I bit into the apple, its taste sweet as the summer-scented air. She plays games with me, this sister of mine.

She takes off her glasses, looks me over approvingly. In my new clothes. She feels my shaven head, her hand warm, I feel the beating of her heart through her fingertips.

She releases her hand, folds them in her lap, faces me, hip to hip. "You look familiar. Have I seen you somewhere?"

I remember the garden. Gnarled old fruit trees and flower beds laid out in intricate shapes and low box hedges with leafy purple lilac bushes.

I remember sitting on a stone in the courtyard, sunlit and golden, statues and fragments of statues, and carved stone slabs bearing inscriptions.

I remember red and blue flowers bursting from lead cisterns, leafy plants and bronze-backed ferns, in little pots hung on lines of string tied between sculptures.

I remember looking out and seeing the ocean, the magical, sun-drenched ocean. I remember my heart was bursting because my pencil couldn't stop sketching.

A great wooden door led to the book filled library, where I saw my father in a chair, reading a leather-bound book to the girl sitting in his lap, the girl Mia, in a red vest embroidered in gold. I have never seen my father so happy. This little girl has a way with him.

The way he is lost as he stares in her face, the beautiful blue eyes, how there is something sublime, like a white silk ribbon binding their hearts.

I don't understand, I remember my father takes me aside, leads me outside to the stone balcony, looking out at the Adriatic.

He tells me the girl is Alessio's daughter, Miraja is just a friend, but something inside me tells me he is lying.

The sun breaks through the trees, my eyes adjust, as her face finds mine.

"Let me help you."

She gently removes the bandage from my nose. She takes out a pocket mirror from her handbag, holds it to my face.

"You see, you have a new face."

I touch my nose, run my forefinger along the smooth new flesh, feel no bumps, as she says, "I have something to tell you: the DNA test came back negative."

A pause as I take this all in.

"I am not your sister."

She walks off, leaving me alone.

* * *

Sitting alone on a bench, just staring out over Oslo, from the lookout known as 'Scream'.

Today would have been my father's birthday. *The 29th of July.*

I found him, a bullet in his head. Why did he kill himself?

And then, why do I live? I could have jumped into the maelstrom when I had a chance. No one would have mourned my passing.

Not Levi, who called my father a drunkard.

Not Torbjørn, who says I am going to hell. Not even Tor-Inge, who says something changed inside me.

Perhaps Lena would mourn a few seconds, as an afterthought on my half-spent life, there was a harshness to her after she discovered my letter to Tor-Inge.

In a man's arms, and tight embrace, in the shadow of the pub, where no one stares, where his voice quiets me. He says I need the surgery; he says he is not worried; I am not infected. I don't have AIDS; he would never enter a relationship if I was ill. He would see to it I received the help I needed; I was not a monster. Yes, I had late syphilis, I was born with the disease, and it could reawaken, it left its mark only on my face, where the nose melted away. The nose will be repaired, I would just have to watch myself.

Even with a new face, in new clothes, my head shaved and glistening, in a stylish lambskin jacket, with aviator sunglasses, all this, and then?

The same haunting thoughts, as if my life has been one long train ride in a dark tunnel. And now I have come to the end of the tunnel, the light blinds me, and I am afraid of what I see.

I tremble inside, staring out over the fjørd, blood-red, as the sun stabs down, and for the life of me I want to stab my heart, and kill my awful thoughts.

All these years the guilt of living has weighed on me.

There are shadows watching me now, I see them from the corner of my eyes. Mia tells me she is not my sister.

I see tongues of fire, the sky splits apart and blood drips through the great, splintered crack, I hear boys screaming, kicked naked into the building, the hell house washed red.

The concentration camp near Prijedor.

How I, a boy seven years old, happened to end up there, with my father, how I was witness to evil, these facts have marked me. People cannot forget what they did here. I want to forget, but I cannot.

What is good is always taken away from us

I stand up, walk to the lookout's edge.

Around me a phalanx of onlookers, perhaps waiting their turn. All those Jesus freaks in the valley, how they go down on their knees and shout their saintly hosannas, yet they forget how to really love a man.

I am not the real freak.

I start screaming.

I sense Mia stares at me in the shadows.

I sense her weeping, her tears dropping like small crystals on flagstones, where the sound of their breaking is like the breaking of my heart.

I scream because Levi lusts in his heart for this white Jesus, this figment of his imagination with an alabaster face, whose mythic life he spins week after week, in that pine-timbered church, where my painting will hang.

That painting of Jesus, whose face was Eirik's.

His soft blue eyes locked by the woman's stare, the woman who came to me in the forest, wrapping me in her feathered embrace, whispering I will paint a masterpiece.

Eirik, the man I loved and kissed, whose whispers on the pine-timbered bed carved with rose petals struck me through and through.

Whose whispers betrayed fear, because he was afraid to go back to his little town up north, where the people said hurtful things.

I scream because Abdi tells me they cut off his leg, and I want to kiss him now.

I love this black man.

In the dark room, in that haunt of mine, the bathhouse Hercules, where I enter off the street, a Saturday night, the receptionist knows me, I am a regular customer. I walk down a flight of steps. The strong scent of aftershave, the air perfumed, the walls damp to the touch, the dark room I enter, barefoot, a clean white towel wrapped around my waist.

"Abdi?" I whisper.

A hand grabs mine. He pulls me close. I feel his robot leg, the metal warm against my flesh. He has been waiting for me.

He tells me to place a wet towel across his back, that way I can hit him as hard as I like without leaving a bruise. Abdi tells me he knows the sound skin makes when it is ripped from the body. I tell him I have seen evil; I am afraid, I can't live in a world where a man tells me to paint a white Jesus.

Because I know this man has been sneaking up on me, I see a shadow in a window, I think I will kill this man.

This man in a priest's garb will never know the real Jesus. This little man with raven eyes, this hypocrite who I saw once, many years ago, abusing that boy. He made me promise not to tell old Torbjørn.

Torbjørn would find me if I revealed his secret. Old Torbjørn, who said I was going to hell, as I shouted Jesus was gay, as my mother sat frozen in the church.

Levi didn't say what Torbjørn would do with me. He would just find me.

I was just nineteen, I was a weakling, Levi was shorter than me, but stout as a bull.

And now he has found me again, in the little church by the bend in the river where I have spent night after night with my brushes, painting my masterpiece. He spies on me, I feel his presence, there is a trembling in me which Abdi stills.

And then, this Jesus, who lives in my heart.

This man whom I love, this Dorian who whispers my sufferings will end, whose eyes watch over me. In my grandfather's room, in the old house, where one day I leaned all my paintings against all the walls in all the rooms of that old house. There were over three hundred acrylic portraits, a portrait of every face, everyone in the village, scattered in every room on all three floors. I had painted everyone in the village. Levi, and Torbjørn, the Lady from Eiken, Lena, Ida, the face without a name. And in the attic the nudes, several hundred, like a museum. That's how I left the house, so when the thief comes back to visit, they will bear witness to his crime. Abdi says he writes his name, Abdi, on the taxi window, when the dew lays on the glass. He writes my name on the window, he draws a circle around our names.

It is a teardrop which washes away, as it rains, the window wipers wipe the window, so the glass is wiped clean.

The river you drown in, there you will drink.

The river will sweep you out to the sea, the sun rises and sinks, the moon pales, as you slip down, in the black.

"I will weep for you, Andreas" he says. Abdi knows my secret.

Freshly fucked, lying by my side, in the dark room.

"Love is like this, it hits you, blow after blow, you strike your fists at me, Andreas."

He whispers I must not hate; I must let my anger fly off, wash it from my body. He says what is good is always taken away from us.

They say I am touched

I scream because my father hid what he feared, from me, thinking it wouldn't fester like a sore, thinking he could protect me. Blaming my night terrors on syphilis, and the hallucinations they spun in my brain.

And now the woman from the island of Pag, the girl Mia, the woman with olive skin and eyes the colour of the sea, who rescued me, not once, but twice, tells me she is not my sister.

She steals my heart, yet I feel I have nothing to give, because there is one more secret to tell.

It is the same to me, as I told Mia, sitting on the bench outside Gaustad, whether I live or die.

What is life but a thousand pinpricks of pain, from the moment you come screaming from your mother's womb, the mother who gave birth to a little monster?

They say I am touched.

Yes, I am touched, what I witnessed, the facts of the case, have touched me.

The evil that men do, lives after them.

My father tried to bury the Balkan tragedy, when he slapped me in the face, then I knew. What he had been writing all those years, at the desk in my grandfather's room, was not fiction, it was a confessional.

I take out the crumbled piece of paper I had found attached to my father's letter to me. My eyes are now sharp, for some reason my eyesight has come back in full strength. It is a shock, that is why I told Mia I need to sit down alone, on this bench, to gather my thoughts.

The hatred men have in their hearts, because you are different, because you love a man, because you are white, and your neighbour is black, lives after them. The hatred men have for their neighbour, the neighbour from Eritrea, or Kosovo, or Asmara, because he speaks another language, and your face is white, and your hair is blonde, and your eyes are the colour of the sea, that hatred lives after them. I love this man Abdi, he whispered in my ear, as I mounted his hard-muscled body on the pine-timbered bed, the way the headboard shook, as shouted those unintelligible Eritrean words, flowing in a melody like a river, surging in the winter, when the snow melts, and the water charges cold and strong. He made me promise to keep our little secret to ourselves.

When I close my eyes, there is silence.

They are not shadows, they are cold facts, how my father took me away, how my mother abandoned me, how it was my father who really cared for me, enough to get me the penicillin shots, in that faraway place, where he got caught up in a civil war.

The mother who threw you a pencil, and locked you up in an old jail cell, iron bars as thick as broomsticks, cold to the touch, where my hand slid up, and down, up and down, as I heard my finger's tapping, like the pencil tapping on the paper, where there appeared her face, her beautiful face, when I closed my eyes.

I want to say so many things. I want to tell her I am in love.

I want to tell her that on the night she lay by the fire when I saw her naked, I knew I had always loved her, that my affair with Eirik was something I couldn't explain.

That yes, I love a man.

Perhaps because I fear loving a woman more.

I feared loving a woman because I was afraid of losing her, losing someone I cherished, like when I threw that stone in the river, that stone where I sketched her likeness.

In the white-water where the falls splash down over the rocks, where my little stone disappeared, and I thought I will never see this woman again, this woman with olive skin and blue eyes, because our hearts will break.

I can tell Mia senses I am at a loss for words.

I had taken her in my arms, when the nurses let us alone, when my eyes opened. I wanted to kiss her, I told her so much, but she pulled away, something was not right, she said she would move to Oslo, or maybe even back to Croatia, because she told me she had become afraid again.

There was something she saw in me. I wait for her to enter my dream.

Here, the hanging sculpture gleaming in the sun. *The Couple.*

Faceless bodies encoiled by polished metal, like a giant snake encoiling its victim, sun reflecting off the polished metal, in this place where not a sound is heard.

The coiled, faceless lovers of Ekeberg.

The way I feel, in just a moment she will reach a hand to my face, and still my soul. She told me to find her in this place.

Where she will look upon my face, where her finger made her mark. In that stone villa, on the hilltop in Pag, where the sun flooded in the arched stone way, where the old man lay on the bed, and she lit a cigarette, and placed it in his mouth.

I lay down in the grass, looking up at the sculpture.

I think of my grandfather, Olav, lying in that dark cell, in the work camp in Fannrem. On May 9, 1945, he and some two hundred and fifty Norwegians were set free from the Nazis. It was the happiest day in his life. Regaining his freedom.

Grandfather Olav lying on his back, looking up in the ceiling where threads hung from the rope where the previous cellmate hung himself.

Will I regain my freedom?

What is there to gain if I really never had it to lose?

What is it, that is free, but for this unspoken passion to take up a pencil, and my paints, and my sable, in a room hidden from the light, where the sound of my sketching fills me, like a glass overflowing?

I think, who is really free, but the artist, or the writer, who can spin a story, or sketch a likeness, or kiss a man on his lips, and lay with him?

Is Levi free, this round little man with a fleshy face and a cross on his lapel, who tells me Jesus was white, who pays me twenty thousand crowns to create a masterpiece, this fake white Jesus, this Judas Levi, who betrays the real man Jesus? The way they spin their wild fantasies of this bearded man, who touches their hearts, and I think these women have never, ever been loved.

The way they come to me at night, in my grandfather's old pine-timbered house, I hear their footsteps. The Syphilis Artist, in the shadow, a candle burning on a small table, by the stool, where the robe drops to the floor, and they sit, waiting, and not a sound can be heard.

But for the wind outside, blowing in the valley, a full moon, a fire glows in the Jotel, the kettle boils, the roiling of the water, the whistling of the kettle, the pouring of tea, into a little white porcelain cup, as she sips, and waits, as I sharpen my pencil.

The Syphilis Artist.

* * *

This man Jesus, who hung on a cross, he was free.

If he was here now, lying in the grass, I would kiss him.

He would see my face, touch his finger where the bone and flesh has healed, and lightly tap his fingers to my forehead, and trace my eyes, touching lightly, so the light no longer stabs.

Healing the scar that cut into me, when my mother locked me in the jail cell, and threw the pencil in.

It was then I lost my eyesight, I didn't want to see any more.

The sound of the iron bars as thick as broomsticks slamming shut, the clicking of the lock's iron bolt, the sound of the pencil being sharpened, as my fingers trembled, and I cried out, "Don't lock me in!" and my mother's hard footsteps down the steps, the slamming of the front door, as I just sat, and grasped the iron bars, tears running down my cheeks, on my ugly face.

I remember her face, like Munch's 'Scream', aghast staring at my infant face, where the nose was broken, at my birth.

What did I do wrong?

Treponema pallidum, that word clangs in me like a drumbeat. It is the lifeless bell hanging in the church tower, ringing, and ringing, and ringing.

I look up, this sculpture like a giant glistening knife, how the sun glints off the polished metal, the way light glints off broken glass.

I think of finding him, in the rocking chair, on that terrible day, my father lying on the floor, a gunshot in his temple.

I know I will lose her

Lying in the cool grass staring up at the floating sculpture known as *The Couple*, in Ekeberg park. Lying, staring up, how the minutes pass. How all this is hallucination.

"You think I'm going to lay here like some Madonna, quiet, when in my heart, every day, I see my mother's face?"

It is Mia. She lays down next to me. Speaking softly. "Tell me, Mia. Tell me something."

"Let me tell you something, Andreas Olav Hansen. At night, soldiers shined flashlights into the cars while bragging of all the children they had already killed. That's how she saved you, and your father, my mother hiding you and me in the trunk, your father was in the front seat, luckily, they allowed us pass into Croatia. They took my brother, Marko."

She stares up at the floating sculpture.

"They were raped, they were beaten, by those animals. Women in Pristina and Prijedor and Omarska and Srebrenica who were too afraid to leave their homes for milk because they would be shot down in the streets."

Turning to me, as I turn to her. Face to face.

Eyes locking eyes.

Feeling her wide hips touch mine.

Feeling her bare feet touch mine, the way she touches. The way her sweet breath stills me.

The way her heart wraps mine. I know I will lose her.

There is a moment I am lost. In her words, as my vision fades, as she whispers, "The worst thing a victim of suffering can do is to pretend it didn't happen."

"Why did you believe you were my sister?"

"I discovered letters to my mother. Your father had an affair with my mother when he visited Vienna."

She studies my expression, her voice sings softly a melody. *"Deep blue sea, tell the world, That a Croat loves his homeland. While the fields are kissed by sunshine, while the oaks are whipped by wild winds, while the dead are sheltered in graves, while his live heart beats."*

I can't look into her eyes.

I know how this story will end. "While my heart beats, Mia."

She pulls a silver chain from one of her pockets. It is a chain with a crystal blue teardrop pendant. "I have been saving this for you, Andreas."

She places the pendant around my neck.

My eyes searching her eyes, the way tears form, something pains her, something unspoken.

There are so many things I want to tell this woman. I am a man torn in two pieces. I whisper, *"Has anyone told you of the shine that sparkles from a kind woman's heart?"*

Her eyes lock with mine.

In her eyes my face's reflection, the way the light strikes down and passers-by are mere shadows. There is a moment when the shadows just vanish in the light of day. Like now, when tears form in Mia's eyes, those blue-green eyes cut like lapis lapida, the way they cut into me, because I know in my heart I have always been in love with this woman. Mia, the girl in the red vest embroidered in gold, who appeared to me in a dream.

"Yes, that was real, as real as you, lying here in the grass." A moment of silence.

"We are going on a motorcycle trip."

The good that men do is forgotten

I got up early in the separate little guest room, showered, dressed and shaved, put on the nice clothes, the new lambskin jacket, fried an egg with bacon and sat down at a table in the tiny kitchen.

The smell of bacon, how hungry I had become, the taste of coffee, I cannot tell you how these sensations have a way with me. My fingers pick up the knife and fork, I hold the silver instruments close to my face.

Looking at the sharp-edged knife, feeling its edge. I have a crazy thought, I could take the knife to my neck, with one deliberate motion end it all. Bleeding out here, on this table, where the sun will rise, she will find me.

I cannot hurt her, I will not hurt her.

What is life but a line drawn by a pencil, a stroke in time, the line a connection of infinitely small points?

Memory connects the little points, and then I think in the end, it doesn't matter, does it?

The line runs off the paper, into the unknown. Heaven, hell, what lies for me?

I want nothing but her memory, as she placed her finger on my face, and whispered.

I want nothing but her face, floating up in the clouds, as I rise up, in the air, my limbs outstretched, as Marko's arms, as he fell in the forest.

As I saw him, hiding with Mia, this man whose last words were not of hate, but love.

I could *not* make up the evil I witnessed, among the Serbs and Croats, the wild-eyed men drunk on hate.

I could *not* hallucinate such evil.

The evil that men do, that will live after them.

And the good that men do, what happens with that? The good that men do is forgotten.

The good that comes from a hand outstretched, pulling up a beggar, lying in the street, whose dirty face, and eyes black, hide a sorrow.

The good that comes from kneeling next to the *innvandere* sitting cross-legged on a yellow pillow outside the store, the dark little gypsy woman in her colourful scarf holding a miserable little handwritten sign full of misspellings and a paper cup.

The good that comes from not placing a coin in her cup, but a little slip of paper with an address.

Where she can come, and be greeted with open arms, and be served a meal. Where she will tell her story, and make friends, and learn Norwegian, and learn we are an open society, and no one is allowed to spit in her face.

The good is forgotten, it ends up not in the newspaper, or on social media, because it is boring, and the masses would rather read about a murder.

III

I LOVE YOU, MIA MIRAJA

In Mia's embrace, her tears running with mine, she knows I am saying goodbye.

I kiss the wind

I take out from my jacket a pocket book. *Writings by Kafka.*

I open the thumb worn pages to a place I marked last night, as I sat alone reading, on the balcony.

I whisper the words, so as not to awake her.

"What are we to do with these spring days that are now fast coming on? Early this morning the sky was gray, but if you go to the window now you are surprised and lean your cheek against the latch of the casement. The sun is already setting, but down below you see it lighting up the face of the little girl who strolls along looking about her, and at the same time you see her eclipsed by the shadow of the man behind overtaking her. And then the man has passed by and the little girl's face is quite bright."

Around my neck, the pendant teardrop, crystal, how I feel it between my thumb and forefinger.

Inside the crystal her mother's tears. Mia told me the story last night.

Her mother had discovered Jedranka, her mother's best friend, was killed in the conflict.

How can I describe to you, my reader, what Mia told me, not in words spoken, but the way she held me tight, her face cheek to cheek, her eyes so close her tears ran with mine?

As she tells me she recites her mother's words, by memory, word for word, transfixed on that terrible scene, in the basement of that hospital, in Vukovar, where gentle Jedranka was found with her patients, hiding from the evil young men in red caps.

Men with raven eyes and bloodied uniform.

Young men not quite twenty years who have never loved, men whose eyes are dead, whose touch is cold, whose heart is stone.

Who discovered her, as she fell to her knees, as she whispered a prayer in her language, Arabic words flowing melodious like a river, gentle, impassioned words flowing as melodious as black ink, running off the page?

Beautiful words startling the drunken soldiers, for a moment, before the knife falls on this woman.

Beautiful Jedranka, for whom I weep, as I write these words, in pencil, in this notebook.

A notebook I will place in the desk drawer, in my grandfather's room, where my little notes are hidden among the scraps and drawings.

Where the wood is stained from my tears.

My heart is wound like a spring, as tight as a bow, and tell me, reader, what is a man to do?

In Mia's embrace, her tears running with mine, she knows I am saying goodbye.

As when the little girl's tears ran, her fingers outstretched to her mother, whose hands stretched to reach hers, and their fingers touched, as the soldiers in red caps pulled the good woman away, at the roadblock near Srebrenica, as she yelled to my father that he had to drive us back to the coast, as I hid my face, in Mia's embrace. As the evil men took her mother, and my frightened father sped away, the smoke of distant burning fields rising like black snakes, spiralling into the grey, darkening sky. The burning houses, the burning haystacks, the corpse-strewn streets and the sounds of gunfire and how Mia hid my face as my father sped us away, in the red Lada. Escaping to the coast, from this hell on earth, as my little boy body shook in terror, as Mia cried in my lap for her mother, as my father sped past armoured vehicles and tanks and refugees.

She knows all this will end; she knows something in me sets me apart. I am not made for this world. I do not fit in this time.

I am a shadow, I kiss the wind, it sighs back, I tap the air, the grandfather clock ticks, not a sound is heard but the shaking of the bedpost.

As he lies under me, his eyes locking mine, full of fear, as I kiss him, and he cries because he says I will die one day, and he will be left alone, and no one will hold him, like I have.

He will have to escape, into the shadows, because he has been spat on, they tag him with cruelties unspoken, as when the old priest Torbjørn matter of factly told my mother my gay friends were Satanists.

"Fuck Torbjørn!" I shouted at my mother, as I ripped myself from her arms, at the church altar.

Jedranka feared no one, did not break, as they tortured her, and the sounds of her voice was as the wind blowing when the leaves fall from the trees.

The evil men feared the emptiness of their hearts, so they filled the empty space with hate. My heart breaks, it is full, a cup overflowing with tears.

I weep because I am happy for Mia, she had found herself a nice place. I weep because this thing that hung over me, that hallucination, is a memory.

You touched me

The way Mia connects the points for me, what happened, in the Balkans, the shadow stalking me.

I had grown up on the east side of Oslo, in that poor section, my father struggled to pay the rent. I didn't see the filth, I smelt it, felt it, when my mother suddenly disappeared, my big sister Vilde started smoking, disappeared for days on end.

There was a rumour she had an abortion. My father locked himself up in his room the day my mother ran off.

I had looked in on Mia, she slept contently, naked, atop the covers. The sight of her, lithe and svelte, a dancer's tight, muscled body, lying on her side, hourglass hips, firm breasts warm and smooth to the touch, quickened me.

They wonder if we make love, they wonder what a man like me has to do with a fine woman like Mia.

We have kept our secret to ourselves, not a day passes where her presence doesn't fill me, like the way you open the door in the morning, and the dark room fills with light.

Yes, I had loved my share of men, there is one who pulls at my heart. Eirik, this young man who came to me, in the night, frightened.

Whose face looked up, there at the altar, as I lifted my filbert to the canvas, and painted the face of Jesus, the Nazarene whose voice calls for me.

I cannot put words to this longing, Mia senses it, I am what I am. "There is no heaven, there is no hell," I whispered.

Eirik wept, he held me tight, his shaking was like an epileptic fit. It was all too much for him, I was just too intense.

On Mia's nightstand in a small crystal vase the pink flower, the palo borracho, that special flower I found in that little hidden shop, in Grünerløkka, when I went out alone, and searched for hours.

When I came back to the apartment, Mia was sound asleep. I hand wrote a poem, placed it on her night table in an envelope, with the flower, so she would find it when she awakened.

A fir tree drops to the ground. A boulder drops to the sea.

A woman's voice, filled with ecstasy, echoes, in the mountains. You touched me.

You placed your finger on my face and awakened me. You whispered how a pencil

Creates a line.

How I did not need my eyes to draw, But only my…

Heart, only my heart. You have stolen my heart, Mia Miraja.

I whisper these words, to you now, lying beside you, in this bed. Whose headboards are carved with rose petals,

So, the touch of my fingers, on the carved wood, smooth to the touch, Is as my touch.

On your face, where my eyes meet yours. Where my eyes close, and I see you.

Lying still, in the meadow of wildflowers, in the sunlit valley, where we have walked barefoot.

Where we lie in the warm grass, and look up, in the sky, And I hear your voice,

As the sighing wind.

I love you, Mia Miraja. I love…

Only you.

I love you, Mia Miraja

The rising sun is just a faint glowing orb peeking distant atop the hills, a half-dark morning where I can walk alone before all the traffic and the rushing-by of trams.

I stand outside on the second-floor balcony, the railing is black, cast iron, in the figure of a swan.

There are clay pots of all sizes and dimensions, full of blooming summer flowers.

The way my fingers feel the ironwork, fingers gliding on the cold metal, the sun will rise, Mia will rise, she will put on her white velvet robe, sipping a cup of tea, standing here at the balcony.

Here on *Middelthuns gate*, where it is early morning and dark, the streetlights still aglow. I need a smoke, so I roll myself a cigarette, light up the fag, it glows in the dark, and the smoke tendrils up, straight, a ribbon of white unmoved.

The day calm, not a sound but the rushing by of a taxicab now and then. I feel strong, something has come over me.

There is a calmness settling over me.

I have gained weight, when I saw myself naked in the wall mirror this morning, I couldn't believe my eyes.

I didn't recognise myself, but for my big tattoo cut into my chest.

My head is close-shaved, my face clean-cut, with the designer sunglasses and my new sharp clothes I am thinking, "What the hell did I do to deserve all this?"

I told Mia I didn't want any handouts; I would see to it that I paid her for the clothes.

No it was a gift.

She says I have a new start in life, she is so happy to start working with the dance company, her dreams are coming true. She is so excited!

This is the sightseeing she has been longing for.

She says it will take fifteen days, biking North, along E16 skirting the Swedish forests, along scenic backroads up North to Mo I Rana, and then crossing west to the coast, up to the islands, riding the gentle shoreline roads, hopping on ferries, to Lofoton, and turning back down in Andøya.

She says she has been planning the trip for months, she has been saving money for years.

"I thought about you, Andreas, and I saved my money."

The new clothes I am wearing, the ones I found on the bed this morning, feel strange. I am not a man used to dressing up, my self-imposed exile from the world clothed me with thoughts hanging on me like my grandfather's old fisherman's coat.

She said we are going to take a long walk over to Grünerløkka, she wants to visit the galleries.

She says I will eat good food, there is a restaurant she will take me, she says I need to walk, and smile, and not hide my face, any more.

On the way back there is a friendly pub on Rosted's gate, she wants me to meet some of her Oslo friends.

"Orlando's pub?" I have been there a few times with Lena.

It's a change from the London Pub, I wonder if the owner will recognise me.

* * *

Up the whole night, slow sipping red wine, picking at a salad from a crystal bowl, just staring into one another's face, not saying a word.

Holding the hand mirror to my face, seeing her smiling reflection, then how her smile left her.

I know what she is thinking.

The way I touched her face, the way she placed my hand between the space, between her legs. The way the girl looked into my eyes, in that great library of books, in that stone villa, on the island where the sea swept its scent into me, into my deformed nose, where she touched her finger.

Taking a wad of gum from her mouth, forming it into a little ball, tapping it in place, so my little nose looked normal. I whispered words, to assuage her frightened look, as suddenly my touch aroused her, her olive skin flushed, her eyes looked away, and then back, where I saw something had changed inside her.

"*I love you, Mia Miraja.*

I love you because you are not afraid of me.

I love you because I love the sea, I love the wind, I love the way the birds circle overhead, alight in the summer's wind.

I love you because you are still, because you still my heart. I will always love you, Mia Miraja, from the island of Pag."

The way I spoke those words, so long ago, in that place my mind made me forget, because the memory awakened a horror.

She has come back to me, this girl in a red vest embroidered in gold, hair like Konavle silk, black as the raven's wing, when it sits atop the church tower, and all I can think about is the way her fingers touched my face, how I could die, in that moment, and that would be enough for me.

A faint and swelling melody I hear distant

I will walk to Frogner before the sun slants through the apartment window and touches Mia's face.

Sweet slumbering Mia, for whom my heart awakens.

There is a sphinx rising from the ashes, as the sun rising anew, I sense something in me, like Grieg's Sonata in A minor stirring in my grandfather's house from his spinning phonograph.

A faint but swelling melody I hear distant, growing stronger as my walk quickens, the hard tap of my shoes on the sidewalk echoing in the narrow alleyways as I cross the streets toward the park.

There is something about walking around in Oslo, here in this part of town, at this early hour, entering the tree-lined park.

The sun has risen above the tops of the tenements, I see my fingers, like pencils, aglow in the strengthening light.

The stone walk rises gently to the distant raised plateau, where the great monolith sits, erect, this writhing mass of humanity, naked, entangled and rising, to the great vault of sky, where the sun has newly risen.

The monolith looks like a distant shard of glass, the way the light touches it now, the way my heart beats faster.

As I run past the splashing fountains, past a homeless person digging in a bin.

"Do you have a smoke?" the ragged old man calls out, as I stop in my tracks, turn to him, walk over, and pull out a little box of unopened L and M cigarettes. I remove my glasses, this old little man in his dirty clothes, who looks at me fondly, handing him the cigarettes and a box of matches. There is an apple in my jacket, I hand it to him, the way he hungrily chews it, the way the juice drips down his stringy beard.

This homeless man could be me.

There is a moment he searches my face; I think I have seen this man before someplace.

His liquid blue eyes are lovely, the way they search mine, the man could be thirty or sixty, I don't know, but before I turn from him, I draw close to his face, and kiss him on the cheek.

This man who has fallen on hard times, this shadow in the park, starts to weep, as I pull away, and turn to the rising plateau, and I hear the man's shouts "Come back! I know you!" as I run faster, there is an expectation I will find the answer, there at the monolith, where the fountains splash, and the scene is more than I can handle.

Because it was here that I pulled my father, when I was a boy, wearing those dark glasses, it was here at Frogner at that sculpture where I raised my trembling hand, and touched her face.

At the monolith, the sculpture of the man, kneeling, naked, above the woman, his hands grasping her head, the woman naked, and kneeling, the granite smooth to the touch. Where I stretched out my fingers to the woman's face, sun-warmed granite, how my fingers tapped the stone, as I felt for my pencils and sketchpad in my knapsack.

As I sketched the sculpture, sitting on the stone steps, my father by my side, silent, the hours passed, as I sensed a crowd watching me, I heard my father explaining to the American tourist that I am blind, I have been sketching since I was a small child.

"This boy of yours, he has a real talent. Wow, that is one incredible drawing!"

* * *

There are so many loose thoughts hanging like threads.

Like lines drawn, when you have sharpened your pencils, the moment comes, you think, touching the canvas with the pencil, outlining a form, what happens next?

Lines that define a shape on one side of the outline carve out space on the other side. A form can never exist alone. It only becomes visible when viewed in the context of the other forms.

The words of my art teacher, *one-armed Anders*, who lost his left arm in a car accident, his calming words I remember, they come back to me now, walking toward the park in Vigeland, where often we strolled, not a word passing from our lips.

He said the drawing of a line with a pencil, in the creation of forms, involves the concepts known as *observation*, and *perception*.

That man Anders whom I secretly loved, who thought me my art, in the art high school not far from me, now, this quiet man who waited for me at night, and unlocked the door, and let me into his studio in that graffiti filled alleyway in Grünerløkka.

Who guided my hand on the canvas, when I was seventeen, unsure of my ability, as my eyesight came and went, and I started wearing those thick sunglasses to hide my nose, because the sight of my face frightened my friends, who left me, because they said I had AIDS?

I weep, with each step I approach to that special place, that holy place, where I have lifted my hands. The monolith rising, the great granite monolith, Vigeland's master work.

* * *

"I knew you would be here." Mia's voice.

"Mia."

She sits on the stone steps, by this sculpture, this sculpture of a kneeling man embracing a kneeling woman, in the shadow of the monolith, where the tourists are busy snapping their photos.

I close my eyes.

"Andreas, don't talk. Let me feel your hand."

Lifting my hand from the sculpture, from the young woman's granite-cold face, to her warm hand, grasping mine, tight, as the summer sun breaks above us, my eyes tightly closed, I don't want to see again.

I have been waiting for hours, here, sitting and waiting, she knew where to find me.

I don't want to see because what I feel is a broken heart, as her words are spoken, I sense a crowd of onlookers staring at us, the way Mia holds me now, not caring the whole world watches, as they snap and make their silly little videos, as she embraces me, and kisses me, and our passion is more than I can take.

They cannot understand, they have not awakened in the night, when the rain blows in, and the thunder rolls, and I cry out for her, the girl in a silken red vest embroidered in gold.

They do not see us, embracing, hiding under the broken altar, as the evil men shot that little boy, and threw him at our feet, as Mia hid my eyes, and cupped my ears, as the soldier's fired their Kalashnikovs.

The deafening sound was thunder, the blood spattered and running down the walls were tears, as Mia comforted me, whispered her mother would find us. *What Mia and I have held onto, all these years.*

We have never let go of one another.

As she has found me, as she holds me, because she is afraid, she told me last night, her grandfather was a Nazi; her mother told her the dark secret, there was a picture of him in a uniform.

It was a picture of the old man, the man with no legs. In the picture he was a young man. In a Nazi uniform. The girl in my dream lays her head down, and weeps, and no one hears her cry, except me, peeking out of the shadows.

Her voice, whispering, as I kiss her passionately, she responds, kissing uninhibited in a manner, as if we were alone, as onlookers take their silly, forgotten pictures. One does need a picture of something to remember. *The eyes see, the ears hear, the fingers touch.*

The onlookers will not see the reflection of my face, on the mirror, as I stretched out my hand, and touched the place where the bone melted away.

Where Mia's fingers placed a wad of chewing gum, the spittle running down my check, and mixing with my tear, because I was just a boy, and this girl in a red vest embroidered in gold took pity on me, in a stone villa, on a hilltop in Pag, where the wind blew in through the open arched doorway.

They will not see the old man, on the train, the man smoking two cigarettes, whose hard stares caught my father's eyes, as he told us to go back, and my father told me he would not return to Norway until I got the shots, there was a kind woman who would help me. She had a daughter, my age, I would meet her, my father was sure we would become friends.

They will not see when we fled Prijedor, a mass of startled humanity pushed and shoved and driven into trucks and buses, where my father dragged me into Marija's vehicle, where she had fought off the soldiers, as she struggled to pull us into the car, as gunshots drilled into the car doors, and Mia screamed, and the windshield exploded.

It is all coming back, those scenes from the Balkan war.

The war I witnessed, and chose to forget, because my mind played tricks. What is memory, what is hallucination?

She whispers in our embrace, there sitting hip to hip on the ascending stone staircase, at the altar of the monolith, in the shadow of the onlookers, as we make out, in the open park.

"I am afraid, Andreas. It is all coming back. The hatred, the walls, the evil."

"Mia, the hatred, that has always been with us. It is in me, in you, it only needs to be awakened."

Opening my eyes, the crowd around us, among them a blank-faced woman with longing eyes, locking on mine, my eyes wet with tears.

About to take a picture with her phone, then lowering her phone, as something comes over her, and she says, "I am sorry," and she turns, and walks off, the crowd startled, because suddenly there is a stillness among them, as Mia helps me up, pulls me away.

"Let them watch. I don't care if the whole world watches. Let us go back to the apartment."

Andreas, you must not die

In her apartment, in Majorstua, twilight.
    In her bedroom.
    The light from a candle playing my shadow on the wall as I kneel on the floor, my hands folded, my head bowed down on the sheets.

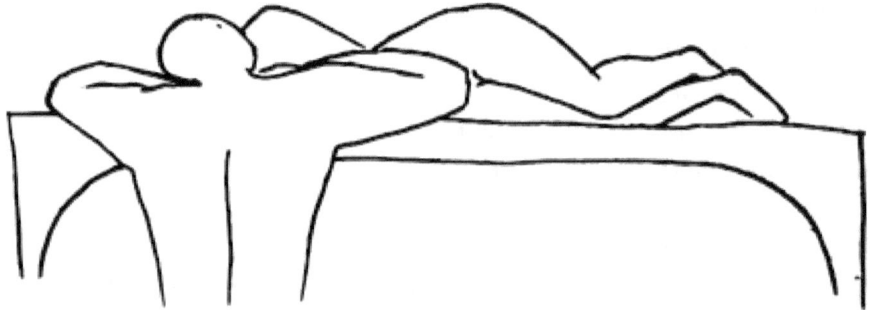

A man praying. A man weeping. A man who sees a vision.
    On the shore, a summer's day, walking hand in hand, barefoot, the waves playing at our ankles.
    In our eyes the sun plays our shadows on the sand, no one sees us, it is just our shadow, hand in hand.
    The gentle lap of waves, the blowing of the wind, the smiling sun, and sky hard blue, hinged on the horizon like a giant plate of glass, cobalt blue.
    Near the shoreline, half-hidden in the rocks, a cave, where the light enters as a shaft, so that when we enter, her body is hidden in the shadow, my clothed body aglow, in the light.
    As she removes my clothes, the cawing of the seabirds fade, there is the smell of sea salt, the whispering of a prayer, from her lips.
    I will take you to the island, Pag, to our villa on the sea, I will hold your hand, and take you to the courtyard, where the stones are smooth.

Where there are flowers in cisterns overflowing, and the wind whispers your name. I will lay a rose on a stone for your father, and a rose for your grandfather, and I will tell you the secret that was hidden in my mother's heart.

She will whisper to me, what I have known all this years, Andreas Olav Hansen. "La vita è più dolce con te," she whispers, her shadow entering into the light, as Mia's clothes drop to the sand, and I enter the darkness, where the air is cold, and

I long for her embrace.

Mia has known about me all along, my father had sent her copies of my drawings, drawings she had hung in her room.

Drawings she did not consider pornographic. Sensitive drawings that made her feel alive, as a young woman, when she was most ashamed to be with a man.

I just need somehow to forgive, and come out of the shadows, because no matter what happens in life there is always a new day.

There is always hope.

She whispers the letters of the word to me, and I glance down below her left shoulder where they are tattooed, just above her breast, and she places my hand over the letters, allowing me to feel them, allowing me to feel lower, as she whispers, she is a dancer, and an artist, and a voice speaks inside her, a gentle voice.

My hand glides, now as she arches her neck, lying down in the sand, in the cave where our bodies linger in the shadows, as she calls my name, and I think this woman is not real, that she is a figment of my imagination, that all these years this disease has played tricks on me.

The way the light finds its way in this cave, the way I catch the scent of olive oil and lavender, the floral tattoo running below her breasts, vines of roses spinning around her navel, the way it is just her and me, and our footprints in the sand.

Footprints washing away, as time washes away, and I hear a melody playing in the distance, as she stretches her hand to me, and she tells me she has an apartment in Oslo, where she walked alone in the park at Ekeberg, and saw the sculpture hanging in the air.

A man, a woman, entwined.

She tells me she has been entwined with me ever since that day in Split, when I drew her likeness, and she discovered the drawing some years later under a flagstone in the courtyard.

Incense, lavender, and rose petals

The smell of incense, lavender, and rose petals. She appears at the door, naked.

She comes to me, I rise from the bed, where I have been sitting, my thoughts a tangle, like yarn spun and twisted and knotted, because I had said goodbye to Eirik.

* * *

He didn't understand, his tears ran, as I kissed him, in that little hidden corner in the London Pub, where he had been waiting for me.

"I am here to say goodbye, Eirik."

The way this young man can without speaking inform me of his innermost thoughts, the way his face can change, from a half-smile, to sadness, with a longing in the eyes, like the way he looked at me, as he posed at the church altar.

This beautiful man, Jesus, with a face of alabaster, because Eirik had lived his life in the sunless shadows, the boys spat at him, called him a fag, he escaped.

"Don't you understand, Andreas, I love you!" his voice breaking, his fist hard on the table. My hand gently grasping his closed fist, opening his hand, holding his fingers to my face, where I guide his forefinger to a tear running down.

My voice breaking, my heart swelling, my fingers trembling. I truly love this man. I must say goodbye.

"What we have shared, Eirik, no one can take from us."

I rise, turn my back, walk out of the pub through a back door, into the dark street, into the dark alleyway, and back out onto the crowded lit-up street, full of music, and the distant sounds of traffic, sidewalks filled with the riotous drunken laughter of pedestrians streaming by, as I make my way back to her apartment.

* * *

I tremble inside and I know this night will be like no other. By her expression, she knows it too, as she undresses me.

She allows herself to stand here, naked, in this candlelit room, where my heart sings a song.

In this little apartment where the window is open, the sounds of traffic distant, laughter and shouting in the streets.

Mid-summer's intoxication, the wild Oslo night, my countrymen all wound up, the smell of chocolate and lavender and wine, sweet on my lips.

In a land touched by the summer's spell, when the sun spins its intoxication and this woman comes to me with an iris in her hair.

One day I watched as a moth entered a candle's flame.

Peeking behind her right ear, the flower she calls *Hrvatska Perunika*. Her accent tickles the letters, and she pulls up close, as she removes my shirt, and unbuckles my belt. As I remove my clothes, and underwear, and we sit hip to hip on the bed's edge.

"Har-vat-ska Per-un-i-ka," she whispers the flowers name.

I gently kiss her, her forehead, her nose, her oiled skin, aglow in the candle's flame, as she begins to sigh, and we lay back, on the bed.

I mount her, grinding slowly, gently, in a manner like a wave, on the shoreline, rising, falling, rising, falling, her voice trembling, my voice heaving, a sound I have never heard before, an ecstasy no man has shared.

It is like the way the wind is warmed, in that meadow called Salmetid, when it blows into the sun-warmed valley, when the sun is high in the sky.

And you walk barefoot, hand in hand, and her voice, like the wind, echoes. Where the moss is soft under my bare feet, where the wind blows in warm, where crags of stone run smooth, boulders huge as houses and pebbles small as chestnuts. Where lichen touches the big stones, marking them, in blotches half grey, and brown, and mauve, colour splattered all around as if the heavens had opened.

A fir tree drops to the ground. A boulder drops to the sea.

A woman's voice, filled with ecstasy, echoes in the mountains.

Mia's voice, as my lips gently kiss her breasts, swollen, her voice a tremor, a climax lingering.

I will draw it from her, as I draw a sketch, it will be hours before we will rise again, from this bed.

She whispers slowly, her voice trailing, and building, there is a sadness mixed with fear.

"There is a small violet-coloured snail, born blind, living on the sea, on the surface. When it grows up it makes a raft of mucus, and bubbles, and if it slips below the sea, and sinks, it will die."

She takes my hand from her breast, to her lips, as she kisses, her voice now pleading, weeping, words tinged with an inner pleading.

"Andreas, you must not die."

The tears dropping from my eyes, *I know now, I can never go back. I have known this truth my whole life, the truth from the heart lying below mine, I feel her quickened heartbeat.*

I have always loved Mia, I have loved men because I was too afraid to release myself in her arms, as I do now.

Because we together are so intense, we burn too bright. She has a way with me.

* * *

The way the wind stirs, the way I was blinded by the sun, the way I have come out of these shadows and she places her hand to my face, and her fingers traipse from my forehead to the bridge of my nose, that nose made anew by the surgeon's art.

A fire burning in my fingertips. "I live now for you, Mia."

I place my hands between her legs, in that soft, smooth place where there lies a longing, as the way the ocean longs for the shore, and her voice now rising, as her sighs flow with mine, and we grind, slow, like the rising and falling of a conductor's wand.

I hear Grieg, I hear a piano, it is my father, in my grandfather's old house, the echo of his fingers tapping the keys, the windows are open, the curtains flutter.

I am a happy boy, on the stone doorstep, sketching a single rose, as it hangs alone on the trellis.

The way all this happens, and the barely noticeable trembling of her lips as she whispers, she loves me, makes me whisper a prayer.

When she sees my lips tremble, I see in my mind's eye a bird, a great seabird, with silver wings, and the light captures me like a spark.

She tells me we can be married in the church in Fannrem, where my grandfather's name is engraved in gold, in the baptismal font where the names of the prisoners were inscribed, the Grini prisoners, heroic men who lived to see their country break the yoke of fascism.

She will wear a red vest with gold braid. I tell her I will wear a traditional Norwegian costume, and then my words strike me, that here, a woman whom I have known just a short time, has just proposed to me, and I have accepted.

She tells me we are not so different, we are full of passion, and one day I will forgive, and enter a church.

And there I will kneel and take communion.

IV

WE GET AWAY

I am blinded by the light, I hear her words, spoken softly, lost in the moment.

We get away

It was a no-joke German machine, a BMW 1200, Mia zipped up her leather jacket, adjusted her helmet.

"We need to get away. Far away. Andreas, it is time for the wind in your face."

"It is time to look out to the sea. I need this as much as you."

Getting upon the saddle, adjusting the helmet, my head swimming from the night before.

"Where do we go?"

"Along the coast. We are going up North. I want to see the sea. Let's go! We are on the road!"

Before I have time to hold tight, she starts the bike, it's humming like a Swiss watch, off we go, speeding off into the dark and empty street, the bike's headlight casting its electric beam into the blackness.

* * *

I can tell you about the wild ride taking the backroads, taking E16 up north along the Swedish border, going east to Oppland, on the sideroads, up to Bjoneroa, along route 245 to 33, then 251 up to E6 and Dovre.

I can bore you with the travel log, up route 63 east to Geiranger, leisurely coasting north along 710 and 715 toward Lofoton, on those beautiful, winding roads.

I can tell you how the wind struck my face, the sensations of taking off the helmet, the blast of Arctic wind, the unspeakable joy seeing Norway through Mia's eyes, blue as the ocean, and the sky, weather perfect, cloudless skies and unseasonably warm.

As when we stopped at that lookout on the coast in Tranøy, and Mia looked at her iPhone and read the temperature. Thirty-one degrees Celsius! It was warmer here, than on the Croatian coast!

I can fill my diary with loose scraps, the little drawings, my knapsack filled with crumbled paper, because I had written poems, and I couldn't bear reading them, it was all too intense, as when she crept up on me, there under the three stone statues in Tranøy.

The windblown hair, of the three stone women, eyes locking the sea, the windswept sea.

I thought of Jedranka, and Mia's mother Miraja, and this woman, Mia.

My poem for Mia, the little scribbling of my pencil, a sentence I remembered, written by Franz Kafka, whose words I spoke, not knowing she listened, "You are the knife I turn inside myself. That is love."

Just simple, idle words heard by Mia, she had crept up on me, and she whispers, "I missed you."

And then, there, under the shadowless statues, where the sun sat overhead, we just stare, the tension of the moment frozen in time.

The way she extends her finger to my face, the face made whole by the surgeon's hand, how minutes pass, there is no distraction, eyes locking eyes, as if our faces were stone.

That is how I want us to be remembered, our gazes locked, our hands on one another's face, the touch that lingers.

* * *

Kneeling here, on a blanket under the shadow of these stone women of Tranøy, as the sun sits on the sea, we have come back to this holy place.

Mia stands, she goes to the statue, the one closest to the sea, the women with black, windswept hair, whose waist sits on a granite rectangle, a woman with arms elbow-bent to her chest, over her heart.

"This is Jedranka. This woman, beloved by my mother." Mia kisses the statue's stone lips.

She takes her hands to my face, her palms pressed gently on my cheeks. The warmth of her hands, the dark, moist eyes, how they pierce me.

"A killer always comes back to the scene of the crime, Andreas. We must get back, to your grandfather's house."

"The police report said it was a suicide." Mia looks away.

"My mother once told me a fable. It frightened me. I don't know why she told me, I was a girl, it was a story her father once told her. It was about a boy, a demon child. He breaks into houses at night. His name was Malik Tintilinic. He was unbaptised, that is why he was a demon."

"What are you saying?"

Mia turns from me, stands, walks a step or two, facing the ocean.

There is a moment, it is as if she is a bird, the way she stretches out her arms, lifting them up, to the sky, her face to the cloudless sun, the light striking her.

I am blinded by the light, I hear her words, spoken softly, lost in the moment.

* * *

It has been a day of laughter, and escape. We played a children's game, hide-and-seek, seeing her escape into the lighthouse, running up all those flights of steps, finding her waiting for me.

Looking out to sea. "What will become of us?" she asked, turning to me, as we kissed, and the passion moved me, as nothing mattered any more.

"This love I seek, this love is unreachable." I whisper, as she pulls away, her face revealing hurt.

"You are wrong, Andreas Olav Hansen. It is not unreachable."

I took off my sunglasses, shut my eyes, the sun blinded me, I saw her figure. Against the horizon, leaning against the railing, opening and shutting my eyes, thinking I see an angel, an angel with gossamer wings, I can't help myself, this damn sensitive beating heart of mine, grasping for something I am too afraid to touch.

I reach my hands out to her, she reaches hers to mine, there are words spoken, she is telling me something in a language, it is Arabic, words I have never known.

I go to her, grasp the iron rails, the sun sits atop the sea.

She is singing, singing to the ocean, the words are broken, full of sadness, a song as I have never heard, beautiful, flowing words.

She has come to the end of the song, her voice softens, to a whisper, turning to me, her eyes full of tears.

"There's a fire of desire that burns, from the bottom of my heart, who can put it out except the sea of your love? That was Jedranka's song."

Then I discover words, something my father said, how he had written on a scrap of paper *I am not her father*, how I found that scrap of paper, and asked if he had something to tell me.

Why was he writing all the letters to this woman, was that why my mother had left us?

I was seventeen, he had discovered my secret. We were in the big room downstairs in my grandfather's house, it was a summer's night, the room glowed from the light coming in the open windows.

I had come in the front door; my father was there to meet me. "I am sorry, Andreas."

"Sorry about what?"

"Sorry I have not been a better father. Sorry I have kept things from you. I just wanted to protect you from yourself."

Sitting on the sofa, how his eyes locked with mine.

The way his intelligent, searching eyes met mine, as I felt a stirring in me, like the hearing of a distant voice, his words spoken in the night. Words rising like curls of smoke, up through the cracks in the rotten floorboards, stinging my nostrils, because I was just a boy, and my father spoke to me, in the dark. As I lay still in my grandfather's bed, on a midsummer's eve, waiting until the sun would set, when the walls turned black, and the shadows of my fingers appeared, when they grasped the pencil, and I heard her voice calling. How my father secretly crept up on me, thinking I slept, but I was awake, I knew he was in the room. How he touched my face, how my nose was changing, collapsing, how this disease has awakened, slowly, without my knowing, because it sneaks up, like a shadow. His finger touches the place, he weeps, I hear his voice.

"I am sorry, little Andreas, I am sorry. Sleep, little friend, sleep, and dream how the river rushes to the sea. How the sun rises, how one day you will forgive me, and then forget."

The stars, the moon, a shooting star

I felt your beating heart next to mine.

The rolling sea.

I know where I am. I know you are lying next to me under a blanket on this boat deck under a million stars.

There is a flash in the sky, a glowing ribbon dancing. Phosphor whips between the white capped mountains, a word hangs on my lips.

It is your name.

Mia Miraja.

Mia, *meaning mine.*

I spell it now, each letter a whisper.

I can make out shapes, and a midsummer's glow, and feel the mountains of Lofoton and the way the clean air fills my lungs.

You said my heart had stopped when you fished me up from the bottom of the lake.

Now it beats again.

You kissed my lips, blew air into my lungs, brought me back to life.

* * *

I know the secret you have kept from me.

Because last night you spoke it in your sleep, and I tell you this now, as you listen, as I feel your breathe on my skin, on my chest, where you have lain your head.

You will bear a son.

We will name him Marko.

So, you weep now, as I speak with you, and there is nothing to say but to listen to the wind, and the waves breaking on the bow.

Tomorrow we will pass through the Troll fjørd and touch those great cliffs, where our cruise ship, the *Midnight Sun*, slips by, as we take in this beautiful landscape.

I can tell you about our trip on the Hurtigruta.

Up along the west coast of Norway, from Bergen all the way north to Norway's tip at North Cape.

The way a woman moans, the way a ship swells on the sea, the way a glass of white wine numbs you to your troubles and this woman whispers she fell in love when I first touched her, all this sets me to think. I can die tomorrow, but today I have lived, and that is meaning enough for me.

How words cannot express how I feel because I never felt this hunger before.

Is it a crime to lie with a man?

The police office is above Hansen's bakery, up one flight of steps, down a hallway to the door with the sign *'Lensmannskontor'*.

I feel stronger in my legs now that I have gained some weight, I carry a leather bag with the money.

I carry a leather satchel with a locked metal metal box with the money.

When I enter the office, I see a man's back turned to me at a desk shuffling papers.

"Excuse me, officer. I am Andreas Olav Hansen."

Above him on the wall, a dozen old black-and-white photographs in stylised gold frames of the town's sheriffs, going all the way back to my great-grandfather. Hans H.- in his high white cravat, bushy sideburns, pince-nez glasses, and that stern look, the same look staring at me from his painting in my grandfather's bedroom.

Officer Brandahl is big muscled, about thirty-five, wears glasses, is as stiff as they come, in a crisp, tight fitting blue short-sleeve shirt. *Amazing, how I can see colour.*

He looks up from his papers, stares at my face for a moment, removes his glasses, stares some more. He is startled by what he sees. I know what he thinks. It is my face.

My beautiful, smooth face, my new clothes and shoes, my hair cropped short.

I could have escaped, no one would have recognised me. I have been on his radar for months, ever since they showed up at the house, the night they found Ida.

"Andreas Olav Hansen?"

The skin on his face is not smooth, it's dry, full of white, ugly stubble, like he hadn't time to shave, or look at himself in a mirror.

I remove my sunglasses. I place the leather bag on the counter.

His eyes lock with mine, he clenches his teeth, the way the facial muscles tighten, he is like a spring, winding himself up.

Brandahl is not one who reveals his feelings. He keeps them inside, all bottled up.

There must be just one important thought inside his brain, he sees me, The Syphilis Artist, standing here, this crazy artist, who lies down with men, who has walked the streets at night, a shadow, who has been visited time and again by the police.

Now, with a new smiling face, what has come over me?

The officer tries to form words, his lips twitch, he is caught up in something.

"Officer Brandahl," I ask, "is it a crime to lie with a man?"

The colour leaves his face. "Excuse me?"

"I said, is it a crime to lie with a man?"

There is a grimace, a tightening of muscle, his upper lip twitches. "No, homosexuality is not a crime in Norway," he says matter-of-factly.

"Officer Brandahl," I continue, "I have a confession."

I see I have caught his attention.

"I have a confession. I confess I was born guilty of a crime."

"And what crime might that be?"

"I live, that is my crime."

It is that unsolved murder, poor Ida, found hanging upside down, her ankles bound, poor, naked Ida, swinging back and forth, like a pendulum, because the wind was strong when they found her.

"Your face. You have changed."

I take out from my leather satchel the metal box with the hundred thousand crowns. Brandahl eyes the box. "Come with me into my office."

He gets up from his chair, I follow him down the hallway to his tiny office, where he sits down, turns on his computer; after a minute, he stares hard at me, with his grey, emotionless eyes, and I realise suddenly why I would never be able to draw his face, because it is blank, there is nothing there but facts and figures.

I recounted the morning I found the cardboard box of money on the doorstep, how I counted the money and was amazed there was over one hundred thousand crowns. How it was from old man Svein Torkildsen.

"Svein Torkildsen, Trond Torkildsen's father?" Something piqued the officer's attention.

I didn't know Trond, the butcher from Sirdal, the man who took Lena from me, except that he lived in the next town, had moved to a small farm where he raised sheep, chickens, and some cows.

He slaughtered the animals, dressed the meat, sold it, here in town.

Officer Brandahl opens the metal box, sees the hundred notes stacked in wads and tied together in rubber bands. He takes the money into a new envelope, seals it shut, labelling it with a black marker, and locks it into a drawer.

"Before you go you will sign some papers. If you give us permission, we will keep this until the investigation is over."

"What investigation?"

Officer Brandahl pulls out some files from a drawer.

I put on my thick glasses and make out Trond Torkildsen's name on one of the files.

He spreads out old newspaper clippings on the desk, there must be over one hundred pages in the file, which Brandahl is now poring over.

"Have you ever met Trond Torkildsen?"

"I saw him once with my girlfriend."

I see a newspaper clipping from the Agder paper with a headline about a woman who had been raped.

"Do you know his father, Svein?"

I tell Brandahl I recall how he came to the house when my father was younger. They would go on trips together; I knew they were drinking buddies. One hot summer night when I was a teen, Svein came barging into Grandfather's house, drunk, swinging his arms around, because he told my father he had been in a fight, and he needed a drink. A few of his front teeth were knocked out. My father gave him a cup of coffee. He struck my father, taking with him a bottle of whiskey, as my disillusioned father stood at the doorway, shaking his head, as Svein disappeared back into the forest.

"This money you found at the doorstep, why did the old man give it to you?

"Do you know? Was there an explanation? Have you spoken with him?"

I knew Brandahl was familiar with my father's case, he was the officer who had written the report, how it was a suicide. That is what the medical report had concluded and there was no need to investigate the report further.

"We are short of staff; it was smart of you to get those crowns out of the house."

I am beginning to like this Officer Brandahl. I get up to leave, walk back down the steps.

"Also, one more thing."

I turn around, he stands looking down from the top of the stairwell. "There is someone breaking into homes, crawling through open windows. You wouldn't know anything about that, would you?"

I walk back up the steps. My legs bear my weight, I feel strong. My knees no longer ache. From my leather shoulder bag, I remove an A4 envelope. I hand it to him.

He takes out the pencil sketch, studies it, his mouth goes slack. "Is this a photograph?"

"No. It's a pencil drawing."

* * *

In the distance I spy a silent black mass around a grave, where I see the priest's long white robe fluttering, like the white ribbon that fluttered from my father's grave, a silky white banner trimmed with gold, with a name, and a final greeting, written in black marker.

The barn is on fire!

I awake to the tick-tock of the grandfather clock.

The clock chimes eleven times, we have slept late.

The window is open, the new snow-white lacy curtains, the ones she hung last night, billow in.

The house is full of the smell of wildflowers, the ones she picked in the garden last night, when we came back from the shore, and she drove all the way to the front door, having discovered the back road that leads to the house. *On that road full of weeds with the rusty gate that now is unlocked and swung open, because she says we will have guests, the house will be painted, the gardens will bloom again.*

On the nightstand two empty crystal wine glasses, an empty bottle of wine, a Frankovka, and a wild red rose.

She told me I will teach again, I will teach modern art, like I did in that private school, and she said last night she had a surprise for me, good news from Oslo. She would tell me today, over a breakfast of homemade pancakes, the flat thin ones I love, and will sip herbal tea, and then we will go for a walk in the woods.

When the church bells ring soon, they will stream into the church, through those double front doors, old Mrs. Gundersen in her floral hat leading the flock.

They will see the painting and wonder who the artist is.

There will be a shudder, it will so quiet you can hear a pin drop.

The balcony overflowing, Levi entering, in that flowing white robe, followed by a stream of children, and the mothers, and their babies cradled in their arms, because there will be baptisms. And mounting the altar, and up again in that little tower, past that little painting of Jesus by the Lubeck artist, that old painting in a gold frame.

There will be dozens in the church, waiting for Levi to pull the curtain string, revealing this masterpiece.

At least that is how it was described in the papers, how it created a local sensation, and people thought it was the work of that other artist in the valley, Frode S.

The floor-to-ceiling mural of Jesus and the angel, the faceless woman with gossamer wings and olive skin, embracing this fair-skinned man with eyes the colour of the sea. This beautiful sensitive face, the face of an artist, framed in chestnut flowing hair, and this angel, in a background of rainbow coloured light cut with a knife.

* * *

I place my fingers lightly on her face, and let them dance downward, to her neck, playfully lower, under the covers.

She awakens. There is a smile on her face. She whispers in my ear.

A woman's voice, filled with ecstasy, echoes in the mountains. The old grandfather clock chimes. I count the bells.

"One... Two... Three... Eleven! — The unveiling of Jesus! We slept late!" On this pine bed with carved rose petals.

I know old Sheriff Hansen looks down at me, from that painting.

I hear the ringing of church bells in the valley. Mia doesn't seem concerned we will walk in late to the service.

"Do you love me, Andreas?"

* * *

"Will you always love me, Andreas?" She lies with her head in my armpit.

Her hair is black silk, I play with the stands, the way they slip and fall between my fingers.

I turn my head and face her. She has a worried look.

"And now you love this man Jesus. You love him, Andreas. Don't you? You love him because he is a man, a beautiful man, like the way you loved Eirik."

She looks at the ceiling, and her words are worried, and I know what she thinks.

"I found the letters you had written to him."

I thought I had burned all of them. That day I found him in the hospital, that night I found the letters and tossed them in the fire.

There are tears welling in her eyes.

"Andreas, I accept you. But you must tell me now, honestly, that you can commit to me, I am old fashioned that way, I need to know, now."

Before I have time to form my words, I hear something downstairs. "Did you hear something?"

My question startles Mia, she gets out of bed, puts on a robe.

I am out of bed in my underwear and wool socks, I walk noiselessly to a crack in the door.

"There are footsteps."

Mia's expression reveals fear.

"I will call the police! Don't go downstairs!"

"No, Mia, don't call the police. I think I know who it is."

I wait and listen, and hear wheezing, like some dog, out of breath, it is an animal noise, and then there is coughing, a violent, guttural cough, and words spoken in anger, swear words slurred, echoing loudly.

I walk down the steps to the landing, the door is open, the sunlight stabs in, there is the ringing of church bells in the valley. The smell of smoke.

"Do you smell smoke, Mia?"

The bells stop ringing, as my eyes adjust to the light and I make out a short, dishevelled figure in a stained white linen garb, standing in the open doorway. The figure is holding a red plastic can in one hand, a lighter in the other.

Mia yells, "The barn is on fire!"

Now that all is dark again

The following events are so startling, recalling them now in this hospital bed, in a room full of a rose's scent, that I cannot help to think it was a hallucination. Leo will come soon. He will take me to the shore.

Now that all is dark again, now that I have received the news, there is a lightness of being, like the way a bird's feather floats. I am spent. My winged spirit has taken flight, the black-eyed raven atop the church's tower shadows me no more.

Memory has had a way with me, things have happened, like the way I can sketch with my pencils for hours, and I have drawn just a few lines, then I tear up the paper, disgusted with the idea.

The memory of a cloud passing.

With a snap of my fingers, I quit myself with those violent scenes, what happened between those pine-timbered walls the colour of dark tea can no longer disturb me.

Now that the killer's mystery has been solved, now that poor and gentle Ida, the girl who just needed a warm embrace, can rest, in the grave in the churchyard where the river bends, this is enough for me.

I placed a rose by the wood cross marking her grave, I knelt, the ground was cold to the touch. "I am sorry, Ida" I whispered, "I am sorry this happened to you, I am sorry my sweet Ida, forgive me."

How Abdi's gentle words whispered behind my back because he came to me, out of the shadow of the church tower, as I knelt, his touch on my shoulder was enough.

"There is a saying that might is right. But I say right is might. You are right to forgive, Andreas, in that you are a mighty man."

* * *

The way my tears fell, how that simple and profound word 'forgive' shook me to the bone, how light I felt afterwards.

In the shadow of the church tower, Jesus spoke to me, I felt whole. Something of me will linger on, when I am gone, for that I am happy.

The doctors tell me the shock of the events in my grandfather's house, in the old jail cell, the violence of my reaction, and the unsettling quiet lingering after the final blow, was enough. Somehow, I accept that fact.

Mia Miraja doesn't know.

The absolution of knowing who killed *Little Harold, the only father I have ever known*, the events surrounding his father's struggle with that madman, the confession and the fitting consequence following, is enough for me.

V

LEVI

To describe what I did next shakes me; when I was finished with him, I felt pity for Mia, because I know she watched, and things would never be the same again.

His face was downcast

My eyes focused, it was a short man with downcast eyes, in a priest's white linen surplice.

The garb was stained with wine, and dirty, like he had been out rolling in the dirt.

His face was downcast, a shadow.

I was frozen, because the image in front of me was like something I had dreamed once, a night terror. There is a knock at the door, you go down and turn the key, there appears a shadow, faceless.

I stretch out my hand to feel, but there is nothing there, it is a ghost of my imagination.

When this shadow finally lifted his face from the floor, I saw it was Levi, wearing his reading glasses.

"I don't know how many times my fish-lines got stuck in that goddamn bush

- one day I'll grab gasoline and a lighter and sacrifice the whole fucker to Satan!" his voice slurred, as he steadied himself in the open doorway, reaching his hand to a shelf. Levi's fleshy face was contorted in anguish.

I brushed his glasses off his face.

"Levi!" I yelled, shaking him by the shoulders.

Then I remembered. I would be late for the unveiling.

Levi's black beady eyes like a raven, sunken in his skull, he has aged since I saw him last, there are black, tired circles under his eyes.

"The ceremony! The unveiling of my painting! Explain yourself!"

"I killed Ida," he says, matter-of-factly, as he collapses in my arms, lets out a wail.

It is a cry of anguish, as I have never heard before, like an organ's bellowing wail.

There is a moment when I gather my thoughts, it all comes back to me. How I would wake up in the night, seeing Ida hanging head down, her ankles bound by rope. Lying in the snow, seeing this shadow.

There is an anger inside me, I don't know if I can control myself, it is like all these years the anger has been building, and building, and now this man who I called a friend says that he has killed gentle Ida, who came to lie next to me one cold winter night. The young woman Ida whose blood led to the front door of this old house.

I grabbed Levi by the stained robe, found the strength to drag him up the steep and narrow steps into the jail cell.

I locked us inside the cell. Mia had put on some clothes, started to yell and bang on the broomstick iron bars; all I remember is Levi's face, that fleshy, round face, the shock of it all as his beady raven eyes opened wide.

My eyesight was knife sharp, as I grabbed this round little man by his throat, threw him against the bars, finding in me a strength summoned from some dark place.

"Stop, Andreas!" Mia's shouting fading, as I ignored her.

"What do you mean, you killed Ida!" I yelled.

I released my hold on his neck, allowed him to speak. His face had turned lobster red, his black eyes bulged, locked onto mine.

"I took her into the barn." His confessional voice, monotone, as cold as ice.

"What- did- you- do- in- the- barn, Levi?"

My voice was firm, and controlled, my anger welling up like a maelstrom, like water rushing from a fresh winter's melt.

The idea that this kindly man whose face I once slapped, who turned the other cheek, as I slapped it, and saw the kindly face of my white Jesus, hard blue eyes upturned to the heavens, killed gentle Ida, was too much for me.

"Andreas, I called the police! Open the door!" Mia's shouting, her fists banging on the bars, her yells fading as my shouting increased in volume, as Levi's cries wailed like a howling wolf.

"I raped Ida in the barn. She was screaming, I became frightened, I tried to sooth her, her screaming wouldn't stop. I cupped her mouth with my hand, she bit it, I got angry and cut her throat."

To describe what I did next shakes me; when I was finished with him, I felt pity for Mia, because I know she watched, and things would never be the same again.

Levi had tried to escape like some cornered animal, his drunken round little body was no match to my anger.

"You killed Ida! How could you kill Ida!" I yelled, with a voice so loud the spittle sprayed from my mouth.

He broke a beer bottle against the bars, when he attacked me, I knocked him to the floor with a right hook landing squarely on his jaw. He awakened something inside me, an animal violence, he saw this, as I stood over him, as I removed my clothing.

"Take off your clothes!" I yelled, as he trembled in the corner, obeying my command, as I rolled a cigarette, taking my time, feeling a numbness come over me like the clouds gathering in the valley.

There was the distant crack of thunder.

There was a sore inside my mouth, a lump like a hazelnut, newly formed, I discovered it not long ago.

Now it throbbed, it was the only thing I felt, as Levi hesitantly took off his clothes.

Off came the stained white linen surplice, off came his pants and shirt and underwear, as his fat round body trembled alabaster white in front of me, his tiny balls hidden by folds of stomach flesh.

I followed his eyes, how they locked on my chest, where I had carved my tattoo, where once the blood ran from the knife, because I had locked myself in this room. Because I was weeping, they had called me names, dirty little disgusting names,

when they discovered my secret.

Levi's raven eyes lock onto my tattoo, 'ARTIST'.

I go over to him, grabbing his right hand, making his trembling fingers feel where I cut myself, as I bend down so my head is level with his, and I kiss him, violently, so his eyes bulge, those beady raven eyes full of hate.

Eyes full of hate, eyes shadowing me all these years, sneaking behind my back, looking in the window.

Raven eyes hunting me, spying on me, as I painted this white-faced Jesus, alone with Eirik on the altar, where he removed his clothes.

Where he and I made love, under the little Lubeck cross, where Jesus's unfinished face looked up to the heavens, and Eirik's cries of joy struck me, because I knew I was being watched.

I knew one day I would get my revenge.

During the act, before everything went black, I looked into Levi's face, full of impenetrable sadness, the like of which I have never seen before.

His raven eyes black, staring cold and frozen, his teeth clenched tight, the pain of my violence causing him to bang his right fist on the floor, the banging keeping tempo with my penetration as my words fell like angry hammer blows.

"The old priest Torbjørn called me a Satanist! He told my mother I was going to hell because I slept with a boy! Who is going to hell now!"

Levi's whimpering, this sorry little man who raped Ida in my grandfather's barn, in the shadow of those mountains.

"There is no heaven! There is no hell! Except what we create here on earth!" I cried.

Levi's fist banging louder, his hand knuckles bloodied, a sudden thunderbolt flashing, the room exploding with a sharp flicker of light, then extinguishing, the heavens cracking open, as raindrops hit loud on the windows.

The summer's midday was filled with blackness like the night, the church bells had stopped ringing; the locals would wonder what has happened to Levi.

The window angrily blowing open, the smell of smoke from the burning barn, the rain driving into the room, on our naked bodies.

The violence of my attack throbbing deep inside him, as my shame fled, and my heart was filled with hate, a terrible, awakened hate.

"My mother hated the day I was born! She locked me up in this cell, she infected me with syphilis! And who infected her? It was Torbjørn, the old priest, whom you have been protecting all these years!"

Levi's wailing's now, increasing, as he has given up his protests, his body limp on the floor, I sense there is not so much difference between us, both tortured souls.

When it was all over Levi lying on his side, bruised and naked and cut up on the floor, curled in a foetal position, staring blankly, the only *sound his heavy breathing and the nervous shaking of his hands on the floor, like he was having a seizure.*

I knelt on the floor, laid beside him, my face a hand's length from his, I felt his clenched right hand, forcefully opened it, though I was now all blind.

I saw not even a shadow, something had exploded in my head, during the act. I felt alive, wonderfully and dangerously alive, I knew I would never see again. I opened his clenched fist; took the little crucifix he had held on to.

"Is it contagious?" he asks, with a voice feeble and broken, as my fingers lightly tap his forehead, running down to his whispered question, as my fingers circle his mouth, and I am thinking I could never sketch this man, this little priest, because he has no soul.

"Is it contagious!" his broken tremulous voice now pleading, as I forcefully open his mouth, and I kiss him, with a deep, tongued kiss, the violence of the act heightened by his protest, the way he tried to break my hands grasp, as I clutched his face, and finally withdrew my tongue. The way he just lay there, this fat-bellied little priest murderer as I bolted up, the utter silence, as I got up to my feet, and said, responding calmly to his question,

"What do you think?"

I have learnt to love the darkness

How we began the bright day with a lover's unbridled expectation, not knowing, or caring, nothing mattered, but to lie the whole day, in each other's embrace.

The doctors said my sickness was cured, Mia asked me for commitment.

I felt I was ready to give it to her. The letters were written, in India ink, on that special handmade paper, written on my father's desk, each letter accompanied by a pencil drawing.

There was a letter to Tor-Inge, and Eirik, a long one to Abdi with a pencil drawing.

There was *this novel*, these words I write, with a pencil, writing on a pad of yellow lined paper, the way I have been writing all these months, at my father's desk.

In a house where I had cut the wires, Mia filled the house with little candles, the way the house glows at night, the way the windows sparkle—Mia said it is like Saint Stefan's church, in Vienna, where her mother knelt on her knees. And asked for forgiveness.

Mia tells me in the dark we create our own light. In the dark we touch one another, minutes, hours, time passes, not a sound is heard but her whispers and the patter of rain on the windows.

Mia says she is not afraid I could infect her; she has been going to the doctor for check-ups, she would not sleep with me if I was sick.

I have learnt to love the darkness in the shadows. I have learnt I can live without machines.

But I cannot live without passion, I cannot breathe without lifting a pencil, and drawing a line.

All I knew on that fateful day when Levi showed up at the doorstep was the fact that there was unfinished business of my father's suicide and Ida's murder.

It was as if I had already known.

I was not a murderer, this horror I imagined in the forest was a ghost of my daydreams, it was an hallucination.

Maybe I wanted to be the murderer.

There was the heavy guilt of living, I wanted secretly to be put behind bars. After all, that is what my mother wanted, to put me away.

Yes, I had been with Ida, I was awakened by her yelling, coming from the barn, I had gone outside to the doorstep where I saw the blood, followed the trail into the forest.

Where I saw Ida hanging lifeless from the tree, and a shadow, only an hallucination would spare me from contemplating the awful fact that this evil was real.

There was a pencil drawing by that artist M.F. from the other valley. 'Adam Leaving Paradise' is the title.

A downcast figure, a man's face hidden by an elbow raised and bent, shrouding the eyes, cast from the mythical garden.

I was overcome with grief. Levi at my feet, blankly staring. The police and fire trucks would take forever to get here.

A hand placed on my shoulder. Mia, weeping, on the other side of the bars. My hands reached out to her face, she firmly grabbed my right hand, pushed it away, her voice a whisper stabbing into me.

"What you have done is wrong, Andreas- Olav- Hansen."

She cries, tears dropping, dropping onto my fingers. Her voice, a sorrowful lament on a summer's day, whispers softly, as her words are spoken with deep meaning, as if she has spared me for this moment.

I burned your father's book

There was a letter from my father to me, he had written about the book, I had nothing but some letters, and my journal.

"Your father had written a story about two Norwegians on holiday, in Vienna, in 1985. In a little bar they had met a woman, a medical student and artist, whose name was Marija, my mother's name. This captivating woman Marija invited the Norwegians to her apartment where they both raped her."

"What are you telling me, Mia? What do you want me to know?"

"The names of the Norwegians were Harold Hansen and Svein Torkildsen. He used his own name. *This book was not a fictional book,* Andreas. It was a confession. I was born nine months after Marija's rape. I was conceived in that little room full of flowers, in that apartment in the shadow of Saint Stefan's Cathedral. The man, *Svein Torkildsen,* is my father."

Svein Torkildsen was the old man who showed up on the front step with the cardboard box of money.

"Your father believed he, Harold Hansen, was the father. It was him who sent my mother money, but she lied to me, said Alessio was my father, a man I never knew. When I found the letters your father had written, I finally knew the truth."

Levi's voice, a wail, awakening.

"Svein, the butcher from Sirdal, he will kill me!"

Levi is up on his feet, before I had time to answer there came the sound of sounds of furniture tossed, a deep, strong voice I have heard before.

A man's voice yelling from downstairs, "Levi! What did you do with the money? Levi, you devil!"

Levi recognised the voice.

"The butcher from Sirdal! He will kill me!"

I pull on my jeans, feel my way out the cell, making sure to turn the key in the lock. I brush by Mia, I feel her laying in the bed, my fingers touch her face, I feel tears, I slide myself forward, along the wall, out the doorway, and start going down the steps. I hear footsteps in the living room, the man is searching for something.

"*Fi fann!*"

I am now the wolf, in the shadows. I know this house, I know how to slide up behind him, coming down to the landing. The door is open, I feel a cold wind, hear distant police sirens, weaponed officers will be here soon.

I sense him standing in front of me. Big Trond Torkildsen, the butcher from Sirdal.

"Where is Levi!" he yells, in a belligerent tone.

I am not afraid. I extend my hand up to his head, as my fingers migrate slowly to his bald scalp, then retrace their tapping down the hot, smooth skin of his face, all the while hearing his heavy breathing, knowing he could knock me senseless. I am not afraid, I sense something about him, as my hand migrates down his barrel chest, the shirt is open, my fingers play over his hard-muscled six pack, reaching down his shirt, feeling his muscles tense.

I hear a new set of church bells ringing distant, the bells the church rings for a burial. That is strange, since today Levi and I would have been at the altar for the unveiling of my masterpiece. The bells just ring and ring. They have found out. *Brandahl has told them.*

The bells stop ringing. The police sirens echo loud, then there is silence, they must have parked their vehicles down below the house.

My hand follows the muscled contours of his bare right forearm, the hand and tightly clenched fingers wrapped around the cold steel of a butcher's knife. I feel the razor edge. I hear the man, talking in a calm voice.

"My name is Trond Torkildsen, you know, Lena's boyfriend. Has he confessed? Has Levi confessed to his crime?

"Yes. He confessed. He said he killed Ida."

"Ida? The unsolved winter murder? Was that Levi?" he asks incredulously.

"What are you talking about? What crime are you talking about?"
"Hasn't he told you?"
"Told me what?"

Trond explains he was in the church, in the front pew, waiting for me to show up. Levi was at the altar, lighting the candles, and when he came back to the lectern, he had a crazy look.

Brandahl, the police officer arrived, he had a weapon. Levi fled out the back door, Trond chased him in the forest. He explained he has been secretly employed by Brandahl these past several months to shadow Levi.

"This paedophile evil priest shot your father. I heard him today whispering his confession in the church service."

"Killed my father!"

I crumbled to the floor, as I felt Mia by my side, pulling me up into her lap.

In my tears, my final absolution.

In Mia's trembling lips, her absolution, because in this open doorway, I hear her say, "Trond is my brother. Blood tests were done. Trond is a good man. He has been working with the police. There was a strong suspicion that Levi had killed your father; a court order allowed the police to spy on this house, because the killer always comes back to the scene of the crime. I am sorry, I was going to tell you."

Trond explains his bedridden father told him the story months ago.

Svein Torkildsen had confessed he had gotten carried away one night with my father; they met a beautiful young woman in a bar, in downtown Vienna. She was a medical student and an artist.

The year was 1984. They were invited to her apartment, one thing led to another, they both ended up in bed with the dark-haired woman, Marija. Svein was violently drunk, there was a fight between my father and Svein. Svein raped Marija, she never filed charges, Trond convinced my father that he, and not Svein, was the father of the girl Mia, who was born on the island of Pag, nine months later.

* * *

On the floor, lifting my head from Mia's lap, hearing Trond's explanation, thinking how all these years my good father had been tormented, because he just accepted the fact that he must have been the father by the circumstances of the case.

After all, Svein was his best friend, his drinking companion.

Svein, the coward who couldn't face up to his deed. And my meek father, who just accepted things, like the way he blindly accepted my mother, when she slapped him on his face, when my father drowned his sorrow in alcohol, and she escaped, because she too couldn't face the fact that she had infected her son with syphilis.

And then my sister Vilde escaped, as I started seeing shadows, it is all so much. Mia tells me her mother was ashamed, her Catholic mother who tattooed Mia's arm with mother's milk and honey.

Mia suspected that her mother knew in her heart that my father was not the rapist, her mother must have known all along it was Svein.

But her mother was ashamed, she told Mia Alessio was her father, he had died when she was an infant. My father had been wiring money to Marija's bank account for over thirty years.

Trond had convinced his ailing father Svein to do the right thing and give back the money my father had paid out. The day her mother told her the truth, Mia left for Norway.

I get up, walk back up the steep and narrow steps to my grandfather's bedroom.

I know this house; I don't need to see to find my way to the secret place under the bed where my father hid his rifle.

I don't have much time, any moment the police will show up.

I creep under the bed, feel for the loose floorboard, remove a few boards, pull out the long metal case.

It's heavy, I hear Trond and Mia shouting downstairs, lock the bedroom door, go over to the wall opposite the bed, feel for Sheriff Hansen's big painting, take it down, and there on the nail, find the key.

I take the key back to the metal box, inserting the key, turning, opening the lid, feeling for the rifle. It was my grandfather's unregistered Krag—Jørgensen, a Danish 'long krag'; I remember my father telling me it was an antique, my father kept it as a keepsake, it was never meant to be fired.

I take the rifle out of the box, lay it flat on the floor. I fiddle with the bolt, remembering how to unlock the magazine chamber. I feel the magazine popping open, I feel around for some loose cartridges in the case, I find a few, pop one into the magazine, snap the magazine closed, pull up the cold and smooth bolt handle, the sound it makes startles me.

"What are you doing!" cries Levi, as I lift the heavy rifle, turn to his cowardly voice, going over to the jail cell, so the rifle's long bore is flush against the bars, where I point the rifle down at him.

"Open the door! The police are coming! Open the door, Andreas!" Trond knocking angrily outside the bedroom.

"You- killed- my- father!"

"You killed my father!" my voice like thunder. Lowering the rifle.

I can't do this. I can't take a man's life. He must take his own. He must create his own hell on earth.

There is not much time so I scramble to my father's desk, pull out the drawer so fast it flies on the floor with all the loose papers and pencils. I scramble for a pencil, and a piece of paper, go over to the jail cell, toss the pencil and paper in.

"Write, now!" I yell.

"I am a paedophile! My mother hated me! I have never been loved! I have abused women! I have forsaken Jesus! Write it now!"

The way his scribbling on the paper fill the room, the way his broken voice wails and the window is open, I feel the midsummer's wind, not a sound is heard but footsteps coming from the hallway.

"Write, now! There is no heaven or hell!"

The anger inside me like a spring about to snap. "Write, now! I am a paedophile priest!"

"Noooooo!" Levi's loud, crazy wail, as he tears up the paper.

"I am not the paedophile! My mother loved me! It was not me! It was Torbjørn! Torbjørn is your real father!"

Silence.

Lowering the weapon, placing it on the floor, my face to the bars.

My voice as a whisper. "What are you saying, Levi? *Torbjørn is my father?*"

The front door crashing open, the stampede of boots on the landing downstairs.

"Police!"

"Up with your hands!"

The church door opens, in blows the wind

The church door opens, in comes the light.

I see in my mind's eye a great flash in the sky, a bird of the sea, with silver wings, vanishing into a cloud, a sun breaking through a scratch in the sky.

The clouds vanish, the sun touches my face, Mia's warm hand grasps mine, I think of my next painting, a stone palace on a hill by the sea.

Mia and I standing in the open door, she tells me the altar is sunlit, she tells me she wears a red vest with gold braid.

I feel the thick, silken braid.

I picture her in her traditional Slavic dress. She tells me the Gothic church is magnificent, the way the light strikes the baptismal font, the rising hard wood pillars, arching above the vaulted ceilings, the grey stone of this ancient church.

"I don't need to see, to feel. I don't need to see to know that the altar is sunlit. I feel it, Mia, my beautiful Mia. I love you, Mia. I knew I loved you when you touched my face, and whispered, I knew then, I know now."

"You look handsome, Andreas Olav Hansen. I really shined you up, haven't I?" she says playfully.

Wearing the traditional colourful Hardanger garb of my countrymen.

"The priest is late for the ceremony," she reminds me.

"Don't worry, an hour, a day, an eternity. We are now together. I have promised myself to you. I have promised myself to our son."

My hand reaching to her dress, feeling the slight baby bump. Kneeling at the magnificent baptismal font, feeling the four golden winged angels, hand carved by the sculptor Oscar Lynum, and given as a gift to the parish by the Grini prisoners. A gift for their freedom, presented in 1946, when my grandfather knelt at this altar, and gave thanks. He was a free man.

"Andreas, Andreas. I am sorry, Andreas."

An older woman's voice echoing in the empty church and footsteps meek, coming to me.

I know this voice.

I turn away from the altar, stretch my hand to the woman's face.

I feel wrinkles, the muscles are drawn tight around the mouth, I feel the earrings, the way my fingers play on this worn face, the tapping, the tears, *my mother's tears.*

I know this woman.

"Andreas, forgive me—I must tell you something."

* * *

I cradle my mother in my arms. I feel the wrinkles on her face, feel how she pulls her head back, as I grasp her head gently, and pull her close.

My mother tells me in halting words made with great effort that she was sorry for the pain she caused me.

She was sorry for locking me in the jail cell and throwing me a pencil. How she hid me from the other boys because she was ashamed.

The echo of my mother's voice in that old church is such that tears fall down Mia's face, as I hold my mother close, and whisper in her ear I was thankful she came to the wedding.

I tell her I was thankful she threw me a pencil.

I was thankful for being alone, in a dark room, by candlelight, where all I could do was draw a line on a piece of paper.

"I forgive you, mother, my dear mother."

Mia's voice. "The priest has arrived."

There is a shadow hanging over me, blocking the light.

It must be the priest.

"It was Torbjørn. I am sorry, Andreas. Please forgive me. I am sorry." She tells me I was abused by Torbjørn.

My mother was ashamed, she had an affair with Torbjørn, she wouldn't let me get treatment, otherwise it would all get out.

The wind will blow the crimson petals up and away

"We are leaving in ten minutes, Andreas. Trond is driving his new Tesla X. I am so excited!"

The scent of roses, as my fingers feel the silk petals, feeling up along the wood trellis, where the thornless stems bloom, where my hands stretch skyward, there must be dozens of newly blossomed roses.

The small paper bag is full of petals.

Trond and Mia are taking me to the pulpit. They will bear me up, on the canvas stretcher, I will lay flat on the plateau. I will stare up at the clouds and look out to the sea.

I will stretch up my hand, the wind will stir the rose petals from this paper bag.

The wind will blow the crimson petals up, and away, out to sea, and the tourists will wonder. They will not know.

The police have received a full confession from Levi. It was in all the papers. He murdered my father. And he murdered Ida. My name has been cleared. And the old rotten priest Torbjørn confessed. He had confessed he was indeed my biological father. Blood tests had been done, the results were hidden in an envelope in the desk. In Little Harold's desk, in the room where the lingering hours of my life have spent themselves, like a dying candle flame, where the police discovered the envelope sealed with a wax stamp and marked with my father's flowery handwriting. "To Andreas, whom I have loved like a father. Please forgive me."

The old rotten priest Torbjørn and my mother Wenche had an affair, the contagion syphilis, the little worm passed from his loin to hers. When I was born, Torbjørn threatened my mother, he would stalk her, do terrible things, if I was not put up for adoption. He said she was unfit, he said disgusting things, I was a bastard son. God had touched his finger to my face, to my nose, as a mark. It was Satan's mark, I was condemned.

My mother fled the priest's shadow, her torment was a knife turning inside her womb. No, she would not give me up, she loved me. Harold believed all along that he, Harold, was my biological father. He would read me stories, his father Olav was a kindly man, grew up in a pine-timbered farmhouse down south, in the valley. Where the purple lupins bloomed in the spring, where the white pussy willows bloom in March, where the olive-green moss drips in the rain, and a man can walk barefoot, to the river's edge, and drink the water, cold from the winter's melt.

* * *

These smiling, happy tourists cannot know how I feel, for the only memory I want lingering of me is the touch of my finger on her lips, when I whispered, "Be still."

The gentle girl Ida, who was not frightened of me, who lay in my bed, holding me tight, because she had been shaking from fear.

There was an evil man in the forest, his name was Levi, he had stalked her as a wolf.

She was too afraid to tell anyone.

Ever since she knelt at the altar, and took communion, sipping from the silver chalice, where he had mixed the grape juice with a narcotic, so that she had fallen asleep, and when she woke up, it was in my grandfather's barn.

Where this wolf had sought to hide because I, the Syphilis Artist, was the perfect alibi.

The Syphilis Artist who walked the alleyways at night, in his wool coat, his face hooded, this recalcitrant who lured girls to his grandfather's old house.

I would be the perfect alibi for Levi's crimes.

Levi would kill Ida and drag her body to the front steps, where the blood trail would mark me as the killer.

Levi would awaken me from my sleep, making sure I followed his shadow, deeper, and deeper into the forest, where I hid myself, knowing he could escape faceless back into the shadows, as he bound her ankles and hung her underside down, under the fir tree.

I would be witness to his crime.

Tormented by its terror, waking me up in the night, I would believe I was the murderer, I was a marked man, touched by what I had witnessed in Prijedor, the boys hanging from the trees.

Levi knew I was frail, and scarred, Levi heard my stories, how he gently consoled me, and prayed for me, and whispered God would heal my inner terror.

This poor Ida would not convict Levi, he hid himself in his priest's black vestment; in the dark, he was a shadow.

When her eyes opened, when she felt her nakedness on the straw, the stabbing bristles of dry hay piercing her smooth flesh, when she awakened to his horror, the shadow would stare, from behind his vale, beady small eyes like a raven.

Whose blackness struck me, because they were the same eyes as the raven who watched me, from the church tower, staring down at me, as my eyes followed my father's silk ribbon flutter up, and away.

The funeral ribbon engraved with the gold lettering, and the words, 'I love you, Father'.

The pulpit rock

"Take me to the pulpit. The pulpit rock."

The scent of the roses fills me, sunlight bakes my face.

The sound of scissors clipping rose stems, the way she playfully touches my forehead with a petal, how it teases me, how the slightest touch of her finger awakens me to happiness.

She knows I am happy.

She knows this, by the firmness of my hand's grasp, though the rest of my body is dying.

She knows this, though every passing day I grow weaker, it is hard even lifting a hand, how I have not been able to get out of bed without her assistance.

The doctor told me of the diagnosis. I made him promise not to tell Mia.

Not before I tell her.

Trond has been by my side every day. "Trond, take care of Mia. Watch over her."

Trond kneels by my bed, my grandfather's bed, the window open, the curtain fluttering in.

* * *

Sunlight, the way it touches his hand, when he grabs mine, the way he holds it tight.

The way I make out his hand, holding mine, the way his voice lingers.

It is a lovely, sad voice, forgiving, this big-muscled man whose heart is tender. My father warned me the apple doesn't fall far from the tree.

But Trond is not like his father.

"I want to say, I am sorry, Andreas. I am sorry my father hurt your father."

"Come to me, Trond."

I kiss his cheek. "I know you have never loved a man, like I have, Trond. But I want you to know… *I love you.*"

* * *

"Take me above the clouds. Take me below the sea. Take me to the shore."

I am carried on a canvas stretcher up the mountain, to the summit of Pulpit Rock. Trond and Mia, they will do this for me.

Mia says I will lie on the great flat rock, look up in the sky, I will close my eyes, and I will see the glint of light off the wingtips of the gulls, I will see the sparkle of light dancing in the sea, out distant in the fjørd.

I am carried on a stretcher on the shore, I feel the sun on my face. I hear the waves gently crashing, the scent of the sea.

I dream I am on the island, in a stone villa, in a great stone palace.

Mia whispers she wants to go to the forests of Fontainebleau and lie down in the grass. She whispers about the old man who visits rich friends with fezzes, and plays draughts and drinks black coffee, and ends up in Seville, Spain, prostrate in the shadows of the Giralda tower.

She whispers, "When you open your eyes you will see me, Andreas." She kisses me on my lips.

I reply "I don't want to see. I close my eyes, I see you, Mia. I will never open my eyes again."

Lying outstretched, on the flat rock, eyes to the sky.

I open them, there is darkness; when I close them, I see the sky, hard blue, cloudless, I feel her kiss on my cheek, she tells me the priest in the Orkdal church has forgiven me.

She tells me he didn't file a police report, when I attacked him, unprovoked, as my mother fled the church, her face like Munch's Scream.

VI

A FEW LETTERS

I dove down, there was just the deep black sea; when I came back up to the surface he was gone.

Mia' s letter

I found Andreas's untitled novel, handwritten, on yellow lined paper, in a folder, in his grandfather's desk.

I do not know if this novel, like his father's, will ever be published.

I read the story and wept.

Andreas lived with an anger I sought to melt. He lived with a disease haunting him.

He writes, *syphilis can be like a shadow.*

There are some men who cannot stand to see their reflection in a mirror. But Andreas was not like that. He stretched out his hand, saw his reflection, lifted a pencil, and escaped, into his drawings.

Andreas could never understand how I could forgive those murderers, the killers of Prijedor, and Omarska, Vukavar, and Srebrenica, he did not understand that there is not one minute when I do not weep inside, at what happened.

In the Bosnian village Omarska, several hundred men, and women were killed. In the concrete room called 'The White House' no one emerged alive.

The terrified men entered, were beaten with clubs, herded worse than animals, in a tiny room with skeletal heads newly shaved.

Where they rubbed their tear-less faces with the bones of their hands. Where they heard the screaming and killing from outside.

Where the stink of burning tyres and burning bodies filled the air.

Andreas and I were only children; we witnessed this from our hiding place, where I cupped my hands over his ears, we heard the screaming.

Though his eyes were losing their sight from the disease he imagined what was occurring, and this marked him for life.

There is a form of evil without explanation, an evil so dark, its forgetting would be a greater evil.

That was the paradox. Andreas didn't forget what he saw and heard.

And he didn't want to remember.

His father wouldn't let him remember because it awoke the evil that befell my mother. Yes, his father, *Little Harold, in whose heart a secret lay hidden.*

How his father and his drunken companion *Svein Torkildsen* forced themselves on my dear mother Miraja, as she pounded her fists on their backs. How I was conceived through a most egregious rape.

How this man, my father, Svein Torkildsen, hid his rape from Harold, Andreas's guilt-torn father, because Svein wouldn't accept responsibility for his actions.

Nor would he see to it that he, Svein Torkildsen, paid my mother child support all those years.

Because he made his so-called best friend, whom he betrayed, pay the support, creating the lie that Harold was the father.

How through all this time in the shadows lurked that evil false priest, whose name I detest to mention. But I must name him.

Torbjørn.

That old man in a priest's white garb protected by Levi.

Levi kept the priest's secret, hidden all those years. *Levi knew the old man Torbjørn was Andreas's father.*

Torbjørn, the false priest in that dark valley, in that church by the bend in the river, the sorry and pitiful man who raped Andreas.

Andreas was only seven years old.

Little Harold knew all about this, that is why he had to get away. The townspeople called him *Little Harold*, but he was a big man.

I found Harold's diary in the house, in a box of papers and old news clippings. There were handwritten, obscene letters between Wenche and Torbjørn.

Torbjørn had written to her that he had syphilis, she should see a doctor.

They must keep this secret. Torbjørn knew that he was the father.

There were clippings from the newspapers about all the unsolved cases, the children in the valley abused in the night, the stalker who crept in the windows.

Harold wrote in his diary- *"Andreas came to my study last night. He came to me, I raised him up on my lap. Yesterday was his seventh birthday. He had a sad face, something bothered him. He had a sore on his ass. What he told me was so shocking I could not stop shaking. It was the old man, Torbjørn, he had done something to Andreas, in a dark room, in the church. Before Andreas could tell me what happened, the boy had a seizure."*

Harold had written he had a big argument with Wenche. Harold would take Andreas to Zagreb, in his desperation.

Harold took the boy to my mother, so he could get his shots of penicillin. Wenche kept her dark secret hidden.

He had been abused for years by the old priest.

The infection was so virulent, so unusual in his little body.

Because the way syphilis affected his mind, he lost the memory of his childhood.

His mother Wenche would take the blame, such was that old priest's way with her.

* * *

The contagion syphilis, the disease stalking Andreas, in the night, sneaking up behind him, staring through windows, where this deranged man scraped away the ice, because it was winter, and Andreas was sitting with that naked woman, in a candle's glow.

Andreas, whose sightless eyes were locked on his subject, the sound of his pencil scratching the canvas.

The woman spoke, told Andreas what she had seen.

The hours passed, when he was done, she had her masterpiece, she put on her clothes, and left as quietly as she entered.

Andreas had handwritten detailed notes of what the women told him.

There were several young women in the valley who had seen and heard things.

They were too afraid to speak to the police.

But they knew who this stalker was, one night his face revealed itself.

There was a mole on his face, on his left cheek, the size of a pea. A gaunt, whiskered face with thinning, white hair.

Andreas had dozens of little notes, with these notes he had created a sketch. Torbjørn's face.

That stern-faced man with a scar on his neck, where she clawed at his neck.

I found the notes in an envelope with the sketch, the envelope was marked with his handwriting. "For Police Officer Brandahl".

This false priest who stared through the windows, this perversion of a man.

Who had admitted some time ago, as I read in the newspapers, his crimes.

In the jail cell where he went blind.

How the old priest Torbjørn sat on his throne, silent, all these years, this false priest who raped Andreas and countless other boys.

The old man protected by Levi, raven-eyed Levi, who tried to hide the old man's crimes in Andreas's shadow.

* * *

Several women have now come forward and witnessed to their abuse. Torbjørn died last week. *No one went to his funeral.*

The newspapers write Levi has recently been taken ill by a peculiar disease. He has begun losing his eyesight.

Poor Ida, murdered, because this little man Levi couldn't accept what he had done to her in the barn.

In his final act, Levi grasped Harold's hand, the hand whose fingers grasped the German Luger. Levi forced Harold to pull the trigger as Harold held the gun unwillingly to his own temple.

The whole scene witnessed by Grandfather Olav, who died from shock as the fatal gunshot rang out, collapsing in his rocking chair.

Those facts were written down in Grandfather's own handwriting, on paper found in his pocket.

All this was documented in Levi's confession. The media has been all over this story.

How my mother's cries in that little apartment on the Danube, in the shadow of St Stephen's church, awoke no pity in those two men.

In the shadow of the steeple rising like an upstretched hand up to the heavens.

The evil that men do, when they cannot look upon a naked woman, without thinking impure thoughts.

The evil that men do when they, without thinking, rape the woman, without the slightest regard for this fellow human, who staggers home, the pain throbbing between her legs, where she will lay awake every night, for the rest of her life.

Some of the perpetrators of the crimes walk free, there is a man walking behind me, a man whose face looked away from mine, who walked with flowers.

I knew his father; *he was a killer.*

Around Prijedor there is little reckoning of what happened, the typical narrative says, "It was all lies" and the journalists have "made up the stories" and today, a young man who was not even born during the war can say it was 'fake news'.

The taking of a life, the evil rising, among neighbours, the hatred in man's heart.

I could not understand that.

My mother understood she had to prick the consciousness of the men with hatred in their hearts, like so many needle sticks, she had to in some way awaken their conscience.

She had to do this secretly, in that hidden place, where she sat down the soldiers, on stools, facing one another.

Unclothed but for the smell of alcohol on their breath. Without their uniforms and sitting all naked, a man cannot be addressed 'Colonel'.

I admit her tactics were unusual.

She knew inside every man's heart there was a light burning, a hand grasping, a voice speaking rationality.

Just facing one another, eyes locking eyes, unclothed.

A man sees his reflection in the other's face, witnesses the man's nakedness, sees there is not much difference between them.

My mother knew a neighbour fighting on the Serbian side in Kostajnica. Her father was a Croat, her mother a Serb. The Sava River divided them like a knife cutting a loaf of bread in half. They left cattle in their stables, even the washing machine was still spinning. They each fled to their sides, infected by tribal loyalties newly awakened, as if some great plaque had risen among them, some mental sickness.

The only wall separating them, the only wall separating the Croat and the Serb, is the wall built by hatred, like loose bricks stacked one upon the other.

Over time, the red bricks rise, higher and higher; the politicians know they must instil a mindset of perpetual mutual hatred if they are to remain in power. So the wall rises, and neighbours stop looking into one another's eyes, and their eyes turn to the ground, the blood-soaked ground.

The desolate trees sleeping in the rain, leafless, branches skeletal from the burning, torched fields.

Where arms of good men and women from both sides stretch to the sky, their tears falling fruitless to the dead ground, because the politicians have stone hearts, and the once rich soil is blood-soaked.

My dear brother Marko, his arms lifting, to heaven.

As he collapsed, in the snow, in the killing fields of Belgrade.

* * *

I received a phone from a man named Bjørn, he said he was from Jølestø. He says he is from a little fishing village on the southern coast.

He has a little eatery called The Propeller, on the coast in Lista where he would like to meet me.

"I found something, which I believe is yours," he said in a friendly, meek tone, his voice betraying an older man.

He had found something on the shore. He didn't say what it was, I would have to see it for myself.

I jumped in my car, drove seven hours from my apartment in Oslo without stopping. I was to meet Bjørn in his little timbered farmhouse that he had made to an eatery, there on the windswept coast in Lista.

I would have to drive all day; I didn't think twice about going. He was waiting for me as I drove up, it was dark. He stood outside the pine-timbered low building; I saw a candles glow in the window.

"My name is Bjørn. I started a fire, come in and see what I have found. I have prepared a warm meal for you. You see, your name and phone number were on the paper."

He is a clean-shaven man in his sixties, a friendly leather wrinkled face which turned serious as I greeted him.

"My name is Mia Miraja Drovik. I am Andreas Hansen's wife."

"Yes, I know," *he said, humbly, as I stepped out of the cold into the warm darkened room full of little burning candles and the glow of an open fireplace.*

"I found the glass jar in the sand, on the beach where I take my morning stroll." *I smelt the birch fire, the air thick with a pleasing aroma, delicate and sweet,*

a hint of lavender.

A blue clay vase with a single rose on a long rustic wooden table with cast-iron legs and a dozen wood chairs on the planked floor. The pine-timbered walls are roughly hewn, it is a charming place.

"This is my little espresso bar, we call it The Propeller. Would you like an espresso?" *he says, this lanky man standing aglow by the fireplace.*

"Yes, please. I like it strong."

I breathe in the rich aroma, place my coat on a chair, look around, the walls hanging with little wood carvings and pieces of faded paper, curious little oddities.

He places in my hands a little white porcelain cup, warm to the touch.

"I have made a meatless stew, I think you will like it. I am not open every day, but I had to open tonight, for you. Let me show you what I found."

Sipping the coffee, Bjørn points to a glass-framed shadow box hanging on the wall.

"I find things on the shore, they wash up, simple little things. Each little thing has a story to tell" *he says.*

He is talking about the things he finds, each tell a story, there are plastic tubes, unopened condoms, a worn hairbrush, a faded pink undergarment, a cloth purse, faded pink, just pieces of rubbish but to Bjørn little treasures.

The shadow box is about a metre in length, I have lost my breath, my eyes catch right away the small glass jar, a Norwegian mason jar, the metal screw lid beside it.

A flower inside the jar.

I recognise it right away. The pink five-petalled palo borracho. A crumbled white envelope, I make out my letters, in flowing black ink, on the envelope.

"Oh, Santo Cielo!" I make out black, flowing lettering on the envelope. "For Mia Miraja—Here is the letter."

Bjørn sits by the table, in the candle's glow.

"It was wet and falling apart when I found it. I dried it out by the fire."

Trond's letter

I tried to save him.

He was at the shoreline, in a still area sheltered from the pounding surf, where the waves are gentle.

I guess he just wanted to feel the cool water lap his feet.

It was a still afternoon, one of those unusual days in late August when it should have been much colder.

The sun was bright, there wasn't a cloud in the sky.

Some days on the coast the sky and sea can be so still, you hear the surf, the crashing of waves, and the sea is like glass.

I was talking to Mia, just some idle chatting, while laying on my belly in my shorts and bare top, sunning myself on a beach towel.

Watching the burgers sizzle and grill over the smoking coals of the grill, thinking we will have a nice meal together, drive around the shore afterwards.

Mia was sitting on a little beach chair with her portable easel, painting a watercolour.

There was the lighthouse in the background, the distant horizon meeting the sea, seagulls alight in the still air of a summer's hard blue sky.

It was a watercolour she was working on, and she was singing to herself. She said it was an Italian song her mother used to sing, I didn't know the words, Mia said it had to do with love, loneliness, and pain.

"You can't have love without pain," and, "You can't be lonely with love," Mia reminded me, as her beautiful voice filled me like an intoxicant.

I knew now why Andreas fell for her, any sensible, lonely man would, because she fills the empty spaces of the heart without making you feel you owe her anything.

Mia and I had been talking about her plans for the old house. She had such big plans.

The money would just be enough to replace some rotten floorboards, put in new insulation in the walls, redo the old wiring.

There was also the business of tearing down the old jail cell, that was important.

I got up to my feet, looked toward the lighthouse, saw Andreas walk along the shoreline.

"Andreas! Come on back, the burgers are ready!"

It was then I turned to Mia, saw her face change, as she dropped her brush, her eyes fixating on Andreas, then on me, as she gasped "Oh no! Andreas!"

I ran toward him. Mia ran right behind me, shouting for him. Andreas is blind, but is hearing is like an eagle.

He didn't respond to my shouts, nor turn to us, I knew then something was wrong.

He had grown so weak.

I saw him taking off his clothes, entering the surf.

"Andreas!" I shouted, he just kept on walking out, further, and further, until all I saw was the glint of sun on his face, as he swam out.

I raced into the water, swam out, he had swum out a hundred metres, I saw his bobbing head. Then as I shouted again, "Andreas! Come back! We need you!" his head disappeared below the waves.

I dove down, there was just the deep black sea, when I came back up to the surface, he was gone.

Andreas' letter

Tell me what you see.

    My dear Mia. My dear Mia Miraja. Mia meaning mine.

La vita è più dolce con te. Tell me what you feel.

    A fir tree drops to the ground. A boulder drops to the sea.

    I drop below these waves, I see how the sunlight reaches down, touching my face, like your hand, the way it stretched out, to my face, where your fingers touched that special place, where the nose had melted away. How my fingers felt your hair, silky black strands like the blackness of the sea, wrapping me, entwining me. I sink further, and further down, blackness fills my heart.

    I know I am not coming back.

    Please, don't weep for me. You know I have spent my whole life resisting ending it. I have spent my whole life, weeping.

    You know it was too much for me. What we witnessed.

    You gave me life, *but it was not mine to have.* I write these words, here on this old desk, my *father's desk.* A vase of blue lavender stems dried and bundled, this paper I flatten with my palm, as I dip the pen in the black ink. The scratching of the pen on the paper, the tears falling. Oh, Mia Miraja. *I am not a worshipper of Apollo.*

    Embrace Marko, my son. *Embrace* him with my *heart.* Hold him in your lap.

    Read to him.

* * *

In this house, in this room I thought I was alone.

    I scraped the ice from the window. I lit a candle.

    You were here.

    You were always here.

Read to him in that room facing the mountains, where the sun's glow smiles, and the light touches the worn, yellowed pages, where I pressed flowers, where the scent of vanilla rises, and a little blue vase of lavender stems sits, waiting for you.

* * *

Read him these words: There is no greater commandment *than to love one another*.

There was a man once, a man with a dark complexion, eyes-tinged honey brown, a quiet, lingering voice, who raised his gaze to the heavens.

I love this man; he waits for me. They have forgotten him.

There is only one man who could forgive old Torbjørn. There is only one man who could forgive Levi.

That man is not me. *It is him*. He, who asked his father for forgiveness, his eyes gazed up at the heavens, his hands nailed to the cross.

The hatred men have for their neighbour, the neighbour from Eritrea, or Kosovo, or Aleppo, because he speaks another language, and your face is white, and your hair is blonde, and your eyes are the colour of the sea, that hatred lives after them.

The hatred that burns because boys have not been loved by their mothers, and their fathers are drunkards, the little boys born in the cold shadows who grow up with clenched fists.

The Serb boys who grow up, and raise their fists against the Croat boys, who grow up and raise their fists against their neighbours.

The Christian against the Muslim, because each is different, each is afraid of the other, because they have forgotten how to stretch out their hands, and just touch.

They have forgotten the stillness in their hearts, where fingers tap, where the sound a butterfly makes, with its wings, fluttering, as you open the window on a midsummer's night, and it escapes, up into the sky, where the glint of light plays on broken glass, *that stillness fills my heart*.

The tremor I feel is like the distant tremor of an earthquake, you have shaken my heart.

The touch of your flesh, the echo of your voice, in the meadow, where the purple lupins are scattered about like drops from a painter's brush.

There is nothing but love, and the smile of a man's heart, when he kisses a lover, and he knows he is alive, because there is passion, and Jesus has told us there is no greater commandment than to love another.

I love you, whoever you are.

I love you, whatever your colour.

I love you, whatever your religion.

I love you if you believe your soul will fly off, above the clouds, or sink to hell, below the sea.

I forgive my mother. My father, he was a torn man. I cannot forgive Torbjørn.

I knew it was him, after sketching all those women, those frightened women who came to me, and trusted me to keep their secrets.

The small little details, how Ida remembered the mole on the shadow's face. The little gold crucifix, shining in the full moon's glow, the way light reflects off broken glass.

He threatened to cut their necks with the broken glass, as he held them down.

I sketched the old man's face; I found a picture in one of the old books.

It was of my mother Wenche, and the old priest. His face bore an exact likeness to my sketch.

The whiskered, gaunt face, thinning hair, the mole on his left cheek. This was the man who raped me.

How I wept, night after night, these last several days, sketching that face, deep wrinkled like the paper I unfold, and flatten with my palm.

A face masked by evil, because it can smile, and the little old ladies kiss his wrinkled hand.

He can in one instance smile, a lovely, devious smile, and in the next instance change into a joker face, with burning eyes, and teeth hard clenched. Because he has you alone, in the shadow, he has a knife.

I cannot forgive Levi.

There is a special place for such men. *But it is not for me to seek revenge.*

The evil that men do, that lives after them.

I love you Mia, I see a distant flicker, a candle's glow.

I lift a pencil, the line I draw pierces my heart, where my fingers played on your mother's tattoo, made from Miraja's milk and that special ink. Where I felt the raised letters, and you whispered the word, Hope, and I kissed your lips, and whisper *La vita è più dolce con te.*

I love you, Mia.

Mia Miraja, I am sorry. I love you, Father.

I love you, my dear grandfather. Whose voice was silent, but for the song he sang. The song his mother taught him.

Imprisoned in the jail cell, on the cold concrete floor, where the Nazis threw him, and said the last occupant hung himself.

Please forgive me.

The way a spirit lifts, upon saying those few, simple words.

The way the scales fall from my eyes, saying those few words. As the fog lifts, and the clouds pass, and the gull flies silver-winged up, high in the sky, where the sun strikes its wings.

As I sit at this desk, writing these words. I fold the letter, crease the edges, as my tears, drop, again, and again.

On the paper, within whose pages there lies pressed a dried flower.

Lavender, whose flowers lie scattered all about, in the field, where their scent stilled my heart.

As we walked, her hand grasping mine, when she pulled me down in the sun warmed grass, and whispered, cradled in each other's arms. Embracing as the silvered floating sculpture in Ekeberg, in the Oslo park, a man, a woman, intertwined.

"You must not die, Andreas. I cannot lose you."

"Oh Mia, oh Mia Miraja." My tears are falling, as when the sky opens, and the rain falls, and the echo of her voice fills the valley.

A fir tree drops to the ground. A boulder drops to the sea.

The window blows open, the curtain billows gently, its lace touches my face. As when she played the ostrich feather on my forehead, lightly brushing,

whispering those words.

Which come to me now and pierce my heart.

I smelt lavender, and the scent of the forest after a summer rain, when the sun alights atop the trees, and glides down, to touch the flesh. She cups her hands on my face, kisses me ever so gently on my lips. She whispers, "Be not afraid."

Placing the letter in the Norway glass, my hand grasping the metal screw top, and turning the lid, tight. The ache of my fingers, those long, piano fingers, now weakened, as they shake, as when they tried to draw a straight line, at the horizon's edge, where the sea meets the sky.

The flat, sunlit sea, where I will return.

Where the ocean will drown my tears, where her memory is my hallucination, where her touch fades, and lingers.

As I catch the glint of the sun, striking the black-tipped wings of the gulls, as they sail in the cobalt sky, under whose heaven my eyes finally close, because my spirit fills with awe.

As I sink, below the sea, as I whisper my son's name, as I whisper, I will cradle him in my arms, forever.

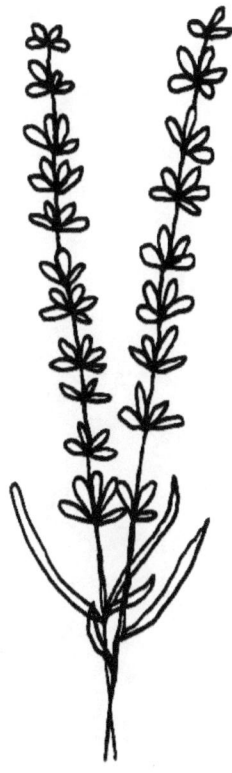

www.ingramcontent.com/pod-product-compliance
Lightning Source LLC
LaVergne TN
LVHW041959060526
838200LV00038B/1290